Praise for Elle Kennedy's Killer Instincts Series

Midnight Alias

"Balances the gritty side of humanity with sizzling passion."
—*Publishers Weekly*

"[Kennedy] shows a real flair for penning thrillers that are passionate, gritty, and extremely suspenseful."
—*Romantic Times* (top pick)

Midnight Rescue

"If you're looking for a chilling, hard-core romantic suspense loaded with sensuality, military camaraderie, and dry humor, why not arrange for a *Midnight Rescue*?" —*USA Today*

"Romantic suspense just gained a major new player!"
—*Romantic Times* (4½ stars)

"Romantic suspense fans will want to get ahold of this book! . . . Elle Kennedy, please write faster!"
—The Book Pushers

continued . . .

"With its dark, edgy tone, passionate love story, and deadly protagonists, *Midnight Rescue* is a surefire win for fans of romantic suspense." —Romance Junkies

"This was a very good romantic suspense. It had all the right elements that I look for in a book like this. The hot alpha men. The strong women they pair up with."
—Fiction Vixen Book Reviews

"Anybody looking for action, intensity, and passion will love this novel." The Book Whisperer

"This is a fast-paced, action-filled, oh-my-God-what's-going-to-happen-next ride and I never wanted to get off."
—Love to Read for Fun

"*Midnight Rescue* has daringly bold characters, precarious situations, and fervent sensuality." —Single Titles

"Action, suspense, adventure, and romance are intertwined superbly to create a wonderful plot. . . . This was an amazing book with a great heroine." —The Romance Studio

Also Available in the Killer Instincts Series

Midnight Rescue
Midnight Alias

MIDNIGHT GAMES

A KILLER INSTINCTS NOVEL

ELLE KENNEDY

A SIGNET ECLIPSE BOOK

SIGNET ECLIPSE
Published by the Penguin Group
Penguin Group (USA) Inc., 375 Hudson Street,
New York, New York 10014, USA

USA | Canada | UK | Ireland | Australia | New Zealand | India | South Africa | China

Penguin Books Ltd., Registered Offices: 80 Strand, London WC2R 0RL, England
For more information about the Penguin Group visit penguin.com.

First published by Signet Eclipse, an imprint of New American Library,
a division of Penguin Group (USA) Inc.

First Printing, August 2013

ISBN 978-0-451-24002-6

Printed in the United States of America
10 9 8 7 6 5 4 3 2 1

PUBLISHER'S NOTE
This is a work of fiction. Names, characters, places, and incidents either are the product of the author's imagination or are used fictitiously, and any resemblance to actual persons, living or dead, business establishments, events, or locales is entirely coincidental.

The publisher does not have any control over and does not assume any responsibility for author or third-party Web sites or their content.

ACKNOWLEDGMENTS

I could not have written this book without the help and support of several people.

My research assistant, Amanda, for making every location, gadget, and backstory come alive. Early readers Travis, Heather, and Mandi for their feedback and suggestions. My family and friends for keeping me sane during this process. And of course, my amazing editor and the staff at New American Library for believing in this series and letting me write it!

Chapter 1

"He called again last night."

Isabel Roma froze. Only for a split second, but a second was all it took to tip off her boss, whose smirk widened. Crap. Noelle was a predator—show her any sign of weakness and the queen of assassins would eat you alive.

"What'd you tell him?" Isabel asked carefully.

"Same thing I've been telling him for the past five months. You're deep cover and can't be reached." Noelle paused, an honest-to-God grin gracing her bloodred lips.

Considering that the woman only smiled right before she killed you, Isabel grew a tad worried. Gulping, she crossed her arms over her chest and said, "Spit it out, Noelle."

"He wanted me to pass along a message." That shit-eating grin got bigger. "He said he never took you for a coward."

A *coward*? The insult prickled her skin, even though she knew the accusation had been Trevor Callaghan's way of provoking a reaction from her. He of all people knew that she was the furthest thing from a coward.

Bristling, she drifted toward the wet bar on the other side of the lavish living room. She was staying at Noelle's Paris penthouse until she found a place of her own, but although she was technically homeless, she had zero complaints about her current digs. The gorgeous two-story apartment was located on the Right Bank, an area known for its spacious avenues, ornate nineteenth-century buildings, and wealthy foreign residents. The enormous floor-to-ceiling windows overlooked the breathtaking cityscape, even more beautiful at night with all the lights twinkling like diamonds. Outside, the silver frost clinging to the streetlamps and the layer of white covering the sidewalks created a magical ambience that Isabel would've taken more time to admire if she hadn't been so rattled at the moment.

With a sigh, she poured herself a glass of Maker's Mark and took a long swig. The alcohol scorched a path down her throat but did nothing to quell the uneasiness that had been rippling in her stomach ever since she'd landed at the private airstrip this morning, where Noelle had been waiting in a silver Mercedes. In that nonchalant, I-don't-particularly-give-a-fuck tone, Noelle had revealed that Trevor Callaghan had been hounding her for information ever since he and Isabel had said good-bye in New York.

Said good-bye? echoed the mocking voice in her head.

Fine. So maybe they hadn't exchanged any good-byes. Maybe she'd just left.

Left?

Gritting her teeth, Isabel tried to silence the exasperating voice by taking another gulp of whiskey, but it didn't work. Guilt continued to trickle into her, along with a pang of shame that made her chest hurt.

Damn it. Maybe Trevor was right. Maybe she *was* a coward. How else could you explain why she'd abandoned him like that?

Five months ago, she'd done some undercover work for mercenary extraordinaire Jim Morgan, which had yet again paired her with Trevor. The first time she'd worked with the former Special Forces soldier, he'd been a ravaged, grieving mess—a man with a death wish, a man she shouldn't have been attracted to but was. The second time around, that attraction had intensified, and Trevor had been a changed man. A healed man.

They'd connected during that second job, really connected. They'd *kissed*, for Pete's sake. And what had she done? She'd deserted him. Left him waiting at her SoHo apartment, hopped a plane, and fled the country.

How long had he waited?

Another rush of guilt flooded her belly as the question she'd been wondering these past five months floated into her head. A part of her hoped that Trevor had figured out the score after an hour or two, but deep down she knew he wouldn't have given up so fast. He would've waited for hours, days even, and when she still didn't return . . . that's when the worry would have set in. The anger. The bitterness.

But again, she knew Trevor—no matter how angry he was, he would need to make sure she was all right, which meant moving heaven and earth to track her down.

According to Noelle, he'd been doing just that.

"Ditching Callaghan like that was a coldhearted move, honey," the blond assassin said with a chuckle. "Giving men the slip is more my style than yours."

Coldhearted. Was that what she was? No. No, she couldn't be. The way she'd ended things with Trevor had been callous, but she'd been motivated by the need for self-preservation, not cruelty. He'd gotten too close. Made her believe that happiness could play a role in her future, that she could actually be a normal woman who had normal relationships and a normal life. But she knew better.

She wasn't destined for normalcy. The most she could ask for was professional fulfillment, and her undercover work provided that. She was good at pretending to be other people. Maybe it wasn't the most honorable profession out there, but she excelled at it. And Trevor, with his perceptive brown eyes and understated charm, with that quiet strength he exuded and his rare but gorgeous smiles . . . he was too big of a distraction. Each time she was around him, she lost her head and dropped her guard—and for a woman who'd spent her entire life perfecting a composed, easygoing front, neither of those responses was welcome.

"You never told me why you bailed on him," Noelle prompted.

Isabel shrugged and took another sip of whiskey.

"It's all right. I already know the answer."

Although the entire exchange was making her uncomfortable as hell, she couldn't fight a spark of wary curiosity. "Oh, do you?"

Lithe as a cat, Noelle slid off the arm of the recliner she'd been perched on and strode across the white Berber carpet. Her tight black leggings and even tighter black tank top contrasted with the all-white color scheme of the penthouse. Isabel wondered if Noelle's interior designer had been making some sort of ironic statement. White leather couch, white armchairs, white carpeting, white walls. The place was very . . . sterile. Cold. Unwelcoming.

The penthouse suited Noelle to a T.

"You left because that man scares you shitless."

Noelle's assessment made her frown. "Trevor doesn't scare me."

Liar.

"Liar." Noelle reached for an empty glass and poured a healthy amount of bourbon into it. She curled her fingers around the tumbler, red fingernails tapping on the glass. "Callaghan was starting to get to know the real Isabel, but we couldn't have that, could we, honey? Because the real Isabel is so very damaged, isn't she?"

Her shoulders stiffened.

"Oh, don't look at me like that, *so* offended and incensed. I'm not saying anything you haven't thought a million times before." The amber liquid in Noelle's glass swished as she headed back to the sofa. With the grace of a ballerina, the blonde sank into the cushions and demurely crossed her legs, balancing the tumbler on one delicate knee.

Isabel couldn't control the rush of indignation that coursed through her. Noelle was a bitch on a good day, but it was rare for one of her "chameleons" to be on the receiving end of that sharp, antagonistic tongue. Isabel had been working for the woman for seven years now, and this was the first time the deadly blonde had unleashed a personal attack on her.

Damaged? Christ, the woman ought to take a good long look in the mirror. Noelle was the freaking definition of the word.

"You think if he sees the real you, he'll realize how flawed you are and run in the opposite direction."

She resisted the urge to slap that amused look right off Noelle's gorgeous face.

"I left because I'm not looking for a relationship," Isabel said stiffly. "That's what he wanted from me, and I couldn't give it to him."

"Mmm-hmmm. What's the next bullshit excuse?"

Her jaw tensed. "These aren't excuses. It's the truth. Look, he clouds my judgment, okay?" Even she could hear the defensive note in her voice. "Back in Manhattan, I was supposed to help one of the girls I met when I was undercover at the strip club. I was taking her to a rehab facility, but I was late because of Trevor. I was late, and that poor girl killed herself."

Noelle offered a long, throaty laugh. "That junkie would've killed herself regardless. You think even if you had managed to get her to rehab, the program would have stuck? How naive are you, Isabel?"

Rather than answer, she raised her glass and downed the rest of her whiskey. This time, the burning sensation only made her feel nauseous. This entire conversation was beginning to piss her off.

"Enough," she snapped. "We're done talking about this."

"Meow."

"I'm serious, Noelle." Isabel took a calming breath, tried to control her rising anger. "Tell me about the fallout from the Ekala job."

Noelle sipped her bourbon. "It's playing out exactly the way we wanted it to. The media is reporting that one of Ekala's lieutenants orchestrated a coup. You did good."

She arched a brow, both surprised and insulted by the praise. "You thought I wouldn't?"

"I worried. You excel at short-term gigs. Deep cover was always more suited to Bailey or Abby."

"Well, I managed just fine."

"That you did. You rid the world of another sadistic fucker. Give yourself a pat on the back."

Sometimes it was incredibly hard to decipher whether Noelle was being sarcastic or not. Isabel decided to treat that last remark as sincere.

Truth was, she was damn proud of herself for the way she'd handled the Nigeria job. Her boss was right—Isabel's strength was the in-and-out gig. Transform herself into whoever she needed to be, go undercover and get the information she was asked to procure, then disappear without a trace.

These last five months, however, she'd been deeply rooted in the mission. Posing as an American journalist, she'd infiltrated Tengo Ekala's camp and cozied up to the man who'd been terrorizing the country ever since he'd come into power. She'd even succeeded in gaining the Nigerian warlord's respect and admiration, under the guise that she wanted to tell the world about his cause.

And when the time had come to put a bullet in the bastard's head, she hadn't stepped aside to let one of the other women take over.

For the first time in her career, Isabel had been the one to pull the trigger.

"Am I officially part of the club now?" she asked drily. "Is there a special assassin membership card I get to keep in my wallet?"

"Sorry, honey. I'm pulling you out."

"What the hell does that mean?"

"Exactly what it sounds like." Noelle set her glass down and got to her feet. "I indulged you with the Ekala job, but you're done now. You're a master of disguise, and that's the only service I require from you. You won't be assigned any more contracts."

The cool declaration brought a spark of anger and a pang of relief. Rather than dwell on the latter, she focused on the former. "I just eliminated one of the world's nastiest warlords without causing so much as a ripple of tension in the international political pool, and you think I'm only suitable for undercover work?"

"You're not a killer, Isabel. Never have been, never will be." Noelle headed for the arched doorway across the room. "Leave the killing to those of us who enjoy it."

She couldn't control her surprise. "You're saying you actually *enjoy* taking a life?"

"When it's the life of a sick fuck who deserves it? Yes." The boss's voice was oddly gentle. "You're not like me, Isabel. We've both suffered. We both came from shitty backgrounds, but see, your crap gave you a bleeding heart. You want to *help* people. My crap crushed my conscience, plain and simple."

This was the most candid Noelle had ever been with her, and Isabel found herself speechless as she stared at the other woman. At five-two, with her long golden hair, ethereal features, and pale blue eyes, Noelle looked like a damn Disney princess, and yet she was the coldest, most lethal person Isabel had ever met. She'd always wondered how Noelle had gotten to be this way and now she finally had an inkling.

Christ.

"So we can waste some more time and keep arguing about this," Noelle said flippantly, "or you can just accept that I'm right. You're not a killer. Ergo, you're not taking on any more contracts. Now, when can I expect you back?"

Isabel blinked. "What?"

"From Jim Morgan's compound. I already alerted my pilot that you'll be using the jet tonight—he's waiting for your call. So when do you think you'll be done there? I need you on recon for Bailey in Istanbul, so don't take too long."

"I'm not—"

"Going to see Callaghan?" Noelle finished. Those blue eyes gleamed. "Bullshit. That's exactly what you're going to do, and you want to know why? Because not only are you not a killer, you're also not a coldhearted bitch. That's my job, remember?"

With that, the blonde sauntered out of the living room, leaving Isabel alone with her thoughts.

Yet again, Noelle was right. The second Isabel had stepped off the plane this morning, her first instinct had been to pick up the phone and apologize to Trevor for the way she'd left things. The way she'd left *him*.

But he deserved more than a half-assed phone call. He deserved a real apology, and no matter how badly she wanted to put distance between them, she wasn't the kind of woman who cowered in the face of conflict. She'd always intended to see him again. To explain why they couldn't be together. Running away from him in Manhattan had really just been about giving herself some time to regroup before they had that inevitable conversation.

You think if he sees the real you, he'll realize how flawed you are and run in the opposite direction.

Was she actually that transparent, or was Noelle too freaking insightful for her own good?

Swallowing her mounting apprehension, Isabel set her glass on the table, dug her cell phone out of her purse, and called Noelle's pilot.

"Holy shit, Holden's wife is *hot*." Ethan Hayes spoke in a low murmur, his hazel eyes glimmering with appreciation.

Trevor Callaghan shifted his attention from the pool table to the raven-haired woman taking up residence on the other side of the game room. This was the first time any of the team had met Holden McCall's wife, and Trevor had no idea why Holden had hid the woman from them for so long. With her wavy black hair and dark eyes, Beth McCall was drop-dead gorgeous. She was also shy, soft-spoken, and completely oblivious to the sex appeal radiating from her tall, curvaceous frame.

"She's really nice too," Ethan added. "She offered to give me some cooking lessons."

Trevor furrowed his brow. "Why would she do that?"

"Because she's a chef, dumb-ass."

"She is?"

"Yup."

Somehow it didn't surprise Trevor that Beth had so easily opened up to Ethan when she'd barely uttered ten words to anyone else at the compound since she and Holden had arrived earlier this morning. With his preppy good looks and unassuming demeanor, Ethan came off as the least threatening man on the planet. But the rookie was far deadlier than he let on, a marine with razor-sharp instincts and honed skills that made him a real asset to the team.

Make that *teams*. As of three months ago, Jim Morgan had expanded his operation. Apparently soldiers for hire were in greater demand these days, and since Trevor's boss was as business-savvy as he was lethal, he'd recruited a second team of operatives. Headed by a fellow mercenary named Castle, B-Team—as Trevor and some of the others mockingly referred to it—was currently in the field working an extraction, while the self-proclaimed A-Team indulged in some R&R at Morgan's compound near Tijuana.

Trevor still found it disorienting to wake up, peer out the window, and not see the Rocky Mountains looming in the distance. He'd lived in Colorado his whole life, calling it home even when his stint in the army had taken him far away and for long periods of time. But even though he got homesick every now and then, longing for the crisp mountain air and the four distinct seasons Mexico seemed to lack, he knew that relocating to the compound had been a smart decision. He'd needed to leave that empty Aspen condo. He and Gina had purchased it together. They'd turned it into a home. *Their* home.

But Gina was gone, dead for more than two years now. It had been time for him to move on, which was why he'd sold the condo to Luke Dubois. The former SEAL was currently off rotation while he got settled in the new place.

It brought a bittersweet pang to Trevor's gut, knowing that Luke and his girlfriend, Olivia, were building a life together in Aspen. The life that had been stolen from him and Gina.

He was happy for his teammate, though. And living on

the compound wasn't bad. He was surrounded by friends, he had a top-notch training facility at his fingertips, the weather was nice year-round, and their housekeeper, Lloyd, was actually a damn good cook.

Oh, and whenever irritating thoughts of Isabel Roma crept into his head, he could easily vanquish them by challenging one of the boys to a Mexican-rum-drinking contest.

Fuck. He'd promised himself he wouldn't think about Isabel today.

The woman was definitely messing with his head. Big-time.

"You taking your shot or what?" Kane Woodland inquired in a dry voice.

Trevor looked at the sandy-haired man on the other side of the pool table, then at the three lone balls sitting on the green felt. "Eight ball, corner pocket," he said absently.

"Good fucking luck. No way you're sinking that." Kane held up his palm to the redhead by his side. "High-five me, sweetheart. He's about to scratch on the eight ball."

Abby Sinclair narrowed her honey-colored eyes, assessed the table, and shook her head. "He'll sink it. Won't you, Callaghan?"

He met the redhead's astute gaze. "Wouldn't have called it if I thought otherwise."

And then he bent forward, lined up his cue, and snapped the eight right into its designated pocket—without scratching.

Kane cursed under his breath. "Damn it. Double or nothing."

"No way," Abby interjected. "You're already out five hundred bucks and two nut shots."

"Nut shots?" Beth McCall's curious voice sounded from behind the group. The black-haired beauty approached the table.

Her husband was rolling his eyes as he came up beside her. "Instead of money, they bet each other a kick in the nuts," Holden explained.

"Or a punch," Ethan said helpfully. "It's the loser's choice."

"And my *loser* husband will be getting kicked or punched in the balls today. Twice," Abby muttered.

Ethan snickered. "You're just mad because you won't be the one doing it."

Trevor wasn't used to hearing the word "husband" come out of the redhead's mouth. A few days ago, Abby and Kane had stunned everyone by nonchalantly letting it slip that they'd secretly tied the knot last week. No wedding, no reception, not even a heads-up—the couple had simply driven to the justice of the peace in town and gotten hitched without telling a single soul.

The covert ceremony didn't exactly come as a surprise, though, since Abby Sinclair loathed being the center of attention. The woman avoided fuss and fanfare like the plague.

Also not surprising was how she began to edge away from the pool table the second Beth McCall got close. Abby had been living on the compound for more than a year now, but the former contract killer still didn't seem comfortable being part of the group. Or being around other women. The only females Trevor had seen her drop her guard around were her ex-boss, Noelle, and her fellow chameleon, Isabel.

That's two.

Grinding his teeth, he pushed aside the latest thought of Isabel and handed his pool cue to Ethan.

"I'll collect my reward later," he told Kane. "First I need a word with your wife."

"Hands off, Trev." Kane's green eyes twinkled playfully, but the note of menace in his voice didn't go unnoticed.

Yeah, right. Trevor had no intention of putting the moves on Abby Sinclair. She was beautiful, sure, but he didn't have a thing for ruthless redheads.

Only cowardly blondes, apparently.

A sigh lodged in his throat. No, that wasn't true. Isabel Roma was the strongest woman he'd ever met. He'd dropped that nasty C-word during his last phone call with Noelle only because he'd hoped that being accused of cowardice would spur Isabel into finally returning his calls.

Hadn't worked, though. She was still "deep cover" and couldn't be reached.

Bull fucking shit.

"What do you need, Callaghan?" Abby asked as she followed him out of the game room.

"What do you think I need, Sinclair?"

They stepped into the spacious hallway and headed toward the set of tall oak doors that opened into the great room. The huge chalet-style space was Trevor's favorite room in the house, probably because it reminded him of the ski lodges his family had vacationed at when he was a kid. Crisscrossed wooden beams made up the high ceiling and the floor beneath their feet was a shiny, dark-stained parquet. L-shaped leather couches took up half the room, while the other side offered a stone fireplace, endless bookcases, and cozy leather armchairs.

Trevor walked over to the large bay window and stared at the reddish brown dirt that made up the front courtyard. Outside, the sun was setting, the sky a fiery shade of burnished copper, nearly the same color as Abby's hair.

"Well?" he prompted when she didn't say a word.

She joined him at the window. "Izzy is in Paris," she admitted.

His heart did an involuntary leap of joy, but the joy faded to anger once the implication settled in. Isabel had wrapped up her job. Which meant she'd undoubtedly received every single one of his messages—and decided to ignore them.

"Are you sure?" he said gruffly.

Abby nodded. "She got in this morning."

He was slightly appeased. All right. She'd gotten in only this morning. She probably had other shit to deal with at the moment. Unpacking, briefing her boss, finding a new place to live . . .

The memory of Isabel's *old* place, the Manhattan walk-up she'd abandoned him in, brought a bitter taste to his mouth. He'd waited all day and night. Sat around like a chump while Isabel went out to help a friend, and as the hours ticked by and her cell phone kept bumping over to voice mail, he'd made excuses for her. She'd lost track of time. Her cell was dead. She was on her way home.

Until finally he'd been forced to face the cold, hard truth—Isabel wasn't coming back.

Of course, his misplaced faith in humankind had led him to think she was in trouble—a pathetic assumption that initiated a frantic, weeklong search that nearly sent him spiraling back into the black hole of depression that Gina's death had banished him to.

Eventually, he'd reached Isabel's boss, who put an end to his needless panic by uttering four very short, very destructive sentences.

Isabel's on assignment. She bailed on you. Deal with it. Stop calling me.

He'd responded with only one sentence of his own: "I won't stop until I find her."

Yeah, maybe it made him a candidate for the most pathetic dude on the planet, but he refused to let this go until he heard from Isabel's own lips why she'd ditched him without a word.

Trevor locked his gaze with Abby's. "Ask her to come to the compound."

Those yellow eyes flickered with discomfort. "I don't want to get in the middle of . . . of whatever the hell is going on with you two."

"You won't be in the middle." His tone became persistent. "I need to see her, Abby."

The redhead didn't answer.

"Pick up the phone and tell her that you and Kane got married. You know she'll be on the first plane out."

A fresh dose of bitterness surged through him. Yep, he had no doubt that Isabel would drop everything to come and offer her best wishes to Abby and Kane. Isabel Roma was loyal to a fault. Not only was she fiercely protective of the people she loved, but she also went out of her way to help total strangers. The woman was a bleeding heart, an unwavering crusader for the innocent.

A total fucking hypocrite.

Because for all her bullshit about helping others, about *saving* others, she refused to help the one person who needed it the most—herself.

And where had her frickin' loyalty been when she'd left him waiting in an empty apartment in New York City?

Abby made a frustrated sound. "Can't I just tell her there's an emergency or something? I'm tired of everyone making such a huge deal over this marriage thing."

"This 'marriage thing'?" Trevor had to laugh. "You don't have a romantic bone in your body, do you, Sinclair?"

"Nope." She shifted in visible discomfort. "Look, I'm sick of the attention and the gifts and the congratulations, okay? Holden and his wife flew all the way here from Montana just to give Kane and me that china set. What the hell are we gonna do with a *china set*?"

Trevor snorted. "Well, not everyone is as thoughtful as D when it comes to gift giving."

Abby's entire face lit up. "It took almost a year and a half," she announced, "but I finally like that son of a bitch."

Yeah, because apparently Derek "D" Pratt was the only person who knew Abby well. As a wedding gift, he'd bestowed a set of razor-sharp hunting knives upon the redhead and they'd brought honest-to-God tears to her eyes.

"Anyway," she said, "I'll call Isabel, but—"

"Thank you."

"*—but,*" she emphasized, "I'm not lying to her. I'll tell her about the wedding and suggest she come for a visit, but if she asks me whether you put me up to it, I'll say yes."

"Fair enough."

They were interrupted by a loud crash from the hallway. A moment later, three chocolate brown Labrador puppies bounded into the room and flew to their mistress's feet.

For the second time in less than a minute, Abby's expression brightened. "Hey, boys. What's got you all rattled?"

She knelt down and proceeded to lavish attention on the dogs in the form of loving petting and vigorous scratching. The little brown bodies wiggled around happily, while Trevor watched with a grin.

The pups had been deposited on the team's doorstep courtesy of Luke, whose love for his girlfriend, Olivia, was rivaled only by his love for his German shepherd. The happy couple had taken the mutt to Colorado with them, but not without making sure there'd still be a few canines running around the compound. And for some reason, anything with fur, four legs, and a tail was obsessed with Abby, though Trevor never would have pegged her as an animal person.

"I swear, these fucking dogs will be the death of me." An annoyed Kane appeared in the doorway. "Every time Hank tells me someone's at the gate, they destroy the house on their way to save you." He glared at the puppies. "I can take care of my own wife, assholes."

Abby lifted her head and leveled him with a toxic look. "Call them assholes again and you're sleeping on the floor tonight."

"It'd probably be more comfortable than the bed, seeing as *someone* lets her three bodyguards sleep with us."

Trevor watched the exchange in amusement, then grew serious when he realized what Kane had said. "Someone's at the gate?"

The other man nodded. "Yeah, Isabel just pulled up. Hank's buzzing her in."

It took a second for the words to register. When they did, Trevor's pulse promptly sped up. "Isabel's here?"

"Yeah, she came straight from the—"

Without waiting for Kane to finish, Trevor marched out of the room.

Chapter 2

He was waiting on the porch for her.

And he looked good. He looked *really* good.

Isabel's heart was beating fast as she killed the engine of the SUV she'd arranged to have ready for her at the private airstrip outside Tijuana. Although the sun had set and the sky was an inky black, the front courtyard of the main house was lit up like Fort Knox. Floodlights affixed to the high concrete fence surrounding the compound illuminated every inch of the yard, but the porch lighting was softer, a pale glow that cast a yellow halo around Trevor Callaghan's head.

She'd never been attracted to anyone the way she was attracted to Trevor. Everything about him spoke to something hot and primal inside her. His short dark hair. His eyes, the color of rich whiskey with flecks of gold around the pupils. His tall, muscular body and chiseled features.

His compassion, his strength, his loyalty . . .

Yes, it was more than his handsome good looks that drew Isabel to him. Trevor was the kind of man she'd dreamed about when she was a little girl. The kind of man you married and lived happily ever after with.

He was flawed, sure. Slightly damaged, yes. And yet that made her like him all the more.

Unfortunately, she wasn't a little girl anymore. She no

longer believed in fairy tales. Some people were fortunate enough to get their happily-ever-after, but she knew she wasn't destined to be one of them.

Isabel's nerves were getting the best of her as she slid out of the SUV. Palms damp, knees wobbly, pulse racing.

Taking a deep breath, she tried to control the atypical burst of anxiety and headed for the sprawling two-story house.

A set of steps led to the pillared entrance, where Trevor stood on the covered porch. His gaze fixed on her as she approached with confidence that she certainly did not feel.

Isabel ran a hand through her hair, and was slightly flustered when her fingers encountered air once they reached her shoulders. She'd forgotten that she'd cut her hair for the Nigeria job.

And wait. Had she removed the violet contacts before she'd left Noelle's penthouse?

She couldn't remember.

God, what color were her eyes?

Her heart beat faster, her throat suddenly tight. She was a bona fide mess—that was for sure. What kind of woman didn't even know what color her own eyes were?

"Isabel."

Trevor's deep voice broke through her panicked thoughts. He didn't move as she ascended the front steps. Didn't blink as their gazes met again.

"Hi, Trevor." Did her voice sound squeaky or had she imagined it?

"You look good," he said gruffly.

"Thanks. So do you."

"Noelle said you were undercover for the last five months."

"I was."

"And the job went well?"

"It did, yes."

So freaking polite. She couldn't believe they were standing around talking like a pair of acquaintances who'd run into each other at a party. At the same time, she couldn't bring herself to put an end to the silly pretense.

"What about you? Has Morgan sent you on any crazy missions?" she asked.

"Nothing too crazy. Security detail for a politician in Argentina. A couple of extractions."

"Piece of cake for you guys, right?"

Her tone was friendly, but inside, she wanted to scream. Maybe she *was* a coward. That was the only explanation for why her vocal cords seemed incapable of producing the two words she'd come here to say.

I'm sorry.

Two measly words, for Pete's sake. All she had to do was open her mouth and say them.

Yet she knew that the moment she uttered those three syllables, she would witness the condemnation in Trevor's eyes, and she wanted to avoid that for as long as possible. Granted, his current expression wasn't anything to write home about—guarded, veiled, with the barest glimmer of happy-to-see-you—but it sure beat the anger she knew would come.

Or disappointment . . .

God, the notion of Trevor being disappointed in her made her heart ache.

"Come inside." He took a step to the door. "Abby'll be happy to see you."

Isabel stayed rooted in place. "Can we sit out here for a while?"

After a second, he nodded. They drifted to the other end of the porch and sat down in a pair of comfortable wicker chairs. Even at night, the air was hot and humid, and Isabel regretted not changing out of her tight jeans, long-sleeved shirt, and high-heeled leather boots back at the airstrip. March in Paris meant coats and boots, but March in Tijuana was freaking sundress weather.

A silence fell. She spent the time chewing on her bottom lip and studying the half dozen vehicles parked on the dirt. A couple of Escalades, a few Jeeps, and a fire-engine red Ferrari that seemed completely out of place.

She gestured to the sports car. "Whose is that?"

"Sullivan's. It's usually in the garage with Morgan's Lamborghini and D's motorcycles, but Abby and Kane took it for a spin this morning. Good thing Sully's not here. He'd freak if he knew someone was driving his precious car. He loves that thing almost as much as he loves his boat." Trevor chuckled, and the husky sound caused warmth to spread through her.

"I assume he's on his yacht right now?" She couldn't help but smile as she thought about Sullivan Port, whom she'd met for the first time during the job in Manhattan. The big Australian had been charismatic, entertaining, and undeniably sexy.

Then again, most of the men on Jim Morgan's team were sexy, from Morgan himself to the man sitting beside her.

"Yep, Sully's on *Evangeline*, sailing around the world and leaving a trail of broken hearts in his wake. Actually, make that *two* trails of broken hearts. Macgregor's with him."

"Liam Macgregor, the contractor?"

"Morgan hired him on permanently. He's part of the team now." Trevor laughed again. "He and Sully are thick as thieves. Like BFF-friendship-bracelets-and-blood-brothers type of shit."

Isabel wasn't surprised. She'd met Liam on that last job too, and with his male-model good looks and endless supply of charm, he was just as appealing as Sullivan. It made perfect sense that those two scoundrels had hit it off.

"What about Luke? Last I heard, Olivia and her mom moved in with him." She hesitated. "Into your old place."

Trevor's voice went gruff. "Yeah. I sold the condo to Luke."

"And now you live here on Morgan's compound." Isabel glanced at the front door. "Where is Morgan, by the way? Normally he comes barreling outside whenever someone so much as looks at this place."

"He's out of town meeting with some contacts about a job."

It didn't escape her that they were going through the list

and discussing the whereabouts of everyone they knew rather than addressing the only subject that mattered.

Damn it. When had she become an avoider? She'd always prided herself on her ability to tackle problems head-on even if it meant dealing with some unwanted discomfort.

"He's been out of touch for a couple of days," Trevor was saying, "which gets pretty damn annoying, especially when—"

"I'm sorry I left," she blurted out.

Trevor stopped in midsentence. Then he released a breath. "So we're doing this, huh?"

She licked her dry lips. "We're doing it."

"About fucking time." He shifted in his chair and pinned her with a dark look. "Five months, Isabel. You disappeared without a trace for *five months*."

An eddy of guilt swirled inside her. "I'm sorry. I should've called."

"No, you shouldn't have *left*."

"I had to." The words came out as a whisper.

"You had to," he echoed flatly.

"It was moving too fast." A vise of helplessness squeezed her chest. No, damn it. She wasn't allowed to feel helpless. She quickly steadied her voice. "We were moving too fast. I realized I didn't want a relationship, and I chickened out, okay? I didn't want to disappoint you, so I took the easy way out by leaving."

She didn't expect the rush of slow laughter that exited his mouth. "Bullshit."

"Excuse me?"

"You heard me loud and clear, sweetheart. I call bullshit."

Sweetheart?

Her cheeks heated at the endearment. Trevor had never called her that before. Nobody had. And though she wasn't proud of it, she experienced a momentary burst of elation—until she remembered that he'd just accused her of lying.

"Moving too fast?" he went on before she could protest. "We were moving at a snail's pace and you know it. We'd been dancing around each other for months, refusing to acknowledge the attraction between us, and when we finally did acknowledge it, we didn't even take it to the next level. We kissed. One kiss, Isabel. We didn't fool around. We certainly didn't fuck, so don't patronize me."

His raised voice and crude language startled her. So did the anger smoldering in his eyes.

Trevor Callaghan normally epitomized cool under pressure. She'd heard him raise his voice only once in all the time she'd known him—when he'd ripped into her for saving his life in Colombia last year. Back then he'd wanted to die, but he was no longer that angry, broken man. In New York, he'd shown her the real Trevor. The man who wore his honor on his sleeve, the man who led with quiet authority and carefully weighed each word he said.

The man who made her heart pound with just one smile . . .

But the Trevor sitting beside her wasn't smiling. No, this Trevor was furious.

And rightfully so.

"I never took you for heartless, but goddamn it, Isabel. Fine, so you took the coward's way out and left, but did I mean so little to you that you couldn't be bothered to pick up the phone and call me? *Hey, Trev, yeah, I won't be coming home after all, so don't bother waiting around.*"

Much to her embarrassment, tears stung her eyes. "You're right," she said in a wobbly voice. "I was a jerk and a coward. I messed up."

He frowned. "At least have the decency to admit the real reason you skipped town."

"Trevor—"

"You were falling for me."

Her mouth slammed shut. Heart hammered against her rib cage. When she stared into those gorgeous eyes of his and saw the glint of challenge in them, her pulse raced even faster.

"You're wrong," she stammered. "I told you, I realized I didn't want to be with you."

He laughed.

She bristled. "I'm serious. I won't deny there was something between us, because there was. A spark, I guess. But my feelings changed. I . . ."

She trailed off, trying to organize her thoughts, but Trevor interrupted before she could continue.

"The only thing that changed is that Heaven Monroe killed herself that morning."

Isabel swallowed. "You heard about that, huh?"

"Of course I heard about it. I spent an entire fucking week in Manhattan, going out of my mind wondering if you were okay. I even—" He halted abruptly, taking a long, ragged breath before exhaling in a rush. "Forget it. None of that matters. Just don't play me for a fool, sweetheart. We both know why you cut and ran. Fear and guilt."

Her jaw went rigid. It didn't matter that he was right, or that every word he was saying hit its mark. His harsh tone triggered the irrational urge to attack.

"Quit psychoanalyzing me, Trevor. It's over and done with. I left. You're pissed. Can we just move past it and at least attempt to be friends?"

Incredulity flooded his expression. "Friends? Are you kidding me? You honestly think I'm going to let you off the hook that easily? You honestly believe you and I—"

"Ahem."

Both of their gazes flew to the door. The massive body filling the doorway belonged to Lloyd, the compound's housekeeper. With a sheepish look of apology, Lloyd shrugged his huge shoulders and rubbed the bushy red beard that devoured his big, square jaw.

"Sorry to interrupt, but I wanted to let you know dinner's about to be served out on the terrace." The gentle disposition seemed incongruous coming from a man who'd once worked as an enforcer for a Mob outfit in Boston.

"We'll be there shortly," Trevor said.

"Don't take too long." Lloyd glanced at Isabel with a smile. "Good to see you again, Isabel. The bride will be happy you're here."

She wrinkled her forehead. "The bride?"

"Abby," Trevor clarified in a grudging tone. "She and Kane eloped last week."

Isabel shot to her feet. "Are you serious? And she didn't call me?"

"Would you have even answered the phone?" was his muttered response.

She ignored the jab and made a beeline for the door. Before she crossed the threshold, she stopped and turned to meet Trevor's eyes, which continued to flicker with displeasure.

"We'll finish this later?" she said awkwardly.

"Damn right we will."

Her uneasiness returned, following her into the house. She may have gotten a reprieve just now, but she knew this wasn't over.

Oh no. Far from it.

Much to Trevor's annoyance, Isabel was her typical charming self throughout dinner. Chatting with Abby, making small talk with Beth McCall, flirting with Ethan.

And as usual, anyone who had the pleasure of being around her was drawn to her like a bee to honey. Men, women, children—no one was immune to Isabel's spell. No one could resist her melodic voice and warm smile and compassionate blue eyes.

This time around, Trevor saw through the charade. Isabel was the consummate actress. She'd created this easygoing facade to protect herself, to cover up the fact that deep down she was so incredibly vulnerable. Five months ago, he'd almost broken through her defenses. Maybe if he hadn't been equally vulnerable himself, he could've succeeded in convincing her to open up to him.

In his defense, back then he hadn't completely let go of Gina yet. Hell, he probably never would, but nowadays he was far more receptive to the idea of letting another woman into his life.

Not just any woman, though.

He wanted *this* one, damn it.

He couldn't tear his gaze away from her. Her hair was both shorter and lighter than the last time he'd seen her. Shoulder length and pale gold, which he knew was her real color. She'd removed her long-sleeved shirt for dinner, leaving her in a black tank top that contrasted with her smooth, lily white skin. When she wasn't donning a disguise, she looked so frickin' delicate. The sight of her triggered the urge to pull her into his arms and never let her go.

The large stone terrace, where Lloyd had served dinner, was ringed by a steel railing and overlooked the endless stretch of dark, barren land in the distance. The glass table with its wrought-iron legs was laden with the remnants of the group's meal—filet mignon, roasted potatoes, two different types of wild rice, a spicy brisket dish, several bottles of red wine, and a case of Bud Light.

The group sitting around the table was smaller than usual. Trevor and Isabel. Abby and Kane. Ethan and D, their resident taciturn asshole. And Beth and Holden, who were flying back to Montana in the morning. At one point, the compound's three new canines had been part of the fun, but they were eventually ushered inside for barking at Kane each time he touched his wife.

"So what exactly did this mysterious undercover op of yours entail?"

Abby's sharp inquiry jerked Trevor from his thoughts. There was no mistaking the suspicious chord in the redhead's voice or the shrewd glint in her eyes as she stared Isabel down.

Across the table, Isabel's expression remained relaxed. She reached for her wineglass and took a small sip. "It was the usual," she told her former colleague. "Recon, intel, same old."

"It took you five months to do some recon and gather intelligence?" Abby said skeptically.

"Yup."

"I see."

"Do you?"

The entire table was following the exchange between the two women, Trevor growing warier by the second. Did Abby know something about Isabel's last job? And if so, why hadn't she mentioned it to him? God knows he'd been hounding Abby for information ever since he'd moved to the compound.

"What exactly is it you do, Isabel?" Beth McCall asked in that quiet voice of hers.

"Undercover work mostly," Isabel answered vaguely. "I'm sent in to get close to a target or placed in a position where I can watch them, and I gather whatever intel I'm asked to acquire. The target's routine, likes and dislikes, personality traits, all sorts of information."

Information that Noelle or one of her girls then utilized in order to eliminate the target. But Trevor didn't blame Isabel for omitting that particular detail. Beth didn't seem like a woman who would understand or approve of contract killing.

"What do *you* do?" Isabel asked, smoothly steering the subject away from herself, the way she always did.

"I'm a chef at a French restaurant in Helena."

Holden smiled as he reached for his beer bottle. "She's being modest. Beth's the *head chef* at a *five-star* French restaurant in Helena. And she cooked everything we ate tonight."

Trevor felt like a borderline voyeur as he watched Holden and Beth exchange a tender look. The love and pride Holden felt for his wife were so obvious it was damn near poetic.

There was a time when Trevor had looked at the love of *his* life with that same smitten expression.

"You're an amazing chef, then," Isabel said warmly. "The food was delicious."

"I didn't prepare the brisket," Beth said quickly, a sweet flush on her cheeks. "That was all Lloyd." Her dark eyes focused on the empty dishes littering the table. "Actually, I should probably start cleaning up so he can bring out dessert."

On Beth's other side, Ethan immediately scraped back his chair. "You don't have to do that. We can handle it."

"I want to," Beth insisted. Her tone brooked no argument, and Trevor realized there might be some fire beneath that shy exterior.

Holden confirmed it when he turned to Ethan and said, "Don't argue with her when it comes to anything kitchen-related. She'll always win."

With Holden's help, Ethan and Beth cleared the table, then disappeared through the glass doors leading into the kitchen.

The moment the trio was gone, Abby spoke again, her yellow-brown eyes glaring daggers at Isabel.

"I didn't want to say it in front of Beth—that woman's so damn sweet she's giving me a toothache," Abby muttered. "But don't think you've got me fooled for one instant, Iz. I watch the news, you know."

Isabel's lips tightened. "What's that supposed to mean?"

D, who'd been smoking a cigarette by the railing, turned around with a raspy chuckle. "It means that yesterday morning someone put a bullet in Tengo Ekala's head. Gee, Blondie, whoever could have done that?"

Trevor didn't know what came as a bigger shock—D's sarcastic revelation or the fact that the man had joined the conversation at all. D wasn't usually so social. Of all the operatives who worked for Morgan, Derek "D" Pratt was the biggest enigma. With that close-trimmed dark hair, muscular tattoo-covered body, and perpetual scowl, he was downright terrifying at times. Not to mention incredibly hard to connect with.

But Trevor had witnessed a different side to D ever since he'd moved to the compound. Before, he'd thought D was a cold, heartless warrior with a penchant for bloodlust, but he'd soon realized there was more to the man than met the eye. For one thing, D was protective to a fault—he always looked after his teammates, including Abby, if his wedding gift to her was any indication. And when Luke had shown up with the puppies last month, Trevor would swear on his life that he'd seen D stroking one of those soft furry heads with infinite tenderness he wouldn't have dreamed the man capable of.

"If you're suggesting I had something to do with Ekala's death . . ." Isabel just shrugged.

She fucking *shrugged*, which sent a jolt of disbelief to Trevor's chest. "Jesus Christ, Isabel," he said in a low voice. "Were you in Nigeria?"

"Yes."

"You infiltrated Ekala's camp?" The mere thought had his gut going rigid with shock and anger. Ekala was one of the most feared warlords on the globe, a sadist who'd earned that reputation thanks to his spine-chilling torture methods and trigger-happy soldiers.

And Isabel had buddied up to the bastard?

"Noelle assigned you a contract?" Abby sounded as horrified as Trevor felt. "Why?"

Isabel gave another shrug. "She didn't have anyone else to send."

"Bullshit," Abby snapped. "She would've done the job herself before sending you, unless she was persuaded not to. For fuck's sake, Izzy, you convinced her to send you, didn't you?"

Isabel pushed back her chair and stood up. "Can we talk about this in private?"

Abby was on her feet before Isabel even finished her sentence. "Damn right we will."

Those were the same words Trevor had said to Isabel about their own unfinished business, and he noted the irony in the fact that Isabel was alienating the only two people who actually gave a damn about her. Who actually *saw* her. *Her*, not the various masks she wore.

Frustration clogged his throat as the two women stalked off. Their stiff body language hinted there would be nothing polite or civilized about their impending confrontation.

Trevor understood Abby's disapproval. Isabel wasn't a killer. She protected people, *saved* them. She didn't take lives unless it was absolutely necessary—or at least that's what she'd insisted both times they'd worked together.

His blood boiled as he remembered all those annoying phone calls with Noelle. Why hadn't the woman told him she'd sent Isabel on a contract job?

"Why did your lovely bride rush off with Isabel?" Holden asked Kane as he rejoined the group.

Beyond the terrace doors, Beth and Ethan were bustling around in the kitchen, while Lloyd placed a huge chocolate cake on a glass cake dish.

"Girl talk," Kane said lightly. "And you don't have to call Abby lovely on my account. We both know she's almost as scary as this guy." He hooked a thumb at D.

Trevor tuned everyone out, wishing he could be a fly on the wall for Isabel's conversation with Abby.

Fuck. Something was definitely up with the woman. He'd thought the only issue they had to contend with was the way she'd fled Manhattan after failing to help a drug-addicted stripper, but to hop a plane to Nigeria and get tangled up with an African warlord? To put a bullet in the guy's head?

Clearly there was a helluva lot more going on with Isabel than he'd thought.

Trevor didn't get another chance to speak to Isabel that night. She and Abby had disappeared into Morgan's study, and when the two women finally reappeared hours later, Isabel pleaded exhaustion and asked if they could talk tomorrow. Like the gentleman he was, Trevor had shown her to one of the upstairs guestrooms and bidden her good night.

He, on the other hand, couldn't grab a second of shut-eye. He was too wired, and knowing that Isabel was right down the hall pretty much guaranteed he wouldn't be getting any sleep. He didn't know why he was so drawn to her. Why he hadn't been able to stop thinking about her since the day they'd met.

You were falling for me.

As the accusation he'd lobbed at Isabel buzzed in his head, Trevor stifled a groan and slid out of bed. It was three in the morning, but sleep was clearly determined to elude him.

Wearing nothing but a pair of black boxer briefs, he approached the window and gazed out at the darkness-bathed landscape. Dense forest, rolling hills, the dusty trail that led to the outdoor shooting range beyond the trees.

Funny how easy it was to tell Isabel what *she'd* been feeling, yet he couldn't put a label on his own emotions. What exactly did he want from her? Sex? Well, that was a given—he was so attracted to her he couldn't think straight. But what else? Did he want a relationship? To build a life with her?

He had no clear answers for those questions. If anything, each question only raised a new one. But he did know that he liked her. A lot. And that he wanted—no, he *needed*—to explore this thing between them, whatever it was and wherever it took them.

He raked both hands through his hair, suddenly craving a good stiff drink. Insomnia was nothing new to him; he'd had bouts of it ever since he'd joined the army at eighteen. Most women would go crazy dealing with a man who paced the bedroom floor half the night, or who lay on the living room couch at four in the morning blankly staring at a television screen—but not Gina. That stubborn woman would stay up with him, even when she had an early shift at the bank the next morning. They'd sit in the kitchen with their respective glasses of warm milk—or whiskey, when the milk didn't achieve the desired effect. Sometimes she'd curl up against his chest and watch TV with him.

Agony burned in his throat. Ten years. He'd loved Gina for ten years, lived with her for eight, and after her death, not a day had gone by when he hadn't thought of the woman he loved. Now, his thoughts of Gina were no longer as frequent, but when they came . . . Christ, when they came, they made him feel ravaged.

Swallowing the lump of pain, he yanked on a pair of cargo pants and left the bedroom.

Shafts of moonlight from the skylights in the front parlor

cast a silvery glow on the off-white walls and the mahogany banister of the wide staircase. When he neared the living room, he instantly noticed the light spilling from beneath the closed oak doors. Looked like he wasn't the only one suffering from insomnia tonight.

No way of knowing who was behind those doors either. He hadn't heard a single footstep when he'd been lying awake in bed—every last person who lived on the compound moved like a ghost. Silent, invisible, deadly.

Opening the double doors, Trevor stepped into the great room and found Isabel curled up in one of the armchairs.

Her blond head snapped up at his entrance, blue eyes filling with wariness. "Hey," she said. "I didn't wake you, did I?"

"Nope. I had no idea you were even up."

He lingered in the doorway, noticing that her gaze was now focused on his bare chest.

Damned if her appreciative look didn't send a bolt of pure male satisfaction through him. After Gina died, he'd let himself go, totally unconcerned about his growing beer gut because the last thing a man felt like doing after losing the woman he loved was hitting the *gym*, for fuck's sake. He'd also quit the team and become a hermit, and who could forget all the time he'd spent trying to figure out how he could kill himself without making his mom and sister suffer?

Christ, he'd been a pathetic mess.

It had taken more than a year to kick his ass into gear. He'd gone back to work, reconnected with his family, his men, and, yeah, he'd definitely been working out more.

The appreciation flickering in Isabel's eyes made every last push-up, barbell curl, and brutal sparring session with D absolutely fucking worth it.

"Can't sleep?" he said lightly.

She sighed. "Jet lag. My body has no sense of time right now."

His bare feet padded on the hardwood floor as he made his way to the wet bar by the fireplace. He felt Isabel's gaze on him as he poured himself a glass of single-malt whiskey.

"Expensive taste in liquor, I see."

He set down the Bushmills bottle and turned to face her. "It's the Irish in me. I can only drink fine Irish whiskey."

A smile curved her lips. "You never mentioned your Irish roots before."

"That's because my family is as American as baseball and apple pie. My great-great-great-grandfather came over from Ireland, but other than a taste for their whiskey, I don't have much of a connection to the culture."

He flopped down in the chair opposite hers. Isabel started playing with the edge of the thin afghan she'd drawn up over her legs. There was a mystery novel in her lap, but she made no move to open it.

"I can't believe Abby is married." Her expression was indecipherable. "Don't get me wrong—I'm happy for her. I'm really happy, but it's just kind of . . . jolting, I guess. She's always been the most emotionally detached person I know."

"People change." He shrugged. "People grow."

"Clearly." Her voice took on a faraway note. "It gives the rest of us hope, no? If someone like Abby can lower her guard and let another person in, then maybe . . ."

Trevor's fingers tightened over his glass. "Then maybe what?"

He held his breath as he waited for her to finish that thought. If Abby could let down her guard, then maybe Isabel could? If Abby could let Kane in, then maybe Isabel could open her heart to *him*?

Her silence dragged on. He could see her pulse throbbing in the hollow of her throat. She was nervous. It drove him nuts that they couldn't be more open with each other, that they were always skirting around certain subjects, hiding certain emotions.

Would two people with so much baggage ever be able to make a relationship work? He'd been wondering that ever since Isabel ditched him in New York, and the same question arose now, giving him pause, making him uneasy.

Isabel still hadn't spoken. Her beautiful face creased with reluctance, as if she wanted to confide in him but couldn't lower her shield, not even a fraction of an inch.

He found it ironic that she thought *Abby* was the emotionally distant one.

Leaning forward to set his glass on the table, Trevor cleared his throat and searched her troubled gaze. "Isabel—"

An explosion rocked the house.

Before he even had time to register it, a wooden beam broke apart from the rafters and came crashing to the floor, two feet behind Isabel. She cried out in shock and flew off the chair, as the walls rattled and the entire house seemed to vibrate. Chunks of wood and plaster rained down on their heads, the ceiling beams cracking and splintering like thin ice on a frozen pond, about to break open.

"What the hell is going on?" Isabel shouted.

Trevor had no answer for that, nor did he have a chance to give it any real thought, because another beam had separated from the rafters, falling so fast he almost didn't reach her in time.

Fueled by the adrenaline sizzling in his blood, he threw himself on top of Isabel and shielded her with his body as the ceiling caved in on them.

Chapter 3

Sudden chaos.

Deafening explosions, falling debris, and thick gray smoke wreaked havoc on the house, the pandemonium so instant and the situation so dire that Isabel felt as though she'd been thrust into an alternate universe without warning.

To make matters worse, she couldn't seem to draw a single breath into her lungs, but that was probably because she'd just had the wind knocked out of her. One second she'd been vertical, the next she was flat on her back, being crushed by a heavy male body.

Trevor.

He'd thrown himself on top of her, his body absorbing the impact of the beam that had plummeted from the ceiling.

Something started to ring. Her ears? No, those were actual sirens. Where the hell were they coming from?

"You all right?" Trevor's urgent voice fanned over her. His hard chest blanketed her torso, powerful thighs straddling her legs.

"I'm fine," she said breathlessly. "What the hell is going on?"

"I have no fucking idea."

His shoulders and pecs strained as he struggled to get the two of them out from under the fallen beam. A moment later, they stumbled to their feet just as another ground-shaking blast reverberated from the back of the house.

"Jesus! This is a full-blown assault. You sure you're okay?"

"I'm fine," she said again.

"Good." The concern in his eyes transformed into intense focus, and then he was no longer in front of her, but jumping over pieces of wood and overturned furniture. He moved with military precision toward the bookcases spanning the far wall of the living room. He touched one of the shelves, and a second later, the unit popped open to reveal the hidden cabinet built into the wall behind it.

"In case we can't make it to the armory," he said when he caught her staring.

She didn't even recognize him—in the blink of an eye he'd gone from the Trevor she knew to a hard-core soldier, and for some strange reason seeing him in total control like this sent a thrill shooting through her.

He leaned into the deep space and emerged with two nine-millimeter SIG Sauers, one of which he tossed her way.

Isabel caught the weapon and checked the clip. Fully loaded. The sense of urgency in the air didn't dissipate, but only intensified as alarms wailed and muffled explosions continued to go off, most of them sounding like they were coming from above.

Trevor quickly grabbed more weapons from the gun cabinet. An assault rifle he slung over his shoulder. Knives and sheaths went in his pockets. A couple of grenades he clipped to the belt loops of his cargo pants. Spare ammo he shoved into the numerous pockets.

Isabel stood guard in the doorway, peeking out into the front parlor, which was enveloped in smoke. The acrid scent filled her nostrils and made her eyes water, so she ducked back into the living room. She looked up, noting that the ceiling didn't look at all stable. Plaster and splinters floated down like snowflakes, and one of the larger support beams was sagging in the middle, perilously close to snapping in two.

"Trev, we need to get out of here," she said sharply, gesturing north.

He followed her gaze and grimaced, then popped an earpiece in and clicked it on. "Hank, come in. What the hell is going on?"

Hank was one of the techs who ran the security booth—he'd buzzed her in at the gate when she'd arrived at the compound earlier. She didn't know what Hank was saying, but from the expression on Trevor's face, it couldn't be good.

Wood chips showered down on them as the center of that ceiling beam continued to bend from the pressure.

Crack.

"Trevor!" she shouted.

He raced toward her and the two of them dove through the living room doors just as the rafter crashed to the floor like a towering oak tree succumbing to a lumberjack's ax.

In the parlor, Isabel glimpsed bodies emerging from the haze of smoke shrouding the staircase. She automatically raised her gun, then lowered it when she made out Kane's face. Abby and D trailed after him.

All three were armed to the teeth and wearing identical looks of unadulterated fury. The compound's canine residents scampered at Abby's feet, eyes alert, body language aggressive, acting like those squeaky puppy barks could actually ward off potential attackers.

"Did you get Hank's report?" Kane demanded when he spotted Trevor.

Trevor's face was grim. "Two military Jeeps bearing down on us. Almost at the gate."

Another explosion shook the house. The walls around them shuddered, and suddenly the mechanical whir of rotors could be heard through the din. Sure enough, a helicopter flew directly over the skylights, its blades slicing rapidly through the early-morning air.

Isabel caught a blur of motion, a male figure hunched in the open cabin of the chopper, but she'd barely absorbed the sight when the figure raised a hand and—

"Grenade! Get down!" Kane shouted.

It was all the warning they had. Isabel flattened herself on the floor just as the skylights above them shattered into a million pieces. Glass fell from the ceiling like sparkling diamonds. Deadly diamonds. Protecting her head with her arms and hands, she felt the sting of pain as shards of glass pierced her skin. The little nicks wouldn't kill her, though.

No, the real threat came from whoever had launched this unforeseen assault in the first place.

This time her ears did ring from the explosion. She heard the muffled barks of the Labrador puppies as they continued to voice their outrage. Several muted blasts, coming from somewhere far away. And then someone was shouting her name.

"Isabel, answer me, damn it! Are you okay?"

Blinking wildly, she staggered to her feet and met Trevor's frantic gaze. "I'm fine. Just a little cut up." She noticed the blood dripping down his left arm. "You're hurt!"

"Got sliced in the arm. It's no big deal." His dark head shot up as the helicopter made another pass. He touched his earpiece. "Hank, what's the gate situation?"

Trevor, Kane, D, and Abby were all wired in to the security booth, and a moment later, all four let out the same simultaneous expletive.

"*Shit.*"

"What is it?" Isabel demanded.

"They blew up the gate." Kane took a step toward his wife. "You and Isabel need to head for the tunnel. Now."

The redhead protested. "No way. I'm not leaving you. We don't know what we're dealing with."

"The boys and I can handle it. Isabel can't get out alone—she doesn't know the exit protocol. I need you down in the tunnel, damn it." When the dogs started to bark again, Kane's expression pained. "And take the fucking pups with you."

"Incoming!" D barked.

In the blink of an eye, Trevor pushed Isabel toward the hall closet behind them as the chopper flew by and unleashed a spray of machine-gun rounds at the empty space where the skylights used to be. Bullets pounded the debris-covered floor, sending chunks of hardwood and glass spitting in all directions.

"We need to take care of that motherfucking bird," Trevor growled.

"On it," D said. He hurried off and disappeared in the smoke.

Loud footsteps thudded on the stairs. Every weapon in the room snapped up, then lowered when Ethan arrived on the scene. His handsome face was covered in soot, his T-shirt soaked with sweat, and his jeans were unbuttoned, as if he'd yanked them on in a hurry.

"I can't get to Holden and Beth," the rookie reported, looking both upset and exhausted. "Goddamn ceiling caved in and the rubble is blocking the hallway."

"They in Morgan's suite?" Kane asked. At Ethan's nod, he gave one of his own. "Holden'll use the balcony to get them out. I need you with Abby and Isabel. Gather the gear. Head for the rendezvous zone."

Ethan didn't question the orders. "Yes, sir."

The screech of tires penetrated the commotion, bringing a jolt of confusion to Isabel's chest. The soldiers at the gate were approaching. God, what the *hell* was going on?

Dazed, she met Trevor's brown eyes, which reflected nothing but calm. "It'll be fine," he said gruffly. "You'll be safe in the tunnel."

Two feet away, Kane grasped Abby by the chin and gave her a hard kiss. "Love you, sweetheart. See you on the other side, okay?"

Isabel opened her mouth to answer Trevor, but the next thing she knew, Abby was dragging her toward the corridor. There was no time to look back, no time to tell Trevor good-bye, or plead with him to stay safe. With Abby in the lead and Ethan bringing up the rear, Isabel found herself being herded to the back of the house.

When they neared the kitchen, Abby stumbled abruptly, then halted, causing Isabel to slam into her.

"Keep moving," Ethan ordered.

But Abby didn't budge. She pointed at the dogs, uttered a sharp "Boys, *stay*" and then darted into the kitchen.

A second later, gunfire erupted.

"Isabel, get down!"

She heeded Ethan's urgent command and dropped like a stone. As she positioned herself on her side with the barrel of her gun trained on the kitchen doorway, she had a perfect line of sight to what had stopped Abby.

Lloyd.

Dead.

With a sharp intake of breath, Isabel stared at the lifeless body of the giant housekeeper. He was on his back, half leaning against the bottom of the stainless-steel refrigerator, one meaty hand clutching his chest. His undershirt might have been white at one point. Now it was red, soaked with blood, with several bullet holes visible in the fabric. His dark eyes were wide open, a mask of pain and fury frozen on his face.

"Son of a bitch," she heard Ethan mumble, the grief in his voice evident.

Two more gunshots ripped through the air.

Where the hell was Abby?

Isabel couldn't get her bearings. She could hardly see through the smoke rolling out of the kitchen. The temperature was hotter too, as if something was on fire very close by.

She belly-crawled away from the open doorway and slid into a sitting position, flattening herself against the wall, which provided cover from the unknown shooters in the kitchen. Abby's loyal puppies were whining in the hallway, but they didn't make a single move, heeding their mistress's order to stay.

More gunshots blasted from the direction of the parlor. Fists of fear pummeled Isabel's chest. Trevor and Kane.

God, please let them be okay.

A blur of motion whizzed past her peripheral vision and then a loud *thud* echoed in the hall as a stocky man in faded fatigues landed on the floor, spraying a round of machine-gun shells into the wall as he went down.

Isabel raised her gun, but Ethan was already disarming the intruder before she could pull the trigger. The rookie, with his classic good looks and sweet demeanor, turned into a ruthless warrior right before her eyes. His features stretched taut across his face, hazel eyes glittering with rage, thick biceps rippling with power as he got the other soldier in a chest lock. Grunting, Ethan wrapped his hands around the man's neck and twisted.

A sickening *crack* sliced through the air.

Ethan let go of the dead man and the body slumped to the floor. "Abby!" he shouted into the kitchen.

No response.

"Goddamn it, Abby, answer me!"

The redhead appeared in the doorway, her honey-colored eyes lined with weariness. She clicked her earpiece and said, "Three dead tangos in the kitchen." Her gaze drifted to the dead body on the floor. "And we lost Lloyd."

Isabel didn't need to be plugged in to know how Trevor and the other men would react. Rage. Devastation.

The three puppies swarmed Abby. She scooped two into her arms while still keeping a solid grip on the twin Ruger pistols in her hands. "Let's keep moving," she ordered. "Iz, will you grab Brownie?"

Lord. Maybe this *was* a parallel universe. A mere twenty-four hours ago she'd been in Nigeria, slipping out of Ekala's tent and disappearing into the night.

Now she was racing down a smoke-filled corridor with a wriggling puppy in her hands, making her way to a secret underground tunnel.

The next explosion was louder and more powerful than any of the previous blasts. Again, it sounded like it had come from the front of the house.

Fear coursed through her veins. Not for herself, but for Trevor.

Ignoring the paralyzing rush of worry, she kept her head

down, matched Abby's brisk pace, tried not to inhale too much smoke.

And prayed that Trevor would come out of this alive.

Ethan and the women hadn't been gone a minute when the helicopter fell out of the sky.

Through the floor-to-ceiling windows on either side of the front door, Trevor saw the chopper plummet to the dirt in a grinding shriek of metal, blades spinning erratically like the wings of an injured bird. It landed fifty yards from the porch, and when it burst into flames, a blast of heat seared his bare chest. Shit, he needed a goddamn shirt. His skin was covered with soot, glass, and blood, and the razor-sharp glass fragments digging into his bare feet were annoying as fuck.

He and Kane stood on opposite sides of the entrance, weapons drawn, expressions hardened with fortitude. He stole another glance at the window and cursed.

"I count eleven."

"My count's a baker's dozen," Kane reported.

Thirteen men.

Shit.

In the courtyard, the soldiers went on the offensive, getting into formation and fanning out. Two groups of three broke off and moved with military precision toward the sides of the house. Seven made a fearless dash for the porch, using a zigzag pattern that made it difficult to lock in on a target.

Trevor shot out the windowpane and emptied the entire magazine of his MP5 on the approaching intruders. Two bodies hit the ground, then a third as Kane fired from his position.

Damn, he wished he'd made it to the armory. In a gunfight he always preferred the HK416 to the nine-mil submachine gun. Or an RPG. Fuck, if he had a rocket launcher right now, he'd blow these bastards to kingdom come.

As the four remaining soldiers ducked out of sight while maintaining their single-minded advance, Trevor glanced at Kane. "Take the three heading west?"

Kane nodded. "You got this?"

"Yeah, I'm good." He overturned the credenza leaning against the wall and dragged it several feet away, then took cover behind it and clicked his earpiece. "D, you copy? What's your position?"

D's gravelly voice rasped in his ear. "Roof. East side. Did a little bird hunting, rejoining the party now."

"Negative," Kane said. "Three tangos heading your way. We want at least one alive."

"Gotcha." However, D hadn't been radio silent for more than two minutes before he spoke up again. "Three tangos KIA. Fuckers opened fire on me. No choice but to engage."

Kane swore, then went absolutely postal when Abby reported there were four men down in the kitchen.

Trevor maintained his position, but the enemy soldiers seemed to be taking their sweet-ass time. After Abby checked in, he shot Kane a pained look. "Only one needs to stay alive, damn it."

"Clearly that's impossible seeing as we're surrounded by trigger-happy assholes," Kane muttered.

"You know one of those assholes is your wife, right?"

"Oh, I know." Green eyes flickering with irritation, Kane checked his ammo and edged toward the hallway to their left. "I'll neutralize the exterior team and track down Holden."

"Tunnel secure."

Ethan's brusque report brought a flicker of relief to Trevor's chest. Good. That meant Isabel was safe.

"Proceed with exit protocol," Kane ordered as he darted off.

The former SEAL had just turned the corner when a round of gunfire sprayed the front door and the intruders finally made their move. Chunks of wood, paint, and drywall ricocheted off the walls and slapped the front of the overturned table. A second later, heavy boots kicked in the skeleton of the door and bodies burst into the parlor.

Trevor opened fire, aiming for legs and abdomens rather than chests and heads. Two men hit the floor, two agonized shouts slicing the air. Shit, had he killed them? One of those fuckers had to live. One was all they needed to find out who the hell had sent these soldiers to ambush them.

When he popped his head out from behind the table, he glimpsed dusty fatigues, black boots, and a lot of firepower. Were they military? Mercenaries?

Trevor ducked out and fired another round, then took cover to shove a fresh clip into his machine gun. The intruders blasted him with return fire, spraying the credenza with bullets until the piece of furniture was riddled with more holes than a brick of Swiss cheese. Rendering his position ineffective.

Two soldiers remained, firing rapidly and practically trampling their injured as they came closer.

Taking a breath, Trevor dove away from the table, pulling the trigger as he abandoned his post. He connected with his targets—head shots. Both men hit the ground, but not before heat streaked through his bare shoulder. The glass littering the floor cut into the soles of his feet, but he hardly felt it. Adrenaline had dimmed his pain receptors while heightening his other senses.

As his heartbeat steadied, he approached the two wounded men and swiftly kicked away any weapons lying in their vicinity. His gaze focused on the first man, a bulky Hispanic with a shaved head. Eyes wide open. Dead.

Fuck.

"Ohhh." The pain-laced moan had come from the second soldier.

Still alive.

The man's breathing was ragged, wheezy, but his chest was rising and falling. Blood seeped out of both his kneecaps. The cries of agony that left his lips echoed in the suddenly silent house.

No more explosions. No more gunshots. No more grunts, shouts, gasps of pain. From the corner of his eye, Trevor glimpsed flashes of red and orange. The chopper. Engulfed in flames, a hunk of burning metal in the courtyard.

"I've got one alive," he reported. "Status?"

"Four tangos KIA," Kane reported back. His voice went dry. "Guess I'm a little trigger-happy myself. No sign of Holden. Making my way back to you."

"Sinclair?" Trevor asked.

"We're long gone. See you at the rendezvous."

"D?"

"Heading to you."

"Holden?"

No response.

"Hank?"

Silence.

Unease washed over him. Shit. Holden hadn't checked in once since the ambush began, and Trevor couldn't remember when Hank's last radio contact had been. Where the hell was the guy?

Trevor got his answer when D's grim voice filled his ear. "Hank's dead."

A few minutes later, Kane and D entered the parlor from opposite directions—D from the back hallway, Kane through the front door. Both men took a look around and shook their heads in amazement.

Trevor didn't blame them. The enormous space looked like a goddamn war zone. Bullet holes in the walls, smoke thickening the air, glass, debris, and blood staining the floor.

The soldier lying in the middle of the room moaned as Kane gave him a sharp kick in the side.

"Kneecaps," D remarked, his coal black eyes gleaming with satisfaction. "Nice."

"Let's get some answers from this motherfucker and get out of here," Kane said in a no-nonsense tone. "You got this, D?"

"You know it, bro."

The former Delta operative removed a hunting knife from the sheath on his belt and gripped the ox-bone handle. Lithe as a cat, he crouched next to the injured man.

"Now it's D's time to shine," Kane murmured.

"Who hired you?" D's voice was harsh, but the movements of his hand were ever so soft and smooth as he dragged the tip of his knife along the curve of his prey's clean-shaven jaw.

The soldier didn't respond.

The blade danced its way down to the man's left knee.

"You don't remember, huh?" D said sardonically. "Maybe this will refresh your memory."

He dug the tip of his knife into the soldier's shattered kneecap.

Though the resounding cry of anguish made Trevor cringe, he didn't have anything against D's method of persuasion. Sometimes extreme measures were necessary to get the job done.

And no matter how professional a man wanted to be, sometimes that need for revenge clouded every last bit of common sense. All Trevor had to do was remember Abby's dull "We lost Lloyd" and D's curt "Hank's gone" and any sympathy he might have felt for the wounded man in front of them left his body like dirty bathwater spiraling down the drain.

"Who. Hired. You." D's tone was deceptively calm, but the look in his eyes could have terrified even a bloodthirsty animal.

The next silence earned their prisoner a stab in the right knee.

Another scream sliced through the parlor.

Shrugging, D glanced up at Kane. "Time to start cutting off some limbs?"

"Lassiter!"

The hysterical shout echoed in the air, making Trevor's lips twitch. Why was it always the threat of losing a limb that spurred a man to capitulate? Any soldier worth his salt, any soldier who'd been trained right, would offer his hands and feet on a silver platter before giving the enemy a vital piece of intel.

"Lassiter," D echoed in a pleasant voice. "Lassiter who?"

When their prisoner didn't answer, D jammed his knife deeper into the man's knee, eliciting a moan of misery.

"Ed Lassiter. Eddie."

Trevor narrowed his eyes. Why did that name sound so damn familiar?

Beside him, Kane's lips curled in a sneer. "Shit, I know Lassiter. He's a scumbag lowlife who specializes in putting together hit squads."

"Right." Trevor nodded in recollection. Lassiter's name came up often on the merc grapevine. He was a middleman who paired mercenaries up with potential clients. Known to be shady as hell too.

"Who hired Lassiter?" Trevor demanded.

"I d-don't know," the soldier stammered.

D removed his knife from the man's knee and brought it up to his throat. A thin red line appeared as the blade pressed into flesh.

"You don't know, or is this another lapse in memory?" D said mockingly.

"I don't know! I swear! Lassiter assembled the team, told us the objective—"

"Which was?" Kane interrupted. "What was the objective?"

"Kill every man on this compound." The man moaned again, his breathing going shallow.

He was beginning to show signs of blood loss. Mottled skin, sweat dotting his forehead, glazed eyes. Before long those eyes closed and the man went unconscious.

"You wanna keep him alive and try again?" D asked Kane.

Kane, who served as second-in-command in Morgan's absence, shook his head. "He gave us a name. That's enough."

"Do we leave him here?"

"Might as well. It's not like he's walking out of here." Kane slung his rifle strap over his shoulder and unholstered his pistol. "Let's find Holden and get the hell out. The compound's been compromised." He turned to D. "Can you deal with the explosives?"

D nodded, drawing Trevor's attention to the black and red snake tattoo circling the base of his neck. "Find McCall. I'll handle the rest."

As D stalked off, Trevor and Kane exchanged a wary look. "Ethan said Holden and Beth were trapped in Morgan's suite, but there's a balcony there," Kane said in a low voice. "Holden could scale that thing in his sleep."

"Maybe Beth couldn't?"

"Holden was a fucking Ranger. He would have found a way to get her down."

Trevor secured his MP5 and palmed his SIG. "Maybe they made it out. Maybe they're already on their way to the rendezvous." He paused in afterthought. "No, if Holden had found a way out, he also would've found a way to check in with us."

"Even if they did manage to escape, I'm not taking off without knowing for sure," Kane said.

They went outside through the front door, which had been reduced to a naked frame and a pile of wood. The chopper across the courtyard continued to burn, but the fire had lost some of its intensity. Plumes of black smoke spiraled up from the wreckage and were carried away by the cool breeze. The smell of fuel, exhaust, and smoke clogged the air.

Judging by the faint sliver of light on the horizon, dawn was approaching, but the sky was mostly black as they rounded the main house. They stopped only to pop into the detached garage, where Kane grabbed a coiled length of rope from one of the worktables, and then they continued on their way.

It was eerily quiet out, save for the soft hiss of the wind and the occasional crash as another wall or ceiling collapsed inside the blown-to-shit estate Trevor had called home for five measly months.

Morgan's suite of rooms was on the second floor, offering a large rectangular-shaped balcony ringed by a curved steel railing. The balcony was fifteen feet off the ground, give or take. The men gauged the height, then exchanged another look.

"Rock, paper, scissors?" Kane suggested.

"Fuck. Fine."

Trevor threw paper.

Kane threw rock.

Trevor was given the honor of planting his bloody feet on Kane's shoulders and being hurled into the air. His hands caught the railing, fingers wrapping around the cold metal. He heaved himself up and over, soundlessly landing on the concrete floor before bouncing to his feet.

The balcony doors had been shattered. Curtains were half open, the burgundy fabric fluttering in the night air. Trevor prayed that Holden had shot the doors himself for some reason, and that the McCalls had made it to safety, but the ominous humming in his body told him they hadn't been that lucky.

Swallowing his unease, he secured the rope to the railing in a two-turn bowline knot and flung it over the side. The rope stretched taut as Kane shimmied up it. Half a minute later, the ex-SEAL's legs swung over the rail, his boots met concrete, and he joined Trevor at the doors.

Neither man said a word as they raised their pistols. They approached the threshold with cautious steps.

Trevor's gaze immediately landed on the slumped shape beyond the doors. His breath caught, then steadied when he noticed certain details about the dead man on the floor. Buzz cut. Caramel-colored skin. Not Holden.

As relief shuddered through him, he slid into the master bedroom ahead of Kane. It was bathed in shadows. Not a single light, no sounds except for the occasional cracking noises as pieces of plaster dislodged from the ceiling. Whatever firepower that helicopter had been packing—RPGs, Trevor suspected—had left a gaping hole in one section of the ceiling, revealing the inky, moonlit sky. Broken clay tiles slid off the exposed roof and crashed to the floor, several pieces colliding with the motionless figure on the carpet.

Apprehension skated up Trevor's spine, growing stronger when he got a better look at the lifeless body. The merc's fatigues were soaked red. Looked like someone had unloaded an entire clip into the dude's chest.

"Holden?" Trevor murmured.

Kane had also made a soundless entrance. From the corner of his eye, Trevor saw the other man assessing the scene with a frown.

Morgan's room was a purely masculine space, with dark blue walls and a black and silver color scheme. Expensive furniture, but no framed photographs or knickknacks cluttering the dressers. No art or decoration on the walls except for a massive flat-screen TV.

The thick black carpet felt like sheer heaven beneath Trevor's torn-up feet. Shit, he definitely needed to find some socks and boots before they hauled ass.

"Holden, where the fuck are you?" Kane muttered, frustration resonating in his voice.

A soft rustling came from the other side of the king-size bed.

Trevor raised his gun and moved closer.

This time when his breath hitched, it didn't ease or get released. It lodged in his throat until his lungs burned and his chest ached.

Holden was on the floor with his back against the wall and his bare legs stretched out before him. His broad shoulders were hunched over, shaking uncontrollably as he clung to the woman in his arms. He rocked her as if she were a baby, murmuring silent words as he stroked her black hair and gazed into her vacant eyes.

Kane came to a halt beside Trevor, a ragged burst of air leaving his mouth. "Oh fuck."

Chapter 4

Trevor's heart stopped. He had no words. No idea how to console the man in front of them.

Beth McCall was dead. Her dark eyes were devoid of life, her loose white tank top covered with bloodstains. She'd been shot. Twice from the looks of it, and right in the heart.

"Holden," Kane said gently.

The man looked up at them with blank gray eyes. "Oh. Hi."

Shit.

Shit, shit, *shit*.

Trevor knew that expression. He knew that empty tone of voice. Holden was still breathing, but the man had died the second Beth had been taken away from him. Same way Trevor had died when he got that phone call informing him his fiancée had been killed during a home robbery.

"We've been married for nineteen years. Did you guys know that?" Holden asked them.

Trevor swallowed. "No, I didn't."

With a fervent nod, Holden looked at his wife's pale face again. "I met her when I was eighteen years old. It was at a graduation party at the lake, the day before I enlisted. She didn't want to hang out with me that night. She thought it would be pointless to get involved when I was leaving the next day."

Trevor cast a surreptitious look in Kane's direction. Indecision, sorrow, and frustration dominated the man's green eyes. They had to get off the compound. Trevor knew it. Kane knew it. Holden did too, on some level.

But their teammate was rooted to the floor, his arms wrapped so tightly around his wife it would take the Jaws of Life to pry them apart.

Several more tiles broke off the damaged roof and slammed into the bed, shaking the mattress.

"I convinced her to have a drink with me." Holden remained oblivious to the falling rubble and the urgency stifling the air. "We spent the entire night talking and laughing and fooling around, and by the time morning arrived, I'd managed to convince her to wait for me." Now he sounded amazed. "She knew me for less than twenty-four hours, and she agreed to wait for me. Can you believe that?"

"Sounds like a woman who knew what she wanted," Trevor said quietly.

"We were married a year later when I was home on leave."

A muffled thump came from the balcony.

Trevor turned to see D stride into the room. The big man took a quick look around before approaching the source of the action. When his black eyes absorbed the scene in front of him, D's expression didn't even change, but his voice was unusually bite-free as he murmured, "Fail-safes are in place."

Something cracked. A moment later, another piece of the ceiling crashed to the floor, revealing the support beams beneath the plaster. One of the wooden slats was about to give, if its ominous creaking was any warning.

Son of a bitch. Trevor was getting damn tired of roofs caving in on him.

"Holden, we have to go," he said. "Why don't you tell us the rest of the story later?"

The man ignored the request. "She always worried about me when I was deployed. She wanted me to leave the Rangers. I re-upped three times before I finally agreed to retire. I had the job with Morgan lined up, and . . ." His expression grew tormented. "I promised her working for Jim wouldn't be as dangerous as the army. I promised her I'd be safe."

Trevor's heart squeezed. "Holden. We really need to go."

"No!"

The sharp exclamation made everyone flinch. Even D, who was fazed by nothing.

"I'm not leaving my Beth," Holden said firmly. "So fuck right off."

After several seconds of silence, Kane sighed. "We'll bring her with us. We'll carry her body—"

"Don't you *fucking* call it that! It's not her *body*. It's *Beth*."

Shit, their teammate was unraveling like a tattered sweater before their eyes. Trevor took a step forward and knelt in front of the heartbroken man. At that precise moment, a piece of plaster plunged down from the ceiling and nearly clipped his ear off, but he shifted out of the way before any damage could be done.

"Holden, I know this is hard. I know you don't want to leave her, but that's not Beth. Beth is gone."

He kept his tone soft, but firm. Come to think of it, it was the same tone Kane had used when convincing Trevor to rejoin the team last year. He hadn't wanted to return to the land of the living either, not when the woman *he* loved was dead.

But although Trevor knew exactly what the other man was going through, he refused to let Holden drown in grief the same way he had.

"You can bring her with us, but you know that's not a good idea," he went on, meeting Holden's devastated gray eyes. "You need to say good-bye now, and then you need to come with us."

"No."

"Yes." Trevor's gaze landed on the beautiful, lifeless woman in Holden's arms. "She's gone, man. All you can do now is—"

He was interrupted by another crash, and then a *thud*. He swiveled his head in time to see D hit the floor like a sack of potatoes.

A quick glance north revealed that one of the overhead beams had tumbled down.

Right on D.

Kane immediately dropped to his knees to check on his fallen comrade. "He's out cold," Kane said, sounding both worried and amused. "Jesus. He survives a full-out military assault, only to get KO'd by a two-by-four."

In front of Trevor, Holden was holding Beth even tighter. "I won't leave her," he said stubbornly.

Behind them, Kane sounded increasingly concerned as he attempted to rouse D without any results. "Shit. Trev, he's not coming to."

"Does he have a pulse?"

"Yeah. A strong one. But . . . oh fuck . . . his head's bleeding like crazy."

A ripping sound cut the air. Trevor turned, saw that Kane had torn off his sleeve and was now pressing it to the back of D's head.

Son of a bitch. Son of a *motherfucking* bitch.

Frustration constricted in Trevor's chest, making it impossible to take a breath. This was a clusterfuck and a half. The compound blown to hell. D unconscious with a gushing head wound. Holden refusing to let go of his dead wife.

Trevor's gaze drifted back to Beth. Christ, that sweet, beautiful woman. Dead.

Like Gina.

"He needs to go to the clinic," Kane said briskly.

Trevor let out a breath. "Holden, listen—"

"I. Won't. Leave. Her."

Goddamn it.

"Go," Trevor told Kane. "Take D and get him help. I'll stay with Holden."

Reluctance creased the other man's features.

"I'm serious, Kane. The compound's been compromised.

A second assault team could be making its way here as we speak."

"Trev—"

"Did D secure the perimeter and set the charges?"

Kane nodded, then reached into his pocket and pulled out a detonator. He tossed it to Trevor, who caught it easily. "You sure about this, man?"

"I'm sure. Just get D some medical attention."

"I can't exactly throw this mofo off the balcony," Kane pointed out, frazzled. "I'll have to carry him out the door."

Which meant they needed to move whatever was blocking said door.

God. Fucking. Damn. It.

Wow. He couldn't remember ever having so many expletives buzzing through his brain.

On the floor, Holden had started to rock Beth again, his head bent low as he pressed his chin to his wife's ashen face.

Suppressing another weary obscenity, Trevor stood up and went to help Kane clear a path in the hall.

Isabel was going out of her mind with worry. She, Abby, and Ethan had been waiting at the rendezvous point for what felt like days. In reality, they'd only been in these darkness-drenched foothills for ten, fifteen minutes tops, but the longer the others took in getting here, the more concerned she became.

"Do me a favor?"

She lifted her head at the sound of Ethan's pained voice. She'd been sitting on the hood of the Humvee they'd driven out of the tunnel, but she slid off as the young man approached. Not *that* young, she had to amend, as she noticed the way his sweat-soaked T-shirt clung to an impressive set of washboard abs. She knew he was in his midtwenties, yet for some reason he'd always seemed younger to her. Boyish.

But he hadn't acted like a boy tonight. He'd acted like a man. Pure alpha male, moving with lethal precision, killing without batting an eye.

Apparently he also dealt with injuries the way an alpha male did—by ignoring them.

Isabel stared at the blood dripping from his shoulder and down his bare arm. "Did you get *shot*?"

He shrugged. "Yeah. Don't worry. I'm fine."

"Sure you are," she said, unable to control her sarcasm. "What's the favor, then?"

Ethan held out a pair of tweezers and a small first-aid kit. "Dig the bullet out of my arm?"

Isabel gaped at him. Un-freaking-believable. She knew the men on Morgan's team were expertly trained and macho as hell, but the kid had been walking around all night with a *bullet* lodged in his arm and hadn't shown a single visible sign of pain? She couldn't help but be impressed.

Sighing, she patted the hood and gestured for him to hop up. As he got comfortable, Isabel took a breath, then glanced in Abby's direction. The redhead hadn't left her post since they'd arrived, not even to check on the dogs sleeping in the backseat of the car. She was keeping watch, her concern for Kane evident despite her attempt to hide it.

Dawn was the only time of day when the temperature was actually refreshingly cool, and a nice breeze lifted Isabel's hair and tickled the back of her neck as she gingerly rolled up Ethan's sleeve. He had the letters USMC tattooed on his biceps, done in black calligraphy. United States Marine Corps.

"I always forget you're a former marine," she mused.

"No such thing."

She wrinkled her forehead. "Huh?"

Ethan's straight white teeth gleamed in the darkness as he smiled. "There's no such thing as a *former* marine. Once a marine, always a marine."

"Ah, I see." She removed some antiseptic wipes from the first-aid kit and then returned her attention to his arm. "When did this happen?"

Ethan pursed his surprisingly sensual lips. "Outside the kitchen, when that asshole dove out with guns blazing."

When they'd found Lloyd's body . . .

Isabel pushed the memory aside and concentrated on wiping away the blood caked on Ethan's thick upper arm. Once she cleaned the area, she examined the puckered hole in his flesh, then touched the back of his arm to feel for an exit wound. Damn. He was right. The bullet was still in there.

"You want something to bite down on?" she asked him.

"Naah. I'm good."

"Uh-huh. Of course you are."

Damn macho man.

Gripping the tweezers with steady fingers, Isabel leaned close, brought the tips of the tweezers to the wound, and proceeded to spend the next fifteen minutes playing doctor. It was just the distraction she'd needed. She was so focused on digging the 39 mm slug out of Ethan's arm that she succeeded in blocking out this entire catastrophe of a night.

After she fished the bullet out, she cleaned and dressed the wound, impressed with how still and unflinching Ethan had been throughout the "procedure."

"Thanks," he said gratefully. "I could've done it myself, but it's easier when someone else gets the bullet out."

She shook her head in amazement. "You're welcome."

When the hum of an engine rumbled in the distance, her back stiffened and she went on the alert. Even though Kane had checked in to say he was on his way, Isabel's rigid muscles didn't relax until she glimpsed the familiar blond head behind the wheel of the camouflage Humvee barreling their way.

The relief didn't last long. Kane's report hadn't specifically mentioned Trevor, but she'd assumed the men would be together.

But only Kane got out of the vehicle.

"Where are the others?" she demanded as he approached them with somber green eyes.

He planted a quick kiss on Abby's lips before answering. "D's unconscious in the back of the Humvee. His thick skull absorbed most of the impact of a ceiling collapsing on it and he needs to get checked out ASAP. Trevor stayed behind to deal with the Holden situation."

"The Holden situation?" Abby echoed.

Kane let out a breath. "Beth's dead."

A shocked silence hung in the air.

Finally, Abby frowned at her husband. "Why didn't you say anything?"

"I don't know. Fuck, I guess I didn't want to believe it myself. But she's gone, shot to death. And Holden is a fucking mess."

Isabel could imagine. God. What the man must be going through right now. She'd met Beth McCall mere hours ago, but it was easy to see that Holden adored his wife. He'd mentioned over dinner that their nineteen-year anniversary had just passed. The couple had been together for two decades, for Pete's sake.

Her heart clenched, a wave of grief swelling inside her and gathering strength when she realized what Kane had said.

Trevor had stayed behind to help Holden.

She supposed it was only fitting—if anyone could empathize with Holden, it was Trevor. He knew what it was like to lose the love of your life.

Isabel went on the alert again as Kane's hand moved to his earpiece. "Yeah, I copy," he barked. "What's your ETA?"

He listened intently, as did Abby and Ethan, while Isabel cursed every single one of them for not giving her a damn earpiece so she could stay in the loop.

"What's going on?" she asked. "Was that Trevor?"

Kane nodded. "He and Holden are on their way."

No sooner had the words left his mouth than a series of rapid explosions shook the landscape. Before, Isabel hadn't been able to see the compound—it was too dark, and the compound was too far away.

Now she had a clear view of it.

Her eyes widened as red and orange flames lit up the night. The wind carried with it the sulfuric scent of smoke, and as the compound burned before her eyes, Isabel experienced a strange sense of grief. She'd visited Morgan's property only a couple of times, yet for some reason the blazing conflagration evoked genuine, visceral loss.

The others didn't seem as upset. "It's protocol," Kane explained when he noticed the distress on Isabel's face. Then he turned to Ethan, who was staring at the inferno. "Did you call the airfield?"

Ethan nodded. "We're all set."

"Good. Take the Humvee and make your way there. The sooner D gets on that plane, the better. I'll wait here for Trevor and Holden."

"I'm staying with you," Isabel said immediately.

Abby set her jaw. "Me too."

"You're with Ethan, sweetheart," Kane said with a shake of his head. "He'll need help with D."

Although Abby looked unhappy, she didn't object. Isabel knew that when Kane gave Abby an order, it wasn't as a husband ordering his wife around, but as a superior officer talking to a member of the team. Kane was Morgan's second-in-command, which meant he called the shots when the boss was away.

Still, the couple did exchange a tight hug and a not so professional kiss before Abby and Ethan left in the Humvee. The vehicle raised a cloud of dust and disappeared into the darkness.

Isabel and Kane didn't say much as they waited for the rest of their party. They didn't have to wait long; less than twenty minutes later, a third Humvee appeared at the top of the crest and sped toward them.

When Trevor slid out of the driver's seat, the relief that slammed into Isabel's chest was so powerful she nearly keeled over.

He was alive and in one piece, his tall, muscular frame now clad in cargo pants, a long-sleeved shirt and black shit kickers. His jaw was covered with dark stubble, lending him a feral air.

Without questioning her actions, Isabel eliminated the distance between them and threw her arms around his neck.

"Whoa, easy," Trevor said when their chests collided with a thump. His voice came out husky now. "Good to see you too, sweetheart."

Emotion tightened her throat to the point that she couldn't even swallow. She took a deep breath, inhaling the scent of smoke and death and something that was uniquely Trevor. Woodsy, lemony, male.

"Are you okay?" she asked urgently.

"I'm fine."

"That's what Ethan said too, right before he asked me to dig a bullet out of his arm."

Trevor chuckled. "I'm bruised, cut up, and I think a couple of bullets grazed me, but I promise you, Iz, I'm fine." The amusement in his whiskey-colored eyes faded when a car door slammed.

Isabel shifted her gaze. Her heart stopped at the sight of Holden McCall's face.

Dead.

God, the man was completely dead inside. In fact, he looked very much the way Trevor had when she'd first met him. Vacant gaze and defeated posture. Radiating sheer and total indifference. To his surroundings, to those around him. To life.

"Do your thing, Isabel."

Trevor's soft request caught her by surprise. "My thing?"

"That thing you do. You heal people with your warmth. You make them feel . . . safe." He sounded tired and sad.

When their eyes met, she found herself breathless. Concern. Sorrow. Rage. Tenderness. Heat. So many emotions flickered in his gaze that she didn't know which one to focus on.

Eventually she just broke the eye contact and stumbled away, but she could feel Trevor's gaze boring into her back.

She went to Holden, who didn't even react to her approach. "Come on," she cajoled, holding out her hand, "sit in the backseat with me. We'll keep each other company on the way to the airfield."

At the sound of her voice, Holden blinked several times, as if emerging from a trance. Then his broad shoulders slumped and he nodded.

You heal people with your warmth. You make them feel safe.

Trevor's words floated through her head, and she couldn't quite argue with his observation. She did seem to possess the ability to put people at ease. To soothe them.

The only person she couldn't ever seem to soothe was herself.

She took Holden's hand and led him to the Humvee. When she stole a glance over her shoulder, she found that Trevor was still watching her intently.

Their gazes locked again, and something hot and sweet and confusing passed between them.

But now was not the time to try to decipher that odd jolt of connection.

Wrenching her eyes away, she slid into the backseat next to Holden and shut the door.

D felt like someone had beaten his skull in with a sledgehammer. His head throbbed like a motherfucker, aching with each vibration of his pulse. When his eyes opened, his vision was assaulted by fluorescent lighting that made him grit his teeth. Fighting the urge to close his eyes, he breathed through the pain and examined his surroundings.

White paint-chipped walls. A small square window. That nausea-inducing lighting and the smell of disinfectant.

He was at the clinic, then. But why? Had he been hit? Had one of those motherfuckers shot him in the head?

The world started to spin like a carousel when he tried to sit up.

"Don't be a hero, man. Just lie back down like a good little soldier."

Kane's taunt brought a scowl to D's lips. He shifted his gaze and spotted his teammate standing in the doorway.

"Doc, he's awake," Kane called to someone outside D's line of vision.

"What the hell happened?" he grumbled as the other man entered the room.

"A beam crashed down from the ceiling and connected with your skull. But I mean, of course it did—your big fat head makes an easy target."

"Ha ha."

Damn, he hadn't even been shot? He scanned his brain for the last thing he remembered.

Setting the charges.

Scaling Morgan's balcony.

Finding Holden with a dead woman in his arms.

He swiftly forced away the memories and focused on business. "You took care of loose ends?"

Kane nodded. "Compound's gone. Nothing but a pile of rubble."

"Trev and Holden?"

"They're around here somewhere. Ethan took a bullet to the arm, but he's good. Isabel and Abby are fine."

"Did you call Morgan?"

Before Kane could respond, a little brunette with dark hair and sharp green eyes flew into the room like she owned the place. Well, technically she did. Barely thirty years old, Sofia Amaro was the sole physician at this clinic, a privately funded medical facility that catered to the surrounding villages. The small brick building was tucked away at the base of the mountain, several hours from the city of Oaxaca and isolated enough that it made an ideal place to get fixed up. At one time or another, nearly every man on Morgan's crew had paid a visit to Sofia.

"Good to see you, Derek." She approached the gurney he was lying on, a grin on her face.

"How's it going, Doc?"

She gave a mock gasp. "Wait. Did you actually ask how I was? You must have been hit harder than we thought."

She was right—he normally didn't go out of his way to find out how the people around him were faring. Truth was, he didn't give a shit.

But he'd figured out a long time ago that if you weren't nice to Sofia Amaro, you paid dearly for it.

"Let me do a quick examination." She pulled a penlight from the pocket of her flannel button-down shirt. "Follow the light, big guy."

For the next five minutes, he humored the good doctor,

but only because the last time he'd given her grief she'd retaliated by telling Morgan that D required a week of bed rest, when they both knew he could've been walking around within a day or two. No way was he letting that happen again.

The compound had been attacked, for fuck's sake. Some asshole had hired a middleman to put together a hit squad of mercenaries. Mercenaries who'd been ordered to leave no one alive. So, yeah, he refused to let this sadist of a woman keep him from hunting down the fucker who'd ordered this morning's ambush.

"Pupils look good. Any nausea?"

"Nope," he lied.

"How bad is it?"

D glared at her. "I just said—"

"I know what you said." Sofia arched a brow. "How bad is the nausea?"

"Manageable," he muttered.

"Headache or dizziness? Ringing in your ears?"

"Mild headache."

"Feeling weak? Any trouble breathing?"

"No."

"Good." Those green eyes grew serious. "You lost a lot of blood. You would've died if Kane hadn't performed an emergency transfusion."

D's gaze flew to Kane's, who grinned. "Yup. I did it on the plane. Congratulations, you've got two units of grade-A Woodland blood in you. Be prepared—you're going to feel extra strong from now on."

The doctor rolled her eyes and stepped away from the gurney. "Bed rest," she said, jabbing a finger at D. "A few days, at least. You'll be weak and lethargic because of the blood loss and you need to give your body time to recover."

Not fucking likely.

Aloud, D said, "Sure thing, Doc."

Clearly he wasn't at all convincing, because Sofia turned to Kane and said, "Make sure he stays put for a while."

"You got it."

After Sofia left the room, D made another attempt at

sitting up. This time he managed to do it without feeling like he was going to simultaneously puke and pass out.

The moment they were alone, Kane resumed the situation report. "This is a total clusterfuck, man. And we can't reach Morgan."

D narrowed his eyes. "He shouldn't be out of touch. He went to meet his CIA guy in D.C., nothing high risk about it."

"Well, the bastard's not picking up his phone."

"How long have I been out?"

"Since we left the compound—five hours. But like you said, we should be able to reach him. Even if he was in the middle of a meeting, he would've seen my hundred SOS's and called back. I also left a message with our contact at the CIA. So we'll see what he says when he gets back to me."

Worry churned in D's gut, making him even queasier than before. The boss often disappeared for days or weeks at a time, but never without warning. This trip to D.C. was a routine business meeting, only a two-night thing. There was no reason for him to be AWOL, unless . . .

"Shit," D mumbled.

Kane lowered his voice. "Remember what the fucker said about how they were ordered to kill every man on the compound? *Morgan's* compound, his entire team. Stands to reason that our boss really pissed someone off."

D had been thinking the same damn thing. Which wasn't at all surprising—Morgan had almost as many enemies as D. Men in their line of work usually did.

"This is bad, man." Kane raked both hands through his hair, looking frustrated and pissed off. "Compound's been blown to hell. Holden's wife is dead. Lloyd and Hank are dead. Morgan's gone. We've got men in the field who may also be targets, but I don't know if I should pull them out."

"You got in touch with Castle?"

"Yeah. I told him to watch his back, watch his team, and get the job done as fast as he can. I also spoke to Luke—he was ready to get on the next plane out, but I told him to stay put. Sully and Liam are on call too, until we figure out our next move."

Kane's arms dangled at his sides, a tired look entering his eyes. "Once Sofia clears you for travel, we'll head to the Costa Rica estate. Morgan was intending to use it as a second base camp, if needed. The place is fucking huge, and there's no connection to Morgan. Technically Abby and I own it, but the paperwork is buried deep. I can coordinate with B-Team from there."

D shook his head, then ignored the resulting jolt of pain. "Fuck that. You and Sinclair go. Leave the rest of us here to hunt down that motherfucker Lassiter."

"No way. We can't jeopardize Sofia by staying too long. We'll get on Lassiter's trail from the new headquarters."

"It makes more sense to start the hunt here," D countered.

"Actually," came a female voice, "it makes more sense for you to go to Noelle."

Both men glanced at the door to see Isabel enter the room.

Her mention of Noelle had D's muscles tensing. That same possibility had been niggling at the back of his mind, but he hadn't wanted to voice it.

"Noelle's got a ranch in Northern California," the blonde added. "The property's isolated, but secure. Only a few hours from here by plane."

"Thanks for the offer," Kane said, "but we can handle this on our own. We don't need to involve your boss."

She raised her eyebrows. "Really? Have you located Morgan yet?"

"No," Kane admitted.

"Well, I can guarantee that if anyone can track him down, it's Noelle. She has more contacts than the president."

D spoke up reluctantly. "Blondie's right. Her boss can help." He paused, hating to reveal his hand in any way but knowing he had no fucking choice. "Noelle might have a way to contact Morgan."

Kane's brow furrowed. "How do you know that?"

"Just a suspicion."

"He's probably right," Isabel said. "Noelle and Morgan have a past—we've all suspected as much. If anyone can find your boss, it'll be *my* boss."

Kane still looked unenthusiastic.

"You know this is our best move," D maintained. "You and Sinclair get the new base camp ready and coordinate with Castle. The rest of us will track Morgan and Lassiter using the lady killer's resources."

"Assuming Noelle even agrees to help," Kane said darkly. "That woman is a total fucking bitch." He shot a quick glance at Isabel. "No offense."

"None taken. She *is* a bitch. But trust me, she'll help." The blonde moved back to the doorway. "I'll let Trevor know."

Once Isabel was gone, D reached up and rubbed his aching temples. He hated showing any sign of weakness, but he couldn't deny that he wasn't at the top of his game at the moment.

He'd have to shape up, though. And fast. Noelle would take far too much pleasure in seeing him weak and immobilized.

And no way was he giving that bitch the satisfaction.

Chapter 5

"There you are."

Trevor looked up to find Isabel in the bathroom doorway, her blue eyes lined with fatigue. She wore a pair of black leggings and a black T-shirt, which he suspected she'd found in Abby's go bag because the shirt was far too tight; Abby's breasts definitely weren't as full as Isabel's.

At the thought, his gaze dipped to the aforementioned full breasts, and when his cock stirred in his pants, he was legitimately startled. After everything that had gone down tonight, he couldn't believe he was capable of feeling aroused right now.

"What's up?" he asked.

"Kane and Abby are heading to Costa Rica, but the rest of us are going to Noelle's ranch in California."

"Kane agreed to this?"

She nodded. "And D backed me up. Noelle has a network of contacts you guys can't afford not to tap into."

Trevor wasn't sure how he felt about that. Isabel's boss certainly had the resources, but he didn't trust the woman. Not only that, but Noelle made no attempt to hide her dislike of Morgan. Trevor couldn't imagine her going out of her way to locate the man.

"What if Noelle refuses to help?" he countered.

"She won't. Not if you ask her nicely." Isabel's blue eyes

twinkled for a second before growing serious again. "Noelle is a very powerful woman. If Morgan's truly in danger, she'll be an asset."

"I guess we'll find out."

Isabel lingered in the doorway, pushing a strand of hair behind her ear. After several moments of silence, she glanced at the sink, toilet, and walk-in shower stall as if she'd suddenly realized where she was. "Oh. Were you planning on doing, you know, bathroom stuff? I didn't mean to barge in."

He had to grin. "Bathroom stuff?"

She actually blushed, which he'd never seen her do before. He nearly teased her about it, until he realized now was not the time for lighthearted banter.

Holden had lost his wife tonight.

Lloyd, the gentle giant who'd worked for Morgan for years, was dead.

Morgan could be dead too, for all they knew.

The reminders were more than a little sobering.

"I was about to clean up some cuts," Trevor said, gesturing to the first-aid kit he'd left on the edge of the sink.

"Why don't you ask Dr. Amaro to do it?"

"I don't want to bug her." And besides, Sofia Amaro had the evil habit of forcing unnecessary bed rest on her patients. Trevor had a feeling that if she got a look at his feet, she wouldn't let him leave the damn clinic.

Isabel entered the bathroom and closed the door behind her.

He looked at her in surprise. "What are you doing?"

"Playing doctor. I'm getting pretty good at it." She eyed him expectantly. "So, what needs to be cleaned up?"

Reluctance washed over him.

"It's either me or Dr. Amaro. Take your pick, Trevor."

The stubborn lift of her chin told him she meant business. With a sigh, he bunched up the collar of his shirt and yanked it over his head.

Isabel's answering gasp made him smile. "It looks worse than it is," he assured her. "Seriously, Iz."

"Are you fucking kidding me? You look like you fell into a pit of razor blades."

The anger and concern flashing on her face brought a spark of warmth to his heart. He couldn't remember the last time he'd had a woman worry about him. It felt . . . nice.

"Sit down." She pointed to the closed toilet seat.

Her tone brooked absolutely no argument. He'd never heard that commanding voice leave her mouth. She was usually so easygoing, self-assured, speaking with quiet authority. But there seemed to be a crack in her composure, revealing a rawer, more emotional side to her. He'd noticed that same emotion swimming in her eyes at the rendezvous point when she'd thrown her arms around him without stopping to worry about propriety. At that moment, it was as if she'd forgotten she was trying to keep her distance from him.

Friends. Ha. He couldn't believe she'd even suggested it. Didn't she realize she made his body burn with her mere proximity?

When he looked at her, he didn't see a *friend*. He saw a woman he desperately wanted to hold. To kiss.

Trevor dutifully sat down. A jolt of heat went through him when Isabel sank to her knees in front of him. Jesus. He hadn't had sex in two years, and now that his body had decided to come alive again, it was doing it with a vengeance. His cock stiffened and strained against the crotch of his pants, but luckily Isabel's gaze was focused solely on his chest.

"There are like a hundred pieces of glass lodged in your skin," she murmured in distress. "How are you not in pain?"

"I'm a soldier. I'm good at blocking out pain."

With the most gentle of touches, Isabel went at him with the tweezers. She picked out the tiny shards of glass, dropping each one into the wad of toilet paper in her hand. Silence settled over them as she worked, diligently tending to each cut and scrape. When she reached his left shoulder, she hissed out a breath.

"This is *not* a graze, Trevor."

He glanced down and noticed that the bullet had taken a small chunk of skin with it, leaving the area raw and bloody.

"Flesh wound," he amended.

"And let me guess—it doesn't hurt either."

Her sarcasm made him laugh, but the sound died in his throat when she dumped nearly half a bottle of rubbing alcohol directly on the wound. Without warning.

"Son of a *bitch*," he ground out. His arm felt like it was on fire, and he bit down on his lip so hard he tasted blood in his mouth.

"Oh, did that hurt?" she asked sweetly.

He glowered at her. "That was evil."

"That was aimed to teach you a lesson."

"What, that you're evil?"

"No, that you should tell people when you're in pain!"

She looked so flustered he found himself leaning forward and touching her delicate jaw. When his hand made contact, she jumped, her eyes widening.

"Were you this angry at Ethan when he kept *his* bullet wound from you?" Trevor asked huskily.

"What? Um, of course."

"No, you weren't." He met her eyes in challenge. "You don't like seeing me hurting."

She visibly swallowed. "Of course I don't. I don't like seeing *anyone* hurting."

"So I'm just like everyone else, huh? No more special than Ethan or D or some stranger you encounter on the street?"

He could feel her hand trembling as she wiped away the blood caked on his shoulder. "You're purposely trying to get a rise out of me," she said stiffly. "You're my friend, okay? I don't like seeing my friends in pain."

"We're back to that, huh? Isabel and Trevor, best friends forever." He chuckled. "You really think we're capable of being just friends?"

Keeping her eyes downcast, she ignored the jab and slapped a square bandage on his arm.

Trevor didn't know why he was deliberately antagonizing her. This wasn't the time to resume the conversation they'd started before all hell broke loose. There were more important matters to deal with. Finding Morgan. Tracking the asshole who'd sent those mercenaries to the compound. Getting a new base camp set up.

At least the situation wasn't a *complete* disaster. All their important documents had been stored in the safe down in the tunnel, and they'd raided the armory before taking off, so they were solid in terms of supplies. Money, of course, was never an issue. Morgan was loaded, and the other men weren't hurting for cash either—mercs weren't called soldiers of fortune for nothing. Everything else—clothing, books, and whatnot—could be easily replaced.

Not Beth.

Trevor's heart clenched so hard he winced, an action that brought a rush of concern to Isabel's blue eyes. "Are you all right?" she demanded. "What's wrong?"

"Nothing." He sighed. "I was just thinking about Beth."

The tension that had been brewing between them dissolved like a sugar cube in water. Isabel's expression softened, her touch becoming gentle once again as she taped up his bandage.

"This must be hard for you," she said quietly.

His head lifted in surprise. "Me?"

"I know Holden's loss reminds you of losing Gina. Brings back painful memories."

Her tone was apprehensive, but warm. Isabel radiated warmth like a damn furnace. He'd never met a more compassionate woman, and although he knew her compassion wasn't an act, he also knew there was so much more to Isabel Roma than he'd ever suspected.

Five months ago, she was just beginning to open up to him, right before she got scared and ran.

This time around, he was determined to get to know Isabel. The *real* Isabel. He'd already amassed a few details during his search for her, but he needed more. He wouldn't be satisfied until he knew all her secrets. Until he learned what made her tick, what made her laugh, what made her cry.

Until he got a peek into her heart.

Her *soul*, damn it.

His obsession with this woman was incredibly disconcerting. He felt like it had come out of nowhere, and yet they'd met more than a year ago. The buildup to this moment had actually been slow and steady.

So why did his feelings for her continue to catch him by total fucking surprise?

"It does bring back memories," he confessed. "I know exactly what Holden's going through, but I also know that nothing we say is going to make him feel better right now. He needs to deal with it in his own way."

"Hopefully it's not the same way *you* dealt with it," she said wryly. "After that first job in Colombia, I was so worried about you, you know. I thought you might . . ." She hesitated. "I truly thought you might kill yourself."

"Not much of a stretch, Iz—I *wanted* to die." Shame gripped his insides like a vise. "I couldn't do that to my family, though. But, you know, as more time passed, I realized I couldn't do that to *myself*. Gina was dead, but that didn't mean I had to die right along with her. It didn't mean there wasn't anything left to live for."

He didn't add that meeting Isabel had contributed to that realization. The fact that he'd been able to feel even an inkling of desire for another woman had shown him that maybe he *wasn't* dead inside. That maybe there was hope for him after all. A chance to find something worthwhile with someone else.

Their gazes locked, and he knew she was seeing his thoughts reflected in his eyes. Her breath hitched, her hands dropping to her lap.

"What else needs fixing up?" she asked quickly.

His gaze traveled to her mouth, to those perfect pink lips he'd had the pleasure of kissing. Once. Only once, and it hadn't been enough. Not by a long shot.

"Trevor . . ."

The warning note in her voice didn't deter him. He leaned closer and brought his hand to her face again. He swept his thumb over her silky cheek, gauging her reaction, and when she didn't push him away, he glided his fingertips to her lips and traced the seam.

A wobbly breath flew out of her mouth and heated the pads of his fingers.

Isabel stayed motionless as she knelt there in front of him. He saw her pulse throbbing in her throat, and knew that if he placed a hand over her heart, he would feel its erratic beating beneath his palm.

His heart was beating pretty damn fast, too. He wanted to kiss her. Fuck, he'd wanted to kiss her from the second she'd walked back into his life. Didn't matter that she'd abandoned him in New York, didn't matter that she insisted she didn't have feelings for him anymore. He still wanted her, and if that made him a pathetic chump, then so be it.

Isabel's lips parted as his head dipped closer, as he grasped her chin and angled it.

Their lips were millimeters apart, nanoseconds from meeting, when a loud knock interrupted them.

Isabel jerked back as if she'd been shot by a cannon, almost falling on her butt. She hastily steadied herself and stumbled to her feet.

"Trev, you in here?" It was Ethan, and the rookie sounded unhappy.

Trevor got up to answer the door, ignoring the shooting pains that went through his torn-up feet. His socks were soaked, which told him he was bleeding, but tending to his injuries would have to wait.

"What's up?" he demanded.

Ethan looked startled when he caught sight of Isabel. He looked from the blushing blonde to Trevor's bare chest and said, "Am I interrupting something?"

"Naah. Isabel was just cleaning me up. What's going on?"

"Holden's gone."

"Are you serious?"

Ethan nodded.

"Fuck." Trevor briefly closed his eyes, feeling a headache coming on. "When did this happen?"

"He was outside up until an hour ago, chain-smoking—I've never seen him smoke *a* cigarette let alone an entire fucking pack. Anyway, I sat there for a while, tried to talk to him, but he's unreachable, man. He's completely shut down. Eventually I came in so Sofia could look at my arm. I went out there just now to check on him and he's gone. So is one of the Jeeps."

Alarm skittered up Trevor's spine. Shit. This wasn't good.

He fished his smartphone out of his back pocket and brought up Holden's number.

"I already tried that," Ethan said. "He's not picking up."

Sure enough, after half a dozen rings he got bumped over to voice mail. He tried again, this time leaving a message. "Holden, it's Trev. Where the hell are you? Check in. Now."

They couldn't afford to lose another man. The rest of the team was already scattered all over the fucking place, no one knew where the boss was, and now Holden had taken off? Was nothing destined to go right today?

"What do we do?" Ethan ran a hand through his short brown hair in frustration. "Should we go after him? I can follow his tire tracks, see where they lead."

With Kane leaving, Trevor would officially be the team leader, and these were the kinds of decisions he hated making. *Never leave a man behind* had been drilled into his personal code of conduct during his army stint, but Holden wasn't a missing soldier. He was a grieving husband, which meant he'd be about as helpful as a case of poison ivy at the moment. Not an asset to the team, but an encumbrance. And sending Ethan after him meant they'd be another man down, mission-wise. So maybe it was for the best that Holden was gone.

Unless he'd left so he could blow his own brains out . . . In which case, someone needed to go after him. Pronto.

Before Trevor was forced to decide, his phone buzzed. The incoming text sent a wave of relief slamming into him.

"It's from Holden," he said. "He's at the airfield, just chartered a flight. Says he's going home to see Beth's family."

Isabel's blue eyes filled with worry. "Is that really a good idea? Should we try to stop him?"

After a beat, Trevor shook his head. "Let him go. You saw the shape he was in—he wouldn't be much help to us anyway. If anything, we'd be splitting our focus, trying to find Morgan while worrying about Holden."

She didn't look convinced. "I don't know if he should be alone."

"Trust me, even if he's surrounded by a hundred people right now he'd still be alone." Trevor choked down a familiar lump of sorrow. "He's going to be feeling alone for a long, long time."

Noelle's ranch was a sprawling eighty-acre spread in the California countryside, and of all the homes Noelle owned, this was Isabel's favorite. The property sat at the foot of a redwood forest, the land abundant with native oaks, winding creeks, wildflowers, and endless pastures.

The house itself was reminiscent of eighteenth-century Spanish colonial architecture. Single story with a stucco exterior and a U-shaped floor plan that allowed for a gorgeous interior courtyard. From the outside, it looked harmless, but Isabel knew the place was more secure than a prison. Bulletproof windows, top-of-the-line alarms, motion sensors, not to mention strategically placed booby traps all over the property.

Last time Isabel had come here was when she and some of Noelle's other chameleons met up for a little R&R. An assassins' retreat, Juliet Mason had called it. It had been surprisingly fun, but then again, it was impossible not to have a good time with Juliet and Paige. The two women could drink Isabel under the table—that was for sure.

The group arrived at the ranch in the midafternoon, after a short flight in the twin-engine Cessna they'd rented at a private airport outside Oaxaca. Much to Isabel's surprise,

Trevor had piloted the small plane himself. The fact that she'd had no clue he could fly a plane was just another reminder of how little they knew about each other.

Which raised the question, how was it possible to feel such a powerful connection to a man she hardly knew?

Abby and Kane—along with the three puppies, which Abby had refused to leave behind—were already on their way to Costa Rica to set up the new compound. Trevor, D, and Ethan had come with Isabel to the ranch, despite Dr. Amaro's insistence that D stay in bed. When the good doctor tried putting her foot down, the man had predictably refused to follow orders and heaved himself out of bed, looking so pale and swaying so hard Isabel had almost laughed.

He didn't look any better now. Skin devoid of color, normally sharp eyes glazed, stumbling slightly as he walked. It was incredibly unsettling seeing the tattooed warrior looking so . . . unwarriorlike.

They strode into the living room, which never failed to startle Isabel. It was so very homey with its wood-paneled walls, gleaming windows, and cozy furniture in neutral shades. Each one of Noelle's properties gave off a wholly different vibe, but the sterile Paris penthouse was the only one that actually seemed to suit the woman.

"Noelle lives here?" Trevor's expression was dubious as he looked around.

"Yes, but only when she's not in Paris or Vermont or Tokyo or any of her gazillion other safe houses," Isabel said drily.

Across the room, Ethan had approached the stone fireplace and was studying the barren mantel. "There isn't a single photograph in this house," he remarked. "Doesn't she have any family? Friends?"

"Friends, definitely not. Family, I'm not sure," Isabel admitted. "You'd have to ask Abby—she knows more about Noelle's background than I do."

"Speak of the devil," Trevor said as his phone buzzed. He quickly took the call. "What's up, Abby?" He listened. Frowned. "Are you frickin' kidding me?"

Everyone in the room went on the alert.

"No, she's not here yet . . . yeah, I'll let you know." Trevor hung up with a soft curse and addressed the group. "Morgan never showed up for his meeting."

D and Ethan released their own expletives, the former's far more creative than the latter's.

"According to Breckin—the CIA agent he was meeting with," Trevor clarified for Isabel— "Morgan bailed on the meeting. No phone call, no message. He just didn't show."

From what she knew of Jim Morgan, the man was a professional right down to his core. Skipping out on a meeting didn't seem like his style.

"He left the compound, what, two, three days ago?" Isabel asked.

Trevor nodded. "Three."

"Did you call his pilot? Did the plane actually make it to D.C.?"

"It did. Abby spoke to Sam, our regular pilot. He's been on call at a private airport near Arlington for the past three days. Morgan told him to wait, said they wouldn't be grounded for more than a day, but Sam hasn't heard from him since."

The anxiety in the air was palpable. So was the fatigue. Isabel felt like she had grains of sand lodged in her eyes—she hadn't slept since she'd left Nigeria, and that had been more than forty-eight hours ago. She could barely stay upright.

Lurking in the doorway, D looked on the verge of collapse too, but she knew the man would never admit he might need to rest.

Meeting those veiled black eyes, Isabel walked toward the big mercenary. "You need to lie down," she said firmly. "Let me show you to one of the guest rooms."

That the normally ill-tempered D didn't protest was incredibly telling.

Without a word, he followed her down the wide hallway. His scuffed black shit kickers didn't make a single sound as they traveled over the tiled floor, a mosaic of soft pastels.

Isabel gave him the room she'd used last time, a large space with a queen-size bed, an enormous bay window, and a private bath.

"When's your boss showing up?"

The gravelly inquiry surprised her. She'd noticed that D rarely spoke to anyone other than his teammates, not if he could help it.

"Her jet left Paris an hour ago, so she should be here around midnight."

He just nodded, then lowered his enormous body onto the bed and stretched out on the peach-colored bedspread.

His black muscle shirt left his arms exposed and drew Isabel's gaze to his tattoos. The Japanese-style images on his biceps were gorgeous—a deadly samurai fighting the green-and-black diamondback snake coiled around his forearm. Another snake circled his neck, this one red and black, with a forked tongue and a thick body that seemed to undulate whenever its owner moved. On the inside of each wrist was a mysterious set of dates, which Isabel didn't dare ask about.

God, he was such an imposing man. Terrifying, even. She couldn't imagine any woman being fully at ease with him. He was the kind of man you'd forever be on edge around, constantly waiting for him to snap. If he possessed even an ounce of tenderness, she had yet to see it.

Unlike Trevor, whose touch earlier had been so tender she'd wanted to drown in it.

She quickly pushed aside the memory of their disturbing encounter in the clinic. She couldn't let herself dwell on that almost-kiss. Not if she wanted to keep a level head around him.

"You want help taking off your boots?" Isabel asked, glancing at the black Timberlands hanging off the edge of the mattress.

"No."

With that, D closed his eyes, effectively dismissing her.

Okay then.

Deciding not to push her luck—the stubborn man was

resting, at least—she ducked out of the room, closed the door behind her, and bumped right into Trevor.

"Oh." A squeak flew out as her forehead collided with his collarbone.

He chuckled, catching her waist to steady her. "You okay?"

Damn it. He was touching her again. The heat of his palm sizzled through the soft fabric of the T-shirt Abby had given her, and his woodsy, masculine scent infused her senses and wrapped around her like a warm blanket. He always smelled so good, no matter what.

"D give you any trouble?"

Feeling awkward, she took a step back, which caused Trevor's hand to drop from her hip. "No, he just ignored me and went right to sleep."

"You should get some sleep too. You look like you're about to pass out."

She sighed. "I feel like it too. I haven't slept in days."

They moved away from D's door and continued down the hall. Isabel stopped in front of the next guest room. "You take this one. Ethan can have the room right across the hall. Noelle will commandeer the master bedroom when she shows up."

"What about you? Where will you sleep?"

His voice was so husky it sent a shiver up her spine. It also summoned the memory of the last time they'd discussed sleeping arrangements. That final night in Manhattan.

What do you say, Isabel? Will you let me sleep next to you tonight?

She'd said yes. They'd slept in the same bed that night. There'd been no sex, no physical contact, just a man and a woman lying together in bed and going to sleep, yet somehow that had felt even more intimate than sex. Sleeping with someone required letting down your guard and placing a substantial amount of trust in the other person. And she'd realized the next morning that she must *really* trust Trevor—because that had been the best damn sleep she'd ever had.

But not this time. She couldn't open that door again.

"There's another bedroom next to the den," she said. "On the other side of the house. I'll take that one."

A soft breath left his mouth. God, his mouth. It was far too sensual for someone so masculine.

"All the way on the other side of the house, huh?" He slanted his head. "What are you so scared of, sweetheart?"

Don't visit again, Isabel. I can't stand the sight of you.

Her most recent encounter with her father suddenly flew into her head like a gust of frigid wind. She made an effort to visit him at Sing Sing prison a couple of times a year, though why she bothered, she had no clue. Bernie Roma wanted nothing to do with his daughter. Sometimes, when she was feeling particularly down on herself, she didn't even blame him.

Daddy issues. What a fucking cliché. But it ran deeper than a case of Daddy-never-loved-me. Isabel had known from a young age that her family was fucked up. At seven, she'd watched her father beat a man within an inch of his life. At ten, she'd found her mother lying in a bloody bathtub with her wrists slashed to hell.

When your father was the number three man in the De Luca crime family in Brooklyn, it was pretty much a guarantee that your childhood would be less than conventional. Running away hadn't been an option, not in the physical sense anyway, but over the years she'd developed a different form of escape—becoming someone else.

Now it was all she was good at. All she had.

So what was she afraid of? God, where did she even start?

"Isabel?"

"Stop looking at me like that," she murmured.

"Like what?" he said gruffly.

"Like . . ." She felt frazzled. "I don't know. Like *that*."

"You mean, like I'm concerned about you? Or like I want to fuck you?"

Her breath hitched in shock. She couldn't believe he'd just said that. So candidly, and so vulgarly, and yet his words evoked a rush of pure desire that made her breasts tingle and her thighs clench together.

Trevor the gentleman she could handle. But this Trevor? The sexy one who wore all black and eyed her with raw lust? Whose strong jaw was covered with beard growth and whose muscular body rippled with power?

She didn't stand a chance around this Trevor.

"I can't talk about any of this right now," she told him. "I'm exhausted and I'm not thinking clearly, and that's not the state I want to be in when we have this conversation."

There was a beat, and then he let out a breath. "Fair enough."

She took another step back, desperate for some much-needed space. "Make yourself at home. I'm going to try to get some sleep before Noelle gets here."

Eddie Lassiter loved beautiful women. Sadly, the Nevada trailer park he'd grown up in had lacked that particular commodity. Instead, he'd been surrounded by bleached blondes with overly painted mugs. Freddy-fucking-Krueger fingernails and tight, unflattering outfits.

Trashy and cheap. Those were the women of his youth.

Nowadays he had the pleasure of spending time with more *sophisticated* women. He didn't even mind paying for them, either. Just meant it was easier to kick them out the next morning.

The two brunettes currently sharing his bed had come at a hefty price, but damn, they were worth every fucking penny. Smooth golden skin, big tits, long legs, and tight pussies.

And they were twins. What man in his right mind didn't want to see a pair of identical twins licking each other up like ice-cream cones?

"Oh baby, that's what I'm talking about," Lassiter drawled as he watched the sisters go at it.

He was standing at the window in his robe, blowing a puff of cigarette smoke into the humid night. The tantalizing scene on the bed thickened his dick and made his balls ache. Shit, he wanted to fuck these bitches again. All damn night.

He took a last drag and flicked the cigarette out the open window. On his way to the bed, his cell phone rang, bringing a jolt of annoyance.

One of the brunettes briefly lifted her head and met Lassiter's eyes. "We stop?" Her Spanish accent was as endearing as the sight of her sister's juices glistening on her mouth.

"Oh no, baby girl, you keep going." He wiggled his eyebrows before answering the phone. "Lassiter."

"We've got a problem."

His good mood faded. "What is it?"

"Our guys are dead."

"What the fuck you talking about, Lex?"

"Shanahan didn't check in, so I sent in a secondary team." Lex Delaney, Lassiter's right-hand man, sounded grim. "The compound was blown to smithereens. Nobody could have survived that blast. There were some bodies scattered outside the main house—they were all ours."

Lassiter's dick went soft, while his shoulders stiffened. "What about the target?"

"Hard to say. Our team couldn't check the house, damn thing was still in flames when they got there. He could have been killed during the strike or the blast, but the men found several sets of fresh tire tracks leading away from the property. Someone got away—that's for sure."

"So you have no fucking idea if he's dead or not."

Lassiter's fingers curled over the phone so tightly his knuckles turned white. He'd assembled a crack team for the Tijuana job. How the fuck had they screwed it up?

"Eddie—"

He cut Lex off. "Find out for sure. I don't care if you have to walk through a wall of flames, check all the bodies inside the compound."

"It would help if we had a picture of the guy."

"Well, we fucking don't. He's a slippery SOB. Dude's changed his appearance so many times it's impossible to know what he looks like now—that's why our guys were ordered to eliminate every man on the compound. But you know the basics, height, build, skin color, so for Christ's sake, check those bodies. I'm supposed to call with a report in an hour and he'll want to know that the right man was eliminated."

"I think he got away, Eddie." Lex's tone was apprehensive. "Those were skilled operatives in that facility. No amateurs."

Lex had a point. The target escaping had always been a valid possibility.

"They were supposed to be caught off guard," he muttered.

"Can you ever catch men like these off guard?"

Lex's matter-of-fact answer made his blood boil. The asshole was actually talking back to him right now? After the team he'd been supposed to oversee had colossally fucked up?

"Get me something more concrete," Lassiter snapped. "We need confirmation that he's dead."

He hung up without another word. His angry gaze drifted to the twins, who were tangled in a sixty-nine position on his bed.

"Get out."

Both their faces turned in his direction.

"We stop, señor?"

He clenched his teeth. Fucking broken-English bitches. "Get. Out."

His glare achieved the desired result. The girls flew off the bed and dashed around in search of their clothing.

Two minutes later, Lassiter escorted them to the front door. He slammed it after they left and went out to the back deck of the rickety beach house that overlooked the ocean. He didn't give a shit that it wasn't some beachfront mansion with marble floors and fancy-ass furnishings. If he wanted a mansion, he'd fucking buy one—God knew he could afford to.

But he loved this shitty little shack on the Mexican coast.

Loved how rustic it was, how fresh the fucking air smelled, how the local bar was only five minutes away.

At the moment, however, he couldn't appreciate any of that shit. He was Eddie Lassiter, a man who didn't explain himself to anyone, who didn't care what anybody thought of him, yet a tremor of fear rippled through him as he anticipated Meiro's reaction to this screwup.

Taking an unsteady breath, Lassiter reached for the half-empty bottle of tequila he'd left on the deck. He gulped down a hearty amount, but the alcohol didn't rid him of that growing dread.

Meiro would be very unhappy. Very unhappy, indeed.

Chapter 6

Noelle showed up just before midnight—and she was just as unsettling as Trevor remembered. He'd met her for the first time a few months ago, when she'd come to the compound to see Abby, and he remembered being utterly startled by her angelic appearance. Her long hair was like spun gold, her blue eyes so vivid he'd caught his breath, and her features were downright exquisite. He'd never laid eyes on a more beautiful woman, and yet he didn't feel an ounce of lust in her presence. Only agitation.

As expected, the blonde wasn't at all concerned that Morgan might be in danger. If anything, she looked amused as hell.

"So you lost Jim," she drawled. "Do you need my help putting up MISSING posters around the neighborhood?"

Trevor ignored the sarcasm. "We don't *need* anything from you. But if you want to offer your assistance, it would be appreciated."

"My assistance?"

She sauntered to the French doors that opened onto the interior courtyard, the ice cubes in her water glass clinking. She didn't bother turning around to see if anyone was following her.

"That's our cue to follow," Isabel said wryly.

Trevor stifled an annoyed groan and stepped onto the

huge patio, which featured a large oval table surrounded by wrought-iron chairs and clay pots laden with leafy green plants scattered about. The house's overhanging eaves provided shade on a sunny day, but they didn't need shade at the moment. The night was cool, the sky dark. A breeze traveled through the courtyard, ruffling Noelle's long hair.

As Trevor joined her at the table, a hint of a smile flitted over her mouth. Oh yeah, this woman liked toying with men.

But he wasn't the kind of man who played games. He preferred the more direct approach. Get right down to business and fuck the whole song-and-dance number.

"You were saying?" he said tersely.

"*You* were saying you want my assistance. I was about to turn you down. I have no intention of involving myself in whatever mess Jim has gotten himself into."

"Are you serious?" Isabel came outside with Ethan at her heels. She looked incredibly unhappy with her boss. "What if he's really in trouble?"

"Then he's really in trouble," Noelle replied with a shrug. "Either way, I don't give a shit, and I won't go out of my way to help that bastard."

Trevor met those cold blue eyes. "He helped you when Abby was missing."

"And I returned the favor on your Manhattan job."

"Technically, Isabel was the one who did us a favor."

"Isabel works for me. She follows my orders."

Isabel's snort confirmed that she definitely hadn't been doing Noelle's bidding when she'd helped out in New York.

Before Trevor could voice another argument, D's gravelly voice sounded from the doorway.

"You know it appeals to you, having him in your debt."

Noelle shifted her gaze. She didn't even blink when she spotted D, nor did she seem at all bothered by his presence. Other women might've recoiled at the sight of him; barechested, he was even more menacing than usual, and all those tattoos only added to the deadly air that surrounded him.

"It does sound appealing," Noelle conceded. "But . . ." Another dainty shrug.

D walked up to the table, drawing Trevor's attention to the tattoo on the man's back. An eagle spanning from shoulder to shoulder, done only in black ink but with painstaking detail. Underneath the majestic creature were what looked like tally marks, separated into groups of five. D's skin boasted eight full sets, followed by three individual ticks. Forty-three total.

The question was—forty-three what?

Trevor had no desire to find out.

D looked better, though. His color was returning and his dark eyes looked sharper now. He dug a pack of Camels from his cargo pants and lit up a cigarette, blowing a big cloud in Noelle's direction.

The smoke in the face didn't get a reaction out of her either.

"You're seriously not going to help us?" Isabel asked.

"Us?" Noelle chuckled. "You work for me, honey. If I'm not sticking around, neither are you."

Isabel's eyes flashed. "Like hell I'm not. You weren't there, okay? Those mercenaries had kill orders. Holden's wife is dead, Lloyd is—"

"Why should I give a fuck about people I don't know?"

"Fine, don't help. But if you order me not to, then I'm afraid I'm no longer in your employment."

Trevor blinked in surprise. "We can handle this on our own, Iz. Don't risk your job over it. And you"—he glanced at Noelle—"if you have any way of reaching Morgan, I'd appreciate it if you tried."

"That I can do," Noelle said magnanimously. "But I can't promise I'll get a response."

"Also, if we could use this safe house for at least another twenty-four hours, that'd be nice. We're still trying to track down the man who dispatched that hit squad. We've put feelers out in the merc community."

"Name?"

"Eddie Lassiter."

"I've heard of him. Real dirty fuck, but one of the best middlemen out there." Noelle's tone became grudging. "I'll call around, see if I might make it easier for you."

"Thank you," Trevor said with a nod.

She strolled to the door, ignoring everyone but Isabel. "Come find me when you're done here, honey."

After Noelle was gone, Isabel turned to Trevor with a dark expression. "Can we talk in private, please?"

A minute later, they were behind the closed door of the guest room he was crashing in. Isabel didn't say a word, but her body language spoke volumes. Rigid shoulders, tight jaw, cloudy blue eyes.

"You suddenly don't want my help?" she demanded.

"There's not much you can do at the moment." He shrugged. "Lassiter's the only lead we've got. Once we find him, we'll figure out our next move."

"I can be an asset."

"I have no doubt. But this isn't an undercover op. Your skill set isn't needed."

"Right *now*," she argued. "But you might need me later on."

"And if we do, I'll call you, okay?"

Disbelief swam in her eyes. "I don't get it. All of a sudden you don't want me around. Why?"

A strangled breath flew out of his mouth. "Because you tie me up in knots, damn it."

Her jaw fell open.

"At the moment, my primary focus is finding Morgan," Trevor muttered. "It's all I can *afford* to focus on. You distract me, all right? Not only that, but I'm kinda pissed off at you."

Now her eyebrows shot up to her hairline. "Excuse me?"

"You heard me. You ditched me in New York five months ago, and we still haven't had an honest conversation about it. All you've done is feed me excuses and lines of bullshit about how your feelings *changed*."

"We haven't been able to talk because the compound was ambushed," she said evenly. "And then we were interrupted again at the clinic."

"And then you were too tired. And then after we woke up and had some dinner, you chose to sit around with Ethan. And then you had to check on D." He shook his head in annoyance. "Excuses, Isabel. All I ever get from you is excuses."

She was quiet for several seconds, a wounded look in her eyes.

Shit, he hated hurting her. He didn't even know why he was being such a dick right now. All he knew was that he was tired of talking in circles. Tired of trying to make sense of the confusing emotions swirling inside him. Tired of this aggravating *one step forward, two steps back* dance he and Isabel were constantly engaged in.

"I'm sorry."

Her soft voice brought an ache to his heart.

"I know I can be . . . difficult." Her voice wavered. "I just want to help, but if you don't need me, then fine. I won't get in the way."

She slid out the door so fast he barely had time to process what she'd said.

Staring at the empty doorway, Trevor suppressed a curse and dragged both hands through his hair.

Fuck. She'd retreated again, only this time he'd been the one to send her running.

And this time he didn't go chasing after her.

"I'm disappointed in you."

Noelle looked up to find Isabel in the doorway. Out of all her girls, Isabel was the most skilled at hiding her emotions, so the unmistakable unhappiness clouding her eyes was unexpected.

And unwelcome.

Bringing a cigarette to her lips, Noelle lit up and approached the open window. "Sorry to hear that," she said coolly.

"You truly don't care about anyone but yourself, do you, Noelle?"

"Not really, no." She raised her eyebrows. "And since

when do *you* care so much about Jim Morgan? You hardly know the bastard."

Just saying the son of a bitch's name out loud brought bile to Noelle's throat. She should've killed him a long time ago, but something had always held her back. Now, the mighty Jim Morgan was missing, maybe even dead, and although the notion brought a streak of triumph, it was accompanied by a strange rush of dissatisfaction.

That ruthless, self-serving heartless bastard might be dead—but *she* hadn't been the one to kill him.

Isabel still hadn't responded. She shifted awkwardly before entering the bedroom and shutting the door behind her. "You're right. I don't know Morgan very well, but that doesn't mean I'm not worried about him."

Noelle blew a puff of smoke out the window. "Honey, you've been surprisingly transparent lately."

"What's that supposed to mean?"

"It means that this is about Callaghan again. You don't want to help Jim. You want to help Callaghan." Another deep drag, another slow exhalation. "If you want my help, at least have the sense not to lie to me."

"Fine." Isabel sighed. "Right again, Noelle. I want to help Trevor. Is that what you wanted to hear?"

"Not particularly, no. What I want to hear is that you don't give a shit about the man. That your work for me means more than a handsome face and a fuckable body. What I *don't* want to hear is how one of my best operatives has turned pathetic and weak-kneed over a man."

Silence hung over the room.

Noelle turned away so she wouldn't have to see that stricken look on Isabel's face, but she didn't give a shit if she'd upset the other woman. She'd seen this train wreck coming more than a year ago, right after she'd loaned Isabel to Jim's team so they could save a dozen underage girls from being sold into the sex trade. When the job ended, Isabel's nonchalant inquiries about Callaghan's well-being had been the first red flag. The next warning signs had come when Isabel chose to spend her vacation doing undercover work for Jim.

And now . . . now the woman was yet again diving head-first into another Jim Morgan adventure. For Callaghan.

Love made women so damn weak. Destroyed them like a slow-moving cancer, eating away at healthy cells, attacking organs, taking what was once an intelligent, independent human being and turning her into a pitiful, sickly shell of a woman no longer capable of surviving on her own.

Once upon a time, Noelle had almost been destroyed by love too. But she'd managed to save herself, emerging on the other side stronger and more powerful than ever.

She just hoped Isabel was smart enough to do the same.

"Did you know Abby and Kane got married?" Isabel's change of subject was more than a little abrupt.

"I did." Noelle watched as the other woman began to pace the reddish brown rug in the center of the bedroom. "Big fucking mistake, in my humble opinion."

Isabel laughed without much humor. "There is nothing humble about you. And I think you're wrong. I think Abby made the right decision. Kane loves her."

"For now."

"Forever."

"Oh, honey, don't tell me you believe in fairy tales."

Isabel quit pacing and sank down on the edge of the bed. "I don't know what I believe in anymore."

The note of sorrow in her voice evoked a twinge of discomfort. This wasn't the kind of shit Noelle talked to her girls about. They didn't discuss feelings or do one another's hair or have fucking pillow fights. They talked business. She gave them an assignment, they went out and accomplished their task, then came back to brief her. End of story.

Noelle put out her cigarette in the ceramic ashtray on the window ledge. "I'm already going above and beyond for Jim by tapping my sources to locate Lassiter. Anything more than that—I'm sorry, but I have no interest in wasting my time trying to find that bastard."

"You hate him." Isabel suddenly looked perplexed.

Noelle didn't answer.

"I mean, you really hate him. *Loathe* him even." The blonde's tone grew more and more troubled. "I assumed it was some sort of rivalry, that maybe you'd crossed paths in the past and rubbed each other the wrong way. But it's more than that, isn't it?"

"It's whatever you want it to be, Isabel. Now, I need to make a few calls."

"Is that your subtle way of ordering me to leave?"

"I'm not trying to be subtle." Her jaw hardened. "Leave, Isabel."

Her operative's lips tightened. "You're a real bitch—you know that?"

You don't know the half of it.

Noelle waited until Isabel was gone, then headed for the walk-in closet. She hadn't had a chance to change since she'd arrived at the ranch, having been ushered into the living room by Isabel as if the damn sky was falling. For fuck's sake. Jim Morgan was off the grid—hardly a national emergency.

She unzipped her knee-length leather boots, extracting two knives and a small derringer pistol from the custom sheaths sewn into the footwear. Her fitted black jacket was next, a garment that was nearly as dangerous as she was; it, too, housed a multitude of weapons.

Her tight pants and tank top, she kept on, but she didn't bother removing the various surprises underneath.

It was always prudent to be prepared around the man she was about to see.

She moved soundlessly. She'd been trained by the best, after all. Trained to be invisible, trained to be deadly, trained to protect herself at all costs. As the memories rose to the surface, they brought forth a surge of fury. These days she didn't get hung up on the sorrow or the grief associated with her loss.

Just the rage.

The hallway was bathed in shadows. No light spilled beneath any of the closed doors. Callaghan and Jim's other man, the rookie, had crashed for the night. Isabel was in the room next to the den and wouldn't hear much from all the way over there. Not that it mattered. If Noelle didn't want anyone to hear her, then they wouldn't.

She slid into his bedroom without making a solitary noise.

And yet his eyes snapped open the moment she closed the door.

"You're wasting your time, baby." His raspy voice cut through the silence, those black eyes glimmering in the darkness. "I'm not in the mood to service you tonight."

With a chuckle, she approached the bed. "Not what I'm here for, honey. I just wanted to see you like this. Weak and pale and hurting."

D's features hardened into steel. Such handsome features too, completely unsuited for this man. His face ought to be feral to match his personality, and yet he was handsome—sharp cheekbones, straight nose, strong jaw, and well-shaped mouth.

"Take a good long look," he mocked. "But we both know I could snap your neck in a heartbeat, *honey*. I might be pale, and I might be hurting, but I ain't weak."

Oh no, he wasn't. Derek Pratt—if that's what he was still calling himself these days—was power personified. A warrior, just like her. Heartless, just like her.

They watched each other for a moment. Shadows danced over the rugged planes of his face and the well-defined muscles of his bare chest. When her gaze lowered to his groin, she glimpsed the unmistakable bulge beneath his pants. A dark thrill shot through her. It'd been far too long since she'd had this man. Five months, if she recalled correctly.

"You just gonna stand there like a mute, or are you gonna say something?" he taunted.

She shrugged. "What do you want me to say? Would you like me to agree to help your boss?"

"Ah, so that's why you're here." He slid higher on the

bed, his abdominal muscles tightening and rippling. "You want me to beg you to help Morgan." D laughed. "Not gonna happen, baby."

"No?"

"Hell, no." A note of challenge entered his voice. "So if you're not here to blow me, then get the fuck out."

She couldn't help but laugh. Her relationship with this man was . . . complicated, to say the least. But boy, did she enjoy it. D was a worthy opponent, the male version of herself—cold, callous, empty. How this game had even started still eluded her, but each time they crossed paths, a new move was made, a new strategy employed.

Slowly and methodically, she climbed on the bed and straddled his rock-hard thighs. "Blow you, huh? Is that what you want me to do?"

The erection pressing against her ass made her pussy ache. Fuck, she was wet. She wanted him. No, she wanted his submission.

But men like D . . . men like Jim . . . they didn't submit. They resisted and fought until their last breath.

"I don't want a damn thing from you," he said with a soft chuckle. "Stay, go, disappear from this earth—I don't give a shit, Noelle."

Offense prickled her skin. Narrowing her eyes, she grabbed hold of his zipper and dragged it down. Son of a bitch thought he could win this round? Well, he could think again.

"Interesting," D murmured as she encircled his stiff shaft with her fingers.

"Is it?" she murmured back.

"You wouldn't be here if it wasn't."

The cryptic exchange was nothing new. Noelle had spent enough time with him to know there was an ulterior motive to his every action, a hidden meaning behind his every word.

She was exactly the same way.

His eyelids closed as she pumped him. He always closed his eyes, and they always stayed closed, no matter how hard she tried to achieve the opposite result.

Her hand moved up and down his cock in a lazy tempo. He didn't make a single sound, but his breathing grew irregular, his impressive chest rising and falling as he began thrusting into her hand.

Licking her lips, she dipped her head and took him in her mouth.

He jerked, fisting the sheets with his hands.

A salty drop seeped from his tip and coated her tongue. Fighting a smile, she laved him with her tongue, then sucked hard, grazing her teeth against his sensitive underside. Each time he tried to take control by pushing deeper into her mouth, she retreated and enjoyed his answering curse.

Her body tingled with feminine power. *This* was where men were weakened. Women were destroyed by love, but men, well, they were destroyed by sex.

Wrapping her hand around the root of him, she brought him closer and closer to the edge, using her mouth and tongue and hands, long licks and sharp pumps that elicited husky sounds from deep in his chest. His cock filled her mouth, big, throbbing, pulsating with need, but she refused to let him come. Not until she made him beg.

She squeezed his cock, hard enough to hinder his impending release.

D's eyes flew open. His expression glittered with menace. "Finish me."

"Ask me to help." A smile stretched across her mouth.

"Fuck you. *Finish me.*"

"No."

"Fine. Then I'll finish myself." With a growl, he uncurled her fingers from his dick, shoved her hand away, and replaced it with his own.

Annoyance slammed into her as she watched him jack himself.

"Stop," she said tersely.

His defiant look triggered another wave of indignation. "No."

He jerked his cock faster, harder, his breathing becoming erratic once more.

But he didn't let himself go yet. He just continued to stare at her with those heavy-lidded, challenge-riddled black eyes. "Well?" he taunted.

Her blood boiled, her jaw so tight it hurt. She didn't want to surrender to him.

So she didn't.

"Fuck you." With a shrug, she climbed off the bed.

His voice stopped her before she could reach the door. "Help us find Morgan."

Surprise jolted through her. She turned around and met his eyes. "Interesting."

"Isn't it, though?" D assumed a prone position again, propping his muscled arms behind his head. His still-hard cock jutted out proudly, but he seemed indifferent to it.

"Why should I care what happens to Jim Morgan?"

"Because you do. Deny it all you want, baby, but you don't want him to be dead. You can't torture and toy with a dead man."

Noelle smiled. "Who says that's what I'm doing?"

"Oh, let's not play any more games tonight." D smiled too, a wide, feral smile, white teeth shining in the darkness. "Don't think I don't know what's going on here."

She met his gaze head-on. "Meaning?"

"You're only fucking me to stick it to Morgan."

"Believe what you want."

"I'm wrong?"

"I fuck you because you're hung like a stallion and you make me come." She paused. "And to stick it to Jim."

D's laugh was surprisingly genuine, bordering on mirthful. "Good. Then you'll help us track him down."

She pursed her lips for a moment, then flashed him another smile, this one loaded with smug satisfaction. "Well, if you insist."

Trevor was pouring himself a cup of coffee when Noelle marched into the kitchen wearing a cornflower blue sundress that made him gape. Who would have thought the woman actually owned a dress, let alone one that wasn't black? However, the skimpy not-black dress wasn't as shocking as the words that came out of her mouth.

"We've got two objectives. Locate Jim, and track down whoever ordered the attack on your compound."

Trevor glanced at the big cedar table on the other side of the country-style kitchen, where Isabel, Ethan, and D were seated. Isabel looked as bewildered as he felt. Ethan, confused. And D, utterly expressionless, as usual.

"I take it you've decided to come on board," Trevor said drily.

Noelle brushed past him and prepared a cup of coffee. "On two conditions."

Intrigued, he joined the others at the table. "Which are?"

"One, I call the shots." She took a long sip, eyeing him over the rim of her mug. "We do things my way, and when I give you an order, you follow it."

Un-fucking-likely. He wasn't about to take orders from this woman, no matter how vast a resource network she possessed. But when he looked over at D, the dark-eyed man gave an imperceptible nod.

Trevor was hit by another dose of shock. Since when did D agree to take orders from *anyone*, let alone a stranger? The man barely listened to Morgan as it was, and Morgan was his boss.

"What's the second condition?" Trevor asked suspiciously.

Noelle hopped up on the counter, luring every male eye to her bare legs. Smooth and shapely, the color of peaches and pale honey.

He quickly looked away, but not before he saw Isabel watching him with a strange expression on her pretty face.

Was that . . . jealousy?

"I want a favor in return. From you." Noelle locked gazes with him. "Carte blanche, Callaghan. Whatever I ask of you, you do it."

What the fuck?

Tension rolled through the kitchen like tumbleweed. D's shuttered eyes made it impossible to decipher his feelings on the matter. Isabel was easier to read—she didn't like Noelle's caveat one bit.

Trevor wasn't thrilled about it either. Carte blanche? Did he really want to owe this woman a favor, and one he couldn't refuse?

Who says you can't refuse?

Good point. He could always agree to her terms, then tell her to fuck right off when she came to collect. What was she going to do if he refused, kill him?

"Don't test me, Callaghan." Noelle's blue eyes gleamed knowingly. "And feel free to ask Isabel what happened to the last man who reneged on a deal he'd made with me."

He let out an annoyed breath. "Fine. Whatever you want, Noelle. You've got yourself a deal."

"Good."

He figured the nods they exchanged had sealed the deal, but the blonde clearly disagreed. She set down her mug and slid off the counter, her strides downright predatory as she made her way toward him.

Noelle wasn't a tall woman, but her presence was commanding. She loomed over his chair, extending one deceivingly delicate hand.

Trevor eyed her outstretched palm. After a beat, he reached out and shook it. Her firm grip surprised him. So did the way she held on for much longer than necessary, running her red manicured fingernails over his palm.

He was the first one to pull away. Shit. He was thirty-three years old. He'd experienced battle, taken countless lives, witnessed atrocities no human being should ever have to see, yet those ten seconds under Noelle's touch actually terrified him.

"Anyway, I've already left a message for Jim," Noelle said, "so in the meantime—"

"How?"

She turned to glare at Ethan, the source of the disruption. "How what?"

"How did you leave Morgan a message? On his cell?"

The edge of her dress swirled around her knees as Noelle walked over to the sink. She grabbed a pack of cigarettes from the window ledge above the counter, some fancy European brand Trevor didn't recognize.

"How old are you, darling?" She appraised Ethan like she was planning on purchasing him. "I didn't realize Jim hired children for his crew."

Ethan visibly bristled. "I'm twenty-five, ma'am."

A peal of laughter flew out of her mouth. " 'Ma'am.' Oh, that's priceless. What a sweetheart you are." The amusement faded sharply. "I have other means for contacting your boss. I don't know if he checks that particular system anymore, but let's hope he does."

She didn't offer any further details, and Ethan didn't push. In fact, the rookie avoided her gaze completely as he reached for his coffee.

"In the meantime," she continued, "we locate Lassiter. We know he specializes in recruiting soldiers and assembling assault teams. What we don't know is who hired him."

"Morgan has a lot of enemies." Trevor spoke up. "At this point, I can't even hazard a guess as to who would want him dead."

Noelle chuckled. Probably, he assumed, because she counted herself among those who wanted to see Morgan six feet under.

"I've already got one of my girls looking into the Lassiter thread," she continued.

"Paige?" Isabel joined the conversation in that no-nonsense tone she used when talking business.

"Who's Paige?" Trevor asked.

"She's our tech geek," Isabel explained. "The female equivalent of Holden, I guess."

At the mention of Holden, Trevor experienced a pang of sorrow, but he forced it away. Holden had texted when he'd arrived in Montana, safe and sound. For now, there was no point in worrying about him and nothing Trevor could do to make things easier for the man.

"I'm also bringing Juliet in," Noelle said, glancing at

Isabel. "In the event that Lassiter needs a little convincing. I was told he has a weakness for beautiful brunettes."

Trevor was about to point out that Isabel was perfectly capable of transforming herself into a beautiful brunette, until it registered that Noelle had placed a helluva lot of emphasis on the word *convincing*.

Good call, then, keeping Isabel out of it—because if Eddie Lassiter so much as touched Isabel in a less than professional capacity, Trevor would kill the motherfucker.

Okay. Whoa. Maybe he ought to get the murderous thoughts under control.

Silencing his inner caveman, he focused on the woman who'd commandeered his entire operation. "I need to call a few contacts," he told Noelle. "There's a private military company based in Texas that has worked with Lassiter before. They'll probably know how to reach him."

Noelle shrugged. "Knock yourself out."

He scraped his chair back and stood up, doing his best not to gaze too long in Isabel's direction. He'd been making a pointed effort to keep his distance. He hadn't lied before—he was sick of listening to her excuses.

Not only that, but he was sick of the way she made him feel. Gina had never aroused these kinds of troubling emotions in him. He was tied up in knots. Frustrated. Desperate for Isabel. Goddamn it, *desperate*. To hold her, kiss her, bring a smile to her lips.

His life with Gina had been angst-free. It had been easy and comfortable, filled with light and laughter and *hope*, damn it.

It wasn't like that with Isabel. It was a million times harder, a million times more intense, and he was tired of trying to make sense of the hot rush of emotions constantly threatening to choke him.

Morgan. His focus had to be on Morgan now.

He would try to make sense of his feelings for Isabel later. Right now, all that mattered was figuring out what the hell had happened to his boss.

* * *

The phone rang at seven a.m., but Lassiter wasn't sleeping. He'd been up all night staring at the waves as they crashed against the white sand a hundred yards from his deck.

Lex hadn't been able to confirm a goddamn thing. The team they'd sent to investigate had discovered a dozen charred bodies inside the burning compound. The ones wearing dog tags were Lassiter's mercs. Of the other four, one might've been a woman, the other three definitely men.

Million-dollar question was—was one of those men the *right* man?

No answer for that, and no way of determining it. Couldn't exactly run a DNA test or pull dental records. The only way to know for sure was if he surfaced again. Until then, they had to assume he was either dead or had gone underground.

Meiro wasn't going to like this.

Dread climbed up Lassiter's throat like strands of ivy. Dragging a hand through his hair, he finally clicked the TALK button and lifted the phone to his ear. "Lassiter."

"You fucked up."

The smooth, accented voice sent a shiver of fear along Lassiter's spine. He hadn't expected to be hearing from Meiro himself. This didn't bode well. Not in the fucking slightest.

"There were skilled soldiers living in the facility." He winced at the feeble note in his voice. "We knew it would be difficult to—"

"To what?" Meiro said pleasantly. "Carry out the task I entrusted you with? The task you were paid rather handsomely for? The task you assured me would go off without a, what did you call it? A hiccup?"

"Well, we didn't take into consideration—"

"Who is *we*, Mr. Lassiter? Are you implying that I am partially responsible for your mistake?"

"No, of course not," he replied hastily. "You're right, Mr. Meiro. I fucked up. It was *my* mistake. But don't worry. I'm already assembling another team. They'll track the whereabouts of the men who escaped during the assault and—"

"Don't trouble yourself. Your services are no longer required."

He gulped. "Mr. Meiro—"

"What do you say I give you a head start?" Meiro's tone was downright amiable. "An hour? Two?"

"No, please—"

"One hour it is."

Click.

The phone fell from Lassiter's hands and clattered to the sand-covered deck. As panic took hold in his chest, he dove into the house like his very existence depended on it.

Because it did.

Chapter 7

Isabel found Trevor on the front porch, staring at the thick cluster of lemon trees growing at the side of the house.

"Hey," she said tentatively.

He turned at her approach. "Hey."

She came up beside him, fixing her gaze on his clean-shaven jaw and damp hair. He must have just come out of the shower, and gosh, what an appealing visual that made. She pictured Trevor's naked body under the shower spray, water sliding down his sculpted pecs and clinging to the dark hair on his chest, then following that line of hair lower and lower . . .

It took a serious amount of effort to banish the naughty images from her mind.

This was the first time she'd experienced such a raw, primal case of lust. It hadn't been this bad in New York. She'd desired him, yes. He'd made her heart pound, definitely. But it certainly hadn't been as powerful as this.

Everything about Trevor Callaghan teased her senses. His heady scent, his incredible body, his intense brown eyes. And his lips. She couldn't seem to quit staring at his lips. She kept remembering how warm they'd been when he'd kissed her all those months ago. Warm and firm and seductive, and his tongue . . . God, his tongue had been so skilled, so damn greedy . . .

"Were you the one who talked Noelle into helping us?" Trevor's voice interrupted her totally inappropriate thoughts.

Hoping she wasn't blushing—her cheeks felt too damn hot—Isabel shook her head. "I didn't do a thing. She was dead set on letting Morgan fend for himself when I spoke to her last."

"I wonder what changed her mind."

"Don't even bother. Noelle operates on her own twisted logic. Normal people could never understand how that woman's brain works."

They went quiet, Trevor's gaze once again returning to the trees. The early-afternoon breeze rustled the branches, and a sweet lemony scent wafted in their direction. From the corner of her eye, Isabel saw him take a deep breath.

"It's so odd, isn't it?" he said absently. "How certain smells trigger certain memories?"

Without waiting for an answer, he left the porch and headed toward the trees. It wasn't until he realized she hadn't followed that he stopped and glanced over his shoulder. "You coming or what?"

Isabel had to smile. "You didn't exactly ask me to take a walk," she said as she joined him.

"I thought it was implied."

When he offered an easy grin, her heart skipped a beat. Damn him for having such an amazing smile.

"So, what's your lemon memory?" She kept her tone casual, her gait relaxed.

They wandered into the thicket, where it immediately got shadier and the scent grew stronger.

"Gina's hands. Every summer, they smelled like lemons. She loved fresh-squeezed lemonade. Made it herself."

Isabel studied his profile, anticipating tight muscles and tortured eyes, but all she saw was sadness and resignation. He no longer looked like he was about to fall apart each time he spoke of his fiancée.

"How did you two meet?" she heard herself ask. "I don't think you've ever told me the story."

Trevor laughed. "It's not much of a story. She was a bank

teller, I was cashing a check. I thought she was hot, so I asked her to dinner."

The straightforward account made Isabel grin. "How romantic."

"Sorry it's not the meet-cute you were looking for."

They moved deeper into the grove, walking side by side, not touching, but not crazy far apart either. Isabel was so tempted to reach for his hand. She wanted to kick herself for even thinking about holding hands with this man, but she couldn't seem to control the mystifying emotions swirling in her stomach like a pack of panicked butterflies.

Friends. That's what she'd told Trevor she wanted, and she needed to stick to her guns. Friendship was the best option for them. The safe option. Anything more than that scared her, threatened the life she'd built for herself.

"If I'm being honest, we were kind of a boring couple," Trevor confessed. "I was gone so often that—" He stopped suddenly. "Want to sit down?"

He gestured to the wooden bench ten yards away, tucked beneath a pair of trees with low-hanging branches that provided a canopy of shade.

"Sure," she said.

They settled on the bench, a foot of space separating them. He had big thighs, she noticed. Firm, muscular, hugged by the fabric of his camo fatigues. And he'd changed into a snug white T-shirt that outlined every masculine contour of his chest.

Heat spiraled through her, and her hands trembled with the need to touch him. She clasped them in her lap instead and forced herself to concentrate on the man's words rather than his tantalizing body.

"You were saying you were gone a lot?" she prompted.

He nodded. "I was twenty-one when I met Gina, still serving a four-year hitch, so the beginning of our relationship took place via e-mails, phone calls, and video chats. We tried the whole romantic handwritten-letter crap, but I have atrocious handwriting, so Gina finally ordered me to stop writing letters." He laughed before going serious again. "It was tough making it work at first, but we managed to stick it out. Once I left the service, it got easier."

"You were together for a long time, huh?"

"Ten years." He paused. "What was your longest relationship?"

Isabel bit her bottom lip, tried to keep her composure. "A few months."

"Really? So short?"

"I didn't have a lot of opportunities to date."

She fiddled with her hands, wanting to change the subject, but at the same time feeling that she owed him something in return for the way he'd opened up about his fiancée.

"Once I hit puberty, no boy was allowed to come near me," she confessed. "I was Bernie Roma's daughter, Joey Roma's little sister. The boys at my high school didn't dare get close to me."

"Shit. That must have sucked."

"Yup. I didn't even touch a member of the opposite sex until my senior year. One of my brother's friends started hanging out at our house in Brooklyn. Sometimes he'd stop by and wait for Joey to come home from the restaurant, and the two of us would talk." A sad smile tugged at her lips. "He was my first love. His name was Michael."

She jumped when Trevor covered both her hands with one of his, gently stroking her knuckles with his fingers. "What happened to him?" he asked.

"I gave my virginity to him, and Michael made the mistake of confiding in Joey about it. Joey told our father, and Dad had Michael brought to the back room of the restaurant." Pain squeezed her heart. "And let's just say the back room wasn't the place you wanted to find yourself in."

"Fuck."

"My father broke both of Michael's hands, ordered his goons to beat the shit out of him, and I never saw him again." Before Trevor could offer words of sympathy, she hurried on. "After that, I stayed away from Joey's friends. From all men, actually. I went out with a couple of guys in college, but it didn't last. Once I joined the bureau, I dated a colleague for three or four months—that was the relationship I was referring to. But it didn't work out."

"Why not?"

"According to him, I was 'emotionally unavailable.'"

Trevor ran his fingers over her knuckles. "And was he wrong?"

Wrong? Isabel almost laughed. Brett's parting words had hurt, but the man had been right on the money. She kept her emotions locked up so tight you'd need a team of professional bank robbers to crack open her emotional vault. That guardedness had started in childhood and followed her all the way to adulthood.

She was spared from answering Trevor's question thanks to his buzzing cell phone. A quick glance at the incoming text, and then he was on his feet.

"What is it?" she asked.

"We've got a lead on Lassiter."

The tip came from the head of the military company in Texas, a man by the name of Russ Pollack, with whom Trevor had crossed paths a few times previously. Pollack was a former Green Beret who'd gone private and was now making cash hand over fist training mercenaries down south—and he'd lost three men during the ambush on Morgan's compound.

"Shit, Callaghan, if I'd known Lassiter was aiming to take out Morgan, I wouldn't have sent him any men."

Pollack's apologetic words put a bitter smile on Trevor's face. "A soldier for hire with a moral code. How rare."

"I mean it, Trev. You know my past with Morgan—I owe that prickly bastard my life. If it weren't for him, I wouldn't have such a great gig down here."

Trevor knew Pollack wasn't bullshitting him. Rumor had it, Russ Pollack had suffered a complete mental breakdown after his Special Forces stint and subsequent discharge. Trevor wasn't sure what Morgan had done exactly, but there was no bigger Morgan supporter in the merc community than Pollack.

"Well, maybe next time you can ask for more information before agreeing to do business with men like Lassiter," Trevor said pointedly.

"I will." There was a beat. "You'll make sure Morgan knows I didn't deliberately try to fuck with him?"

"Sure thing, Russ. And the address you gave us—you certain it's current?"

"Should be. My sources say Lassiter's been living at the beach house for the last two years. You need backup checking it out?"

"Nah, we're good. Later, Russ."

He hung up and drifted to the central courtyard of the ranch house. Noelle and D were at the table, smoking in silence, while Ethan cleaned his rifle nearby. Isabel stood by a bed of pink tulips, her expression sharpening when Trevor walked out.

"Do we know where Lassiter is?"

"Holed up in a beach house near Baja." Despite himself, Trevor couldn't help but smirk at Noelle. "Our contact scored the intel faster than yours did. One point for Morgan's team."

She smirked right back. "Your team captain is most likely worm food. I'm very much alive. Please remember that."

Trevor just laughed. The more time he spent with Noelle, the less terrifying she became.

Casting him a shrewd look, she pursed her lush red lips. "Oh, Callaghan, please don't make the same mistake other men have made."

"And what mistake is that?"

"Underestimating me."

With her cigarette dangling from her graceful fingers, she rose from her chair and sauntered up to him. Smoke curled in his direction and floated into his face, but he ignored it. Noelle was so close their bodies were nearly touching. The top of her head brushed his chin, her silky hair tickling his flesh.

She brought her lips right up to his ear. "I'm capable of

killing you in a hundred different ways, honey. I know at least seven methods that focus heavily on a man's testicles. Want me to show you?"

Trevor's shoulders stiffened. There was no mistaking the heat in the blonde's blue eyes. Was she flirting with him?

Noelle dragged her fingers over the curve of his jaw before resting her palm on the center of his chest. "What do you say, Callaghan? Want me to show you some tricks?"

Fuck, she *was* hitting on him.

"Leave him alone, Noelle."

Isabel's annoyed voice summoned a throaty laugh from Noelle. "Oh, Isabel, you're no fun at all." With that, she broke the contact and returned to the table, taking a careless drag on her cigarette.

When Trevor met Isabel's gaze, her cloudy expression didn't go unmissed. Was she jealous of the inexplicable attention Noelle had been paying him ever since she'd arrived at the ranch? Because that sure looked like jealousy darkening Isabel's blue eyes.

"All right," Noelle said, back to business. "Callaghan and the kid will check out this lead. Can you boys be ready in an hour?"

Trevor ignored her use of the word "boys" and offered a nod.

"I'm going with them," D said stiffly.

"You're a liability," Noelle retorted. "You stay behind."

D looked ready to murder her, but Trevor quickly intervened before the man lost his shit. "She's right. Give yourself another day to rest, man. You're still white as a sheet, and don't think I didn't notice you swallowing half a bottle of ibuprofen this morning. Head still hurts, huh?"

D just scowled at him.

"Well, then I'm going," Isabel spoke up.

Noelle's eyes flickered with irritation. "For fuck's sake, is everyone here deaf? I said Callaghan and the kid. And if you keep questioning every fucking decision I make, Isabel, I'll sideline you entirely."

Trevor's hackles rose. He wanted to lay into her for talking to Isabel like that, but Noelle was suddenly reaching for her phone. Her lips curved as she glanced at the screen. "Good. Juliet's here."

Isabel looked surprised. "Already?"

"She was in the air an hour after I summoned her."

"You say jump, and your chameleons jump, huh?" Isabel sounded oddly bitter, but when Noelle gestured for her to follow, she did so without protesting.

After the two women disappeared, Trevor met D's eyes, then Ethan's. "I don't like this," he admitted.

"Me either." Ethan glanced uneasily at the French doors. "Let's hope this Juliet chick is more like Isabel and less like Noelle."

Ethan didn't get his wish—the woman who strolled outside a few minutes later took one look at the rookie and released a peal of laughter.

"Oh, aren't you adorable," she cooed. "I didn't realize Morgan was recruiting them out of high school."

Ethan looked at Trevor as if asking for permission to kick some ass.

Fighting a grin, Trevor gave a slight shake of his head.

He took a minute to appraise the newcomer, who—no surprise—was an absolute knockout. She looked to be in her early thirties, with a head of thick dark hair that fell down her back in tousled waves, eyes the color of dark chocolate, a willowy body, and a damn nice rack. Her dark blue jeans were plastered to her long legs like plastic wrap, and her arms, bare thanks to her black tank top, revealed a pair of matching tattoos on her biceps. A cluster of nautical stars, feminine yet edgy.

"Guys, this is Juliet," Isabel said. "Jules, this is Ethan, D, and Trevor."

The brunette studied D first. Well, more like eye-fucked him. She damn near licked her lips too.

Then that seductive gaze landed on Trevor, who suppressed a sigh and managed a half smile. "Nice to meet you," he told her.

"Oh, the pleasure is all mine." She grinned, and he noticed she had a little mole right above her mouth.

Okay. He wasn't even gonna try to deny it—the woman was hotter than a five-alarm fire. But although he was able to appreciate her on a wholly masculine level, she didn't get his blood going the way Isabel did. Not even close.

"So you're one of the chameleons." He kept his tone polite. "Another master of disguise?"

"Among other things," she said vaguely before turning to her boss. "What did I miss?"

Noelle quickly filled her in, finishing with, "Don't bother unpacking. You'll be accompanying Callaghan."

Isabel frowned deeply, but she didn't question her boss's latest decision.

"Isabel, I want you to contact the Reilly brothers," Noelle continued. "Tell them to look into Lassiter's movements for the past couple of months. I want to know where he went, what he did, who he met with."

As the blonde barked out a few more details to Isabel, Juliet sidled up to Trevor and flashed him a smile. "So you and I are going for a little airplane ride."

"Ethan too." Trevor gestured to the rookie, who was eyeing Juliet with visible mistrust.

She waved a hand. Her fingernails were short and rounded, painted a dark blue that added to the bad-girl vibe she was throwing off. "We'll just pretend he's not there," she whispered with a conspiratorial wink.

Trevor couldn't help but laugh. The woman had balls—that was for sure.

But his response earned him a dark look from Isabel, who he knew was listening to the entire exchange even as she nodded at Noelle's instructions.

She *was* jealous. There was no mistaking the red hue to her cheeks, the tight jaw, the flash of irritation in her blue eyes.

Everything she'd confessed out in the grove returned to his head now, reminding him of the insight he'd reached right before they'd been interrupted. He'd realized there was a reason for Isabel's emotional detachment, for her fears and insecurities. There was a reason she'd run away from him all those months ago.

As frustrating as her excuses were and as annoyed as he was by her determination to keep him at arm's length, backing off was the *last* thing he ought to be doing.

In fact, he suspected it might be time to push her. It wasn't a strategy he usually employed—he believed in letting people deal with their issues in their own time, in their own way. But Isabel's problem was that she refused to deal with a damn thing. Instead of letting herself be vulnerable, she hid behind her various disguises.

He wasn't sure he even blamed her. If he'd grown up with a mobster for a father, a man who solved problems not with words but in a *back room*, he'd probably have some issues of his own.

A push, he decided. Just a little tiny push.

"You can sit in the cockpit with me if you want," he told Juliet, keeping his tone casual but loading a touch of heat into his expression.

She let out a delighted laugh. "Oh, I would *love* to sit on—I mean, *in* your cockpit, baby."

He shot her a crooked grin. "You're a sassy one, aren't you?"

Noelle's razor-sharp voice put an end to the flirty exchange. "For fuck's sake, Callaghan, put your dick back in your pants and gather your gear."

"Yes, ma'am." He turned to Ethan. "Come on, let's do this shit."

The two men went inside and ducked into their respective guest rooms. Trevor was just about to shut the door when he heard her footsteps.

Hiding a smile, he poked his head out and said, "Hey, come to say good-bye?"

Isabel's blue eyes burned with anger. "What the fuck was that, Trevor?"

"What was what?" Nonchalant, he beckoned her to enter.

She practically stomped into the room. He'd never seen

her so pissed off, so rattled. Normally she hid her emotions behind those easygoing smiles of hers, but not now. Now her face displayed everything she was feeling.

She looked fucking gorgeous.

"You were flirting with Juliet," she said in accusation.

"So?"

With a shrug, he crossed the room and unzipped one of the large duffels he'd liberated from the compound. As he began putting together a go bag, he felt Isabel's incensed gaze boring a hole into his head.

"So?" Incredulity dripped from her voice. "That's all you have to say?"

"What else do you want me to say?" He checked the clip of his SIG, then tossed her a quick look. "Should I apologize for flirting with another woman? We're friends, remember? There's no reason why I can't flirt with your colleague, Iz."

"Since when do you play games?"

He stood up and stripped off his T-shirt.

Isabel sucked in her breath.

The desire that heated her eyes did wonders for his ego, but he forced himself to stay the course he'd set, no matter how turbulent it might get.

"I'm not playing games," he lied. "I happen to find Juliet very attractive."

"Oh, really?"

"Really."

He strapped a Kevlar vest to his torso before reaching for his discarded shirt. Shoulder holsters went on next, guns slid inside, and then he cocked his head and glanced at Isabel. "I'm about to drop trou. If that's something you don't wanna see, I'd leave now."

"I'll stay," she said tightly.

He fought a grin and unzipped his pants. They hit the floor with a soft thud.

This time, when her breath hitched, he knew it had everything to do with the unmistakable erection straining against his boxer briefs. Yep, he was harder than a concrete block, and it had everything to do with the beautiful blonde glaring daggers at him.

But it wouldn't hurt to imply otherwise.

"Like I said, Juliet's attractive. Sexy, in fact." He plopped down on the edge of the bed, strapping a holster on one ankle and a knife sheath on the other.

Isabel moved closer. "You're just trying to get a rise out of me."

"Am I?"

"Yes, you are. And it's damn childish of you."

His gaze dropped to the hard ridge of his crotch. "There's nothing childish about me, sweetheart."

Her cheeks turned the sexiest shade of pink. He could see her pulse hammering in her throat, and when he met her eyes, the need he glimpsed in them took his breath away.

"Don't." Her voice was softer than a whisper.

He puckered his brow. "Don't what?"

"Don't sleep with her." She paused. "With Juliet, I mean."

At first he thought she was kidding. He nearly laughed out loud, but then he saw the sheer misery on her face and realized she was genuinely worried that he might screw Juliet. A woman he'd known for all of five minutes.

Aw, hell, perhaps there was a reason he didn't play games.

The direct approach was so much more effective.

"I'm not going to sleep with Juliet," he said gruffly. "Fuck, Isabel, do you really think I'd sleep with someone who . . ." He trailed off, suddenly feeling awkward.

"Someone who what?"

Trevor let out a ragged breath. "Who isn't you."

Her mouth formed a cute little O.

"*You* are the one I want," he reiterated.

He still hadn't put on his pants, and his erection was at full salute as he stalked toward her.

"Trevor," she started.

"Kiss me good-bye."

Those blue eyes widened. "What?"

"You heard me. Kiss me good-bye." When she just stood there like a mute, he quirked his lips. "Who knows what'll be waiting for us at Lassiter's place? I might never see you again—do you really want to deprive me of one last kiss?"

"Don't say things like that. This isn't good-bye, and you know it."

"All I know is that it's been five months since I had a taste of you."

He moved closer, bringing one hand to her cheek. Lord, her skin was softer than silk. His gaze fastened on her mouth, and damned if she didn't lick her lips.

But her expression continued to flicker with reluctance.

"I won't take it from you," he said softly. "You've gotta give it to me, sweetheart."

"I . . . can't."

His hand dropped from her face. "And I refuse to make it easy for you. If you're determined to cling to the idea that we're just friends, then go ahead and—"

She kissed him before he could finish, stunning him speechless.

A groan slipped out of his mouth when their lips touched. Christ, he'd forgotten how warm and pliable her lips were, how sweet she tasted. How *real* she was.

Most of the time, she could hide the real Isabel, fool him with that confident, professional disposition of hers, but right here and right now, with her mouth pressed against his, she was beautiful and genuine and incredibly vulnerable.

Trevor felt her hands trembling as she braced them on his chest, and when his tongue delved into her mouth in one smooth motion, hers responded tentatively, innocently.

His entire body burned with need. Unable to resist, he backed her into the dresser near the door and ground his aching erection into the cradle of her thighs. Isabel's answering moan stoked the fire in his groin, bringing a husky groan to his lips.

She twined her arms around his neck, then lifted one leg and hooked it around his hip, deepening the connection between their bodies. He groaned again, his tongue exploring her mouth with hungry strokes, his hands gliding up her waist to cup her breasts over her tank top.

What was supposed to be a harmless good-bye kiss had spiraled into something hot and uncontrollable, and it took all of Trevor's willpower to pull away.

They were both breathing heavily as he took several steps backward.

"I can't be your friend," he said roughly. "You get that, right?"

Isabel was wide-eyed again, her chest rising and falling rapidly. "Just because you want to sleep with me? What, so if we don't have sex, we can't be friends?"

"You want to sleep with me, too."

She began to look agitated. "Yeah, but if I had to pick one, I'd choose our friendship over sex any day."

"Then it's a good thing nobody is making us choose. We can be both, Iz. Friends *and* lovers. That's what I want from you." When she didn't respond, he let out a breath. "I need you to do something for me."

"What is it?" she said warily.

"Think about it. Think about what you want from me. What you want from *this*. If it really is just friendship, then I'm sorry, but I can't give that to you." His voice sounded so raspy he paused to clear his throat. "You're the first woman I've wanted since I lost Gina. The *only* woman I've wanted."

He could tell she was biting the inside of her cheek. "I know."

"I can't be satisfied with friendship. It would be too damn hard being around you, when we both know I want more."

"I know," she said again.

He put on his pants, then reached for his bag. "All or nothing, Iz. Think about it, okay?"

Her voice stopped him just as he reached the door.

"Trev?"

He glanced over his shoulder, a tiny balloon of hope inflating in his chest when he glimpsed the flicker of vulnerability in her eyes. "Yeah?"

The longer she stayed quiet, the more hopeful he became, especially when she took a tentative step forward and raised her hand slightly, as if she wanted to reach out to him.

Except then that hand dropped to her side, and the only words that came out of her mouth were, "Be careful."

Pop. The hope burst, replaced with a pang of disappointment.

"I always am," he muttered.

And then he left the room.

Chapter 8

D waited until Isabel was busy in the den before making his way to the master bedroom. The others had left for the airfield an hour ago—without him, much to his displeasure. But he was a man who knew how to pick his battles, and a routine visit to Lassiter was hardly worth expending his energy on. Might as well let the boys handle it. In the meantime, he'd regain his strength and play nice with Noelle.

For Morgan's sake, anyway.

When he entered her bedroom without knocking, she didn't seem at all surprised to see him.

Their eyes met from across the room.

"You're playing with fire, baby," he said roughly.

"Oh, am I?" She plucked a bottle of bourbon off the dresser. "Drink?"

"No." He locked the door and walked toward her, not giving a shit if his scuffed boots dirtied up her rug.

Glancing around, D didn't bother hiding his distaste. A canopy bed with a peach duvet, antique furniture, a shitload of flowers. Dudes like him didn't belong in rooms like this.

Neither did the lethal bombshell standing before him. She might be wearing a dress, but Noelle was no lady, and these girlie surroundings didn't suit her.

"So tell me, how am I playing with fire?" She tipped her head back and wrapped her lips around the bottle's rim.

Her long, elegant throat worked as she swallowed. She made a contented purr of a sound, then put away the bourbon and reached for the bottom of her skimpy blue dress.

"We both know you're purposely toying with Trevor. The question is, why?" His eyes never left hers, but he heard the rustle of fabric as her manicured fingers lifted her dress.

"Maybe I'm just bored."

Yeah, Noelle was definitely the kind of woman who'd get a kick out of tormenting men in her free time, but D knew boredom was not the reason she'd targeted Trevor. He also knew he would never get a straight answer out of her, so he didn't push.

"What did you think of Juliet, by the way?"

D raised his brows. "What does it matter what I think of her? Did you bring her here for me? Would you like me to fuck her too?"

Noelle laughed. "If you want."

The blonde pulled her dress over her head and let it drop to the carpet.

His gaze dropped south. Her full breasts, tipped by small pink nipples, gleamed in the dim lighting of the room.

Noelle's thong came off next. Her blue eyes sparkled as she strode toward him.

Naked.

"You're angry that I didn't let you go with them, aren't you?"

"*Let* me? I chose to stay behind. Make no mistake, if I wanted to be on that plane, I would've been on it."

"Why did you stay then?"

The curvy blonde sat at the foot of the bed and watched him with interest. Propped one knee up a little, revealing her glistening slit. She always did shit like that, trying to unnerve the other person, remind them of her power.

D wasn't unnerved. He was perfectly capable of standing his ground even while his gaze ate up what she was attempting to distract him with. "To keep an eye on you."

She traced her kneecap with one red fingernail. "Because you don't trust me? You don't believe I'm sincere in my offer to help find your missing Morgan?"

He shrugged. "Of course I don't trust you. I'd be a fool if I did."

"Oh, honey, who are we kidding? You don't trust women, period."

She sounded far too amused by that, and it raised his hackles. But rather than utter a denial or an argument, he kept his mouth shut. The bitch was right anyway. He'd never encountered a female he'd been able to trust. He'd learned at a young age that women were duplicitous creatures, far more dangerous than their male counterparts. Particularly the ones he'd found himself surrounded by in recent years.

Noelle.

Abby Sinclair, who, he had to admit, had slowly begun to win his respect. Not his trust, though.

Olivia Taylor . . .

The thought of Luke's girl had D's chest knotting with discomfort. He and Olivia had shared an unsettling moment in Manhattan, and the woman's perceptiveness had disturbed him on a whole other level. Her sympathy had infuriated him, her kindness had annoyed him. And her gentle embrace . . . Jesus.

He forcibly shoved the memory from his brain.

"Let's not talk about trust," D finally said. "Just know that I'm watching you."

She gracefully rose from the bed. "Watch all you want." Her tongue darted out to lick her bottom lip. "Now shut up and take off your pants."

He didn't appreciate the commanding note in her voice, but again, he was quite skilled at picking his battles. Fact of the matter was, he could use a quick, uncomplicated lay, and Noelle, with her no-bullshit policy and smoking-hot body, was uncomplicated.

She was also the most complicated person he'd ever met. Figure that shit out.

Rather than take her on the bed, he led her to the small

sitting area near the set of doors that also opened onto the courtyard. But the drapes were shut, giving them privacy.

He yanked on his zipper. Didn't bother removing his black muscle shirt or even taking off his pants. He simply shoved them down so his erection sprang free, and rolled on the condom Noelle handed him. A few seconds later, he spun her around and bent her over the glass table. Without hesitation or warning, he slid into her with one deep stroke, but she was more than ready for him. Wet and tight, the heat of her surrounding his hard length.

This thing between them, it contained no tenderness. Neither of them was capable of that. They'd never even kissed, for Christ's sake. Nope. What they had was straight-up, hard-core fucking. Hard thrusts and heavy breathing and low groans.

And always from behind.

His balls slapped against her ass as he screwed her, and when she squeezed her inner muscles against his dick, he growled and slid his hand between her legs to fondle her clit. She responded with a deep growl of her own and wiggled her bottom, meeting him thrust for thrust.

It lasted all of five minutes, and then they were both coming. Digging his fingers into her hips, D closed his eyes and let the release take over, pounding into Noelle until he was totally and utterly spent.

Damn. He'd needed that. He'd been too wound up lately, angry as hell and with no outlet for it.

Catching his breath, he withdrew, peeled the condom off and flicked it on the rug. Any other woman would've reamed him out, bitched that the floor was not a garbage can, but Noelle didn't seem to care.

Without getting dressed, she plucked a pack of smokes from the table he'd just drilled her on and brought a thin cigarette up to her pouty lips. It was some European brand, and when she held out the pack, he extracted a smoke and leaned in so she could light it for him.

Shoving the cigarette in the corner of his mouth, D tucked himself back in his pants and zipped up.

"What?" he muttered when he noticed the mocking glint in her eyes.

"You ever done it face-to-face?" She blew a set of flawless smoke rings. "Looked a woman in the eye while you screwed her?"

He didn't respond, which seemed to amuse her.

"Someone messed you up pretty bad, didn't they, honey?"

"Probably as bad as they messed you up."

Her smile was toxic. "Well, aren't we a pair?"

He exhaled a cloud of smoke. "There's no we, *honey*. There's you and there's me, and that's all there is to it."

Still smiling, she sauntered over and palmed him over his pants. "I know exactly what this is."

"Good." He took one last drag, jabbed out his smoke in the ashtray, and left the bedroom without another word.

It was dark out when they exited the hangar. For the most part, the flight had been uneventful, aside from Juliet's relentless flirting and Ethan's brooding. By the time the Cessna touched down on the dirt runway, Ethan had looked ready to murder the sexy brunette, who'd taken great delight in teasing him about his rookie status during the two-hour flight.

The car they'd arranged for was waiting near the gate, a beat-up Jeep that had seen much better days. They tossed their gear in the back, which was also where Juliet banished Ethan by usurping the passenger seat.

"You know, you could stick around here while we check out the house," Trevor suggested. "There's really no reason for you to come along."

In fact, he doubted they'd even require Juliet's assistance on this op—what did they need her feminine charms for when he and Ethan were perfectly capable of extracting intel from Lassiter using the good old-fashioned kind of persuasion?

Juliet clearly disagreed. With another one of those lazy grins he'd decided were her trademark, she buckled her seat belt and lifted her legs onto the dashboard. She'd changed into an all-black getup, and she looked like one of those kick-ass heroines you saw in action movies.

"Trust me, you might need me, depending on Lassiter's security situation."

Ethan spoke up from the backseat, a bite to his voice. "We know how to bypass alarm systems."

"Yeah?" She twisted around to look at him. "What's your preferred method for disarming the new Global Switch TR26 PIR unit?"

Ethan's blank look brought another grin to her lips. "That's what I thought, kiddo."

Trevor joined the conversation before Ethan could blow a gasket from that "kiddo" comment. "So, what, you're a professional thief?"

He drove along the dusty road leading away from the airfield. Nearly every streetlight on this stretch of highway was busted, and the Jeep's headlights didn't illuminate shit, they were so damn weak. Keeping his eyes on the road, Trevor headed in the direction Ethan had mapped out for them. Lassiter's beach house was only thirty miles west, and fortunately, the full moon helped light the way.

"Former thief," Juliet responded. "Now I just kill people for a living."

Trevor rolled his eyes. "How old are you exactly?"

"A lady never reveals her age," she said demurely.

In the backseat, Ethan snorted.

Juliet shot Trevor a sidelong look. "But enough about me. Let's talk about *you*. You're the one who got Isabel shot."

Her words brought a jolt of surprise. "Pardon me?"

"Last year in Colombia. Izzy was shot saving your ass in Blanco's compound." Juliet's tone sharpened. "Isabel's like a sister to me. You catch my drift, Callaghan?"

"If you're implying that you'll fuck me up if I hurt Isabel, then, yes, I hear you loud and clear."

"You don't think I'm serious?"

"Doesn't matter either way. Trust me, I'd throw myself in front of a firing squad if it meant keeping her safe."

His firm proclamation surprised him as much as it did his passengers, both of whom went silent.

Shifting awkwardly, Trevor peered at an approaching road sign. "That should be the turnoff up there, right?" he asked Ethan.

The rookie nodded. "Yeah. We drive through town for half a mile, and then there's another turn."

Town ended up being a less than apt description for the shithole they encountered. The narrow street could barely accommodate both the Jeep and the beat-up vehicles parked on either side of the road. Most of the storefronts were boarded up or covered with graffiti, and it seemed that the only establishments capable of staying in business in the "town" of Pelegro were the cantinas, the pawnshops, and the lone strip club at the corner.

A burst of loud laughter echoed in the night air. Trevor slowed the Jeep to let a group of teenagers pass.

Four dark heads swiveled toward the windshield as the teens eyed the vehicle with visible distrust. A few Spanish sentences were exchanged, low murmurs that Trevor couldn't make out. After a second, the young men quickened their pace and ducked into a bar with a neon pinup-girl sign blinking over the door.

"This place is a fucking dump," Juliet commented as they passed several more groups of nefarious-looking characters.

Fortunately, Pelegro was as small as it was shitty; minutes later, the town was a speck in the rearview mirror and they were on the road to Lassiter's house.

The beach house was nothing more than a glorified shack. Splintered wood and a tin roof made up the exterior, and the front yard was littered with old tires, piles of two-by-fours, and the skeletons of two old Chevys.

"Isn't this dude supposed to be loaded?" Ethan asked.

"Yeah, but maybe he's not into showy displays of wealth." Trevor shrugged. "Can't help but respect him for that. And now we don't have to worry about encountering any fancy-pants security systems."

"Stop the car," Juliet said sharply.

Trevor slammed on the brakes so hard Ethan nearly sailed out of the backseat, but neither man questioned Juliet's outburst. Whether they liked it or not, she was part of the team, and Trevor never second-guessed a team member's instincts.

"What's going on?" he demanded.

The Jeep had stopped fifty yards from the front door of Lassiter's place, which was shrouded in darkness. Not a single light spilled out of the various windows, but the Dodge pickup truck parked in front of the attached garage seemed to indicate someone was home. Unlike the other vehicular corpses on the property, the pickup looked brand-spanking-new, red and shiny and boasting silver rims that sparkled in the moonlight.

Next to him, Juliet unbuckled her seat belt and peered at the trees on either side of the dusty path.

"We've got motion sensors. There, there, and there." She pointed out the various locations. "I can disarm them, but it'll take some time. Five, ten minutes."

"Don't bother." Trevor continued to stare at the dark house in the distance. Something was off about the place. "I think we're too late."

"I'm thinking the same thing," Ethan murmured.

Trevor brought his foot back to the gas pedal and veered off to the side of the road, driving right into the canopy of trees. He killed the engine and they all slid out of the Jeep.

He could hear the ocean now, the muffled crashing of waves, and a salty breeze wafted toward them. If they'd triggered those motion detectors Juliet had spotted, you wouldn't know it. No alarms wailed, and the house remained dark and quiet.

"Take the rear," he told Ethan. "Juliet stays with me."

He decided to forgo the M16 and carry his SIG instead. He doubted they'd be greeted by a dozen armed mercs; everything about this situation screamed *you're too damn late*.

While Ethan darted off and vanished in the shadows, Trevor and Juliet approached the house through the trees.

The scents of salt and seaweed grew stronger, the rhythmic pounding of the waves getting louder. Lassiter's shack might be an eyesore, but hell, location, location, location, right? Having the ocean in your backyard probably boosted the place's market value.

Juliet moved like a pro, communicating with him via hand gestures and gripping her black Beretta with confidence. They crept along the ramshackle exterior toward the front door, where Trevor signaled for her to fall back.

He held up three fingers in a silent count.

She nodded, waiting.

Three seconds later, Trevor kicked open the door. The thing flew right off its hinges and went crashing to the weathered wooden floor in the house's tiny entryway. Another crash reverberated from the back of the house as Ethan let himself in under similar circumstances. No point in using stealth mode here; Trevor didn't have high hopes as he moved through the shadows.

The coppery scent of blood reached his nostrils long before they found the body.

Yep, too damn late.

"He kinda looks like Mickey Rourke," Juliet remarked. Her dark eyes swept over the dead man on the floor. "Yeah, he's definitely Rourke-esque."

Trevor did notice the resemblance. Eddie Lassiter was a big man—thick chest, bulky arms, muscular legs. His skin had the leathery look of a man who'd spent too much time in the sun, and his dirty blond hair was long and stringy.

As far as death masks went, Lassiter's was actually kinda comical—the man looked entirely pissed off, as if he couldn't believe someone would have the gall to murder *him*. Trevor recognized Lassiter from the grainy photo Noelle's girl Paige had e-mailed them earlier, though the man in that photo hadn't been quite so . . . dead.

He approached the body and studied the dime-size bullet hole in Lassiter's forehead. A pool of brownish red blood, now beginning to dry, surrounded his head, and one red line trickled out of the wound and down his nose.

"Seeing as the back of his head is still intact," Trevor said drily, "I'd wager he got popped by a small-caliber pistol."

Ethan's hazel eyes took in the scene from the doorway. "Not point-blank, either, considering the lack of powder residue. The shooter was standing a few meters away."

The rookie's gaze landed on the open suitcase on the bed, then the .45 pistol lying on the bedspread.

"He burst in while Lassiter was packing and caught him off guard. Lassiter didn't have time to go for his weapon," Ethan mused.

"Did you learn crime scene analysis watching *CSI*?" Juliet drawled. "That's so adorable."

Ethan narrowed his eyes at her. "You do realize I'm a marine, right?"

She looked amused. "So?"

"So I can kick your ass without batting a fucking eye."

Uh-oh. Trevor knew the young soldier swore only when he was seriously pissed off.

Juliet, of course, fueled Ethan's anger by laughing. "Go ahead, kiddo. Do it." Challenge lit her eyes. "But we both know a sweet thing like yourself would never hurt a lady."

"Yeah, keep calling yourself that, sweetheart. Maybe if you say it enough times, you'll magically transform into one."

Her delighted laughter echoed in the room. "Well, well, the kid's got a backbone. Ain't that sweet?"

"Enough," Trevor barked. "You two search the house for anything that might be connected to Morgan or the compound. I'll check the body."

Ten minutes later, it became glaringly obvious that both Lassiter's corpse and his shitty shack had been cleaned. Either that, or Lassiter didn't keep anything of value here.

No documents, no cash, no hidden compartments as far as they could tell. His pockets were empty, his wallet containing nothing but an expired driver's license and a folded-up birth certificate that revealed the tough guy's middle name as Marion—Juliet got a kick out of that one.

By the time they reconvened on the rickety front steps,

Trevor felt like this entire trek to Baja had been a total waste of time. No hint as to who might have hired Lassiter. No evidence pointing to who wanted Morgan and his men dead.

Waste of fucking time.

"Call Noelle," he told Juliet. "Tell her we've got shit all." He holstered his gun and released a pent-up breath. "Let's hope the Reilly brothers have something better to offer."

Chapter 9

"Lassiter's dead."

Isabel's head jerked up in surprise as her boss walked into the den. "Since when?" she asked Noelle.

"Callaghan's guessing he was popped five or six hours ago."

"He was shot?"

Nodding, Noelle sat down in a big leather easy chair. The den was as cozy as the rest of the house, with a pair of overstuffed couches, an electric fireplace, and the antique desk Isabel was sitting behind.

"The person who hired him was clearly tying up loose ends," Noelle said. "Or, if that person is anything like me, he was punishing the imbecile for his royal fuckup. The men Lassiter recruited were clearly incompetent."

Isabel pictured Lloyd's lifeless body sprawled on the bloody kitchen floor.

And she couldn't even begin to imagine the scene Trevor had found in Holden McCall's bedroom.

"They weren't totally incompetent," she murmured.

"They left the majority of their targets alive," Noelle retorted. "In my book, that's amateur hour."

"Did they find anything useful at Lassiter's place, at least?"

"It was clean. If Lassiter kept any records, he stashed

them off-site. Call Sean and tell him to look into it, find out if Lassiter's got a safe-deposit box or storage locker, or hell, a lawyer."

"Got it. Oh, and Sean wanted me to pass along a message."

"Oh, really?"

"He said, and I quote, 'Tell your boss to fuck right off.'"
Isabel grinned. "What'd you do to him?"

"He was trying to find Bailey, and Bailey didn't want to be found, so I may have fed him some false intel that sent him on a wild-goose chase."

A sigh slipped out. "Well, I wish you hadn't done that because now he's being all sulky about it and charging us double for this latest intel."

Then again, the Reilly brothers employed an arbitrary fee schedule that didn't make much sense to begin with. A pair of former mercenaries who may or may not have been tangled up with the IRA at one point, Oliver and Sean fancied themselves the best information dealers currently operating on the globe—and they probably were. Isabel had yet to meet anyone with a bigger network of contacts than the Reilly brothers. Those Irishmen possessed the ability to produce information out of thin air.

Oliver had helped her and Trevor in New York on that last job, and in all honesty, Isabel wished she was dealing with Ollie again; he was the nicer of the two, playful and down-to-earth, while Sean was the rogue, a cocky flirt who didn't quit once he had you in his sexual sights.

"Wait. Why is he looking for Bailey?" Isabel asked, wrinkling her forehead.

Of all her colleagues, Bailey was the most mysterious, ten times the chameleon Isabel herself was, and a stone-cold killer when she needed to be. Since Bailey was customarily assigned deep cover jobs for prolonged periods of time, Isabel rarely ever saw the woman.

"They crossed paths a while back," Noelle said vaguely. "Sean took a liking to her."

"And let me guess: Bailey didn't return the sentiment."

The boss laughed. "Nope."

"Okay, well, now he's annoyed with us, and we can't afford to be on his bad side when we need his help."

"Has he found anything yet?"

"It's only been a few hours since I contacted him. He said to give him at least twenty-four hours."

Noelle rose from the chair. "Find me when he gets in touch. I need to return Abby's call."

"She and Kane made it to Costa Rica okay?"

"Yes, and I've been informed that Dubois, Port, and Macgregor are on call should we need their assistance. Once we learn who Lassiter was dealing with, I'll consider bringing them in to track Morgan." Noelle's tone grew sarcastic. "See how cooperative and charitable I'm being? And all to find a man who can rot in hell for all I care."

"Why are you doing it, then?"

"Why do you think? The idea of that bastard being indebted to me is quite a lure."

"I see. And the flirting with Trevor part . . . what's your reasoning for *that*, Noelle?"

She was rewarded with a genuine-sounding laugh rather than the mocking one the boss usually doled out. "Oh, honey, if you haven't figured it out for yourself yet, then I'm damn well not going to tell you."

Still chuckling to herself, Noelle left the den.

Everyone was still awake when the trio returned to the ranch. Trevor found Isabel reading a book in the living room, and Noelle and D chain-smoking in the courtyard. The pair sat at opposite ends of the glass table, each one gazing elsewhere, neither one saying a word, yet the sight gave him a funny feeling. A sneaking suspicion that something was going on with them.

After a moment, he dismissed the thought, realizing just how insane it was.

Isabel glanced up at his entrance. "You're back."

He smiled. "I'm back."

She was on her feet in a heartbeat, moving toward him

as if she wanted to embrace him, but at the last second she halted and kept a couple of feet between them.

"So Lassiter was a dead end," she said wryly.

"Literally."

"Noelle says you didn't find any evidence to indicate who may have hired him."

"We didn't, but hopefully Irish and Irish-er have better luck."

She grinned. "Did you come up with that nickname all by yourself?"

"Yep."

"It's not particularly creative."

"Well, I did fail both ninth-grade art and tenth-grade writing, so clearly creativity isn't my strong suit."

Isabel let out a laugh. Then she furrowed her brow as if something had just occurred to her. "You know, I can't picture you in high school. I mean, I want to say you were a jock, but you've also got this serious side that makes me think you might've been a bit of a nerd."

He gave a mock gasp. "A nerd? How dare you?"

"Am I wrong?"

"Actually, no. You'll be surprised to know that I was the first-ever jock-nerd in existence. I think I even started a trend."

That got him another round of melodic laughter, and damned if he didn't feel a spark of male pride. He liked making her laugh. He liked bringing that twinkle to her eyes and seeing her let down her guard.

"What sports did you play?" she asked curiously.

"Keep me company while I change my dressings and I'll tell you."

Her hesitation lasted only a few seconds. Much shorter than usual, he noted in satisfaction. She followed him to the guest room, where he flopped down on the bed and unlaced his boots.

All traces of humor drained from Isabel's eyes when she saw the blood on his socks.

"What the hell?" she demanded. "What happened?"

He waved off her concern. "This? It's nothing. I was barefoot when the shit hit the fan back at the compound."

Anger colored her cheeks. "Why didn't you tell me when I cleaned you up at the clinic?"

"Holden had just taken off, and then I had to deal with D not listening to Sofia, so, yeah . . . I forgot." He peeled off his socks and rested his ankle on his thigh so he could study the sole of his foot. "Ah, it's just this one nick that reopened. Everything else is starting to scab over."

Isabel wasn't listening to him. She'd marched into the bathroom, and he could hear her rummaging around in the cabinets beneath the sink. When she returned, she held a wet washcloth and a first-aid kit.

"Why do men always insist that every injury is no big deal?" she grumbled.

" 'Cause we're stubborn?"

"And foolish," she said darkly.

"And foolish," he echoed with a grin.

Although his feet really weren't as bad as Isabel seemed to think, Trevor decided to humor her. He sat patiently and without a single complaint while she cleaned the sole of his foot and taped a fresh piece of gauze to that one obstinate cut that refused to heal.

Once she was done, Trevor stood up and peeled off his shirt.

Isabel huffed out a breath. "Why are you constantly undressing around me?"

"Are you complaining?"

"Are you implying that I *shouldn't* be complaining because your body is so dreamy and therefore I'm lucky to be around it?"

A laugh rumbled from deep in his chest. This was the Isabel he liked—the confident, funny Isabel whose compassion drove her to tend to his injured feet and whose candid nature never failed to inspire him. The other Isabel, the one who hid behind her various disguises, was *too* confident. Too easygoing, too composed, too perfect.

He didn't want that version of Isabel. He *wanted* a woman

with flaws, a woman who wasn't scared to be vulnerable around him.

It was a damn shame she couldn't grasp that.

"My body is just a body," he answered with a shrug. "Flesh, blood, bones, muscle." He couldn't resist teasing her. "I'm happy to know you find it dreamy, though."

When he unzipped his pants, she grumbled again. "Seriously, will you stop getting naked all the time?"

"I'm not naked. I'm in my boxers." He tossed his discarded clothes on the chair next to the bed before heading to the bathroom. "Give me a sec."

A few minutes later, after he'd used the john and washed up, he returned to the bedroom and was pleased to find that Isabel hadn't budged from her perch at the foot of the bed. He'd half expected her to sneak off while he was in the other room.

But when he stretched out on top of the duvet, she shot to her feet. "What are you doing?"

"I was planning on catching some shut-eye. It's three in the morning in case you hadn't noticed."

"And yet you lured me into your room under the pretense that you were going to tell me about your high school years."

He stacked two pillows behind his head and got comfortable. "It wasn't a pretense. I still plan on talking your ear off. It'll just be after we wake up."

"We?"

Patting the empty space beside him, Trevor met her suddenly panicked eyes and loaded a whole lot of challenge into his voice. "What, you're too scared to take a nap with me?"

She visibly swallowed.

"Come on," he coaxed. "What's the worst thing that could happen? You'll fall asleep? Good, because the dark circles under your eyes tell me you're exhausted."

"I am," she admitted.

"Come lie beside me."

His pulse kicked up a notch as Isabel approached the bed again. She wore a loose blue shirt and black leggings, and she stopped to kick off her sneakers before gingerly getting on the bed beside him. She lay down, but maintained that same aggravating distance.

This time, he refused to give it to her.

Reaching out, he wrapped his arm around her shoulders and tugged her against him. When she yelped, he simply chuckled and said, "This is happening, Iz. Deal with it."

He expected another objection, but what he got was a soft laugh. Then, to his extreme surprise, her limbs relaxed and she rested her head on his bare chest.

Warmth spread through him. Isabel snuggled closer, her silky blond hair tickling the bottom of his chin. It felt nice. It felt damn nice.

Like an idiot, he'd forgotten to turn off the lights, but he didn't want to get out of bed. He feared that if he moved, Isabel would change her mind and bolt like a frightened deer, and he didn't want this opportunity slipping through his grasp.

He absently stroked her back, but the cotton fabric of her shirt served as an annoying barrier. Before he could stop himself, he yanked the shirt up a few inches and ran his palm over her bare skin.

Her quick intake of breath echoed in the bedroom.

"We're just lying here, sweetheart. Nothing to freak out over." He moved his fingertips over her warm, supple flesh.

"Okay," she murmured.

He felt her relax again. Her arm came out and folded against his chest, her delicate hand resting on his right pec. When he covered her hand with his own and held it there, she didn't jump or flinch. A quiet breath left her mouth and heated his skin.

As they lay there in silence, Trevor was overcome by a hot rush of emotion. His throat tightened, making it hard to draw a breath. His hand trembled over Isabel's. He hadn't cuddled with a woman in two years. He and Isabel had shared a bed in New York, but it hadn't been like this. Back then, he'd allowed her the distance she'd craved.

Tonight was different. He was so achingly aware of her

nearness. The flowery scent of her shampoo, the sweet fragrance of her skin, the rapid beating of her heart vibrating against his chest.

The last woman he'd been this close to was Gina. His feisty, beautiful Gina, whose face no longer haunted his nightmares. Nowadays, he didn't dream of a curly-haired brunette. He dreamed of the blue-eyed blonde who'd managed to sneak past his defenses before he'd even seen it coming.

"Trevor?"

"Mmm-hmmm."

"This is nice."

Serenity washed over him. "Yeah, it is."

He held her until she fell asleep. Listened to her quiet breathing and the steady vibration of her heartbeat. For the first time in five months, he felt utterly at peace again, and that feeling of tranquillity followed him into the best sleep he'd had in a long, long time.

Tomas Meiro was a man who was used to making things happen. He didn't sit around and wait for good fortune to come his way. No, he made his own luck.

Most of the VIPs staying here at the Crystal Palace shared that mind-set, but not all. Not the hungry faces currently gracing the wall of monitors on the security floor. Not the groups of tourists who streamed into the casino and told themselves they'd be leaving it as millionaires.

Those people were fools. You didn't rely on games of chance to make you rich. You relied on your intelligence, your cleverness, your drive.

Sometimes, though, you had no choice but to enlist another man to do your bidding.

And sometimes, that man you placed your trust in was a total fucking idiot.

"You took care of the problem?" Meiro said into his cell phone as he absently studied the security screens.

"Lassiter is no longer in business," Roussel assured him.

"Good. And our little friend?"

"There's no way of confirming whether he died during the

attack, but if he didn't, our people will find him." Roussel paused. "Perhaps we can use the woman to lure him out."

Meiro's tone sharpened. "You've found the woman?"

"Not yet, but I suspect she'll surface now that our friend has disappeared."

"Will she, though? They're no longer together—she might not care about him anymore. Do we know why they went their separate ways?"

"No, but if they are enemies now, we can use that to our advantage," Roussel pointed out. "Use them against each other."

Meiro wasn't as convinced. "First find the woman. Then we will discuss what to do with her."

He disconnected the call and turned back to the dozens of screens that occupied the enormous space. A flash of silver winked at him.

"Zoom in on Table Eight." He directed the order at Keller, one of his most trusted security experts.

As commanded, Keller enlarged one of the screens, and a raven-haired woman wearing a red strapless gown and half a million bucks' worth of diamonds appeared on the monitor. She was young, early twenties, maybe late teens. And she was spectacular.

As his groin stirred, Meiro glanced behind him and said, "Who is she?"

There was a flurry of activity as the staff manning the computer banks worked hard to get him an answer.

"Alicia Montoya," one of the techs announced. "Nineteen years old, daughter of the Spanish ambassador."

"Staying in the Emerald Villa," someone else said. "With her mother and younger sister, Magda."

Meiro examined the screen. The lovely Alicia was all alone at the roulette table. No mother or sister in sight.

He swiftly headed for the door, where his two bodyguards awaited him. "Invite Alicia Montoya to the VIP lounge," he told the assistant who greeted him outside the security room.

"Right away, sir."

* * *

There was a hand on her breast.

A big male hand.

Cupping her breast.

Isabel's eyelids flew open as the thought registered. Almost immediately, her pulse went off-kilter and her breath got stuck in her lungs.

She and Trevor were spooning—how the heck had that happened?—and either she had the dirtiest imagination on the planet, or there really was a long, hard cock pressing against her ass.

A low groan broke the silence, and suddenly that thick bulge was grinding into her buttocks and Trevor's hand tightened over her breast, squeezing hard.

She moaned before she could stop herself.

And just like that, his hand was gone, his rock-solid body no longer nestled behind her.

"Shit, I'm sorry," came his husky voice. "Didn't mean to do that."

She gulped. "It's okay."

They both sat up. Isabel rubbed her eyes, ignored her pounding heart, and glanced at the window. The sun had already risen, the sky a gorgeous, cloudless blue. She checked the clock on the bedside table and saw that it was nine thirty. Wow. Some nap—they'd slept for more than six hours.

She just hoped that no other catastrophes had occurred during the night.

"Baseball."

Isabel blinked at the abrupt announcement. "What?"

"I played baseball in high school." Trevor wore a sheepish expression. "And rugby. Oh, and I was on the honor roll every semester, except for the years I took art and writing."

She had to laugh. "You really were a jock-nerd, then."

"Yep."

He climbed out of bed and raised his arms in a stretch that made every mouthwatering muscle on his bare chest ripple. He was in amazing shape, posing a seriously alluring picture as he stood there in nothing but a pair of boxer briefs that hugged his impressive package. A shiver ran through her at the knowledge that his erection had been straining against her butt only minutes ago.

Damn it. The lust was back, stronger than ever. Pressure gathered between her legs, and the raw need coursing through her stunned her with its ferocity.

"I haven't had sex in three years," she blurted out.

Her out-of-the-blue announcement caused Trevor's dark eyebrows to shoot up to his forehead. Raking one hand through his sleep-tousled hair, he stared at her with bewildered eyes.

"Um . . . all right." A faint grin lifted the corners of his mouth. "It's been two years for me."

She nervously licked her lips. Felt the heat of embarrassment staining her cheeks. "I don't know why I said that."

"Sure you do." The grin widened. "You were turned on, you got scared, and you felt compelled to make it known that sex isn't something you treat lightly."

Her jaw fell open, even as amusement danced over her. "Oh, really?"

"Yep."

She rolled her eyes at his careless, somewhat smug tone. At the same time, she was caught completely off guard. She'd thought she had Trevor Callaghan all figured out back in New York. He was the strong, serious type. Honorable and sweet and tender.

Well, he was still all of those things, only now he was showing her a few more unexpected facets of his personality. Playfulness. Sensuality. Pigheadedness.

He was opening up to her. Revealing a new side of himself with each private moment shared.

And in return, she was revealing . . . nothing. Absolutely nothing, as always.

Despite the rush of self-loathing that flooded her body, she managed an uneasy smile. "I guess I just wanted you to be aware of it."

"I told you I wanted all or nothing, but I didn't say I

wanted it all right this very second. It's not a race to the finish line, Iz. I'm a patient man, and I'm willing to wait as long as you need."

Tears pricked her eyes. She quickly averted her gaze and ordered herself to pull it together.

But . . . wow. Who *was* this man? And what the hell was the matter with her that she couldn't lower her guard and give him what he wanted? What they *both* wanted?

He deserves better.

Pain lodged in her chest. And there it was, the root of the issue. Trevor deserved someone better. Someone less . . . flawed.

Taking a deep breath, she pasted on another smile and slipped into her sneakers. "I'm going to take a quick shower and get changed. I'll catch up with you later."

She could practically hear Trevor's thoughts as she darted out the door. She was thinking the same damn thing.

Coward.

Chapter 10

Later that morning, Trevor finally had a chance to speak to D and Ethan away from prying eyes.

As much as he appreciated Isabel's help, he didn't feel entirely comfortable around Noelle. Or Juliet, who'd spent the past hour picking every lock in the house simply because she was "bored." Eventually Isabel had dragged the brunette into the den, claiming she wanted to catch up, but Trevor suspected Isabel was looking for new ways to avoid him.

Ah, well. He would let it go for now. He'd given her a lot to think about, not just last night but this morning, and now he simply had to wait and see if he'd gotten through to her.

The three men were alone in the central courtyard. It was another hot and beautiful day, which made Trevor wistfully think of home. The streets in Aspen would still be covered in snow, the late-March chill still lingering in the air. Christ, he wished he was there instead of here.

He noticed that D and Ethan looked as frustrated as he felt. None of them liked waiting around with their thumbs up their asses, but until they had a lead on who Lassiter had been doing business with, their hands were tied.

"That woman pisses me off," Ethan muttered.

Trevor chuckled when he realized Ethan's frustration was about more than the absence of action.

"You know she only keeps needling you because you're such an easy target," he told the guy. "Stop taking the bait."

"Hard to do when everything is a frickin' game to her," Ethan retorted. "She doesn't give a shit that Morgan's AWOL."

The rookie's concern was palpable, and when Trevor glimpsed the steely determination in Ethan's hazel eyes, he realized the man was a lot more shaken up about this whole mess than he'd been letting on.

Made sense, though. To Trevor and the others, Jim Morgan was a boss and a friend. To Ethan, Morgan was a father figure.

All Trevor knew about Ethan's background was that the kid hailed from a small town, had no family, and was recruited by Morgan after one tour in the Marines. But since the day Ethan had come on board, it had been obvious to everyone that he viewed Morgan as a role model of sorts. And he was incredibly protective of the boss.

"Forget about Juliet," Trevor advised. "All that matters is that *we* give a shit." He glanced at D. "Have you spoken to Sullivan today?"

When D shook his head, the snake tattooed on the base of his neck seemed to ripple as if the deadly creature had come alive. "Nah, but I spoke to Kane. He and Sinclair have everything under control at the new base. B-Team's still heading up the extraction in Kabul. They ran into a few snags."

"Yeah, I heard." Trevor rubbed his temples, feeling a headache coming on. "Luke's going nuts in Colorado. He's pissed that there's nothing for him to do."

And since there was nobody who craved action as much as Luke Dubois, Trevor could understand why the man didn't appreciate being grounded.

"There's nothing for any of us to do," Ethan said in aggravation. "Where the fuck is Morgan? Why the hell hasn't he checked in?"

No one had an answer.

Trevor reached for his coffee mug. The liquid was lukewarm from sitting out, but he gulped it down anyway, needing the caffeine fix. When footsteps sounded, the men's heads shifted toward the door.

"Sean's on the phone. He says he's got something for us." Isabel walked out with brisk strides. She was trailed by Noelle and Juliet, who didn't look so bored anymore.

Trevor's muscles instantly tensed. "What did he find?"

"Don't know yet." She quickly spoke into her cell. "Hey, Sean, I'm putting you on speaker."

A moment later a deep male voice greeted everyone. Sean Reilly sounded exactly like his twin brother, Oliver, whom Trevor had met in New York. Same Irish brogue, same deep timbre, same sarcasm.

"You sound well rested, luv. Could it be because you weren't up all bloody night, chatting with every slimebag in the mercenary cesspool?"

Isabel laughed. "Hey, you're the one who chose to go into this line of business."

"Yeah, well, I'm charging you double."

"Quit being a brat and tell us what you've got," Juliet said.

Sean sounded delighted. "Jules, is that you? How come you don't visit me in Dublin anymore?"

"Oh, Sean, you know I've always been partial to your brother," Juliet said mockingly. "Now what the fuck did you come up with?"

Reilly's tone went from flirtatious to professional in a split second. "Can't be one hundred percent on this, but I think the man you're looking for is Tomas Meiro."

Frowning, Trevor set his mug on the table. "Tomas Meiro? Doesn't ring a bell."

"Who am I talking to?"

"Trevor Callaghan. I work for Morgan."

"Callaghan. Yes. Right. You dealt with my brother last year."

"I did. Now who's this Meiro dude?"

Noelle, who was smoking a cigarette near the terrace doors, was the one who answered. "Casino owner. Originally from Lisbon, but based in Monte Carlo now." Usually so composed, she now seemed troubled. "I haven't been able to get a read on him. He appeared on the scene fairly recently, a year or two ago. Came out of fucking nowhere."

Sean's voice joined in. "I can't tell you much more than that, but like I said, I think he's the one who hired Lassiter."

"You got evidence to back that up?" Trevor asked.

"I've traced Lassiter's movements for the last three months—I figured this hit on your compound, it had to be a recent transaction, right?"

"Most likely," Trevor agreed.

Unless the ambush had been in the works for months, years even. In which case . . . fuck, he didn't even want to consider that possibility right now.

"Lassiter's last few deals were with a Dominican cartel, a new outfit that needed some muscle to prove a point to the Haitians. I didn't find any connection between Morgan and the cartel—granted, I only did a surface probe, but I don't think the Dominicans give a shit about Jim Morgan." Sean paused, as if collecting his thoughts. "Anyway, after half a dozen meetings with the cartel, Lassiter flew to Monaco. He stayed at the White Sands, was spotted in the casino, the bar, the fitness center. On his last night, casino security cameras caught him in what looked like a hush-hush meeting with Claude Roussel. Roussel is Meiro's number two. He's ex-military, worked as a bodyguard for a while, now serves as Meiro's henchman and representative."

"Did Lassiter set foot in Meiro's casino?" Noelle inquired.

"Negative. In fact, our man Eddie visited every casino *but* the Crystal Palace, which I find mighty suspicious." A rustling noise filled the line, followed by the unmistakable sound of a lighter being flicked and a cigarette being inhaled. "I e-mailed a copy of the security footage of Lassiter and Roussel to Paige, and another copy to you, Iz."

Isabel pursed her lips. "So we think Roussel was meeting with Lassiter on Meiro's behalf?"

"Roussel handles the shadier aspects of Meiro's business. I can't imagine why else he'd be dealing with a middleman like Lassiter if not to hire the man's services. Again, couldn't find a connection between Meiro and Morgan, but I'll keep digging. Oh, but how's this for fishy? The day after Lassiter met with Roussel, your boss Morgan dropped off the face of the planet. Last known whereabouts were D.C., right?"

"Right," Trevor said warily.

"My brother's going to check it out, see if he can track Morgan's movements, but don't hold your breath. Jim Morgan can be very sneaky when he wants to be."

No kidding. And Morgan had taken off on his own so many times before that Trevor and the others had no way of knowing if the boss was truly in trouble or simply off on another one of his secret missions.

Granted, Morgan usually did inform Kane when he planned on being out of touch. A heads-up he certainly hadn't given this time around.

"That's it for now," Sean said. "I'll stay here for another day or so to chat with a few more folks. See if I can find a stronger link between Lassiter and Meiro."

"Wait—you're in Monte Carlo?" Isabel asked.

"Yessiree, luv. I flew in a couple of hours ago. And FYI? I expect compensation for the five grand I lost at the craps table earlier."

"The check's in the mail," Noelle drawled.

Isabel spoke up again. "Thanks for everything, Sean. Call when you have more, okay?"

"You got it, sweetness."

The call disconnected with a click.

Trevor rose from his chair, suddenly feeling on edge. He paced the dusty clay-tiled floor in the open courtyard, his brain filtering through the details Sean had just fed into it.

He addressed Noelle. "What else do you know about this Meiro guy?"

The blonde lit another cigarette and sank into the chair Trevor had abandoned. "Like I said, he's new on the scene. He owns a chain of casinos, or rather his wife does. He married a French heiress, a really unfortunate-looking girl. But

Wifey's daddy was filthy rich, and she inherited the family casinos after his death. Daddy also ran a high-class prostitution ring and dabbled in human trafficking—I assume Meiro deals with those aspects of the business as well."

"So he's bad news," Trevor said flatly.

Noelle turned to Juliet. "You crossed paths with him in Lisbon last year, didn't you?"

Nodding, the brunette reclined in her chair and twined a long strand of hair around her fingers. "He's very charming," she admitted. "Smart, too. And he has no shortage of mistresses. I met him at a charity gala. He showed up with his wife." She grinned at Noelle. "You're right. The woman is plainer than oatmeal. But I hear he only brings her out to serious, media-heavy events. We both wound up at the after-party, and Wifey was nowhere to be found. He brought a delicious piece of arm candy to that party."

"They do say he has a weakness for beautiful women," Noelle said thoughtfully.

"And he's very mysterious," Juliet added. "Debonair, sexy in a dangerous sort of way. Very Gatsby-esque."

Trevor had to smile—he rather enjoyed Juliet's comparisons—but his good humor faded fast. "I've never heard Morgan talk about a Tomas Meiro." He checked with the other men. "You?"

D shook his head, then dragged his hand over his buzz cut. "Not a peep."

"Maybe they have a history we don't know about," Ethan said in a tired voice.

Noelle's throaty laughter made them all frown. "Oh, you boys. So fucking naive. Haven't you figured out by now that Jim has a history with *everyone*?"

Trevor lifted a brow in challenge. "Including you?"

She ignored the question and kept talking. "If there's a connection between Jim and Meiro, the Reilly brothers will find it. For now, we have to explore the Meiro-Lassiter link. We need confirmation that Meiro was the one who hired Lassiter."

"Recon," D said curtly, getting to his feet. The man was

in fighting form again, his head injury nothing but a fading red scab at the base of his skull, and he'd been looking antsy all morning. Itching for action.

"I haven't been to Monte Carlo in *ages*." Juliet's almond-shaped eyes twinkled like dark gems.

Ethan shot her a surprisingly evil look. "This isn't a vacation, sweetheart."

"Gosh, I love it when you call me that. It makes you sound so grown-up."

Noelle held up a hand before the bickering could start. "Either get a room, you two, or shut the fuck up." She spared D a pithy look. "Yes, recon. My pilot's on call—we can be up in the air in two hours, tops." She turned to Trevor. "Arrange for your men to meet us there. Port and Macgregor."

Trevor nodded. Sullivan and Liam would be happy to hear that; they'd been chomping at the bit to join the group. None of the men on Morgan's crew enjoyed sitting idle, and the two mercs had been calling to bitch all morning, just like Luke.

"What about Luke?" he asked.

"Tell him to stay put for the time being. We'll hammer out a more solid plan once we're in the air. For now, let's—"

Isabel's phone buzzed, causing the glass tabletop to vibrate. She leaned in to check the display, then frowned. "It's Sean."

A second later, the Irishman's voice once again floated out of the speaker.

"Me again." He sounded downright chipper, but Trevor picked up on the grave note beneath that cheerful brogue. "We've got ourselves a little development here, boys and girls."

"What is it?" Noelle said sharply.

"Seems like a couple of policemen fished a body out of the marina about an hour ago."

Trevor's stomach clenched. Oh shit.

"Unidentified male. Caucasian, late thirties or early forties. That's all I know. Body was taken to the morgue." Sean sounded momentarily jazzed up. "It's been years since I broke into a morgue. Send me a current photo of our man Jim and I'll see about identifying the stiff."

The click on the line indicated that Sean had hung up.

Trevor exchanged a look with D, whose expressionless black eyes didn't fool anyone. The man was worried about the boss, just like they all were.

Well, maybe with the exception of Noelle—the woman hadn't even blinked when Reilly mentioned the dead body in the harbor.

A long silence descended on the group as nobody voiced what they were all thinking.

Finally Ethan pushed his chair back with a loud grating noise. "It's not Morgan," he said firmly. "And we're wasting time. Come on, let's get this fucking show on the road."

Chapter 11

Isabel sat next to Trevor in the cabin of Noelle's private jet, a thirty-two-million-dollar toy that never failed to impress her. The plane accommodated ten passengers and a crew of two, and offered a wide cabin with double club seating, a galley, and a full-size lavatory.

Every time Isabel set foot on the jet, she felt like Donald Trump. Or Oprah.

They were two hours into the six-hour flight to Monaco, and she was watching the security tape of Eddie Lassiter and Claude Roussel for the second time. When the tape neared its end, she entered a few keystrokes to slow down the footage. A few seconds later, she pressed PAUSE.

"Watch this," she told Trevor.

Trevor leaned in close so he could study the laptop screen. The citrus-and-wood blend of his aftershave surrounded her, made her feel light-headed and weak-kneed. Fortunately, she was seated and therefore in no danger of keeling over from the overpowering desire coursing through her like an electric current.

"What am I looking at?" he asked.

She rewound the segment and played it again. "Look at their hands. Roussel slips something into Lassiter's hand before they go their separate ways. It looks like a flash drive, maybe."

"Good eye. You're right. He definitely handed Lassiter something. Question is," Trevor mused, "did the exchange have anything to do with the attack on the compound, or was it completely unrelated to Morgan?"

"We'll find out soon enough, I guess." She bit her lip. "The body in the marina . . . It can't be Morgan, right?"

There was a split second of hesitation, which told her he wasn't a hundred percent sure in his response. "Of course not."

"Isabel." Noelle's commanding voice wafted from the other side of the plush cabin, and then the blonde was striding toward them.

"I've booked Valerie a suite at the Crystal Palace," Noelle said briskly. She settled in one of the two seats opposite Trevor and Isabel. "Peterson's shipping your papers, but there's a chance they won't arrive until tomorrow morning. If that's the case, Valerie will show up at the hotel tomorrow."

"We should do that anyway," Isabel mused. "Checking in a day late is just Valerie's style. She never sticks to a schedule."

Trevor cleared his throat. "Who exactly are Peterson and Valerie?"

"Peterson's the lawyer who keeps my various identities straight," Isabel explained. "And Valerie is one of those identities."

Trevor didn't look happy as he glanced at Noelle. "You're sending Isabel in?" His gaze briefly shifted to Juliet, who sat across the aisle and was listening to their conversation. "Not you?"

"I already told you what my specialty is, and it's not transformation," Juliet replied. "Isabel's better at creating an entire persona."

Trevor's jaw seemed unusually tight. His brown eyes flicked back to Noelle. "So Isabel's job is to cozy up to Meiro. What about the rest of us?"

"We'll be the eyes and ears. I want at least three of us on the casino floor, the rest posted outside on the strip. Reilly will stick around and gather intel on Meiro and his business dealings, and Reilly's twin is following the Morgan thread."

Noelle looked annoyed. "Every source I've got knows I'm looking for the mighty Jim Morgan. That son of a bitch is gonna owe me big. That is, if it wasn't his body floating faceup in the Monaco harbor."

Looking positively uplifted, Noelle headed back to her seat. "We'll formulate a firmer plan of action when we know more," she said over her shoulder.

Normally Trevor relaxed once Noelle left the scene, but Isabel noticed that his jaw remained tense. She shifted in her seat so her back was to the aisle, but since the new position offered only the illusion of privacy, she still lowered her voice when she spoke. "What's wrong?"

"Nothing," he muttered.

She suppressed a sigh. "You're not happy that Noelle assigned me to Meiro."

"Not particularly, no."

The breath she'd been holding slipped out. "This is my job, Trevor. I work undercover."

He just shrugged, a response she had no clue how to interpret.

"Trust me, you're going to like Valerie." Grinning, Isabel slipped into the flawless British accent she'd perfected over the years. "She's a sassy little thing."

Trevor cracked a smile, but a second later another black cloud floated into his expression. "Just out of curiosity, how similar is Valerie to Paloma?"

She wrinkled her brow, unsure where he was going with this. He was referring to Paloma Dominguez, the alter ego Isabel had used in Colombia the year before. Make that Paloma Dominguez-*Martin*. During that job, Paloma had just married Julian Martin, Trevor's alter ego. They'd gone undercover as the newly married couple to rescue a dozen innocent girls from Luis Blanco, a twisted arms dealer who also had his fat fingers in the sex trade pie.

"Similar, how?" she asked.

"You know, personality wise. Sexpot wise . . . ," he said grudgingly.

"Aw, come on, Paloma's not *that* big of a sexpot."

His voice lowered as he leaned in close. "As I recall, Paloma had no problem giving me hand jobs in public. Just wondering if Meiro can expect the same kind of special treatment from Valerie."

His breath was hot on her ear, and once again his intoxicating scent grabbed hold of her senses. She was suddenly hit with the vision of waking up to the feel of Trevor pressed up against her, and goose bumps broke out on her bare arms.

Damn it. She needed to get this attraction under control. Pronto.

"Valerie won't be giving anyone a hand job," she assured him.

"You sure about that?"

"I don't use sex to gather intel. Just charm and minor seduction."

"Same thing."

"Different thing. Look, Noelle knows where I stand on this—if the target demands sex, I walk away. That's not how I operate."

Although he looked relieved, his dark eyes continued to flicker with what she was starting to suspect was jealousy. "Why can't we go in as Paloma and Julian?"

"Wouldn't it be fun if we did?" She couldn't help but grin. "I miss those two. They were such an entertaining couple. But I can't use Paloma again, not unless she and Julian get a divorce."

"Not necessarily. I used Julian's ID to do some minor recon on the Argentina job a few months ago. I just dropped mentions here and there of my feisty wife, Paloma, said she was back home spending my money."

"So the cover's still intact."

"Yes." He cocked his head. "Which means there's no reason why we can't use it again."

"We can't do it because Meiro likes arm candy. As in, a beautiful *woman* on his arm. Not a married couple."

"I guess."

"You know, I can't figure out if you're jealous that I'll be spending time with Meiro or worried about my safety."

"A little bit of both." He didn't sound happy admitting to either charge.

Impulsively, Isabel reached for his hand. "It'll be fine. I've done this a hundred times before and I always walk out alive."

"Doesn't mean you will this time."

Trevor laced their fingers together.

Isabel didn't stop him.

Truthfully, it felt nice. She couldn't remember the last time she'd held a man's hand.

She stared at their intertwined fingers and her heart did a little flip. God, why did she turn into such a sap when Trevor was around? The man had the uncanny power of making her believe anything was possible. That a messed-up person like herself could actually find peace. Love, even.

When she noticed him watching her with an intense expression, her heart jumped again. "What is it?" she murmured.

"I don't like the idea of you risking your life."

"Yeah? Well, I don't like the idea of *you* risking *your* life, but I didn't try and stop you from checking out Lassiter's place in Baja."

"It's my job." Her pointed stare brought a sheepish flicker to his eyes. "I get it—this is *your* job."

"Yep," she said lightly.

"Still, doesn't mean I can't worry."

He gripped her hand tighter.

And didn't let go until the jet landed in Monaco four hours later.

It was early evening by the time the team got settled at the White Sands Hotel, which was located across the street from Meiro's establishment, the Crystal Palace. Posing as three couples excited to gamble their life savings away in Monte Carlo, the six of them checked into a block of suites on the fifth floor. Isabel wouldn't be staying long, though.

She'd be moving to the Palace tomorrow, and as much as Trevor hated the thought, he knew he couldn't do a damn thing about it.

He also felt incredibly uneasy about using a hotel as their base. He would've preferred a more secure location, but Noelle had insisted they needed to stay close to the Palace.

Needless to say, he was acutely aware of the security cameras in the wide, elegantly carpeted hallway. Years of training had him ducking his head so the cameras didn't get a clear view of his face.

"You and D bunk in the other room," Trevor told Ethan, dropping his duffel in one of the bedrooms of the adjoining suite. "I'll crash here. Sully and Liam can battle over the other bed when they show up." He paused in afterthought. "Though knowing Sully, he'll be in Juliet's bed ten minutes after he meets her."

Ethan's hazel eyes narrowed. "You think so?"

"You gotta admit, she's exactly Sullivan's type."

"Yeah, what's that?"

Trevor snorted. *"Hot."*

The younger man didn't look thrilled at the prospect of their teammate taking their new ally to bed, but whether his displeasure stemmed from jealousy or concern for Sully, Trevor couldn't be sure.

He drifted to the window and studied the scene below. Monte Carlo came alive at night, the streets teeming with luxury vehicles and the well-dressed elite, the casinos lit up and the air thick with excitement. The city had a classy ambience, attracting the rich and richer, moguls and politicians and socialites looking to spend daddy's money.

Trevor had visited Monaco several times while playing the role of Julian Martin, the billionaire playboy who traveled the world and spent money like there was no tomorrow. And each time he came here, he was floored by the sheer opulence of it all.

Foreboding climbed up his spine. Was Morgan somewhere in this city?

Or was the boss lying on a slab in the morgue, waiting to be identified?

Trevor moved away from the window and left the room. Noelle's suite was across the hall, and he strode in without knocking. He found all three women in the suite's enormous living area.

"Where does Meiro live?" he asked in lieu of greeting. "Does he own a property in the city? Does he live in the hotel?"

"Paige is looking into it," Noelle said with a careless wave of her hand.

He gritted his teeth and looked at Isabel, who was on the couch with her laptop. "You're not going in blind, Iz. We need to know everything we can about Meiro before you go near the man."

She smiled. "Don't worry. We'll have a dossier thicker than an encyclopedia by the time Paige is done. She's the queen of background searches. And Sean is on it, too. We'll have all the intel we need, or at least enough for me to wing it."

Wing it? A knot of frustration twisted up his insides, but he forced himself to keep his cool. Isabel was a professional. Like she'd said, she'd done this many times before. Hell, she could probably pull off an undercover op more successfully than he could.

Yet he couldn't seem to curb the protective instincts that shouted for him not to let her out of his sight. They didn't know enough about this Meiro character, but if Meiro was the one who'd sent that shooter to Lassiter's beach house, then clearly the man was no regular old casino owner. Any man capable of ordering another man's death was probably capable of a whole lot of other crooked shit.

A knock on the door had everyone going on edge.

Trevor reached for his SIG, but his hand fell to his side when he heard a familiar voice on the other side of the door.

A moment later, he let Sean Reilly into the suite, all the while battling a feeling of overwhelming déjà vu. He'd known the Reilly brothers were identical twins, but usually there was some way to tell twins apart—a mole, a hairstyle, a variation in weight.

But not in this case. For all Trevor knew, he was sharing space with the same man he'd met in New York five months ago. Unruly blond hair, dark green eyes, scruffy facial hair—if he ever wound up in the same room as Sean and Oliver Reilly, he truly wouldn't be able to tell the two men apart.

Wait. The smirk. Sean's smirk totally gave him away; Trevor remembered Oliver's grin as being more playful and less mocking.

"I come bearing gifts," the Irishman announced. The man radiated pure energy as he strode into the room. "But first, give me some sugar."

The flirty request was aimed at Isabel, who laughed as she rose from the couch to greet Sean with a warm hug.

Trevor had to resist the urge to yank her right out of the other man's arms. Jeez. Where the hell was this behavior coming from? He knew he harbored a protective streak, but possessiveness? He scanned his brain, but couldn't think of a single instance when he'd wanted to rearrange a man's face for hugging Gina.

But Sean Reilly? Trevor's hands were frickin' *tingling* with the urge to do some rearranging.

Fortunately, Sean released Isabel before stupidity ensued. The embrace the man exchanged with Juliet was far more seductive and lasted a lot longer, which put Trevor at ease. Good. Let Reilly lust after Juliet. Isabel was off-limits to that scoundrel.

"Did you go to the morgue?" Noelle asked the new arrival.

"Sure did."

"Was it Morgan?" Isabel's expression creased with reluctance, as if she didn't want to know the answer.

"You tell me," Sean answered.

The Irishman reached into the inner pocket of a faded army surplus jacket that Trevor suspected was concealing a lot of nasty surprises. In fact, the very way Sean Reilly moved told him the man was as deadly as they came. Precise and predatory, whereas his brother's gait had been far more relaxed.

Apparently there *were* ways to tell them apart.

Sean produced an iPhone and tossed it to Noelle, who took one look at the screen and scowled.

"Well, then," she remarked.

A second later, the phone sailed through the air toward Trevor. He caught it easily and studied the picture.

The stiff's face was blue and bloated. Bloodshot eyes, and a gaping hole in the right cheek, most likely the result of a slug from a high-caliber pistol at close range.

Relief swelled in Trevor's gut as he noted the eye color—brown—and then the slight double chin and shaved head.

Morgan's features were chiseled, his dark hair cropped but not shaved, and his eyes were a dark shade of blue that burned like liquid metal when he was furious.

The man in the picture was not Jim Morgan.

Isabel came up and peered at the screen, then let out a relieved breath. As she leaned forward, a few strands of silky blond hair fell over Trevor's bare forearm.

His groin clenched with need, throbbing even harder when he remembered how they'd woken up this morning. Isabel's firm round ass pressed up against his aching dick, her full breast filling his palm, her soft hair tickling his cheek.

Not the time, man.

"It's not him," he announced, before looking at Reilly. "Did you get anything more on Lassiter? Like where he keeps his documents?"

"No safe-deposit boxes in his name and I can't find a lawyer on record, but the little bugger must have used someone to manage his money. I'll keep looking."

"What about Ollie?" Isabel asked. "Does he have any news from D.C.?"

Sean shook his head. "Just what we already know. Our man Jim got off the plane, told the pilot to stay put, got into a rented Escalade and dropped off the face of the bloody earth."

"He must have gone *somewhere*," Trevor said in frustration. "Bought a coffee, checked into a hotel, talked to a homeless dude on the street. He can't have just disappeared."

"Sorry, old boy, but I've got nothing else to give you at the moment." Grinning, Sean flopped down on the couch like he owned the place. "So what's our next move?"

Laughter danced in Juliet's dark eyes. "Now you get the hell outta here and give us something we can use."

"I want more on Meiro," Noelle added. "Ollie can stay on Jim, but I want you here in the city gathering as much data as you can on Meiro, Lassiter, and Roussel."

Sean gave a mock salute and got to his feet. "Yes, ma'am."

"I'll walk you out," Juliet told him, linking her arm through his.

Once the Irishman was out of earshot, Trevor shot Isabel a surreptitious look. "You sure we can trust these guys?"

"You asked me the same thing in New York. My answer hasn't changed since then."

She touched his arm, and damned if his cock didn't twitch from that teeny bit of contact.

"Sean's harmless," she assured him before taking a step away.

"Where are you going?"

"To transform. Becoming Valerie will take a while."

He hid his disappointment. He'd been hoping to spend some time with her before their brains kicked into mission mode. "What's 'a while'?"

She let out a sigh. "Trust me. Don't wait up. This could take all night."

Chapter 12

It was midnight when the knock sounded on his door. Trevor had been asleep, but he'd long ago mastered the ability to snap out of slumber to immediately function at a high level of alertness. He reached for the gun on the bedside table just as he heard her voice.

"Trev, can I come in?"

He relaxed. "Yeah."

The door opened and she appeared, the light from the living area silhouetting her in the doorway.

The woman that entered the room was not Isabel.

Instinctively, he grabbed for the nine millimeter again, then let out a laugh. "Valerie, I presume?"

"Pleasure to meet you, luv." Isabel closed the door behind her and headed for the second twin bed in the room.

Trevor leaned over and flicked on the lamp between the two beds. As he got an even better look at her, he was overcome with awe and a touch of arousal.

Christ, she looked sexy as hell. Gone was the blue-eyed blonde he'd spent the last few days with. This woman had flaming copper-colored hair in a chin-length bob. Straight bangs slashed across her forehead, drawing his attention to her bright green eyes and liquid ivory skin that displayed a hint of freckles. Her face was rounder, too, and when he peered closer, he could swear her nose looked more upturned than usual.

"Jesus, did you get a nose job?" he blurted out.

Isabel's laughter filled the bedroom. "I saw you five hours ago. Do you really think I underwent rhinoplasty and *healed* from it in that short a time?"

"I don't know—you work for Noelle. Maybe it's possible."

"Yeah, well, it's not. Remember I told you that makeup can modify a person's features depending on how it's applied?"

He remembered, but he still couldn't imagine how a few dabs of bronzer and concealer and powder could produce such a drastic transformation.

His gaze swept over her face once more. "Your cheeks look fuller too. Also thanks to the makeup?"

"Partially. And these."

He saw her tongue moving behind her cheek and then she opened her mouth and stuck out her tongue to reveal a cylindrical piece of plastic, similar to the rolls of cotton that dentists stuff in their patients' mouths.

"Cheek pads," she explained. She used her finger to pry both pads out, swiped a tissue from the box on the table, and placed the plastic pieces on it.

Trevor shook his head, still amazed. He had no fucking clue how she did it. It wasn't just the face and the hair—it was the whole damn package. The entire persona, Juliet had called it.

The way she moved, the way she spoke, the way she interacted with others. If Isabel had moved to Hollywood all those years ago instead of going to work for Noelle, she'd have a dozen Oscars on her mantel by now.

"What about the clothes?" he couldn't help but tease. "I figured Valerie would be more sophisticated than that."

Isabel gestured to her leggings and oversize T-shirt. "Oh, Valerie wouldn't be caught dead in this outfit. She only wears haute couture. And jewels. She loves her jewels."

She spoke those last few words in an upper-crust British accent, making Trevor laugh.

"Anyway, I'm exhausted." Isabel reverted back to her normal voice. "It took hours to make myself look this way."

"I can imagine."

With a little sigh, she stretched out on the bedspread, curling up on her side and crooking her arm so she could rest her head on it. She watched him, a rueful look entering her now green eyes. "I'm sorry if I woke you up. I'm tired, but I don't think I can sleep yet. I thought we could talk."

Trevor pushed the covers away so he could roll onto his side too. As they lay on their respective beds watching each other, he couldn't fight the wave of pleasure that washed over him. She'd come to him. Willingly. And, yeah, maybe she'd chosen to get comfortable on the neighboring bed instead of jumping on top of him and ripping her clothes off, but this was definitely progress.

"You don't mind, right?" She searched his face as if she was truly worried he didn't want her here.

Silly woman.

"Of course not," he said gruffly.

"Okay, good. So what'd you do all night?"

"Spoke to Kane, called a few old army contacts."

"Army contacts?"

"Some Rangers, active duty and retired. My former CO, a couple of guys that went private. Pretty much anyone who might have a lead on Morgan."

"And?"

"And nothing. I'm wondering if Morgan really did drop off the face of the fucking earth."

Isabel spoke in the soothing tone he'd grown used to, the one that calmed his very soul. "So what exactly *do* we know? Morgan was supposed to meet his CIA man in D.C., what, four days ago? We know he made it to D.C. because his plane landed sometime in the morning. He then ordered the pilot to wait for him at the airfield."

"Right. But he never made it to his meeting, which was scheduled for that evening."

"Which means he would've had to kill time all morning and afternoon until his contact was available to meet with him. Something must have happened during that time. He must have met with someone else, or received a phone call, or . . ."

"Gotten abducted."

"Do you honestly think Jim Morgan would let himself get abducted?"

"Maybe he didn't have a choice. Who knows what happened?" Trevor said grimly. "Hell, a sniper could've blown his head off, and his body might be in a Dumpster in D.C. for all we know."

Isabel's tone was firm. "I don't think he's dead."

"I sure as hell hope not." Releasing a breath, Trevor sat up and ran a hand through his messy hair. "I also spoke to Holden tonight."

The sympathy that flooded Isabel's eyes came as no surprise. She was the most compassionate person he'd ever met.

It was funny—even though her eyes were now green rather than blue, when he gazed into them he still saw Isabel. Yes, she could fool him at first glance, trick his eyes into seeing the persona she projected, but if he looked hard enough, if he peered close enough, he glimpsed the woman behind the mask.

She couldn't fool him anymore, Trevor realized.

"How's he doing?" she asked softly.

"Beth's funeral was this morning. They buried an empty coffin."

"Oh, God. Poor Holden."

"He said Beth's entire family was there, but not his. When I asked, he told me Beth was the only family he had. He didn't sound good, Iz. His voice was . . . empty. Do you know what I mean?"

"I imagine he sounded exactly the way you did when you and I first met."

After a second, he nodded. "I *was* empty back then. Losing someone you love . . . it rips you apart, you know?"

"Yeah, I know."

The pain in her voice triggered a memory. The image of

him and Isabel sitting in a hotel room in Bogotá. The annoyance in Isabel's voice as she snapped at him. *It's not like you're the only one who's ever lost someone, Trevor.*

"You once told me that your mother committed suicide."

When she shot up like a jack-in-the-box, Trevor jumped out of his own bed and plopped down on the edge of hers before she could flee.

Taking her hand, he forced her to stay put. "You don't have to tell me the details if you don't want to. Just know that if you want to talk about it, I'm here. Okay?"

Isabel looked sad as she met his eyes. "Sorry. You just caught me off guard. I guess . . . shit, I guess we can talk about it."

She suddenly looked incredibly vulnerable. Biting her bottom lip, using her free hand to toy with the hem of her T-shirt.

"She killed herself when I was ten. I found her body."

"I remember you telling me that." He reached for her other hand, which she'd curled into a fist. He gently pried each finger out of that tight hold. "What was she like?"

"She was . . . very, very fragile. I was just a kid, but even I could see how delicate she was. It's funny, she wasn't crazy-skinny or even all that petite, but I could so easily picture her getting blown away by the tiniest gust of wind. She looked like she'd break if anyone touched her with even the slightest bit of force."

Trevor knew the type. He'd met both men and women who exuded that same fragility. No inner strength—that's what it boiled down to, but he didn't want to paint a black spot on Isabel's mother's memory by insinuating she wasn't strong.

Then again, he had come damn close to killing himself after Gina's death, so he wasn't exactly in a position to judge.

"I found her in the bathtub. She slit her wrists, and the water was . . . Jesus, it was so red. I remember thinking at first that it was fruit punch or something, and I couldn't understand why she was taking a bath in juice." Nothing showed on her face, but bitterness had crept into her tone. “I started shaking her, and when she still didn’t wake up, I realized it was blood.”

Sympathy clogged his throat. He let go of her hands and wrapped an arm around her, pulling her close. “Do you know why she did it?”

Sighing, Isabel rested her cheek on his shoulder. “She left a note. I never read it, but years later, my father told me what it said. Apparently she was tired of life.”

He waited for her to continue, but she didn’t.

“That was it? That’s all she wrote?”

“There was some other stuff, but it’s not important,” Isabel said vaguely.

Trevor’s eyes narrowed with suspicion, but he didn’t want to push her for answers. He was scared that would only push her right out of the room.

“I don’t blame her for being tired.” Isabel laughed, but it sounded hollow. “I was a bundle of energy when I was a kid. She was constantly running after me, begging me to sit still.”

An alarm went off in his head. “Isabel . . . you don’t blame yourself for her death, do you?”

“Of course not,” she said quickly.

Too quickly.

Before he could press, she hurried on. “Anyway, after she died, I went to live with my grandparents in Jersey, and honestly? I was relieved. I loved my dad, but I always sensed the danger in him. Know what I mean?”

“I can’t even imagine what it would be like growing up with a mobster for a father.”

“What did your dad do?” she asked curiously.

“He worked at a lumber mill.”

“I don’t think I’ve ever heard you talk about him. Is he still alive?”

“He died during my first tour of duty. Lung cancer. The doctors said inhaling all that shit at the mill might have been a contributing factor. The man didn’t smoke a day in his life.”

“Oh, I’m sorry.” She paused. “What about your mother?”

"Alive and kicking." He grinned. "She lives in Denver, remarried about five years ago. She and Gina were shopping buddies."

"They were close?"

"My mom adored Gina. So did Krista—that's my younger sister. Kris moved to Wyoming a few years back when her husband got transferred for work."

"Do you keep in touch with them?"

"I've been making an effort to call and e-mail this last year, but right after Gina died . . ." His heart constricted with pain. "Well, you saw the shape I was in. I pulled away from them, same way I did with everyone else in my life." He searched her eyes, which were so unfamiliar and familiar at the same time. "What was it like in Jersey for you?"

Another cloud of sadness floated across her face. "I had some good times there. Went to school, made a lot of friends. My grandfather died of a heart attack when I was fifteen, so after that it was just Nona and me. She died a few years later. We got in a car accident." A pause. "I was driving. There was nothing I could do. It was the dead of winter, the roads were a mess, and we were rear-ended by a snowplow. Our car shot forward and smashed into a pole, and Nona died on impact."

Trevor touched her cheek. "I'm sorry."

She gave a little shrug. "It was a long time ago. I was eighteen when she died, so I didn't need a guardian or have to move back in with my dad. I went to NYU, studied criminology, and was recruited by the FBI."

The reminder was slightly jarring. He kept forgetting that she'd been a Fed before she went to work for Noelle. He could totally picture it, though. Isabel in one of those tight-fitting suits those female Feds loved to wear, her blond hair pulled back in a tight bun, a standard-issue Beretta holstered at her hip.

Damn, why was that image so frickin' hot?

"And you got assigned to the organized-crime unit," he finished for her.

"Yup."

"Using your family history to infiltrate the De Luca organization."

"Uh-huh." She fidgeted beside him, then ducked out from under his arm. "I'm tired of talking. Actually, I'm tired, period." She began to rise. "I should go to my—"

"Stay," he cut in.

Her eyes widened in surprise, but he didn't give her the chance to protest. Grabbing her hand, he yanked her down, right into his lap. Then he cradled the back of her head, brought her mouth to his, and kissed her.

Even if she'd wanted to object, Isabel couldn't conjure up the ability of speech. She couldn't think, couldn't breathe, couldn't move. Trevor's mouth felt like heaven against hers. His lips were firm yet soft, gentle yet rough, and his kiss was both tender and greedy. The contradictions made her mind spin, sent her pulse careening.

She kissed him back with a fervor that surprised her. She didn't try to stop him, didn't push him away, didn't pretend that she wanted to be doing anything other than this.

God, *this*. His tongue licked its way into her mouth, bringing a moan to her lips. He swallowed the desperate sound and angled his head to deepen the kiss.

"I love the way you taste." His mouth broke free, his voice so hoarse and thick with desire that her heart beat even faster.

When he cupped her breasts over her shirt, they both groaned.

"And I love the way you feel," he rasped, sweeping his thumbs over her hardening nipples.

She wasn't wearing a bra, and each touch, each gentle pinch, sent a jolt of heat right down to her core. Their ragged breathing moistened the air as their mouths broke apart again. She sucked in a breath, only to inhale Trevor's incredible scent.

With a soft whimper, she gripped his strong jaw and brought his mouth back to hers, needing that connection again.

Needing *him*, damn it.

Her fingers trembled as she touched his face. The stubble shadowing his chin abraded her fingertips, serving as a reminder of his sheer masculinity. He was so very male—broad shoulders, solid chest, sexy beard growth.

A thrill sizzled through her as Trevor gently lowered her onto the bed and covered her body with his. They were both fully clothed, yet her skin was on fire, tingling and pulsing, little sparks crackling in her nerve endings.

"I haven't done this in so long," he said huskily, then moved his mouth to her neck and sucked.

Isabel shivered. God, that felt good. So good she could barely focus on what he was saying. "Done what?"

His lips kissed a path up to her ear. "Made out with a woman." His tongue tickled the shell of her ear. "I feel like I'm totally out of practice."

Somehow, his sheepish admission put her at ease. Her fingers were no longer trembling as she traced the hard line of his jaw.

"Me too," she confessed.

They kissed again. Long and slow, tongues dancing, bodies arching and straining to get closer. With a groan, Trevor thrust one firm thigh between her legs and ground against her. He wore a T-shirt and a pair of boxers, but the material of those boxers was thin, so thin it was impossible to hide his arousal. Isabel moaned when she felt that thick erection pressing into her thigh.

Thrilling. Terrifying. She couldn't decide what this was.

All she knew was that she didn't want it to stop.

She wrapped her arms around his shoulders and hooked one leg around his trim hips, a move that deepened the contact between them, intensified the friction. Every inch of her ached. Breasts. Nipples. Clit. Even random body parts she wouldn't have associated with arousal throbbed with exquisite agony. Her neck. Her belly. The backs of her knees.

She'd never experienced anything like this before, this overpowering need to have a man inside her. To be claimed. Possessed.

"No sex."

Her eyes flew open as Trevor's half growl, half moan of anguish registered in her head.

An instantaneous gust of disappointment blew into her. "What? You don't want . . . ?"

"Oh, I want. I want it very, very badly." His whiskey brown eyes gleamed with such passion it took her breath away. "But not tonight. Not when it's so late, and definitely not when it'll have to be rushed." That gaze burned hotter. "I want to take my time with you, sweetheart."

Her pulse raced. "Yeah?"

"Oh yeah."

He slid his hand down her body and cupped her mound.

Isabel nearly bucked off the bed. "But you just said . . ."

"I said no sex." His laugh was surprisingly cocky. "But that doesn't mean we can't do . . . you know . . . other things to take the edge off."

To punctuate that, he rubbed her aching core in slow, teasing glides.

Pinpricks of pleasure danced over her flesh. When he applied pressure on her clit, she moaned softly, her hips beginning to move in a restless rhythm. The tension building inside her was unsettling, unfamiliar.

Male satisfaction darkened his eyes. "You're so beautiful, Isabel."

Her cheeks heated with embarrassment. "I don't even look like me."

Trevor smiled, an odd, secretive little smile. "Yes, you do. You look exactly like you, baby."

What on earth did *that* mean?

She didn't have time to dwell on her jumbled thoughts and confusing emotions because Trevor used that moment to slip his hand underneath the waistband of her leggings. His finger dipped inside her panties, and they both groaned when he encountered her bare sex.

"Christ, that's hot," he choked out. "Are you always like this?"

She managed a nod, though it was getting harder and

harder to concentrate, what with Trevor's fingers deftly moving up and down her slit.

"It's easier to wax it all off than dye the carpet to match the drapes every time I change hair color."

He stiffened, a flash of pure possessiveness setting fire to his eyes. "How often do your targets get a peek at the *carpet*, Isabel?"

A laugh burst out. "Not often. But now I'm always prepared, thanks to the French Riviera fiasco."

"What happened on the French Riviera?"

"The man I was tailing loved nude beaches. I didn't have time to hit a salon so I used some dye that ended up being way too strong. It burned like a bitch, totally wasn't meant for such a delicate area."

Speaking of delicate areas, Trevor's hand was still between her legs, except he wasn't stroking anymore.

"You walked around naked to get close to the asshole?"

"Yup." She rolled her eyes. "Now can you ask Jealous Trevor to leave the room so we can concentrate on more urgent matters?"

The humor returned to his eyes. "Urgent, huh?" He dragged his fingers along her folds and toyed with her wet opening. "You're feeling a sense of urgency?"

She gasped when he pushed one finger inside her.

He chuckled.

Heart pounding, she watched Trevor's face as he pleasured her. His gorgeous eyes glittered with heat, lust, satisfaction.

And he was watching her right back, his gaze never leaving hers as his finger moved in and out and his thumb tended to her swollen clit.

It should have felt intrusive, that ravenous gaze fixated on her face. She should have felt exposed and vulnerable, but she didn't. His hunger just fueled her own.

"Fuck, you're so wet," he mumbled.

He added another finger and quickened the tempo, leaning in to kiss her as those talented digits worked her tight channel, as the pad of his thumb rubbed her clit in a persistent circle.

Trevor's blistering kisses only stoked the fire building down below. Isabel clung to him, rocking her hips into his wicked hand. Her pulse drummed a frantic beat in her ears, her lungs working overtime to process the oxygen she was inhaling in shallow bursts.

"Come on, Iz, let go." His hot breath tickled her nose, and then his mouth took possession of hers and she got lost in another reckless kiss.

Her muscles coiled tight, the pressure between her legs becoming so hot and unbearable she thought she'd die if she didn't get some relief. This was uncharted territory for her. And it scared her, so much so that she found herself desperately trying to suppress the rising waves of arousal by focusing on Trevor, on *his* pleasure.

She reached out and fumbled with his boxers. "I need to touch you. I need . . ."

She gave up on talking and focused on wrapping her fingers around Trevor's shaft.

His answering groan was loud and laced with desperation. As his fingers thrust deeper inside her, his cock thrust into her hand.

The haze of pleasure in his eyes floored her. He was the sexiest man she'd ever met, and suddenly her new goal in life was to make him come apart.

"Oh, Iz, that's good." His voice was strangled, hoarse. "A little faster, sweetheart."

She tightened her grip and stroked him faster, teasing his engorged head with the pad of her thumb on each upstroke. They were both breathing heavily, their foreheads touching, hips moving.

Soon his expression became tortured and a low groan left his sexy mouth. "It's been too long, sweetheart. I'm . . . fuck, I'm gonna come."

As he trembled with release, her own pleasure mounted, the pressure increasing, but then his passion-glazed eyes locked with hers and that pressure spontaneously receded, the climax retreating as it always did. But God, she'd come so close to . . . well, to *coming*. How was that even possible?

"Christ, Isabel. That was . . ." He suddenly halted, narrowed his eyes. "You didn't . . ."

"No," she admitted.

"Well, we'll just have to fix that."

When his expression turned sensual again and his fingers slid deeper into her core, she stilled his hand and smiled. "Trust me, it won't happen tonight. I'm way too exhausted." Noting his visible unhappiness, she hurried on. "I promise you, I enjoyed this as much as you did. It was . . . gosh, it felt incredible, Trevor."

"Really?" he said hoarsely.

She gave him one last stroke, then released his cock and pressed a gentle kiss on his lips. "I've never been more turned on in my life, Trev. I don't need an orgasm to verify that I just had my world rocked. And believe me, my world was totally rocked."

She wasn't lying, the way she was usually forced to do, and Trevor must have picked up on her sincerity, because he shot her a crooked grin.

"Fine, but next time we see each other, you'd better be well rested, sweetheart, because I plan on keeping you up all night."

Her smile faltered, but she didn't think he noticed. Just in case, she broke the eye contact between them and slid up to a sitting position. Her hand was wet and sticky, prompting her to reach for the tissues on the bedside table. As she cleaned up, she noticed Trevor watching her.

"What?" she said awkwardly.

"I'm glad you stayed."

A tentative smile curved her lips. "Me too."

He sat up to brush his lips over hers. When he drew back, he looked slightly troubled.

"What is it now?" she teased.

"Just wondering whether you're going to pull away from me again, or if this time you'll actually stay the course."

She opened her mouth to respond, but he pressed a finger to her lips. "Don't," he murmured. "Don't say anything. Just kiss me good night, Iz."

Trevor captured her mouth and kissed her, and Isabel's heart did the impossible—it leapt and sank at the same damn time. The mention of the future dampened her spirits, but the kiss . . .

The kiss was pure passion. Pure liberation.

"You should go." He gave her one last kiss before helping her to her feet. "Tomorrow's gonna be a long day."

They walked to the door, Isabel hesitating before turning the knob. "Trevor . . ." She trailed off, uncertain.

"Don't overthink it," he said gruffly. "Okay?"

After a long beat, she nodded. "Okay."

But ten minutes later, when she was lying in her own bed and staring up at the ceiling, overthinking was exactly what she did. Overthinking, analyzing, agonizing . . . and wondering if letting Trevor in tonight had been the biggest mistake she could've made.

Or the best decision of her life.

Chapter 13

The next morning, Isabel found a ninety-eight-page dossier on Tomas Meiro in her e-mail inbox. Paige had outdone herself this time—she'd gathered so much intelligence that Isabel's head spun as she sifted through it all. Photographs of the man were conspicuously absent save for one, which was perplexing. With all the charity events and galas Meiro supposedly attended, one would think his picture would have been snapped a lot more than once.

She studied the photograph on the screen, acknowledging Meiro's undeniable good looks. Tanned skin, dark hair, caramel-colored eyes. According to Paige's notes, he wasn't an exceptionally tall man, but his body filled out a suit rather nicely.

His wife, Renee, was also in the picture, a plain woman with a long, thin nose, too-close-together brown eyes, and acne scars that she attempted to cover with makeup. Isabel didn't consider herself a cynic, but there was only one reason a man like Meiro married a woman who looked like that—and it started with *m* and ended with *oney*.

"Reading the Meiro file?"

Trevor entered the suite's living room wearing faded jeans, a black T-shirt, and black boots. His hair was damp from the shower, and a few water droplets glistened on his forehead.

Isabel's cheeks heated slightly as she remembered what they'd done last night, but she maintained a friendly expression. Juliet was across the room drinking her morning coffee, which meant they couldn't exactly discuss yesterday's encounter.

She resisted the urge to bite her lip in dismay, still confounded by the all-consuming desire Trevor had evoked in her. For the first time in a long time, release had been within her grasp. But why? Why *this* man? Past lovers couldn't even get her halfway to orgasm, let alone to the brink of it.

Isabel banished the troubling thoughts and focused on Trevor's question. "Yeah, I'm reading it for the second time. I asked Paige to forward it to you and the guys." She spoke in her British accent, as she'd been doing all morning. She was immersed in the role of Valerie now, and would be until this job ended.

Trevor didn't comment on the accent, but she noticed his eyes twinkle in amusement. "We got it. I've been skimming it for the past hour actually."

He headed for the table where Juliet was sitting and grabbed a mug.

Room service had brought up coffee and breakfast pastries, but Isabel hadn't had a chance to eat yet. Her head wasn't on food; it was on the mission. In a couple of hours, she'd be checking in at the Crystal Palace and attempting to make contact with Tomas Meiro. She couldn't afford any distractions at the moment.

"I'm not done with it yet," Trevor said as he poured himself some coffee. "Fill me in on what you know?"

"Sure. Pour me some of that?" She gestured to the coffee carafe in his hands.

A moment later, he handed her a cup and sat down at the other end of the couch. "So what's Meiro's deal?"

"Pretty much exactly what Noelle and Jules uncovered," Isabel answered. "Originally from Portugal, moved to Paris when he was a teenager, but it's unclear what he did for the next decade or so. He met Renee Beaumont about a year ago, married her, and won over her father."

"Michel Beaumont."

"Yes. Multimillionaire, owns a dozen casinos all over Europe. The Crystal Palace is the crown jewel of the business, though. It's where Beaumont spent most of his time before he died last year, and Meiro is following in his father-in-law's footsteps."

Across the room, Juliet left her seat and perched on the arm of the couch. "Not just the legitimate footsteps," she added, tossing her long brown hair over her shoulder. "He owns dozens of upscale brothels, one in nearly every major European city, including one here in Monte Carlo."

Trevor took a quick sip of coffee. "The dossier said something about human trafficking? Tourists getting abducted?"

Both women nodded, and Juliet's dark eyes flashed with disgust. "Meiro's goons target female tourists. They scour the clubs, bars, raves, pretty much anywhere you find cute girls. Usually blond, usually American. The men slip them a roofie, get them in a car, and the girls are never heard from again."

Trevor's jaw tightened. "Shipped to whorehouses or private buyers, I assume."

"Most likely, yes."

Like Juliet, Isabel shook her head in anger. It never failed to amaze her how many sadistic men and women resided in this world. What was the *matter* with people?

"Anyway," Juliet went on, "Paige wasn't sure how involved Meiro is with his little side enterprises. He definitely calls the shots, but he seems to delegate a lot of the responsibility to his henchmen."

Isabel drained her coffee, then stood up to grab another cup. She was feeling too damn sluggish this morning. Probably because she'd barely slept a wink last night. Sleepless nights seemed to be the norm when Trevor was in her life, and the realization brought a pang of irritation. A woman in her line of work couldn't afford an Achilles' heel, but she suspected she had one in Trevor Callaghan, which was a damn unwelcome notion.

"He can usually be found at the casino," she said, joining the discussion. "He stays in the hotel penthouse most of the time."

"What about the wife?" Trevor asked.

"She lives in the family mansion. It's a huge estate in one of those nouveau riche areas of the city."

Juliet grinned. "The West Egg."

Trevor wrinkled his forehead before nodding. "Right. Gatsby."

"I told you, Meiro is very Great Gatsby," Juliet insisted. "Came out of nowhere, self-made rich, handsome and mysterious."

"Anyway," Isabel said, "the Meiros inherited the mansion from Beaumont after he died. Renee was Beaumont's only child and sole heir. It's got to be a loveless marriage, though. Doesn't seem like Mr. and Mrs. Meiro spend any time together at all."

Juliet snorted. "Hey, you saw the picture of his wife. Do you blame the man for getting his jollies elsewhere?"

Something buzzed, causing Juliet to stand up abruptly. She pulled a phone out of her back pocket, glanced at the screen, and then disappeared into the bedroom.

Isabel didn't comment on her colleague's hasty departure; Juliet wasn't the kind of woman who offered explanations. She did what she wanted, when she wanted, without consulting a soul.

On the couch, Trevor had a thoughtful look. "So how do you plan on getting close to him?"

"That's the beauty of it—I won't even have to go to him. He'll find *me*."

"How are you so sure?"

"If you're a high roller, Meiro personally seeks you out. At least according to Paige's intel. All I have to do is flash some cash and Meiro's staff will notify him. If Paige's sources are right, then Meiro will come down from his castle and introduce himself to me."

"And if he doesn't?" Trevor countered.

"Then it's time for Plan B."

"What's Plan B?"

"I'll let you know when I come up with it."

Trevor looked torn between laughing and voicing his disapproval. He didn't get a chance to do either because the phone next to the couch rang.

Isabel picked up the phone and dropped the English accent. "Yes?"

"Is this Ms. Jensen? I'm calling from the front desk," a brisk female voice said.

"No, Kelly is out on the terrace. This is Brittany," Isabel replied in a bubbly tone.

They were all traveling under fake American passports, Isabel's bearing the name Brittany Matthews, a blond advertising executive from New York. It was her least favorite alias, but hey, Brittany got the job done.

Didn't matter anyway—in a few short hours, she'd be Valerie Parker-Smith. It was funny, but she could already feel her confidence level rising as she adopted Valerie's mannerisms and personality.

Why was it so easy for her to become another person?

And why did she feel truly whole only when she wore another woman's skin?

Banishing the disturbing thoughts, she listened to the desk clerk, then hung up and turned to Trevor with a dry smile. "The rest of our party is here."

"Sully and Liam?"

"I believe they called themselves Kirk and Brody. Our bros from the Big Apple."

Trevor snickered.

Two minutes later, a distinctly male knock sounded on the door, followed by an overly high voice calling, "Room service!"

Rolling his eyes, Trevor went to let his men in.

Sullivan Port and Liam Macgregor entered the suite with a level of enthusiasm that didn't surprise Isabel—those two possessed a scary amount of energy. What did startle her was their appearance.

The two men looked like a pair of spoiled preppy kids

who'd spent the summer sailing around St. Barts on their daddy's yacht. Tanned skin, scruffy facial hair, muscular bodies clad in T-shirts, board shorts, and flip-flops. The oversize duffel bags they dropped on the carpeted floor didn't mesh with the carefree nomad vibes the men were emitting. Isabel didn't even want to know what deadly secrets those bags contained.

"Took you long enough." Trevor greeted the two men with back slaps and handshakes.

"Stubborn Susan over here insisted we dock in Nice and catch a flight from there." Liam's vivid blue eyes twinkled playfully when he glanced at Isabel. "Is that you, Blondie, or am I still drunk from all that Jamaican rum?"

She'd forgotten she was wearing a blond wig, which was ironic considering she'd taken such pains to go from a blonde to a redhead yesterday. But since she'd checked in as the blond Brittany, she needed to keep up appearances whenever she was in this suite. Not just for the staff's sake, but for anyone who might be peering through a high-zoom lens from some balcony across the street. They'd all been avoiding the terrace, save for D and Noelle, who went out there to smoke.

"It's me," she told Liam. "Good to see you again."

He gave her a hug and a quick kiss on the cheek, then flashed a dimpled grin that would have made her heart flutter if she was the kind of woman who went for the male-model type. Because Liam Macgregor? Drop-dead gorgeous. Those Black Irish good looks belonged on a movie screen.

Sullivan wasn't hard on the eyes either. The six-foot-three, dirty blond–haired Australian hugged her next, his gray eyes gleaming with appreciation as his gaze skimmed over her face, down the length of her body, and then back up. The way he was checking her out, you'd think she was wearing skimpy lingerie rather than faded jeans and a white T-shirt.

"You look good, Isabel," Sullivan told her, casting that rogue grin of his.

"So do you." She grinned back. "You left *Evangeline* in France, huh? What, you didn't want to introduce her to me?"

At the mention of his yacht, Sullivan's expression went serious. And oddly defensive.

"I didn't want to moor her in the marina here. What if things get tumultuous?"

Liam hooted. "Tumultuous? Is that your vocabulary word of the day?"

"Zip it, Boston. I'm friggin' serious. If this op turns into another clusterfuck and shit gets blown up? I don't want Evie anywhere near us."

Isabel could honestly say she'd never met a man who loved his boat more than Sullivan Port did.

At the word *clusterfuck*, the mood in the room grew sober.

Liam ran a frustrated hand through his spectacular hair, which was thick and dark and more lustrous than a shampoo model's. "We tried to reach Holden on the radio when we were making our way here, but we couldn't get him."

Trevor sighed. "He's not feeling very social at the moment. He needs time to grieve."

Anger etched into Sullivan's features. "What the fuck happened, Trev? How did those fuckers manage to launch an assault that you didn't see coming?"

"It was a blitz attack. Dead of night, bird overhead. The ground troops took out the gate while we were being hit with a wave of RPGs. We weren't expecting it." Trevor released a harsh curse. "Lloyd, Beth, and Hank lost their lives, Sully. Trust me, we're all kicking ourselves for letting that happen."

Sullivan had the decency to look shamefaced. Good thing, too, because Isabel had been about to come to Trevor's defense. The only people to blame for the strike on the compound were the mercenaries who'd attacked it, and she'd be damned if anyone tried to lay the burden of blame on Trevor's shoulders.

"Sorry, mate. I'm not assigning fault here. Just trying to make sense of it, y'know?"

"I know," Trevor said quietly.

"Any word from the boss man?" The inquiry came from Liam.

"Not a peep."

The newcomers glanced around the empty suite. "Where are the others?" Sullivan asked.

"D and Ethan are across the hall. Noelle and Juliet are around here somewhere," Trevor said.

"Juliet?" The tall Australian looked intrigued. "She sounds hot."

Isabel laughed. "You can tell just by her name?"

"Hell, yeah."

Liam concurred. "A name tells you a helluva lot, Blondie."

"I'll take your word for it." She left her empty cup on the table. "I should get going."

Trevor was at her side in a heartbeat. "Can we have a moment alone first?"

When she nodded, he turned to the new arrivals and said, "Give me a sec." Then he followed Isabel into the bedroom she'd shared with Juliet last night.

"What's up?" she asked.

"I want you to be careful," he said sternly.

She couldn't help an indulgent smile. "I'm always careful, Trevor."

"I know but just . . . be extra careful, okay?"

"Okay."

"Do you have everything you need to back up your cover?" His tone was brisk, professional, but it didn't quite mask his concern.

"Valerie's documents arrived this morning, and her bags are already in the limo I'm taking from the airport."

She stifled a sigh, knowing the next few hours would be tedious as hell. To give credence to her backstory, they'd chartered a private plane and paid the pilot to file a bogus flight plan to give the appearance that Valerie Parker-Smith had left London this morning. She was due to "land" any moment now; Isabel would make her way to the private airfield and then come right back to the strip, which was annoying but necessary.

"I'll be fine," she assured him when she saw the deep groove in his forehead. "This will all go off without a hitch."

Rather than answer, Trevor took a step closer and planted his hands on her hips.

And rather than flinch or shy away, she found herself sinking into his embrace. She rested her head on his sturdy chest, listened to the steady beating of his heart, and wondered what the hell she was doing.

Why was she letting this happen?

Why had she allowed them to go so far last night?

She'd left Trevor in Manhattan for a reason—because she couldn't imagine the two of them ever having a future.

Because her feelings for him threatened her work and her peace of mind.

Because . . . because she was *scared*, damn it.

None of that had changed, and yet instead of keeping him at arm's length and trying to view him as nothing more than a friend, she was doing the exact opposite.

Trevor dragged his hands up her bare arms, his touch leaving goose bumps in its wake. He cupped her chin and dipped his head to kiss her. It was a gentle kiss, fast and sweet, and it left her wanting more.

"Don't do anything reckless," he said gruffly.

I already have.

"I won't," she promised.

Night didn't come fast enough for Trevor. He'd been on edge ever since Isabel left, and he knew he wouldn't relax until she was safely back in her room tonight.

Clearly he was in the minority, though, because nobody else seemed worried, least of all Noelle, who was barking out assignments in a commanding voice that would have made any drill sergeant proud.

He resented the fact that the blonde had taken charge,

and yet she was running the op precisely the way he would have run it, charging each team member with the same task Trevor would've assigned.

D would be posted on the exterior, since those tattoos of his would stand out like a neon sign amid such posh surroundings. Same went for Sullivan and Liam, who drew attention wherever they went, usually from the ladies.

And just like Trevor would've done, Noelle had split up the dynamic duo, ordering Sullivan to the strip and Liam to the Meiro house, which Juliet had dubbed the West Egg Mansion. Along with Ethan, Liam would be monitoring the movements of Meiro's wife, Renee, and watching the place in case Meiro decided to pay her a visit.

"Callaghan, I want you on the casino floor," Noelle said brusquely. "You're handsome in that understated kind of way, so you'll be able to fly under the radar."

Handsome in an understated kind of way? Was that how women viewed him?

"Jules, you're inside too. Gauge the security situation, not just in the casino but in the hotel itself. We might need to find our way up to Meiro's penthouse."

"Paige's file mentioned some security procedures, but she wasn't as thorough as I would've liked," Juliet said. "I'll take a gander and see what we're working with."

Trevor noticed every male eye dip to Juliet's cleavage when the woman bent to adjust the high slit of her black cocktail gown. He had to admit she looked incredible. The satin dress outlined every curve of her willowy body, and her stilettos added height to her already tall frame. With her dark hair piled atop her head to reveal her long, graceful neck, and her breasts practically pouring out of her bodice, she was sex personified.

Sullivan and Liam had been panting over the brunette from the moment they'd laid eyes on her, which seemed to annoy the shit out of Ethan, who now wore a perpetual scowl that made him appear both older and meaner.

"What about you?" D asked in a mocking tone, cocking

his head at Noelle. "Where will our fearless leader be throughout all this?"

"Around," she said vaguely.

In her black leather pants and tight black turtleneck, with her blond hair cascading down her back, Noelle didn't look like she would blend in anywhere, but Trevor didn't doubt she had something up her sleeve.

"Anyway," she went on, "get in position, people. I want this bullshit over with as fast as humanly possible."

The tête-à-tête broke up as the team went to gather their gear. Everyone was wired in via the transmitters Noelle had produced out of thin air; the earpieces were flesh-colored, no bigger than a watch battery and barely discernible unless someone with an ear fetish decided to stick his face in Trevor's ear. The most advantageous part of the transmitter was that it could be switched off with the press of a button; its signal would disappear in a nanosecond if Meiro or his casino staff decided to sweep for bugs.

If anyone was subjected to a search, though, it would be Isabel, whose transmitter and mic would be embedded in her earring just in case Meiro did get a closer look . . . while nibbling on her delicate earlobe perhaps?

Trevor's entire body tensed at the unwelcome thought. Shit. It was going to be tough watching Isabel charm Meiro. Listening to her flirt with the man. Hearing her melodic laughter trill in his ear as she giggled at Meiro's jokes.

It's her job. Deal with it.

Taking a calming breath, he ducked into the bedroom to find his passport. He was Wes Murray tonight, a Wall Street trader who was gambling solo because the rest of his party had decided to listen to some jazz at the Blue Note. Wes didn't do jazz, however. He was all about the Benjamins.

Clad in a tuxedo, and with a wallet full of cash, Trevor left the hotel and strolled down the boulevard toward the Crystal Palace. The area was bustling with activity. People dressed to the nines wandered in and out of the majestic hotels lining the street. Expensive cars whizzed along the road, and every now and then, a sleek limo pulled up in front of one of the casinos.

The city teemed with life, oozed wealth and indulgence. Trevor could easily understand why so many people caught the gambling bug and were blinded by the glitz and glamour. They couldn't help it; the lure of riches, the dream of gaining affluence were too great. And here, in a city like this, that dream seemed so attainable.

An illusion, of course. Only the established aristocracy, the already wealthy, would return to their suites and villas as millionaires tonight. The others, the ones who were here for the dream, would end the vacation deeper in debt.

When Trevor strode into the lobby of the Crystal Palace, he was nearly ensnared in the same seductive trap as everyone around him. The floor beneath his feet was black Italian marble streaked with veins of ivory, the ceiling above him vaulted and boasting at least a dozen crystal chandeliers.

The men and women who walked past him looked like characters straight out of a Bond flick. Tuxedos and designer cocktail gowns were the norm, which meant that anyone who'd committed the faux pas of not wearing either stood out like a kid at a senior citizens' home. The casually dressed were rewarded with snooty looks and deep frowns of disapproval, but since the hotel didn't have a formal dress code, the rich folks couldn't openly revolt.

The casino, however, did enforce a dress code, allowing the wealthy crowd to feel right at home. Trevor slid through the enormous arched entryway and found himself surrounded by the dings and chimes and whirs of slot machines, the continuous drone of voices, the whoops and cheers of lucky winners.

Bypassing the slots area, he headed across the lush red carpet toward the table games. The gaming floor was made up of several staggered levels; low sets of steps led to various areas, with a crowded bar spanning one wall, and the cashier cages on the other.

Trevor followed a well-dressed couple to the blackjack tables and dragged a hand through his hair, making sure to get close to his ear. Another nifty trick to Noelle's spy gadget? The microphone was motion activated, so all he had to do was move his hand near the mic for it to switch on. Once he finished speaking, the mic turned off but the receiver stayed on, which ensured that the feed wasn't constantly swamped with voices or pointless conversation between him and, say, the blackjack dealer who was about to rob him blind.

"Getting in position," he murmured, his lips barely moving.

Juliet's throaty voice slid into his ear. "I see you, stud. Two o'clock."

As Trevor took the last available stool at the table, he cast a discreet look at the spot Juliet indicated. Sure enough, the brunette was positioned at the bar. Sipping a martini and attracting her fair share of admiring glances from the men around her.

Tossing five hundreds on the table, Trevor greeted the male dealer with a nod.

The man nodded back and uttered a polite hello, ran his fingers over the bills and counted them out. "Changing five hundred," he called.

Since Trevor had chosen a table with a minimum bet of twenty-five dollars, his cash garnered him twenty red chips. As he placed his bet, he noted the presence of a tall man in a dark suit behind the dealer. Pit boss, judging by the hawklike gaze he swept over the dealers and players in his vicinity.

"Dealer has fifteen."

Trevor absently glanced at his cards. Queen, king. The other four men at the table each took another card. When it came around to him, he waved his hand over his cards to stand pat.

The dealer drew a king.

"Dealer busts."

There was a blur of hands and chips and cash, and then the man slid two red disks in Trevor's direction, and the whole cycle started again.

He fucking hated casinos. He knew Luke and Sully flew to Vegas a couple of times a year for their "bro retreat," and Morgan had always been partial to the ponies, but Trevor considered gambling a total waste of time and a needless waste of money. He might as well be taking a hundred-dollar bill and wiping his ass with it, for all the good it did him.

"On my way down."

Isabel's voice filled his ear, momentarily startling him. Her British accent was so polished he would've believed she was an Englishwoman if he hadn't known better.

From her two brief check-ins, he knew she'd spent the day in her lavish suite, had ordered room service for lunch and dinner, and had inquired of the hotel staff about the kind of perks offered to VIPs, a tactic that served as a not so subtle reminder that she was a wealthy woman who warranted extra attention.

And she got plenty of attention when she strolled into the casino moments later.

Trevor's breath lodged in his throat at her entrance. He recovered quickly and shifted his attention back to the blackjack game, but the image of Isabel had already been burned into his brain like a cattle brand.

As he waited for the dealer to start the new round, he snuck another quick peek and his entire mouth went dry. Isabel's floor-length, pale green dress clung to her hourglass figure, the strapless bodice emphasizing her full breasts while the slinky material hugged her firm ass. She'd accessorized with silver high heels, dangling diamond earrings, and an emerald pendant that sparkled in the soft lighting of the casino. With her flaming red hair, she stood out against a backdrop of blondes and brunettes.

She was stunning.

Juliet spoke up in awe. "Iz, you know I don't swing both ways, but right now? I would totally fuck you."

Several male chuckles sounded in Trevor's ear.

"No fair," Sullivan complained. "Why am I always stuck outside while everyone else gets to have all the fun?"

Fun? Was that what this was?

Because Trevor could honestly say this was the farthest thing from it. Seeing Isabel standing across the room looking like a million bucks and knowing he was about to watch her charm the pants off another man?

Yeah, about as fun as getting your legs waxed.

"Get in position," came Noelle's sharp order. "It's time to set the trap."

"On it," Isabel murmured.

The flash of green that blurred past his peripheral vision told Trevor she was making her way to the roulette area.

He tapped two fingers on the felt tabletop to indicate he wanted another card from the dealer, then hunkered down and prepared for a long night of losing money and worrying about Isabel.

Let the games begin.

Chapter 14

Tomas Meiro swept his gaze over the monitors dominating the walls of the security floor. Everything looked good, but then again, it was still early. Every night brought a new series of issues, a new round of complaints, and a new collection of problematic customers.

It was bound to happen—place people in a room where cash flowed freely and even the most levelheaded individual turned into an irrational motherfucker. Greed was a powerful tool, a man's worst enemy.

And Meiro's greatest ally. Without greed, he wouldn't have any of *this*—a packed casino, a booked-to-capacity hotel, a fat bank account, and standing invitations to every prestigious event in Europe. Renee's father had capitalized on that greed to build an empire, and now that the old man was dead, Meiro was reaping the benefits.

"Zoom in on the man in the purple blazer," he told Keller. "Blackjack, Table Fifteen."

Keller enlarged a screen at the bottom right corner of the wall.

Meiro took a step closer and peered at the image. "Left hand."

The monitor zoomed in on the hand resting on the patron's knee. After a moment, Meiro relaxed. Nothing but a nervous twitch.

"Harmless," he said absently. "But keep an eye on him."

He did another quick examination of the screens, then gave a pleased nod. "I'll check in later. Inform me of any developments."

"Yes, sir."

He'd just stepped away from the monitors when a flash of red snagged his attention. He turned back to the main wall, then sucked in a breath.

"Zoom in on the west grid. Roulette. Table Eight."

Keller swiftly executed the command, and Meiro stared at the screen for several long moments.

"Who is she?" he asked slowly.

Behind him, the usual commotion ensued.

"Valerie Parker-Smith," one of the techs announced. Fingers moved over a computer keyboard in fast, rapid clicks. "She checked into the Lavender Suite this morning."

"Where did she come from?"

"London, sir." More typing. "License lists her as twenty-six years old. There's a note from the front desk in her file—she paid for the suite with a black AmEx."

Intrigued, Meiro watched as the exquisite redhead threw her head back and laughed with the older man beside her. A pear-cut emerald dangled from the silver chain around her long, graceful neck, the sparkling jewel nestled in her spectacular cleavage.

"Who is the gentleman with her? Did she arrive with him?"

"No, sir. She is the only occupant of her suite, and she entered the casino alone."

Meiro pursed his lips. "Zoom in on the eyes."

Keller did as he was told, and suddenly a pair of mesmerizing green eyes filled the screen. Dancing with delight. Twinkling with mischief. Gleaming with *life*.

"Incredible," Meiro murmured.

He was oddly reluctant to look away, but he forced himself to sever the thread of fascination tying him to those big green eyes.

His pulse was unusually fast as he headed for the door,

where his two expressionless bodyguards stood. In the corridor, he was met by the young male employee he paid for the sole purpose of sticking close and delivering his messages.

"Anything I can help you with, Mr. Meiro?" the man asked eagerly.

"Yes. Invite Ms. Valerie Parker-Smith to the VIP lounge."

Her gambling partner was annoying the shit out of her.

Isabel had been trying to edge away from the loud, obnoxious man for the last ten minutes, but the oil tycoon refused to let her out of his sight. When she'd attempted to sneak off to the bar, he'd snapped his fingers and hollered at every waiter in a ten-foot radius until a flute of champagne was delivered into Isabel's hands. When she'd feigned boredom with roulette and announced that she was in the mood for some craps, he'd accompanied her to the tables and forced her to blow on his dice for good luck.

She was two seconds from spilling her drink all over the man's Armani tuxedo trousers when she felt a discreet tap on her shoulder.

She turned around to find a lanky, brown-haired man in his early twenties standing there. He had on the black blazer and gold tie worn by every employee at the Crystal Palace, from the hotel bellhops to the dealers to the waitstaff.

"Good evening, Ms. Parker-Smith. May I have a moment of your time?"

She gave him a broad smile. "Of course, luv."

The oil tycoon received the briefest of apologies from Isabel before she followed her savior to the wrought-iron railing sectioning off the craps tables from the other games. The casino was one unending wave of sound, and the staff member's words were drowned out by a sudden wave of cheers.

"I'm sorry. I didn't hear you," she told him. "Is something wrong?"

"Not at all, madam. In fact, I've been asked to extend an invitation."

Her lips curved enticingly. "Oh, really?"

"Mr. Meiro requests your presence in the VIP lounge."

"Mr. Meiro?"

The young man looked surprised at her question. "The owner of the Crystal Palace Hotel and Casino. He is a very important man, and it is a great honor to be invited to share his company."

Still smiling, Isabel swiped a glass of champagne from a passing waiter. "And what can I expect to find in this VIP lounge, aside from the honor of Mr. Meiro's presence?" She took a slow sip and eyed him over the rim of her glass.

"Stop eye-fucking the kid." Trevor's low grumble slid into her ear, briefly distracting her. "The target is Meiro."

The "kid" flushed under her seductive scrutiny. "You'll find the surroundings are more comfortable. Private tables, higher buy-ins, fine wine that Mr. Meiro reserves for elite patrons."

"By all means, then, lead the way, luv."

With an expectant arch of her brows, she held out her hand and waited for Meiro's errand boy to take it. His cheeks turned redder, his Adam's apple bobbing, but finally he clasped her hand and tucked it in the crook of his arm, guiding her across the casino floor like a true gentleman.

Isabel got a kick out of her companion's evident embarrassment and the look of infatuation that had entered his eyes. Valerie wasn't as blatantly sexual as some of Isabel's other personas, but the Brit was playful as hell, and she loved making men squirm.

Her four-inch Louboutins clicked as they ascended another set of steps, this one leading to an area that housed several large tables with poker games in progress. Most of the players were men, with the odd female tucked between them, and from the size and color of the chips stacked on each table, Isabel suspected they were dealing with serious money here.

Her escort led her to an arched, curtained-off doorway. The red velvet drapes made it impossible to see what lay beyond the door.

"Visual on Meiro." Trevor's voice again, rapid and straightforward. "Just entered the main floor. Stopping to talk to the pit boss."

"This way," Isabel's companion said.

She followed him into a large room that clearly catered to high rollers. Everything looked more expensive here, from the furnishings to the liquor to the wagers.

"Mr. Meiro will join you shortly." Leaving her to her own devices, the young man ducked out of the VIP lounge.

A waiter came by to take her drink order, but she waved him off and headed to one of the blackjack tables instead. When she started to open her silver clutch, the stoic-faced dealer gestured for her to put her money away.

"Any transactions made here will be charged to your room, Ms. Parker-Smith. How much would you like to play with?"

It didn't surprise her that the dealer knew her name. She suspected every employee in this room had been alerted to her impending arrival via the earpieces tucked into each staff member's ear.

"Twenty-five thousand to start," she replied in a careless voice. "I'm feeling lucky tonight."

"Target's heading for the lounge."

Trevor's voice continued to leave her disoriented. She wasn't used to being plugged in like this on a job, and his deep voice was a distraction, jolting her out of character each time she heard it.

The blackjack dealer pushed a stack of chips across the green felt. Isabel was the only player at the table; the rest of the high rollers milling around the lounge seemed more interested in the dice games on the other side of the room.

Isabel placed her bet. She hit blackjack on the first hand, doubling her thousand-dollar wager. She let out a delighted laugh as she reached for her winnings. "Told you I was feeling lucky," she purred.

The dealer's smile was polite.

She played another hand, won another grand.

"Target's coming your way."

Trevor's report was unnecessary—the nape of Isabel's neck had begun to tingle the moment Tomas Meiro entered the room. She felt more than saw him come up behind her. She caught a whiff of expensive cologne, a hint of cigar smoke.

She didn't turn to appraise him. Instead, she played through the next hand, issuing another throaty laugh when a risky double down paid out.

"The lady knows her stuff." His surprisingly deep voice was as smooth as cream.

Slowly, she met Tomas Meiro's caramel-colored eyes, allowing a little smile to play over her lips. "The lady makes a point of mastering any game that makes her richer."

"I see." Meiro's mouth curved in an answering smile. "Is that what excites the lady, then? Money?"

A snort sounded in her ear.

Yet again, the intrusion knocked her off balance. If she could turn off her microphone, she'd be able to avoid Trevor's running commentary, but unfortunately her transmitter was embedded in one of her diamond drop earrings, which happened to sway whenever she moved her head. The constant movement kept triggering her mic, which meant Trevor and the others could hear every word she exchanged with Meiro.

Trying to shut out Trevor's presence, she focused on the man in front of her, who happened to be much more handsome than that one grainy photograph had conveyed. Not a tall man—he was only an inch or two taller than her, and her heels put her at five-eight—but definitely attractive. Chiseled cheekbones, sensual mouth, amazing hair, and very broad shoulders beneath his tailored suit jacket.

"Of course money excites me," she told Meiro. "It is the single greatest aphrodisiac."

"I could not agree more."

He had a slight accent, likely Portuguese, since he was originally from Lisbon, but it sounded Latin American to her—and Isabel had a keen ear when it came to languages. She was fluent in seven of them, one of which happened to be Portuguese. But accents changed and evolved over time, particularly if a person moved around often.

"Allow me to introduce myself." His smile widened, grew more seductive. "My name is Tomas Meiro. I happen to be the owner of this establishment."

"And I happen to be a fan of this establishment," she teased. "You have a beautiful hotel, Mr. Meiro."

"Please, call me Tomas." He lifted a dark eyebrow. "And what shall I call you?"

"Valerie. Valerie Parker-Smith." She extended her hand, and the square-cut emerald ring on her fourth finger winked in the soft overhead lighting.

Meiro brought her hand to his lips and kissed her knuckles. "It's a pleasure to meet you, sweet Valerie."

Sullivan's laughter poured out of the transmitter.

"Smooth," Liam piped up.

Isabel ignored them both. Wished like hell she could find a way to stop her swinging earring from activating her damn mic.

"Are you traveling alone?" Meiro inquired.

"Unfortunately, yes. I was supposed to be here with friends, but my party abandoned me at the last minute."

"You poor thing."

She waved a hand. "Your sympathy is appreciated but unnecessary. Truthfully, I prefer traveling alone. This way I get to indulge my own whims and no one else's."

"My staff tell me you arrived from London earlier this morning."

Isabel laughed in delight. "Ah, so you knew who I was the entire time. Why did we go through the formality of introductions, then?"

"A gentleman and a lady must always be properly introduced."

"I think it's time we stop referring to me as that." She shot him a mischievous look. "Because I can assure you, there is nothing ladylike about me. I'm a very naughty girl, Tomas."

Meiro's laugh was so surprisingly warm she found herself responding with a genuine smile.

She swiftly had to remind herself that this was no ordinary casino owner. The man abducted tourists and sold them into the sex trade, for Pete's sake.

"I know redheads are rumored to have fiery tempers," he said in amusement, "but are they typically this bold as well?"

"Of course, luv. Us redheads are downright brazen. Shameless, in fact."

The blackjack game was all but forgotten as Isabel rested her hand on Meiro's biceps. "So, I was told you save all your finest vintages for preferred guests." She dragged her fingers over the expensive material of his sleeve. "I'm curious—am I a preferred guest?"

Heat darkened his gaze. "White or red?"

She smiled sensually. "What do *you* think, Tomas?"

"Red it is." Meiro signaled one of the waiters, then addressed the dealer who'd been standing silently during his boss's flirtation with Valerie Parker-Smith. "Arrange for a cashier's check of the lady's winnings to be delivered to the Lavender Suite."

"Yes, sir."

Isabel and Meiro drifted away from the table. She kept her hand on his arm. He kept his gaze on her eyes. In fact, he stared for so long, and so intensely, that prickles of unease traveled over her skin.

"Is something wrong, Tomas?"

He didn't answer.

The lounge offered several seating areas—velvet couches and small tables that allowed for seclusion, some shielded from view thanks to black marble columns or low walls made of frosted glass that were difficult to see through.

Meiro spoke after they'd settled on a plush burgundy couch. "Nothing is wrong. To be honest, I'm captivated by your overwhelming beauty and I'm having trouble concentrating on anything else."

Trevor made a sound of disgust that rumbled in her ear.

Once again, the disturbance snapped her right out of character. For a second, she couldn't formulate a single response to Meiro's gruff admission.

Shit. Fucking *shit.* Flirting came as naturally to Valerie Parker-Smith as brushing her teeth in the morning. She didn't get flustered or hesitate or forget how to string together a few seductive words to create a provocative response.

A spark of anger lit Isabel's belly. This wasn't the way she operated, damn it. She worked solo, not with a team, and she certainly didn't have someone blabbering in her ear in the middle of an op.

"I do tend to have that effect on men," she said cheekily, finally managing to regroup.

When she crossed her legs, Meiro's dark eyes instantly homed in on the creamy expanse of thigh revealed by the dress's perilously high slit. Appreciation and desire washed over his face, fueling her returning confidence.

His voice lowered to a smoky pitch. "Tell me about yourself, *chérie*. I want to know everything about you."

She raised her eyebrows. "Everything?"

"Everything." Meiro slid closer. So close she could smell his spicy aftershave again, feel the heat of his body. He placed a hand on her knee, his touch possessive. "I want to know you inside and out."

Sullivan laughed in her ear.

Isabel had officially had enough.

Fortunately, the waiter chose that exact moment to approach their table with a bottle of Romanée-Conti and two wineglasses in his hands.

Meiro insisted on uncorking the expensive vintage himself, and Isabel waited until he was focused on the task before reaching up and unclipping her right earring. She let the dangling string of diamonds slip through her fingers and land in her lap, then released an exasperated squeal.

"This bloody clasp!" she huffed. "This is the third time tonight it's come undone by itself."

Meiro glanced over with an indulgent smile. "Perhaps the hotel jeweler can take a look at it."

She feigned annoyance. "Yes, I might need to get it fixed. For now, I'll just take them off before I end up losing one."

With a sigh, she removed her other earring and proceeded to drop both into her clutch.

Then she snapped the little purse closed.

Effectively cutting off contact with the team.

Son of a bitch.

Trevor had no clue what Isabel was up to, but he was so furious his vision turned into a red haze. He tried to concentrate on the spinning roulette wheel, but it was hard to cheer for a fucking ball to land on black when one of his team members had deliberately gone dark.

"What is she doing?" Sullivan demanded.

Trevor scratched the side of his face to activate his mic and muttered, "No clue, man."

A chorus of cheers rang out as the ball landed on black thirteen.

"Lucky thirteen!" the dealer announced before raking the unlucky chips off the table.

Rather than place another bet, Trevor left the game. His gaze gravitated to the curtained archway a hundred feet away.

"Don't even think about it," Juliet's voice warned. "Down, boy."

An unexpected vise of panic squeezed his chest. Fuck. He didn't like knowing Isabel was in that lounge with Meiro. Tossing suggestive remarks his way. Batting her eyelashes and flashing him coquettish little smiles. Flicking an imaginary piece of lint off the man's lapel, touching his arm in a teasing caress.

Each thought made Trevor's gut clench. He'd worked with Isabel before. He was well aware that she was a pro. Well aware that she could take care of herself, and that she utilized certain methods to pry information out of her targets.

At the moment, however, that awareness was overshadowed by a streak of jealousy and the rush of protectiveness currently wreaking havoc on his body.

Tomas Meiro sounded like a total slimeball. The man was

too smooth, too confident, and clearly this was a routine of his—invite beautiful female guests to the VIP lounge, shower them with compliments and pump them full of expensive wine, all for the purpose of luring them into his bed.

Trevor promptly saw red again.

If that son of a bitch so much as touched a hair on Isabel's head—

"For fuck's sake, Callaghan, what are you doing?"

Juliet's incredulous voice penetrated his irrational train of thought, made him realize he was fifteen feet from the VIP entrance. His legs had carried him there of their own volition, similar to the way he would sometimes drive home on autopilot and find himself in his driveway without remembering how he'd gotten there.

He inhaled a calming breath. Shit. What was the matter with him? Why couldn't he control the tornado of panic swirling inside him?

He quickly repeated a silent mantra.

Isabel was fine. She was a professional. He had to stop worrying about her.

Fine. Professional. Stop worrying.

"Hey there, darling. Buy a lady a drink?"

Trevor's head jerked up at the sound of Juliet's femme fatale voice—which hadn't come from his earpiece.

No, the brunette was standing directly in front of him, a come-hither smile on her lush mouth. He hadn't seen her leave the bar, yet here she was, blocking his path.

"What are you doing?" He summoned a smile to his face even as a bite entered his voice.

"Damage control." She kept up the flirtatious act by letting out a loud, musical laugh, then moved closer and brought her mouth right up to his ear. "You're this close to fucking blowing this, Trevor. I'm pulling you out."

He perpetuated the charade by laughing in return and linking his arm through hers. All the while grinding his molars.

"Says who?" he asked cheerfully.

"Me. I made an executive decision. So now you and I are going to have a drink and calm ourselves down."

The only reason he allowed Juliet to lead him toward the bar was because he didn't want to make a scene. Not with the pit boss standing ten feet away, not to mention the various floor supervisors whose cagey eyes flicked over them as they strolled past.

A few minutes later, a bartender placed a glass of scotch in front of Trevor and a martini in front of Juliet.

One look from the brunette and Trevor's ass sank into one of the high-backed stools, but his jaw was tighter than a drum as he raised the glass to his lips.

"Good boy." A resigned look settled over Juliet's face. "And now we're not moving an inch until Isabel has concluded tonight's business."

Trevor drained the rest of his scotch and ordered another.

The next hour was pure torture. Neither Isabel nor Meiro reappeared on the main floor, which told Trevor that Isabel must be making headway in the VIP lounge and had succeeded in hooking her target.

Her *target*.

The word loitered in his head like an unwanted visitor. Christ, he didn't want Isabel anywhere near someone like Tomas Meiro. A man who passed himself off as a legitimate businessman, all the while operating in the seedy underworld of Europe and treating young women like commodities.

Granted, most of Meiro's brothels were actually legal—but the tourist scheme he had going? His dossier had included far too many details about that particular venture, leaving Trevor feeling sick to his stomach.

Meiro had a standing deal with an Asian crime outfit. The majority of the abducted female tourists were shipped to Hong Kong and Tokyo, where blond hair and Western features were in high demand among the whorehouses that needed fresh meat or the men who were in the market for a sex slave. As far as Trevor was concerned, Tomas Meiro deserved to rot in hell for the role he played in that vile operation.

So, yeah, could anyone really blame him for wanting to protect Isabel from the motherfucker?

Apparently, yes, considering that the woman beside him looked ready to kill him.

"Still haven't calmed down, have you?" she drawled.

He casually sipped his scotch, but every muscle in his body ached from being coiled so tight. "I don't like being kept in the dark."

"Who does? But you're just gonna have to deal with it." Juliet popped her martini olive into her mouth. "Don't worry. She's fine."

"Yeah? Do you have some secret way of monitoring what's going on in there? Astral projection, maybe?"

"Nope. I just have faith in the greatest chameleon I know."

He wished he possessed that same level of faith, but Isabel's radio silence was discouraging. Why the hell had she cut off contact?

"See," Juliet said a second later, sounding very smug. "Just fine."

Relief washed over him as he saw Isabel emerge from the curtained lounge.

On Meiro's arm.

Laughing. They were laughing. And Meiro was taking too many damn liberties—touching her bare shoulder, stroking her upper arm, bringing his lips much too close to her neck.

Trevor tightened his grip on his scotch glass.

Isabel and Meiro strolled across the gaming floor, lost in their own private world.

When he realized they were leaving the casino, panic spiked in his blood again. "Sully," he hissed. "Blackjack's knocking on your front door."

Sullivan, who was out on the street with a line of sight

into the Palace lobby, replied with a brisk "Got 'em. He's escorting her to the elevator."

Some of the panic dimmed. "Is he getting in with her?"

"Negative. She's giving him a kiss on the cheek, getting into the elevator alone. Blackjack is chatting with the concierge now."

Trevor polished off his scotch and stood up, extending a hand to the woman he was supposed to be interested in. "Care to join me for a nightcap in my suite?"

Her dark eyes narrowed, but she still accepted his hand. "I would love to."

He and Juliet had just stepped into the lobby when Isabel rejoined the feed.

"Sorry, guys. Didn't mean to go dark on you. I couldn't stay in character. The chatter on the line was too distracting."

Trevor was in no way appeased by her explanation. She was part of the team, damn it. When you worked with a fucking team, you didn't break communication. Ever.

"Anyway, I'll make my way over to you when I feel like I can slip away," she added in a soft tone. "I'm having lunch with him tomorrow. I'll brief you on the rest later tonight."

And then she was gone again.

I'll brief you.

Damn right she would.

"Hey, Callaghan, flap those wings and fly back to the nest."

For the first time all evening, Noelle's voice finally made an appearance on the comm. And she didn't sound the least bit happy.

"Uh-oh," Juliet said mockingly. "Someone's in trouble."

He stifled a groan. Fuck. Looked like Isabel wasn't the only one who needed to explain herself tonight.

Chapter 15

When Isabel strode into the suite at White Sands several hours later, it took a valiant effort on Trevor's part not to pull her into his arms and hold her tight. He couldn't, though. Not with Noelle's blue eyes already shooting daggers at him.

The "boss" was *pissed.* When he'd returned to the hotel earlier, the blonde had given him a tongue-lashing in a voice so sharp it could have cut glass. She'd finished the scolding by informing him that he was being replaced; Liam would take over casino duty, while Trevor joined Ethan on mansion surveillance.

Trevor hadn't argued with the woman. Because . . . well, fuck. Because she was making the right call. Killed him to admit it, but it was the truth.

He'd nearly blown it tonight by marching into the VIP lounge. His sole focus had been on protecting Isabel from Tomas Meiro, and the man hadn't even done anything wrong. Whatever his past crimes, the only offense Meiro committed tonight was flirting with the woman Trevor happened to be in love with.

Whoa—what?

The thought came out of nowhere, whizzing into his head like a sniper's bullet.

The woman he was in love with?

No. He couldn't be in love with Isabel.

Could he?

He did his best to stop the confusion and shock from showing on his face. He took a breath, tried to focus on the briefing, but his concentration was shot to hell.

He kept sneaking peeks at Isabel, but clearly he wasn't being at all covert, because each time he looked at her, she looked right back.

And each time their gazes held, her expression grew increasingly troubled.

Fuck, why did he get the feeling she could read his thoughts?

Trevor's pulse sped up. Did she somehow know that the L-word had breached his consciousness? That he was, at this very moment, questioning whether he'd fallen in love with her?

How was it possible, though? He'd been in love before, and he didn't remember it feeling like this.

His love for Gina had filled him with an overpowering sense of peace. Yes, there had been passion and arguments, and sure, Gina's kisses definitely made his heart beat a whole lot faster, but at the end of the day, when he'd looked into her big brown eyes he'd seen his best friend and his soul mate, not a woman he wanted to . . . to *possess*, damn it.

So why did he feel this crazy urge to possess Isabel, body and soul? Why were his emotions so much more heightened in her presence? Passion became raw lust. Anger became red-hot fury. Peace became bone-numbing serenity.

When he looked into Isabel's eyes, he saw . . . his other half. He saw a missing piece of himself, and that was beyond fucked up, because he'd never thought of himself as lacking.

What did that mean? And why didn't he feel like he was betraying Gina by considering that he was meant to be with Isabel?

"Keep a close eye on the wife." Noelle interrupted his thoughts. "She might know more than we think."

"I doubt it, but sure," Trevor replied.

As the briefing came to an end, Noelle disappeared onto

the terrace, while Juliet and Liam walked over to the wet bar on the other side of the suite. Sully, D, and Ethan were on surveillance duty, which meant Trevor would be bunking alone tonight.

He glanced at Isabel and lowered his voice. "We should probably talk."

"Damn right." Her dark expression followed them all the way to his room. "What the hell happened tonight, Trevor? Why did Noelle reassign you?"

He closed the door and locked it. He didn't bother with a lie or an excuse; when it came to Isabel, he always found himself being totally honest, no matter how painful or embarrassing it was.

"I didn't like listening to you flirt with him," he said gruffly.

"Are you serious?"

"I got jealous, okay? Your voice was in my ear, cooing and giggling and being all sexy, and it pissed me off." He offered a sheepish shrug. "I may have been on my way to crash the VIP lounge when Juliet stopped me."

"Are you kidding me?"

Her visible displeasure grated. "I wouldn't have felt the need to do that if you hadn't gone dark. What the hell were you thinking, shutting off your comm like that?"

"I told you, the chatter was too big of a distraction. I can't work when I've got half a dozen voices chirping in my ear."

"Well, tough fucking luck. We're here to back you up, and that's something we can't do unless we're in contact with you."

"Tough fucking luck," she mimicked. "I work solo, and I can't do my job unless I have total concentration. How am I supposed to play the part of Valerie when I'm constantly being reminded that I'm Isabel?"

"I won't let you out in the field without a comm."

"You won't *let* me? Sorry to burst your bubble, but you're not running this op. Noelle is, and I follow her orders, not yours." Her cheeks flushed with indignation. "And you know what? Even if you *were* running the show, I still wouldn't give in, because frankly, the request is insulting. I'm a pro, and I work better without a freaking mic in my ear."

He gritted his teeth. "You're not working solo on this op. You're part of a team, and—"

"I can't be an asset to the team if I'm distracted," she interrupted. "Besides, we both know your reaction has nothing to do with a teammate being out of contact. This is about you being overprotective and trying to keep me out of danger. Well, screw that. I've had men thinking they know what's best for me my entire life. My dad, my brother, my supervisor at the bureau. There's no way I'm letting another man run my life, or tell me what I can or can't do in the field."

Trevor fell silent, suddenly feeling flustered. Isabel's blowup was unexpected, but as her angry words hung in the air, he realized she was right. He *was* being overprotective. The mere thought of Isabel anywhere near a criminal like Meiro scared the shit out of him, and yet he wouldn't have batted an eye if, say, Sully or Liam had been assigned to Meiro.

Fuck. He hadn't viewed her as a teammate earlier, but as a woman he cared deeply about and needed to protect, and that *was* an insult to her skills. A really crappy move on his part.

He swallowed a lump of guilt. "Isabel—"

"You're not going to win this one, Trevor. I tried the earpiece thing. It didn't work. From now on, I do it my way. I was a federal agent, remember? I know how to take care of myself."

She sat down on the bed and angrily started to pull out the bobby pins keeping her wig in place. A moment later, the blond tresses slid off to reveal the sexy red bob underneath.

"I'm sorry," he said gruffly. "You're right on all counts. I *know* you can take care of yourself, and I know you excel in undercover work. I guess I just lost sight of that tonight. I was overprotective and jealous and I shouldn't have reacted the way I did."

She shifted, and his gaze landed on the bottom of the black dress she now wore instead of the green gown. It had ridden up to reveal her creamy thighs, and even with the jumble of confusing emotions knotted around his insides, his body was still capable of getting turned on. Saliva promptly flooded his mouth, his fingers tingling with the need to touch all that firm, silky flesh.

"Were you jealous with Gina, too?" she asked, her voice tight.

Trevor slowly shook his head.

"Did she ever flirt with other men in front of you?"

"Sometimes. It wasn't really a big deal, though."

Something flickered in Isabel's eyes. She looked almost . . . wounded.

"What's that look for?" he said roughly.

"I was just thinking you must have trusted her a lot more than you trust me. You must have had complete faith that she would never, ever stray."

Surprise filtered through him. "That's not true. I mean, yes, I trusted her. I trusted her implicitly. But you've got that same level of trust from me."

"Really?"

He approached the bed and knelt in front of her. "You would never stray either. Look, I didn't freak out tonight because I thought you might wind up in bed with Meiro. When you told me you don't use sex as a weapon, I believed you."

Her breath hitched when he rested his hands on her bare knees. "Why did you freak out, then?"

A strangled groan left his mouth. "Because the thought of another man touching you drives me insane. Nobody else is allowed to touch you. Nobody but me."

Astonishment widened her eyes, and then the animosity she'd been radiating dissolved and she let out the warm, melodic laugh he loved so damn much. "I never would've guessed."

"Guessed what?"

"That you're a caveman at heart." She laughed again. "Pure alpha male, just like the rest of your men." She tilted her head pensively. "But you weren't like that with Gina, were you?"

As much as he hated drawing comparisons between the woman sitting in front of him and the woman he'd lost two years ago, he had to acknowledge that Isabel was right.

"Protective? Yes. Possessive? No," he confessed.

With her typical Isabel frankness, she said, "I don't want to be treated like a possession. That's how my father and brother saw me, and I hated it. In their eyes, I belonged to them."

He cleared the gravel from his throat. "I don't see you as a possession or a piece of arm candy or some object I need to conquer. I just . . ." He shrugged helplessly. "I just need you, Iz. I fucking *crave* you."

All the frustration, anger, and jealousy he'd bottled up tonight came spilling out, leaving his body in the form of a desperate growl that had him grabbing Isabel by the hair and kissing her senseless.

He swallowed her surprised squeak with his kiss, thrust his tongue in her mouth without waiting for permission. His heart pounded like a jackhammer, each frantic beat vibrating in his groin, every ounce of blood in his body pooling south, until his cock was harder than steel, thick and heavy and aching.

When her tongue touched his, he groaned and slanted his head to drive the kiss deeper. They were both panting when they came up for air.

Isabel's green eyes were glazed, her chest heaving with each breath, and she was clutching the front of his dress shirt between her fingers as if she couldn't decide whether to pull him closer or push him away.

"I'm sorry," he murmured again. "If you don't want to wear a mic, I won't push the issue. From this point on, I won't question any move you make during this op. I promise you that."

"Thank you." Her fingers toyed with the top button of his shirt, her expression conveying indecision. "I guess I should head back to—"

"Unbutton my shirt." His hoarse demand caused her eyes to widen again.

"I . . . really can't be away from the Palace for too long."

"I know."

Trevor brushed his mouth over hers in a fleeting kiss, then captured her bottom lip with his teeth and nipped at it.

She responded with a tiny moan. "We . . ." She sighed in pleasure when he pressed his mouth to her neck and licked her hot flesh. "We can't . . ."

"We can't what?"

And then he slid his hand underneath her dress and between her legs, and she stopped talking altogether.

Chuckling, Trevor rubbed her over her panties. He loved the dampness he felt on his palm, the way she parted her thighs to grant him better access, the pink flush of arousal that rose on her cheeks.

She made a disappointed noise when he abruptly withdrew his hand.

He laughed again. "Don't worry, sweetheart. This isn't over, not by a long shot. Stand up and turn around."

Evidently she was done searching for reasons why they shouldn't do this, because she stood up without question and offered him her back.

Trevor dragged his hand down the length of her body, trailing his fingers over the fragile bumps of her spine. Her short black dress had a zipper running down the center of her back. He undid the little silver hook at the top, then pulled the zipper down, slowly, one tooth at a time.

His breathing went shallow when her bra became visible, a strip of black held together by a flimsy clasp.

Despite the lust burning in his blood like jet fuel and the internal order to ravish the living hell out of this woman, he miraculously managed to keep his ravishing instincts under control.

Swallowing, he stroked her bare shoulders for a moment,

then tugged on the soft material of her dress and peeled it off her body.

"You're so beautiful," he told her.

Her laughter tickled his ears. "You realize you're looking at my back, right?"

"Mmm-hmmm. And it's a very beautiful back."

He toyed with that intriguing bra clasp, then glided his hands down to her firm buttocks. Deliciously bare, thanks to the dental-floss thong wedged between them.

When he squeezed her ass, Isabel let out a moan that sent a spike of heat straight to his cock. His heart went Formula 1 on him. Every muscle in his body was coiled tight, primed, ready for this.

After he'd lost Gina, he hadn't thought he would ever desire another woman, but he wanted Isabel so badly he could barely see straight. Each time he took a breath, he inhaled her intoxicating, feminine scent. Roses. She smelled like roses.

He gripped her hips and brought her ass to his groin. Rotated his hips, letting her feel how hard she made him, how much he wanted her.

"Trevor." She spoke in a husky whisper, her tone resonating with longing and desire and a twinge of confusion.

He pressed a kiss on her shoulder, enjoying the way she shivered. "What is it?"

There was a long pause, then a wobbly breath. "Why can't I resist you?"

"Because you don't want to."

Before she could reply, he spun her around and kissed her again.

Her arms looped around his neck as he lowered them both onto the mattress. He was fully dressed, his clothing a bothersome hindrance that made Isabel curse as she yanked the tail of his shirt from his waistband.

"You're wearing too many clothes," she mumbled. "Damn it, Trevor."

He laughed at the outrage in her voice. "You're right. This is a travesty."

Working together, the two of them swiftly remedied that, his hands clawing at his tuxedo jacket while her eager fingers tackled his shirt buttons. Soon both items of clothing were tossed aside, followed by his pants and boxers.

Trevor ran his hands over her curvy body, groaning in frustration when he encountered the lacy waistband of her thong. "Now you're the one wearing too many clothes," he muttered.

He grabbed the band of fabric and ripped it off her.

Isabel's jaw dropped. "Those were two-hundred-dollar panties. I hope you realize that."

"Are you shitting me?"

"Nope. I told you, Valerie only buys the best."

"Well, tell Valerie I'll buy her a new pair. Right now I'm more concerned about making Isabel feel very, very good."

Her eyelashes fluttered teasingly. "Wait—how good?"

"*Very* good."

Grinning, he reached behind her to undo her bra, then threw it aside and feasted his eyes on her bare breasts.

Perfection. There was no other word to describe her, no other word that could do her justice. Her breasts were so round, so full, tipped by dusky pink nipples that puckered under his intense scrutiny. His gaze moved to the juncture of her thighs, to her bare mound and perfect pink slit that made his mouth water.

Fuck, he had to taste her. He didn't care that a fire of impatience was burning in his groin or that his cock was pleading for relief. He needed to put his mouth all over this woman.

Now.

Isabel gasped as his mouth took possession of one rigid nipple. While he sucked on the pearly bud, his hand cupped her other breast. Squeezing, kneading, pinching. The soft mewling sounds she made drove him absolutely crazy.

Groaning, he continued to play with her breasts and did his best to ignore the storm of lust raging inside him.

The caveman in him wanted to be set loose. He wanted to thrust her legs apart, plunge inside her, and fuck her so hard neither of them would be able to walk properly for days.

But the gentleman in him overruled the caveman. This was *Isabel*, damn it. He'd been fighting this attraction for a year, struggling with it, berating himself for it.

Well, no more. He wanted Isabel Roma more than he wanted his next breath, but he wouldn't take her until he succeeded in making her feel that same wild and irrational need he'd been feeling since the day they'd met.

"You doing okay, sweetheart?" he murmured when she began to move her hips restlessly.

"Uh-huh."

The heat in her eyes stole his breath. He flicked his tongue over one beaded nipple, eliciting another sexy moan. Isabel's fingernails gouged his shoulders, bringing little stings of pain. He fucking loved it. So much that his cock thickened to a level of hardness he hadn't known possible. His erection was an iron spike, throbbing, pulsing, yelling for him to do something to ease the pressure.

He once again ignored the persistent demand for release and lavished more attention on Isabel's perfect breasts. His stubble left red splotches on her delicate skin, making his inner gentleman wince in shame and that dastardly caveman growl with satisfaction. *His.* This woman was fucking his.

As his heart hammered out a reckless rhythm, he kissed his way down her body until he reached the wet paradise between her legs. She jerked the moment his mouth fastened on her clit, and he quickly braced his hands on her thighs to keep her still. Her muscles quivered beneath his palms, her clit pulsing against his tongue.

"I . . ." She sucked in a breath. "I don't know if . . ."

He glanced up as she trailed off, but he was unable to decipher her expression. "You don't know if what?"

"Nothing," she said after a beat. "I lost my train of thought."

He arched a brow. "Permission to continue?"

She let out a wheezy laugh. "Permission granted."

Over the next ten minutes, he became his own hero, because damn, his herculean effort to go slow deserved to be included in the history books. Somehow, despite the roaring of his pulse and the flames of hunger devouring his body, he managed to drag out Isabel's pleasure until she was begging for relief.

He licked her like an ice-cream cone, drowning in her taste, her scent, *her*. When he pushed two fingers inside her and sucked hard on her clit, her hands came down to tangle in his hair, to hold him in place. He could tell what she liked based on her soft moans and sweet little gasps, and it wasn't long before he felt her entire body tense.

"Oh *God*." Her voice was squeaky, laced with both delight and surprise, and then she was coming, nearly pulling his hair out by the roots as she rocked into his mouth and freely took the pleasure he offered.

"I want you inside me," she burst out, even as she continued to tremble and moan from the orgasm.

Nothing short of dying could have stopped him from donning a condom and climbing up her body. As he positioned himself between her thighs, she gazed up at him almost reverently, as if she couldn't believe what had just happened. Before he could make sense of it, she cupped his cheeks and brought his head down for a kiss.

He longed to feel those warm hands encircling his cock, but he was too impatient. Too desperate and greedy. He plunged inside with one hard stroke and found her so tight he almost passed out from the sheer pleasure of it. Her pussy clutched him like a hot fist, and sweet mother, it felt so good he never wanted to leave her.

But he had to. He had to move.

Christ, he *needed* to move.

Trevor pulled back his hips and withdrew, then thrust right back in, making them both groan.

Isabel's hands slid down to grip his ass. Her nails dug into his flesh. "More. I need more."

"I'm trying to make it last." His muscles knotted,

throbbed from the strained effort it took to try to pace himself.

"It's not about lasting. It's about enjoying." Her breathy words heated his neck and then she was kissing him there, unleashing an explosion of shivers.

"Trust me, I'm enjoying," he choked out.

"Me too." Passion flared in her green eyes. "But I'd enjoy it more if you *moved*, damn it!"

With a strangled laugh, he said good-bye to slow and gave the woman what she wanted. He drove into her over and over again, and she met him thrust for thrust with the lift of her hips.

Trevor's pulse raced, his mind going to that blissful place where nothing existed but pure and utter ecstasy. It had been too long for him, and Christ, how he'd missed this. The sense of connection and belonging, the all-consuming pleasure.

Before long he was hit by an orgasm that rivaled a category five hurricane. It seized his balls and seared a path through his body, so powerful it brought black spots to his eyes. Isabel's answering cry of pleasure stoked his own, bringing a fresh rush of incredible heat that vibrated in his blood until he was reduced to a panting, sweaty mess drained of two years' worth of bottled-up passion.

As he collapsed on top of her, she stroked his back and pressed a kiss to his shoulder. "You okay?"

He made an unintelligible sound and held her tighter.

She laughed softly. "I'll take that as a yes."

Noelle found D on the balcony of the men's suite. He was alone, standing at the railing with his black-eyed gaze focused on the cityscape.

He didn't turn around when she stepped outside, but his sardonic chuckle revealed he knew who'd joined him. "Careful. People will start to wonder."

"Do you care?"

"No."

"Good. Neither do I."

In fact, she'd stopped caring a long time ago what people thought of her.

A bitch. A shrew. Cold, calculating, evil.

Whatever. Let them talk. And let them fear her. If she *had* to evoke some sort of emotion from others, she'd prefer it be terror.

"Give me a smoke," she ordered.

As D shoved a hand in his back pocket in search of his cigarette pack, Noelle's attention shifted to his taut ass, hugged oh so nicely by his cargo pants. There wasn't an ounce of fat on that sculpted body of his. He was spectacular.

Smoking together had become a habit since D and his men had shown up at her ranch. They didn't speak much—talking wasn't something either of them excelled at—but tonight Noelle found herself saying more than usual.

"Callaghan's getting laid," she remarked.

D took a deep pull of his smoke. "About time. You jealous, baby?"

"I don't get jealous, and I don't want Callaghan."

"Yet you've been toying with him since we joined forces, and don't think anyone has forgotten about that special favor you demanded of him." D chuckled. "Have you decided what it'll be?"

"Not yet."

She blew a cloud of smoke into the night. It was chilly out, the wind packing a frigid bite, and she wrapped the two halves of her long black sweater tighter around her.

"Something's bothering me," she said.

"Yeah? What's that?"

She felt D's piercing gaze on her, but she didn't turn to meet his eyes. Lately, he'd been watching her far too often for her liking. Constantly searching and studying, as if he was trying to delve into her psyche and make sense of her, find out what made her tick.

He needn't waste his time, though. Her secrets were buried so deep they may as well be in a bottomless abyss, forever out of reach to anyone but her.

"Meiro. I can't figure him out." She slanted her head. "Did you read his file?"

D nodded.

"Did you notice anything odd about it?"

"No pictures," he said curtly.

It didn't surprise her that his naturally suspicious brain had locked in on the same detail—or lack thereof—that had given her concern.

"No pictures," she echoed. "And it's not like he was raised by wolves—he grew up in Lisbon, for fuck's sake. There should be school photos, driver's license and passport photos, but there's no photographic record of him prior to the age of thirty, and even then, Paige only found that one picture from the charity gala in Madrid. It's like the son of a bitch appeared out of thin air."

D shrugged. "Dude must have a shady past—that's for sure." He paused. "Has Reilly been in touch?"

"Yeah, but he doesn't have anything we can use. He found out Lassiter's finances and records were handled by a business manager down in Florida—Sean's trying to get his hands on the man's paperwork, but it'll take some time."

"What about the other Reilly? The one in D.C.?"

"Oliver's got zilch. Wherever Jim went and whoever he talked to remains a big fucking mystery. And so is Jim's connection to Meiro."

As usual, Jim's name got stuck in her throat like a piece of rotten food. She showed no sign of it, though. Her feelings about Jim Morgan had been banished to the abyss right along with her secrets.

As the image of Jim's intense blue eyes flashed in her mind, a rush of hot anger wrapped around her insides and made her stomach burn. She still remembered the first time she'd seen those magnificent eyes, how they'd hypnotized her, lured her in the way a flame drew a moth.

She had to wonder, were moths capable of acknowledging their mistake before being burned alive, or did they leave the world as oblivious as they'd entered it?

"Don't you look pensive."

D's mocking voice jolted her back to the present. She shot him a sideways glance and swept her gaze over him. His black muscle shirt clung to each and every ripple of his chest. Razor-sharp stubble slashed his jaw, making him appear even more menacing than usual.

"You know, one of the first men I ever killed looked a lot like you," she mused.

"Yeah?" D sounded bored.

"Yeah. He was French. No, Czech. Right, it was Prague."

"Private contract?"

"Government."

D's dark eyebrows shot up. "Which government?"

She shrugged.

"Interesting. So you're telling me that at one point in time, a government agency actually employed a crazy bitch like you?"

She had to laugh. "Shocking, ain't it?"

"I'm curious about something else—that number you have for Morgan, the one you used to leave him a message, where'd you get it?"

Her hands nearly curled into fists before she caught herself. "Just a number I had lying around."

"I'm sure."

"And I'm bored." She stepped away from the railing, her lips tightening in frustration. "I don't like that we still have so many questions about Meiro."

"Well, maybe when Blondie finishes making Trev come," D said in a disparaging tone, "she can go back to work and get us some fucking answers."

"I should go," Isabel murmured, but even she could hear the complete lack of enthusiasm in her voice.

Who was she kidding? The last thing she wanted to do at the moment was disentangle herself from Trevor's embrace and return to her empty suite at the Crystal Palace.

Two orgasms.

She'd had *two* honest-to-God orgasms tonight, all thanks to this man. When the first waves of release had swelled inside her, she'd fought hard not to burst into tears of stunned joy. A part of her wondered if she'd hallucinated those earth-shattering orgasms, but her sated body said otherwise.

"Uh-uh. You're not going anywhere yet." His arm tightened around her shoulders, keeping her in place.

Smiling, she rested her head on his bare chest and listened to the steady beating of his heart beneath her ear. His body was so warm, his presence unbelievably comforting.

But even as she reveled in the extraordinary way he made her feel, she recognized that she was making a mistake. Instead of pushing him away, she kept pulling him closer and closer.

She really had to stop doing that, damn it.

Tomorrow, said the sleepy voice in her head.

Yeah, that was a much better idea. Tomorrow she'd rearm herself against Trevor's magnetism.

Tonight she would simply close her eyes and enjoy this feeling of pure contentedness.

"So who was *your* first time with?" she heard herself ask.

"Sara Malkovitz." Trevor didn't even have to think about it, and to Isabel, that said a lot about his character.

"Sara Malkovitz. Interesting. High school girlfriend?"

"Yep. We lost our virginity to each other in junior year." His husky chuckle vibrated in his chest. "It was a total disaster, but I didn't know it at the time. I thought I rocked it."

Isabel burst out laughing. "Okay, I have to know more."

He stroked her hair, threading his fingers through the red strands. "I planned this whole romantic evening. My parents were out of town, and I bribed Krista to spend the night at a friend's so I could have the house to myself. Then I went all out—cooked a gourmet dinner, stole a bottle of wine from our cellar, sprinkled a bunch of rose petals down the hall and all over my bed."

"Mr. Romantic over here."

"Sixteen-year-old me thought so too. Sara, not so much. She sat through dinner pretending it was the most delicious thing she'd ever tasted, without bothering to tell me that I put waaaaay too much hot sauce in everything—"

"Hot sauce?" she interjected. "What the hell did you make?"

He snorted. "Spaghetti. Yeah, I know. I thought I was creating a cool new sauce that would blow her mind. So poor Sara's sitting there, her face fire-engine red and her nose running because that spaghetti sauce is the spiciest thing on the planet, and she's washing it down with wine. Neither of us were big drinkers, and instead of getting drunk, Sara just got sick. I had no clue though, because she didn't want to upset me, so she ducked into the bathroom to 'get ready' when really she was puking her guts out."

Isabel snickered. "Oh, shit, I don't mean to laugh. It's just . . ." She giggled again. "That poor girl."

"Eventually she came out wearing nothing but my baseball uniform shirt, which was damn hot. We didn't get to the sex part right away. Sara was nervous, so I held her hand like the gentleman I was and we put a movie on. About halfway through, she decided she was ready, and we followed the trail of rose petals to my bedroom, and . . ." He broke out laughing. "I lasted forty-five seconds."

Isabel propped herself up on her elbow. "Aw, that's sad."

"Sad? I thought that was *good*. My buddy Pete said if you went longer than thirty seconds, that was crazy-awesome."

Tears formed in the corners of her eyes as another wave of laughter overtook her.

"Needless to say, Sara Malkovitz's first time was thoroughly underwhelming." He flashed a cocky smile. "Her second time, on the other hand, was mind-blowing. She didn't even have to fake an orgasm."

"Did she fake it the first time?"

"Yep. She really had me going, too. Lots of moaning and shuddering and squealing, a real porn-star performance. If a woman did that to me now, I'd know in a heartbeat that she was faking."

"Oh really? What about me? Was I faking it tonight?"

Isabel regretted the words the second they slipped out of her mouth. Crap. Why had she inserted herself into the discussion? Her past sexual interludes were way too humiliating to share with Trevor.

His whiskey brown eyes took on a smug light. "No fucking way." Then those eyes narrowed, as if he was suddenly second-guessing himself. "Were you?"

"No. I wasn't."

His expression became even more suspicious. "Why do you say it like that? Like you're surprised?"

"I'm not surprised. I was just joking around."

She'd tried to sound casual, but Trevor wasn't buying it. He went quiet for a second, and then his voice took on a contemplative note. "You didn't have an orgasm last night."

She bristled. "I told you, I was exhausted."

He didn't acknowledge her response. "You didn't seem surprised by it, though. It was almost like you expected not to. But tonight . . . you came and it caught you by total surprise, didn't it?"

She supposed she could have lied, but she got the feeling Trevor would see right through her. "Yes. It caught me off guard," she admitted.

His brow furrowed. "Why?"

Embarrassment heated her cheeks. "Because the last person to bring me to orgasm was Michael."

The boy whose hands her father had shattered with a baseball bat . . .

She banished the agonizing memory and focused on Trevor, whose jaw had fallen open. "You mean up until tonight, you hadn't had an orgasm since you were a teenager?"

"No, I've had orgasms." She blushed. "The ones I've given myself."

"But you'd been with other men, right?"

She nodded.

"You faked it with them?"

"Yes."

The admission was accompanied by a pang of shame.

She hated thinking about her past lovers, as few and far between as they'd been.

"It's a shitty thing to do, I know," she said wearily. "But honestly, after a while, faking it was the only option. I would try to explain that the sex was still enjoyable—just because I didn't come didn't mean I was having a crappy time or anything. But men are black and white creatures." She rolled her eyes. "If you're not giving a Sara Malkovitz performance, then they start to wonder if there's something wrong with them, but since no one wants to believe they might have any sexual inadequacies, they immediately deflect the blame. Which means that there *must* be something wrong with me."

She sat up with a sigh, pulling the sheet up to cover her breasts. "They were right, though. There *was* something wrong with me. Hard as I tried, I couldn't let myself relax. Every time things got too . . . intimate, I guess, I would shut down."

Her confession hung in the hotel room, bringing a rush of discomfort to her stomach. She suddenly felt queasy. God, why had she told him all that? What kind of woman talked about her sexual deficiencies and intimacy issues while lying in bed with a sexy, naked man? No wonder she was still single at thirty-two.

She bit her lip. "I don't know why it was different with you. I didn't expect this."

"It's different because *you're* different," he said quietly.

"What does that mean?"

"It means you're not playing a part when you're with me. You're opening yourself up to me, and that makes a difference when it comes to sex. You can't experience true intimacy unless you let down your guard."

"I guess." Feeling uncomfortable, she eased out of bed, still holding the sheet against her like a shield. This entire conversation was unsettling, nearing a line she wasn't ready to cross.

Naked as the day he was born, Trevor hopped off the mattress and caught her by the waist before she could pick up her dress.

"No," he said roughly. "Don't do it, Isabel."

She avoided his gaze. "Do what?"

"Shut down. You did it with the other men in your life, but I'll be damned if you shut *me* out."

Too late. Her guard was back up and higher than ever.

Continuing to avert her eyes, she gently removed his hand from her hip. "I have to go. We're in the middle of an undercover op here."

She felt his frustrated gaze on her as she got dressed, but he didn't say a word, not until she'd slipped on her high heels and was taking a step toward the door.

"This isn't over, Iz. You know that, right?"

"All I know is that I have a job to do. Anything beyond that, I'll figure out later."

"Why do I get the feeling that when this job ends, you'll be giving me a speech along the lines of 'what happens in Monte Carlo stays in Monte Carlo'?"

Her lack of response inspired a muttered curse from Trevor.

"I won't let you walk away from me again," he said.

A weight of exhaustion settled over her. "What do you want me to say? What do you want from me?"

"Everything."

"Christ, who *asks* for that, Trevor?"

He approached her again, and her eyes devoured every glorious inch of him. His sculpted chest and washboard abs. His powerful legs and firm thighs. His thick cock, semihard even now.

"I don't do half-ass relationships, Isabel. Once I'm in, I'm in one hundred percent." He gripped her chin and forced eye contact, holding her prisoner with his intense gaze. "Give me a hundred percent in return, sweetheart."

Little drops of fear trickled down her spine. She felt utterly hypnotized as she stared into Trevor's gorgeous eyes. The man was casting a spell on her. He was somehow breaching each and every one of her defenses, getting closer and closer to the heart she'd locked up tight a long time ago.

He wanted everything.

Damn it, how could he even make such a demand?

Pressing her lips together, she shrugged out of his grip and marched to the door with false bravado. "Like I said, we'll talk when the job is over. Good night, Trev."

She left the room quickly, before he could call her bluff.

Chapter 16

When Tomas Meiro showed up at Isabel's hotel suite the next afternoon, Valerie Parker-Smith didn't waste any time putting the man in his place.

"You're married." Her flat tone and unhappy pout conveyed her precise feelings on the matter.

As expected, Meiro's expression darkened. "You've been asking about me."

"Of course I have. I'm not an imbecile, luv. When a handsome man showers me with attention and invites me to lunch in the private dining room of his luxurious hotel, I ask questions."

She crossed her arms over the front of her red Dior silk blouse, which she'd paired with a black Dolce & Gabbana pencil skirt and three-inch Manolo Blahniks. The peep-toe heels clicked on the parquet as she turned away from Meiro and strode into the suite's living room.

He followed her inside. "I'm sorry, Valerie. I should have told you the truth."

His remorseful tone caught her off guard. Meiro didn't strike her as the type of man who apologized often.

"Well, at least you're not denying it." With a haughty lift of her chin, she walked over to the bar area, picked up the crystal water jug, and poured herself a glass. "Nevertheless, I'm afraid I won't be accompanying you to lunch."

"Ma chérie—"

"I'm not your darling," she interrupted. "I'm also not a home wrecker, so I'm sure you can understand why I choose not to spend time with you."

She sipped her water and eyed him coolly over the rim of her glass.

Meiro looked visibly unhappy. And again, quite handsome. Today he wore a pair of perfectly starched gray chinos and a black V-neck sweater that outlined his broad chest. His thick, wavy hair was slicked away from his forehead, emphasizing his angular features and pronounced cheekbones.

"Will you at least give me a chance to explain?"

She feigned boredom. "What is there to explain, Tomas?"

His jaw tensed, the only crack in his polished armor. He was far more annoyed than he was letting on—that was for sure.

"My marriage is nothing more than a business arrangement."

"How naive do I look?" She rolled her eyes. "You think I haven't heard that before?"

With purposeful strides, he joined her at the bar and splashed a small amount of bourbon into a tumbler before focusing his caramel eyes on her face. "I married Renee for her money."

"That's a very frank thing to say."

"It's the truth. There is no love between my wife and me. Her father was my employer, a very powerful man, but also quite old-fashioned—he didn't think a woman could run an empire, so he was trying to marry his daughter off to a man who could eventually take over the business. I was looking to elevate my social position, so I asked for her hand in marriage and he gave us his blessing."

"And your wife was perfectly willing to marry a man she didn't love?"

"We were friends. That was enough for her. And she recognized that I was a far better candidate than any man her father might have chosen for her."

Isabel watched him carefully, pursing her lips. "I do believe you're telling the truth."

"I am." He drank the contents of his glass, set it down on the counter, and reached for her hand.

She let him take it, but maintained a wary expression.

"Renee and I lead separate lives. We appear in public together when the situation necessitates it, but for the most part, my wife and I are friends and nothing more."

He rubbed the center of her palm with his thumb, slowly, sensually, while those deep brown eyes locked with hers. The man oozed charm and confidence, and damned if he didn't sound sincere. He was smooth—she had to give him that.

"So you see, I am married in name only. In my heart, and in my soul, I am a free man."

Ugh. Gag. All right, so he was as slimy as he was smooth, Isabel amended.

She allowed him to stroke her hand for a few more seconds before withdrawing it from his grasp and taking a step back.

"That is all well and good, luv, but the details surrounding your marriage are inconsequential to me. I'm the kind of woman who cares about one thing—the bottom line. And bottom line? You're a married man. I don't shag married men, and I certainly don't allow them to offer me false promises only to make a fool of me in the end. I had a lovely time with you last night, Tomas, but I'm afraid our acquaintance has come to an end."

A muscle in his jaw twitched.

Oh yes, you don't like that, do you, Meiro?

"If that's what you wish," he said tersely.

She injected some regret into her voice. "It's not what I wish, but it must be done."

Meiro's evident dissatisfaction made her want to laugh, but she forced herself to keep her composure as she walked him to the door.

"Enjoy the rest of your stay, sweet Valerie." Mr. Smooth returned in the blink of an eye, clasping her hand and lifting it to his lips.

"Thank you, Tomas."

After he was gone, she allowed the grin to surface. Gosh, she loved the game. It was such a thrill at times, setting the trap and then sitting back and waiting for her prey to walk right into it.

She didn't miss the irony of that. In her real life, she *hated* games, which was why she was generally upfront about her intentions, honest about her feelings.

Except with Trevor.

For some screwed-up reason, she found it so difficult to reveal what she felt for him—but maybe that was because she didn't know *how* she felt.

All she knew was that whenever Trevor got anywhere near her, she turned into a puddle of confusion, and the lighthearted front she'd worked so hard to construct over the years flew right out the window.

In the bedroom, she unzipped the small compartment at the bottom of her carry-on suitcase and dug out a cell phone. It was the secure one she was using to stay connected to the others, but if anyone ever discovered it, she would simply claim that she traveled with a backup in case her phone got lost or stolen.

She'd witnessed plenty of wealthy folks employing that same system, and the idea of legitimately traveling with backup electronics never failed to make her roll her eyes. People these days were so enslaved to technology, and the sad thing was, they often didn't even realize it.

Again, ironic thoughts, seeing as she was holding an untraceable cell phone at this very moment.

She quickly checked in with Noelle and described the encounter with Meiro, knowing that her boss would relay the update to the others. But she hadn't expected it to happen so fast; less than five minutes later, the phone buzzed in her hand and Trevor was on the line.

"What game are you playing, Iz?"

She furrowed her brow, genuinely stumped. "What are you talking about?"

"Cockteasing Meiro?" he prompted.

"Oh, that."

"'Oh, that'?" He grumbled something she couldn't make out. "You rejected him. Why? We need to hook him, remember?"

An incredulous laugh popped out. "*I* need to hook him, and that's exactly what I'm doing."

"By sending him away?"

Annoyance surfaced in her voice. "Are you seriously questioning my abilities right now? After you apologized for doing the same thing last night?"

A breath sounded in her ear. "No. No, I'm not. I'm sorry. I'm just feeling impatient. I've been watching the West Egg mansion all frickin' night and I'm bored as fuck. I keep thinking how every second we waste is a second Morgan might not have. His life could very well be on the line here."

Isabel relaxed when she realized his harsh words had stemmed from concern rather than criticism of her methods.

"I know you're worried about Morgan," she said softly. "And I'm well aware of the urgency of the situation. But trust me, by the end of tonight? I'll have Meiro eating out of the palm of my hand."

Just as Isabel had anticipated, Meiro was nowhere near done with Valerie. She'd just been seated at a secluded corner booth in the hotel's award-winning restaurant when a shadow fell over her.

She lifted her head from the menu in her hands, hiding a smile.

"Tomas," she said slowly. "What can I do for you?"

Solemn-faced, he gestured to the other side of the booth. "May I join you?"

Isabel pretended to hesitate.

"It won't take but a minute."

Continuing to look torn, she finally nodded. "All right."

As he slid into the booth, she noticed that several pairs of eyes were fixed on them. Well, mostly on Meiro. Seemed like everyone in the room knew who he was, and many of the female guests were gazing at him as if he was a million times more scrumptious than the gourmet dishes before them.

It was to be expected, though. Tomas Meiro was young, rich, and easy on the eyes, married or not. That made him a prize catch for females looking to fill his mistress slot.

The restaurant was busy that evening; the small, square tables on the main floor were all occupied, as were most of the more intimate VIP booths lining the back wall. The bar area to Isabel's right was also bustling, guests taking up residence on the tall stools or leaning against the stainless-steel counter.

Liam Macgregor was among them, looking as dashing as any movie star in his tailored black suit. His blue eyes gleamed with mischief as he flirted with a curvy brunette in a short dress, but Isabel knew Macgregor was sharply aware of his surroundings. Every table, every person, every last detail. She didn't have much knowledge about his background, except that he was from Boston and had been DEA at one point and a soldier at another. But if Morgan had hired the guy, that meant he was damn good.

"I have something for you." Meiro reached into his inside pocket. When she opened her mouth to protest, he held up his free hand and said, "Please, don't object. It's simply a small token of my appreciation, my way of apologizing for not being completely upfront about my . . . situation."

He placed a rectangular-shaped jewelry box on the tabletop.

"Open it," he said softly.

After a beat of reluctance, she reached for the box and opened the lid. Sucked in a breath when she laid eyes on the beautiful emerald bracelet twinkling on the black velvet bed.

"You were wearing the most enchanting emerald pendant last night," Meiro said smoothly. "I thought you might enjoy a companion for it."

Well played, sir.

She gazed at the bracelet again, let her mouth fall open

in astonishment. "Tomas . . . this is breathtaking . . ." Now she blinked a few times, trying to give the impression that she was too stunned to think clearly. "But . . . I told you, I won't go to bed with a married man."

"I didn't come here tonight to convince you to sleep with me, *ma chérie*."

Yeah, fucking right.

"I was merely hoping to express my sincerest apologies for misleading you, and to see if for the duration of your visit you might enjoy spending time with me—as a friend."

"A friend." She repeated the word, slowly, carefully, as if she were trying it on for size.

His tone grew persuasive. "Your party abandoned you, and you mentioned that you don't know anyone here in the city. Well, I would be honored to show you the sights, perhaps take you out on the *Splendid Lady* tomorrow afternoon?"

"The *Splendid Lady*?"

"My yacht." Meiro gently lifted the bracelet out of the jewelry box. "Give me your hand, sweet Valerie."

She made a big production of hesitating before daintily extending her hand.

Meiro's voice lowered to a seductive pitch as he circled her wrist with the bracelet and flicked the clasp. The gems sparkled under the overhead lamp, making her smile.

"So, this is a symbol of our friendship?" she teased.

"I can be a very good friend when I want to be."

"Evidently."

They both laughed. Isabel raised her hand and admired her new bauble. "Well, I suppose there's no harm in—"

"Pardonnez-moi," a rough voice interrupted.

Isabel quickly masked her excitement. She instantly recognized Claude Roussel from the security tape footage that had captured Roussel's meeting with Eddie Lassiter. He looked even more sinister in person, though. Rodentlike features, harsh scowl, thinning hair, and a linebacker's body.

Annoyance flickered on Meiro's face. "I believe I asked not to be interrupted."

Both men were speaking French. Since Isabel happened to be fluent in it, she had no trouble following along.

Roussel looked more bored than repentant. "My apologies, Mr. Meiro. I have some news that bears your attention. May I have a moment alone?"

With a regretful smile, Meiro slid out of the booth. "Please excuse me, Ms. Parker-Smith. There's some casino business that needs to be taken care of."

"Take your time." She pretended to be captivated by the expensive bracelet around her wrist.

Much to her delight, the two men didn't go far. They simply walked a few feet away and stopped by one of the beautiful crystal fountains scattered throughout the room. The fountains were gorgeous, topped by lifelike statues of well-endowed women that were reminiscent of fertility idols of the past.

The fountains were also damn loud.

The water cascading out of the statue's mouth and bubbling at the crystal base made it difficult to hear what was being said. Throw in the standard restaurant noises of voices murmuring and tableware clinking and chairs scraping the floor, and you needed a lip-reader to interpret what the men were saying.

Still, Isabel did manage to pick out a few key words. The word *package* was definitely used more than once.

She picked up her menu and pretended to study the appetizers list, all the while straining to hear Meiro and Roussel. Meiro's goon spoke so quietly she'd given up on him—until a timely lull among the restaurant's patrons allowed one sentence to meet her ears.

"He's definitely still alive."

She continued to peruse the menu, but her mind wasn't on the fifty-dollar appetizers.

He was still alive.

Who was still alive? Were they talking about Morgan?

". . . time and money looking for him . . ."

This time Meiro's voice rose above the din, but it still wasn't enough. She needed more than bits and pieces. She needed something solid, damn it.

Unfortunately, neither man felt compelled to give it to

her. Less than a minute later, their conversation wrapped up and Meiro was striding back to the booth.

"I'm afraid I must go." Looking genuinely disappointed, he walked to her side, bent down and pressed a kiss on her cheek before she could react. "I apologize. An important matter requires my attention."

"It appears I'm already being abandoned by my new friend." Valerie was half teasing, half sulking.

Meiro offered an indulgent smile. "As a woman who claims to appreciate the bottom line, you should understand why business must always come first."

"You've got me there, luv," she said, albeit grudgingly. "Thank you for the lovely gift, Tomas."

"It was my pleasure. Will you reward my generosity by joining me on the *Splendid Lady* tomorrow?"

She mulled it over. "I suppose it couldn't hurt. As long as our involvement is based strictly on friendship and nothing more."

"I simply want to enjoy your company for an afternoon. As a friend," he added.

Pursing her lips, she glanced at the emerald bracelet around her wrist, then back at Meiro. "All right, then. I'll join you tomorrow."

"Wonderful. I look forward to it." His dark eyes gleamed. *"Mon amie."*

"It definitely sounds suspicious," Trevor conceded when Isabel reported in several hours later.

Balancing his phone on his shoulder, he unfastened his pants and let them drop to the carpeted floor. He'd just returned to the suite from surveillance on the West Egg mansion, and every muscle in his body was sore from being crammed in a tree for the past ten hours. Damn Noelle for assigning him to recon.

"Meiro might have been referring to Morgan with that 'he's still alive' part," Isabel said. "And whoever this mystery man is, Meiro has ostensibly gone to much effort to locate him, time- and money-wise."

"Like I said, sounds suspect. But we have no way of knowing if he was talking about Morgan. A tap on his phone would be nice right about now."

"I'm going to see about making that happen tomorrow. If I can get my hands on his SIM card number, Paige has a few tricks she can use to tap his cell."

Trevor frowned. "Don't you need the actual phone for that? I don't want you stealing the man's cell, Iz."

"No, like I said, just the SIM number. She doesn't need more than that."

"You know, I'd really like to meet this Paige."

Trevor headed for the bathroom, where he pulled back the shower curtain and turned the faucet on. As water rushed out of the showerhead, he heard Isabel's intake of breath.

"Are you about to take a shower?" she demanded.

"Yep. Got a problem with that?"

"No." There was a beat. "So, what, you're naked right now?"

"I'm in my boxers, but they'll be coming off any second."

"Interesting."

He couldn't control his laughter. "You totally wish you could join me, huh?"

"Yes." She sighed. "But I can't. Valerie's making an appearance at the roulette tables and then turning in early. She needs her beauty sleep for her yachting date with Meiro tomorrow."

"Yeah, about that . . ." His voice sharpened. "When were you going to tell me about the kiss?"

"What kiss?"

"Don't play dumb. Macgregor told me all about it."

She sounded incredibly amused. "Oh, really? And what did Liam tell you?"

"That Meiro kissed you in the restaurant."

Isabel paused for a moment, then let out a laugh. "Oh, right. On the *cheek*. That doesn't count as a kiss."

"If his lips touched any part of your body, then that's a fucking kiss, Isabel."

To his annoyance, she just laughed again. "Stop being so melodramatic, Trevor."

He had to smile. "Yes, ma'am." After a pause, he grudgingly added, "You were right to turn him away this morning. I shouldn't have doubted your methods."

"I told you I knew how to hook him." She went on with a twinge of sarcasm. "I'm also a trained sharpshooter, a black belt in ju-jitsu, and fluent in seven languages."

He sighed. "And I'm an ass for being overprotective."

"Yup, but I forgive you. Now, tell me how your night was. Did Meiro's wife do anything interesting?"

"She had a few women over for drinks. They looked like the rich, snooty type. Ethan and I were bored to tears."

"Is Ethan still watching the mansion?"

"Yeah, but Juliet went to relieve him. Noelle doesn't want her on the casino floor tonight. Not sure why."

"Noelle always has a reason for everything she does." He could practically see Isabel rolling her eyes. "Anyway, I should go. We'll talk tomorrow."

Would they, though?

Trevor let the question settle as he adjusted the water temperature. He shucked his boxers, stepped inside the glass stall and shut the door. Hot water cascaded down his chest, bringing instant relief to his achy muscles, but there was no relief for the unhappiness weighing on his heart.

He and Isabel might fuck again. They might even share a brief emotional moment or two, but the second she felt him getting too close, she would push him away again. The way she always did.

Christ, Isabel Roma's heart was harder to penetrate than the vault in the Federal Reserve.

He dunked his head under the spray and soaked his hair, ordering himself to quit stewing over this. One, he wasn't a frickin' teenage girl. Two, his boss and mentor was *missing*. So, yeah, Jim Morgan's disappearance trumped Trevor Callaghan's love life, for fuck's sake.

But apparently he wasn't the only one focusing on trivial bullshit. When he stepped out of the bathroom, he found

Liam and Sullivan in the room. Each man was sprawled on a twin bed, and either Trevor had misheard, or the two boneheads were actually discussing whether Juliet would be up for a threesome.

"She's got a wild streak—that's for sure," Liam said thoughtfully. "But she seems like the type who'd take charge in the bedroom. Being dominated by two dudes? She wouldn't go for it."

"Totally disagree with you, Boston. She's a naughty little minx." Sully flashed that cocky grin of his. "And I think she'd dominate us both."

Liam laughed. "Probably right about that."

Trevor cleared his throat. "You guys do realize I'm standing right here?"

"No, Trev, I didn't notice the six-foot-tall bloke in a towel four feet away from me," Sullivan cracked.

"Me neither," Liam chimed in. "Jeez, way to catch us off guard."

He couldn't help but laugh. Forget *When Harry Met Sally*. The day Sullivan Port and Liam Macgregor met, birds had been chirping, angels had been singing, and every single woman on the planet creamed her frickin' panties.

"Seriously, though, you know Juliet won't let you tag-team her, right?" Rolling his eyes, Trevor unzipped his duffel and grabbed some clothes.

"I beg to differ," Sully countered. "I think she'd be into it."

"I still think she'd veto it, man." Liam sat up, those blue eyes taking on a calculated gleam. "You know what? Just 'cause I'm a nice guy, I'll take my hat out of the ring and let you have her."

Sullivan hooted. "You'll *let* me? Fuck right off, mate. Keep your hat in the bloody ring. We'll let the lovely Juliet decide which one of us she wants as her Romeo."

Trevor zipped up his pants. "Do either of you ever *not* think about getting laid?"

The two men exchanged grins. "Nope," they said in unison.

"Just checking."

Liam rose from the bed, wagging a finger at Trevor on his

way to the door. "Be careful, Callaghan. Keep knocking our lifestyle and I'll tell everyone all about your little freak-out sesh from earlier."

That got Sullivan's attention. "What freak-out sesh?"

Trevor glared at Liam. "I didn't freak out, asshole."

"He went bananas when I informed him that Meiro kissed Isabel," Liam told Sullivan.

The image of Meiro's slimy lips connecting with Isabel's silky-smooth cheek had Trevor's hands curling into fists all over again.

Shit. Why couldn't he temper his responses when it came to Isabel?

"You know, Luke mentioned he thought you had a thing for her," Sully said in a pensive voice. "I didn't believe him until just now."

"Since when do you and Luke discuss my personal life?" Trevor asked warily.

"Me and Luke discuss everyone's personal lives."

"It's true," Liam piped up. "Those two are really into gossiping."

"We watch *Gossip Girl* every Wednesday," Sullivan said solemnly.

"Monday," his partner in crime corrected.

The Australian broke out in a fit of laughter. "Now how the hell would *you* know that? Hmmm?"

Despite himself, Trevor found himself laughing. Sully and Liam reminded him of a couple of boys from his former army unit. Every squad had a pair of them, the trash-talking, sex-obsessed, cocky clowns that made you laugh even when you were surrounded by death and suffering and heartbreak.

"Well, tell Luke my love life is none of his business." Trevor fixed each man with a stern look. "It's none of your business either. So drop it."

Now they both shrugged.

"Dropped," Liam said.

"Definitely dropped. Your love life is boring," Sullivan agreed.

Boring? The woman he loved was currently parading around as a British socialite in an attempt to get close to a man who collected beautiful mistresses.

So . . . *boring*?

Yeah, fucking right.

Tomas Meiro's mansion was located in a wealthy neighborhood with sloped streets and commanding houses nestled behind tall wrought-iron gates. The homes outside the city were situated on larger sections of land, set far back from the street and accessible only by long, winding driveways, but the Meiro mansion, here in the city, was clearly visible from the quiet, well-maintained boulevard.

D was hunkered down in the wooded area at the rear of the mansion. He had a clear line of sight to the manicured back lawn and the patio doors, but there had been no activity since he'd shown up to relieve Trevor.

Ethan was manning the street from the roof of a house whose owners were out of town. The team was unofficially using the property to conduct surveillance, but making sure to stay out of sight so the street's other residents didn't detect their presence.

"I'm in position." Juliet's voice echoed in D's ear, her tone mocking as she added, "I got here just in time, too. The rookie was very cranky before he took off."

Since Ethan was still plugged in, his irritated voice came over the line. "I was on that roof for ten hours. Dinner was a power bar and a bottle of water. So forgive me if I'm not feeling as chipper as you are, sweetheart."

"Fair enough. Skedaddle, kiddo. Mr. Cranky Pants needs to put some food in his belly and turn his frown upside down."

There was no response from Ethan, which made D roll his eyes. Their bickering was getting damn old.

He clicked his mic on and addressed Juliet. "Your boss wants you to assess the security situation. You see anything interesting?"

After several moments of silence, Juliet finally responded. "No signs of motion detectors near any of the usual suspects—doors, windows, roof. I can't get a good look at the parlor because of the frosted-glass panels on either side of the front doors, but there's a faint flicker of light through the glass. Blue. Intermittent. They have a regular home alarm installed."

"Anything else?" he barked.

"Give me a sec. Do these field glasses zoom in any closer? Oh, here—okay, I've got it. There's something off about the lighting behind that big bay window—I'm assuming it's the living room window. Hold on." She paused, then chuckled. "Oh, come on, guys. Join the twenty-first century already."

Her lack of clarification was annoying as hell. "What is it?"

"Are you seeing anything red back there? Beams, lights, flashing?"

D peered into his binoculars and studied the patio's French doors, which were shielded by thick drapes. "Can't be sure, but looks like there might be a couple of flickering red beams close to the floor."

"Lasers. Apparently the Meiros think they live in a heist movie." Her snort filled the line. "Nobody uses that form of technology anymore. It's old school."

"So they're motion activated?"

"Yep, which makes them easier to disable remotely. One snip of a wire or click of a keyboard, and the whole system can be turned off. With heat sensors and more complicated detectors, you need to get closer to see what you're dealing with, and getting close is fucking risky."

D narrowed his eyes. "I didn't realize we were considering breaking in."

"What's that Boy Scout motto? 'Always be prepared'?"

"Do I look like I was ever a fucking Boy Scout?" He ignored her answering laugh, suddenly going on guard. "Your boss said to keep our distance. Stay in position."

"I need to get a better look if we want a more comprehensive picture of the security situation."

"Or . . . you can stay in position," he said curtly.

She laughed again. "Yes, sir."

The line went silent, but D couldn't shake the unsettling feeling that Juliet had no intention of staying put.

After a beat, he shrugged it off and resumed his own surveillance. Let Juliet do whatever the hell she pleased. What did he care, anyway? In the end, she was the one who'd have to deal with Noelle's wrath.

Chapter 17

The *Splendid Lady* was a gorgeous eighty-foot yacht with sleek decks, spacious staterooms, and a top-of-the-line galley. Isabel would have loved to be out on the water, to feel the ocean breeze snaking beneath her hair and the salty spray splashing her face, but the weather hadn't been very compliant. Thick gray clouds loomed in the distance, the sky overcast and dreary. Luckily, Meiro hadn't canceled their outing altogether; their lunch had been pushed to dinner, and the *Splendid Lady* would remain in her slip at the marina while Isabel and Meiro dined on the upper deck.

"If it rains, we'll retire to the galley," Meiro said from the other side of the elegantly set table.

It was his third reassurance since they'd sat down more than an hour ago, and Isabel had to laugh. "Or we can just stay out here."

He raised a dark eyebrow and gestured to her thousand-dollar Alexander McQueen dress. "And ruin your dress?"

"It's only a piece of fabric, Tomas." She smiled broadly. "I adore the rain. There's nothing more freeing than standing outside in a downpour and letting those cool drops soak you right to the bone."

"Why am I not surprised to hear you say that? Such a free spirit, aren't you, *ma chérie*?" Chuckling, he refilled his glass and took a deep sip of champagne.

They were still on their first bottle of Dom, most of which Meiro had consumed. Isabel had been nursing her own glass all through dinner, a meal comprising the most delicious veal tenderloin she'd ever tasted, arranged on a bed of wild rice and asparagus. As they'd eaten, she'd regaled Meiro with stories about growing up in London. She'd provided him with numerous opportunities to discuss his own upbringing, but the man remained conspicuously mum about his childhood.

It was beginning to aggravate her, how tight-lipped he was, and as he topped off her glass, she realized it might be time to abandon the get-to-know-you and focus solely on gaining access to the man's phone.

She'd yet to find an occasion, though. Meiro's smartphone sat on the crisp linen tablecloth next to his wineglass. He must have set it on SILENT, because the phone hadn't rung or buzzed all evening.

"It really is beautiful here," she gushed, letting her gaze sweep over the marina.

The light breeze rocked the yacht ever so slightly, but although a storm seemed imminent, the water was calm. The lights gracing the other yachts and vessels moored around them twinkled in the dusky night, making her sigh with pleasure.

"Much classier than St. Tropez," she went on. "Don't you think?"

"Oh, I wholeheartedly concur. Monte Carlo offers a sophisticated ambience that St. Tropez lacks."

"Though the latter is quite perfect if you're in the mood for decadence," she said with a wink. "The nouveau riche crowd is skilled at self-indulgence."

Isabel drained her champagne and teasingly held up her empty glass. "Speaking of self-indulgence, this bubbly is phenomenal, Tomas."

His dark eyes twinkled. "My friends deserve the best."

He placed great emphasis on the word *friends*. In fact, Meiro had gone to great lengths to keep everything aboveboard and platonic between them. His flirting had been subtle, his compliments lacking any overt sexual undertones.

But Isabel knew he still desired her. That sultry gaze lowered to her cleavage at least every other minute, and each time they happened to touch, his fingers lingered a little too long.

"Which do you prefer," she asked thoughtfully, "France or Portugal? You grew up in Paris, but you were born in Lisbon, no?"

"I was."

"Personally, I'm partial to Paris. I find the nightlife to be more exciting. The overall atmosphere is far more suited to my personality."

She leaned in so Meiro could pour her another glass. To her delight, they'd finally polished off the bottle.

"Lisbon is equally exciting, if you go to the right places," he told her.

Taking another sip, she eyed him with interest. "What do you think I'd enjoy in Lisbon?"

"Belém Tower, of course. There are some magnificent churches as well, really beautiful architecture. And I never leave without a visit to my favorite café at Comercio Square."

Isabel dismissed his suggestions with the wave of her hand. "Tourist traps. I don't want to go where all the people are. I want to go where all the *right* people are."

Meiro laughed. "A woman after my own heart. Well, if it's luxury you crave, then you're better off visiting a city like Paris. Lisbon is rather dull in comparison."

"Do you have many fond memories of growing up there?"

"Some. Like you, I'm drawn to the finer things in life, and always have been. As a boy, I would immerse myself in the culture. The museums, the churches, the palaces. I soaked up knowledge like a sponge. Sometimes I would visit the Collectors Wing at the Museum of Art—are you familiar with that wing?"

She nodded. "I am. Private collectors lend the museum pieces for monthlong exhibits, no?"

"Precisely." He played with the stem of his glass. "Beneath each work is a bronze plaque listing the painting's value, where it was acquired, and how long it has been part of that particular collection. I would stare at those placards for hours, and tell myself that one day *I* would own a coveted piece of art, and *I* would loan it to the wing for all to see."

"And have you?" She spoke in a light, teasing voice, yet something was niggling at the back of her mind.

She couldn't figure out what had bothered her about Meiro's speech, but for some reason her internal alarms had gone off.

"No," he confessed. "But that will change when I acquire a work worthy of the wing."

She finished her champagne in one long gulp, needing to speed things up.

Fortunately, she'd grown up in a household where wine was served instead of water, and she'd built up a tolerance for alcohol. Those three glasses had barely made her tipsy, and she knew she could have at least another before she began to feel buzzed.

"Oh, our bubbly is done," she complained after she reached for the bottle only to find it empty. She offered her best little-girl look, the one that never failed to trigger a man's urge to take care of her. "Can we open another bottle? Or is that asking too much of a friend?"

Meiro laughed heartily. "I don't know . . . it might be too big of a demand." His caramel gaze smoldered as he leaned forward to take her hand. "But if you ask me nicely . . ."

She pretended to take a sharp breath, as if his touch affected her in a very primal way. Letting her eyes grow heavy-lidded, she tentatively stroked the center of his palm.

This time, *his* breath hitched.

"Tomas," she murmured, her voice nearly a purr, "it will please me to no end if you could spare another bottle of champagne for me."

A smile stretched across his mouth, and then, in the blink of an eye, he gripped her hand and brought it to his lips.

"Nothing would please me more than pleasing *you*, *ma chérie*."

She met his gaze head-on, letting her lust show, letting him see how much she craved their being more than friends.

"I'll be right back," he said in a husky voice.

He rose from his chair and headed for the set of steps leading down to the main deck.

He'd left his phone on the table.

Isabel wasted no time. The second Meiro disappeared from sight, she nonchalantly reached for his smartphone. The screen was password-locked, but she wasn't interested in breaking into the phone.

As she ran her fingers over the sleek edge, she spared a quick look at the pier. The two guards Meiro had posted at the end of the gangplank weren't paying her any attention, but it wouldn't matter if they were. She'd discovered that sometimes the best way to gather information was to do it right in plain sight.

"Tomas," she called in the direction of the stairs, "can I use your phone to check my e-mail? My battery just died!"

His muffled voice sounded from below. "I'll take care of it for you in a moment, Valerie. I'll be right up."

"Thank you, luv." Her fingers busily pried the SIM card out of its compartment. "Our discussion about art reminded me that I'm waiting for confirmation from my dealer about a piece I purchased at auction the other day."

The tiny square card popped out. With no time to lose, Isabel opened her clutch, grabbed a pen, and quickly jotted down the nineteen digits on the back of a casino note.

"This auction house is rather obnoxious," she babbled on, extra loud. "Quite slow when it comes to delivering their merchandise, even after assuring me the item would be available at once."

She tucked the paper into the zippered pocket at the bottom of her clutch, put away the pen, and closed the bag.

Footsteps echoed from behind her, and Meiro appeared with a fresh bottle of Dom.

He scowled in irritation when he spotted his phone in her hand. "I told you I would take care of it."

She giggled, unperturbed that she'd gotten caught, because hey, she'd done nothing wrong.

"I got impatient. But your phone was locked, much to my displeasure."

His features relaxed, a faint smile returning to his lips. "To keep nosy girls like you out," he chided, but his tone resonated with humor.

With an innocent smile, she handed him the phone. "My account is through my service provider. If you could just open a browser page, I'll type in the details."

"Anything for my sweet Valerie."

It took five minutes to go through the tedious effort of checking the e-mail address that Isabel and Noelle had set up for Valerie years ago. The message in her inbox had even come from a legitimate art dealer, who had indeed procured a painting from an auction house in London. For authenticity, Isabel walked around the table to show Meiro her latest acquisition.

When she told him the price she'd paid, he threw his head back and laughed. "You truly do crave nothing but the best, don't you, *ma chérie*?"

"Of course." A teasing note entered her voice. "Why, you don't believe I deserve the best?"

With the way she was leaning over him, she was practically draped over his chest, and their eyes locked as he mulled over her question. His gaze moved to her breasts, which overflowed from the low neckline of her couture gown, then glided north to her lips, which she licked in anticipation.

Despite the reluctance traveling up her spine, Isabel forced herself to play her part. Had to be done. No other way around it.

"Tomas." Her voice thickened with passion. "I . . . we . . ."

Next thing she knew, he'd thrust his hand in her hair and yanked her mouth to his.

The kiss made her feel absolutely nothing. No desire. No

heat. Not even mild pleasure. It was just another mindless chore, like taking out the trash or vacuuming the living room carpet.

She kissed him back on autopilot, making little sounds of delight, digging her fingers into the nape of his neck, sinking into his chest as if she could no longer support her own weight.

When Meiro's cell phone buzzed, relief soared inside her like a cluster of helium balloons. She'd been about to break the kiss herself, but this interruption was much better.

She quickly straightened up and inched away from the table, as if needing the time to recover from that mind-blowing kiss.

Meiro glanced at his phone display. "I'm sorry," he said, his voice still raspy from desire. "I have to take this."

"It's all right," she said softly.

Rather than take the call down below, he drifted to the other end of the railing. Another stroke of luck—because every word he murmured carried on the night breeze and wafted right into Isabel's ear. She could hear only Meiro's side of the conversation, but it was still enough to make her inner alarms go off.

"You did . . . where? Where was the son of a bitch hiding?" There was a long pause, then a chuckle. "How badly injured? . . . Good . . . deserves to suffer . . . spent more than a year hunting him down . . . What about the woman?" Another pregnant pause. "I see. A falling-out? Perhaps that will work in our favor . . ."

Isabel went on the alert. Her brain worked overtime to sift through the new information, but several details stood out like fireworks in the night sky. The man Meiro was seeking had been found—and he was injured, if she'd heard correctly.

And it also sounded like Meiro was looking for a woman. A woman who'd had a falling-out with the captive man . . .

If said man was Morgan, then who was the woman?

Noelle.

Isabel banished the thought. She couldn't try to make

sense of this now. She still had a role to play, and she couldn't afford to let these crazy ideas distract her from her job.

When Meiro stalked back in her direction a minute later, she didn't let him see exactly how shaken up she was. However, she did convey some uneasiness.

"Tomas . . . you're married," she murmured, making a point of avoiding his eyes. "We shouldn't have done that just now. In fact, I'm grateful for the interruption. It gave me a moment to collect myself, and now I see what a mistake this was."

"Was it?" he said huskily. "Was it really a mistake?"

He moved closer and touched her lips, eliciting a sigh from her throat. Slowly, she stepped out of range of his touch.

"You're married," she repeated, firmer this time. "I refuse to come between a man and his wife, no matter what the state of their marriage."

Frustration darkened his gaze. "What are you saying, Valerie?"

She adopted a sorrow-filled expression. "I'm saying I'd like you to take me back to the hotel now."

"He kissed her again. Tongue this time."

Trevor didn't appreciate Macgregor's updates in the slightest, especially since he knew Liam was only doing it to piss him off. For the past three hours, Trevor had been holed up in the hotel suite while everyone else watched the West Egg mansion, the Crystal Palace, or in Liam and Sullivan's case, the marina where Isabel was having her first date with Meiro.

"Yo? Did you hear me?"

Trevor gritted his teeth. "Yeah, I heard you."

A laugh floated over the extension. "Cool. Just making sure. Anyway, the date's over. They got into a limo and left the marina."

"You and Sully are tailing them?"

"Of course. Looks like they're heading back to the Palace." There was a pause. "Oooh, I wonder if she'll invite him up to her room for a nightcap. I'll keep you posted, bro."

Liam hung up, leaving Trevor to glower at his cell phone. His brain was assaulted by the image of Isabel's mouth pressed against Meiro's.

It took every ounce of self-discipline not to slam his fist into the wall.

Get a grip, man. She's playing a part.

He inhaled a calming breath and went to find Noelle. He and the blond assassin had been alone all evening, yet they hadn't exchanged a single word.

She was on the terrace, her long hair blown around by the wind, which was picking up as the clouds overhead grew thicker and the temperature grew cooler.

Trevor opened the sliding door and cleared his throat. "Liam just checked in. Isabel and Meiro are on their way back to the Palace."

Noelle didn't even turn around. "Good." She paused. "D and the kid are covering the mansion?"

"Yep. And Juliet's off doing whatever mysterious errand you sent her on . . ."

He waited, giving her the chance to fill in the blanks, but she didn't offer any explanations. Instead, she threw him a curveball, as always.

"You're in love with her."

"Juliet? Nope, can't say I am."

"Don't be a smart-ass, Callaghan. You know who I'm talking about."

He didn't answer. Just walked over to the railing and admired the view. He could feel Noelle's shrewd gaze on him, and sure enough, when he turned his head, those blue eyes were probing, seeking.

He expected her to bring up the dreaded L-word again, but she simply threw him for another loop.

"You can't change her," she said emphatically.

He bristled. "I don't want to change her."

"Are you sure about that?"

"I'm sure," he said through clenched teeth.

Christ, sometimes it was incredibly hard to refrain from strangling this woman.

"I disagree." Noelle laughed. "I think you want what you used to have. The sweet, supportive woman who patiently and obediently waited at home while you were fighting wars and saving the world with Jim. What was her name again? Jenny?"

Red-hot fury burned a path through his veins. "Her name is Gina, and I won't discuss her with you. You didn't know her, and you don't know a goddamn thing about our relationship."

"I know you're trying to replace her with Isabel."

He faltered for a moment. His first instinct was to tell Noelle she was dead wrong, but the twinge of guilt he experienced stopped him. Was that really what he was doing? Replacing Gina?

"No," he said slowly.

Noelle raised her eyebrows. "No?"

"I'm not trying to replace her. Gina . . . she *can't* be replaced."

Clarity sliced into him out of nowhere, and he suddenly recognized the truth of his own statement. All this time he'd felt so guilty about his feelings for Isabel, as if falling in love with another woman was a betrayal of Gina's memory, but it didn't have to be that way. Isabel and Gina couldn't be more different, and so was the way he felt about each woman. Loving Isabel didn't take away from what he'd had with Gina. How could it? Gina had given him ten incredible years, and he'd cherished every moment with her.

But it was time to let her go. To start a new chapter of his life.

Conviction resonated in his voice as he met Noelle's eyes and said, "Isabel isn't a replacement. I get that she isn't Gina, and I have no intention of trying to change her."

"Given the chance, you'll do everything in your power to persuade her to abandon her work."

"That's not true," he protested.

Noelle moved away from the railing. The wind lifted her hair, and the sweetest scent he'd ever smelled flooded his nostrils. A garden in full bloom, the ocean, vanilla cupcakes . . . random, contradictory scents, yet somehow they made perfect sense in relation to this woman, who was a walking contradiction herself.

"Your fiancée died."

Those harsh words, spoken in such a blasé tone, split his heart in two.

"You don't have to remind me," he muttered.

"Yes, I think I do. Your fiancée died and the guilt eats at you, doesn't it, Callaghan? You couldn't protect her, so now you're going out of your way to protect Isabel—a woman who doesn't need your protection."

He didn't respond. Wouldn't have been able to anyway; his jaw was so tight he couldn't unhinge it to open his mouth.

"I know she comes off as vulnerable sometimes, but she's tougher than you think," Noelle went on. "She was trained by the Feds, and then by me. Believe me, she can take care of herself."

"I know that."

"Do you?" Noelle suddenly appeared very, very tired. "She needs her work. You can't take it from her."

"You just don't want to lose another operative," he said contemptuously.

"That's not what this is about. It's about Isabel. She *needs* the escape. It's how she functions."

"And you think that's healthy?"

"Why not? Who the hell are you to judge how people deal with their shit?" Now she looked pissed off. "Be careful, Callaghan. Isabel doesn't need a bodyguard, or a man to define her."

"Yeah, then what *does* she need?"

He was rewarded with a husky laugh. "Lord, I'm surrounded by the densest people. Or maybe you're all in denial."

"What's that supposed to mean?"

"It means you know *exactly* what Isabel needs. And if

you don't, then, tough shit, Callaghan, I'm not telling you. Figure it out for yourself."

Isabel found herself in Trevor's hotel room for the second night in a row, once again being glared at by a pair of sexy brown eyes.

Heaving a frustrated breath, she flopped down on the edge of the mattress and glared right back. "Seriously, can we discuss the one thing we *should* be concerned about and not the most unimportant detail of the evening?"

"Unimportant?" Trevor loomed over her with his arms crossed. "That son of a bitch kissed you again."

Despite herself, a smile rose to the surface. "Oh, for Pete's sake, Trevor."

"Did you like it?"

"Like it? I *loved* it. Oh, Lordy, it got me *so* hot I almost had an orgasm."

Those whiskey eyes flashed. "You're making fun of me."

"That's what you get for asking stupid questions." She crossed her arms too, mimicking his aggressive pose. "Now sit the fuck down and tell me what you make of this new development."

After a beat, Trevor's handsome face broke out in a grin.

In response, her heart did a wild somersault before pounding louder and faster than the rain beyond the window. The storm had made an appearance shortly after Meiro delivered her back to the Crystal Palace, but the downpour had actually made it easier for her to slip away. Shielded by a black umbrella, she'd ducked into the White Sands to meet the others without a single snag.

It was the first time she'd seen Trevor since they'd slept together, and her traitorous body had reacted the moment she'd laid eyes on him. The memory of his naked body, his strong arms, his powerful hips thrusting as he moved inside her . . . she'd nearly melted into a puddle on the floor, and it had nothing to do with the rain dripping down the length of her black trench coat.

Oh no. Trevor Callaghan had a scary, debilitating effect

on her. He clouded her judgment, heated her body, drugged her senses.

She'd been trying so hard not to think about the sex and focus solely on this mission, but it was an impossible feat. Her body—and her heart—refused to let her forget.

As Trevor sat down beside her, she put an end to her wayward thoughts and directed the discussion where it needed to go.

"Do you think Morgan's disappearance has something to do with Noelle?" she asked, feeling uneasy.

Trevor rubbed his jaw, which was dotted with dark stubble. The sight of his strong fingers traveling over that sexy beard growth made Isabel's own fingers tingle in response.

Snap out of it.

Right. She needed to focus.

"Well, the way Meiro phrased it—assuming you heard right—does imply that he's hunting down a man *and* a woman. Is that woman Noelle, though? Who the fuck knows?"

"Noelle said that as far as she knows, she and Morgan don't share a common enemy," Isabel reminded him.

But her boss's assertion still didn't sit right with her, in the same way it hadn't sat right twenty minutes ago during the briefing. Noelle hadn't seemed at all concerned to hear that Meiro might also be searching for a woman, nor had she reacted to the news that Morgan might be injured if he was the captive Meiro had spoken of.

"She could be lying," Trevor answered. "Or she could be telling the truth."

"Gee, way to state the obvious."

He cocked an eyebrow. "You know, you're a lot more sarcastic than I realized. I think I might have liked it better when you hid that side of yourself from me."

Isabel grinned. "Once you open Pandora's box . . ."

He leaned in to nuzzle the crook of her neck. Immediately, warmth spread through her body, pulsing in her nipples, tingling in her core.

God, he smelled good. She ought to bottle up that intoxicating scent, package it, and put it in stores. She'd be a billionaire in no time.

"I change my mind." His breath tickled her ear. "I don't want you hiding any part of yourself from me. I want to see all of you." His hands slid down to her waist, gripping it lightly. "I want you wide open."

She suddenly found herself on her back with Trevor's hands beneath her dress, his fingers circling her thighs as he parted her legs.

Leaving her wide open indeed.

The hungry look in his eyes robbed her of breath. "What are you doing?" she murmured. "We're in the middle of a briefing."

Those wicked hands traveled to her inner thighs, teasing the edges of her panties. "I need to be briefed on other matters first."

"Like what?"

"Like, hmmm, how your pussy's going to taste when I lap at it with my tongue."

Oh sweet Jesus.

Never in her wildest dreams would she have pegged this man as a dirty talker. Just went to show that you should never underestimate the quiet ones—and never let your guard down around them either.

Yet as he shoved aside the crotch of her panties and lowered his head, any resistance she might have mustered faded away.

Oh, fine, who was she kidding? *Resistance?* The word played no part in this equation.

Isabel's hips lifted off the bed the second Trevor's mouth connected with her slick folds. She hadn't been a fan of oral sex in the past, never received much pleasure from it. But with Trevor it was a whole other story.

As his skillful tongue licked and probed, and his lips closed over her clit with just the right amount of pressure, she closed her eyes and gave herself over to the pleasure. She moaned when he pushed a finger inside her. So wet she ought to be embarrassed, but Trevor's groan of approval as he moved his finger in and out of her slick channel erased any awkwardness.

Soon she was bumping her hips to meet his thrusting finger and eager tongue. A knot of pleasure formed between her legs. Hot, achy, unbearable. Trevor's tongue flicked over her clit, greedy and persistent, and that knot wound tighter and tighter, tormenting her, making every muscle in her body plead for relief.

"Come for me, Iz."

His raspy command, along with the second finger he pushed deep inside her, was the catalyst for an orgasm that left her gasping for air. She exploded like a radiator cap under pressure, crying out as her body convulsed in sheer rapture. She didn't even get a chance to recover from the all-consuming high, because Trevor ripped her dress off and suddenly he was on top of her, his erection heavy against her belly. She moaned, reached down to bring him inside her, and then she was soaring even higher, her inner muscles contracting over the hard length of him.

A husky groan left his throat, his tongue filling her mouth as thoroughly and possessively as his cock filled her body.

After several long, rough strokes, he wrenched his mouth away.

"Ride me, sweetheart."

No sooner had his words registered than she was being flipped over, her breasts colliding with his chest as he rolled onto his back.

A familiar pang of self-consciousness tugged at her. She didn't usually enjoy being on top. It was easier to avoid her partner's eyes if she was lying beneath him, simpler to just turn her head to the side and squeeze her eyes shut.

This position didn't allow her the luxury. Astride him, she was acutely aware of Trevor's heavy-lidded eyes staring up at her, and yet for the life of her, she couldn't look away. She couldn't close her eyes and shut him out.

She was mesmerized by him. By his chiseled features, stretched tight with pleasure. His sensual lips, parted with excitement. His spectacular chest, heaving with each ragged breath. The tight abs that sucked in the moment her fingers moved over them.

At that moment, she realized she affected him as much as he did her, maybe more so, and with the thought, her insecurities and fear of feeling exposed floated away like a feather in the wind.

She started to move, sighing in pleasure when his big hands reached up to cup her breasts. He pinched her nipples, teased them, got them so impossibly stiff that the tight buds began to ache uncontrollably.

Trevor's gaze locked with hers. "Are you going to come for me again?"

"Maybe," she teased.

"Maybe? Wrong answer, Iz." He promptly lowered one hand to the place where they were joined and idly rubbed her clit.

A bolt of heat sizzled up her spine, making her body arch with delight.

God, why did he know exactly how to touch her?

She could no longer control her movements. Rather than lifting herself up and down on his cock, she began grinding against him, desperately craving release.

"That's it, sweetheart," he encouraged. "Let go for me. Surrender."

Let go. Surrender.

She hated thinking of it in those terms, but there was no other description for what happened next. For the way she locked her gaze with Trevor's, took a breath, and . . . *surrendered* to him.

This climax was stronger, sweeter, better—because Trevor was experiencing it too. The second she let go, she felt him do the same. His hardness pulsed inside her, his release heating her channel and bringing notice to the lack of barrier between them.

No condom. They'd neglected to use one. Luckily, she was on the pill, but still . . . Damn it, why did she so readily hand her trust over to this man?

As the aftershocks of climax ebbed, she collapsed on top of his damp chest. Listened to his heartbeat for what seemed like an eternity, while he absently caressed her bare back.

"Iz . . . we didn't use anything."

"I know." She swallowed. "I'm taking birth control, and I'm STD-free."

"Me too. Well, not the birth control part. The disease-free part." Now he was stroking her hair.

She still couldn't get used to this cuddling thing. For some reason, it felt even more intimate than the sex itself, and as a wave of discomfort swelled in her stomach, she attempted to erase that growing sense of intimacy by bringing up the job they'd come here to do.

"Something about Meiro really bugs me," she commented.

"*Everything* about Meiro bugs me. First and foremost, the fact that his lips are constantly on you."

Troubled, she rolled over and lay on her side. The wetness trickling down her thighs brought a flush to her cheeks, but she was too focused on making sense of Tomas Meiro to clean up just yet.

"Yes, well, that's not what I'm referring to right now. I'm serious. I can't pinpoint what it is, but it's there."

"D said it bothers him that there are no pictures of Meiro in the dossier."

"Bothers me too, but that's not what set off my alarm tonight." Frustrated, she tried to recall the details of her night with Meiro, but the lingering pleasure coursing through her veins at the moment was making her feel lethargic. "I don't know. I just get the feeling he's hiding something. Something big."

"Human traffickers and brothel owners are usually hiding a lot of things," Trevor said wryly.

"I guess." She bit her lip, thought about it some more, then decided to let it go for the time being.

She would give it more deliberation later, when she didn't have Trevor Callaghan's distracting presence to contend with.

"Hopefully this trace on Meiro's phone will help us uncover his dirty little secrets," Trevor said.

"Hopefully. Paige has been monitoring his calls for the past hour, but she said they've all been casino-related thus far. Nothing fishy yet."

"She got that trace working *fast*. And with only the guy's SIM card number on hand. She's even better than I thought."

"Paige is a tech whiz. I don't understand half the stuff she does. Honestly, it scares the shit out of me, all the damage a person can cause using nothing but a computer."

"Where is she, by the way? Why isn't she here with us?"

"Paige is a loner. She lives in a little village in northern England, and usually holes up there like a hermit. She only leaves her cottage when Noelle contracts her out."

"So she's an assassin."

"A very deadly one. She worked for some MI5-type agency before going private. She got sick of following the rules. Fortunately, when you work for Noelle, there aren't a lot of rules."

"Speaking of Noelle," he said lightly, "I spoke to her about you tonight."

Isabel froze.

"Hey, don't tense up on me. It wasn't a big deal. I'm just letting you know for the sake of full disclosure."

"What did she say?" Isabel asked carefully.

He chuckled. "A bunch of antagonistic stuff that I wrote off as bullshit." A pause. "And a couple of things that might have some merit."

"Such as?" Isabel couldn't control her rising agitation.

"That you use your work as a means for escape."

Her lips tightened. "Noelle has no business passing judgment on anyone."

"She wasn't passing judgment. Just offering an opinion." He paused. "I think she's right, to some degree."

"I see."

"Don't give me that betrayed look, sweetheart." Trevor rolled onto his side, then reached out to stroke her cheek.

"You know there's truth to it. Your various disguises allow you to take a break from being Isabel. They offer an escape, a respite. And I get it—sometimes I wish I could tell Trevor Callaghan to fuck off and just pretend to be some other man for a little while."

The need to flee came hard and fast, but Isabel forced herself to stay put. She licked her suddenly dry lips, drawn to the quiet warmth shining in Trevor's eyes, which now took on a self-deprecating light.

"But I'm not as skilled as you. I can't maintain the mask for too long," he admitted. "Sooner or later, I'll show myself. All my flaws and baggage and fucked-up thoughts—you saw the worst I had to offer in Bogotá last year, but you know what? Even if I could have kept that part of me hidden, I wouldn't have done it. You can hide your true self from the world, but not from the person you're in a relationship with. You can't have something real, something honest, if you don't take a leap of faith and let the other person in." His fingertips glided over her bottom lip. "You don't have to hide from me, Iz. Show me your worst, and I promise you, I won't go anywhere."

Her pulse sped up as panic skittered up her spine. "I'm not hiding," she lied.

"Yes, you are. Every now and then, you show me glimpses of the real Isabel, the woman beneath the masks, but the second I get too close, you pull away from me." His voice became husky. "What are you so afraid of?"

She swallowed the lump in her throat and opened her mouth to respond, but the four words that came out were the last ones she expected to utter.

"That I'll hurt you."

Surprise filled his eyes. He slid closer, his naked body pressing against hers, his hands cupping her chin. "You won't."

"You can't know that for sure," she said miserably. "Trust me, Trevor, you don't want a future with me. This thing between us . . . the sex . . . it won't evolve into something deep or permanent." Her next words made her heart ache. "I'm going to walk away from you again when this job is over."

His jaw tensed, but this time he didn't look at all surprised. "I figured you'd say that. But you're wrong. You won't leave this time. And no matter what you think, you would never hurt me."

"Not intentionally. But . . ." To her mortification, tears stung her eyes. "But I have a track record for destroying the people I'm closest to."

"I don't believe that."

"You don't *know*. You have no idea what—"

"I know."

She frowned. "What?"

"I know, Isabel."

"I don't understand. What do you know?"

"Everything," he said simply. "I visited your father in prison, sweetheart. I know everything."

Chapter 18

Shock and horror seized Isabel's body, burned in her throat, churned in her belly. Heart pounding, she sat up abruptly. Fumbled for the dress that was crumpled up at the foot of the bed and slipped it on.

"What do you mean, you visited my father in prison?" Outrage echoed in her voice and pulsed in her blood.

With a weary sigh, Trevor stood up and put on his boxers. "It was a few weeks after you skipped out on me. I hadn't managed to reach Noelle at that point, so I had no fucking idea if you were alive or dead or in trouble or who the hell knew. So I went to Sing Sing to talk to your father. I was hoping he might know where you were, or at the very least, have an idea about where you would go."

Don't visit again, Isabel. I can't stand the sight of you.

Humiliation slammed into her. God, what had her dad told Trevor?

With sympathy flickering in his eyes, Trevor took her hand and led her back to the bed.

Numb, she ordered her knees to bend so she could sit beside him. She finally found her voice, which came out wobbly. "Who did you say you were?"

"Your boyfriend." Displeasure flashed in Trevor's eyes. "He thought I came to tell him you were dead."

She bit hard on the inside of her cheek. "Let me guess—he didn't seem at all upset by the notion."

Trevor's answering silence irked her.

"Don't try to spare my feelings. I know my father hates me." Isabel turned her head and fixed her gaze on the wall ahead.

She couldn't look at Trevor. She refused to see the pity in his eyes. She couldn't *bear* to see it.

You don't put people in prison, do you? You put them in graves.

Her father's voice. Her father's accusations.

"What exactly did he tell you?" she said dully.

"He blames you for the deaths of your family."

A laugh bubbled in her throat. "Trust me, he never lets me forget it."

"Yeah, well, your father's full of shit, sweetheart." Trevor's lips tightened. "He's a bitter old man who made terrible choices in his life but can't take responsibility for any of them. So instead, he blames his daughter for all the crappy things that have happened."

"So he told you everything? He told you about my mom and Joey and my grandparents?"

"Yes, but not in great detail," Trevor answered. "I already knew about your mother's death, since you'd told me about it, but he filled me in on the rest."

Isabel was consumed by a rush of resentment. What kind of father did that, for God's sake? Spewed his venom to a man he didn't even know, a man who'd shown up out of love and worry for Isabel.

A man who lied to you . . .

The resentment grew as she stared into Trevor's eyes. "The other night when I told you about my Nona's accident . . ." A scowl twisted her mouth. "Why the hell didn't you tell me you already knew about it?"

"Like I said, Bernie didn't give me many details."

"But you knew the basics. You just sat there and pretended to be hearing it for the first time." Her hands trembled with anger, and she couldn't help but feel utterly betrayed as she glimpsed Trevor's remorseful expression.

"I wanted it to come from you," he said softly. "I could have forced you to talk about it by telling you about my visit to Sing Sing, but I didn't want you to feel like you *have* to share things with me. I want you to open up to me because *you* want to, not because I'm making you."

She couldn't control her rising bitterness. "So I guess you know about my grandfather?"

"That he died of a heart attack? Yes."

"No, he had a heart attack because I snuck out of our house in Jersey to meet some friends on the boardwalk." Pain sliced into her heart. "He was out of his mind with worry when he found my room empty. My dad said the stress was too much for him."

"The cardiologist's report said otherwise. Your grandfather's arteries were so clogged it was a miracle any blood could flow through them at all. He was a heart attack waiting to happen."

Her gaze flew to his. "How do you know that?"

"You have your tech geek. We have ours. I asked Holden to dig into your background after you disappeared. He got his hands on your grandfather's entire medical history." Trevor clasped both her hands. "Maybe you gave your grandfather a scare that night, but his heart would have given out on him eventually, Iz."

She couldn't respond. The lump in her throat was too big.

"And your grandmother's death? Well, that's an accident if I've ever heard one," Trevor went on. "Your father didn't tell me about the truck. He only said you were driving and she died. But there was nothing you could have done to prevent a snowplow truck from rear-ending you. It wasn't your fault."

Tears pricked her eyes. "Yeah, and what about my mother? Did he tell you what her suicide note said?"

His forehead wrinkled with confusion. "No."

Isabel blinked rapidly, hoping to clear her wavering vision. "Her note said she couldn't handle the stress. *I* was her source of stress, Trevor."

"Come on, Isabel. You know that's pure and total crap. Your mother couldn't cope with the stress of being married to a goddamn mobster. But your father couldn't come to terms with the fact that his wife didn't want to be with *him*, so he laid the blame at your door. A ten-year-old child who happened to be a little precocious." Trevor angrily shook his head. "I'm sorry, Iz, but I've gotta say it. Your dad is a fucking asshole—and the only reason I didn't snap his sorry neck was one, because we were in a damn prison surrounded by guards, and two, because I knew you would hate me for it."

Shock rippled through her. "Trevor—"

"No, I mean it. The bastard had the nerve to give me a grand speech about loyalty and family and protecting the people you love—can you believe that? But did he ever protect *you*, his daughter?" Trevor's expression was more furious than she'd ever seen it. "He didn't protect his son either. What kind of father chooses that kind of life for his son?"

The torment returned to claw at her chest. "I didn't protect Joey either," she whispered.

Trevor let go of her hands and wrapped an arm around her shoulders. "All Bernie said was that Ric De Luca killed your brother and you watched it happen."

Hot agony streaked through her as the memories spiraled to the surface. Sights, sounds, smells, textures—it all came back to her in one grand sweep.

The scent of basil and oregano permeating the air. The plush upholstery of the back booth. The overpowering cologne of De Luca's son Frank and the softness of his expensive wool trousers pressed against her lower thigh.

The scarcely audible *pop* of De Luca's pistol discharging. The hole appearing in Joey's forehead.

"I *let* it happen," she mumbled.

"Could you have stopped it?"

"Not without blowing my cover. Not without dying myself." Shame clogged her throat. "I chose my own life over my brother's."

"Why was your brother on De Luca's shit list?"

"He stole from him. After my dad took one for the team and went to prison rather than give up De Luca, Joey took over my dad's duties. Our restaurant was a front for drug running, and Joey got greedy. He stole from the big boss and stupidly got caught. My dad refuses to believe Joey was guilty, but my brother confessed everything to me."

"Did Joey know you were a Fed?"

Isabel shook her head. "The bureau recruited me out of college. It was very hush-hush—they'd planned on making use of my family connections from the get-go, and even my training at Quantico was done under an assumed name. After I got my badge, I was immediately assigned to the organized-crime unit and sent back to Brooklyn. I asked Joey if I could stay with him until I figured out what I wanted to do with my life, and he put me to work at the restaurant—he was happy to let me take over his manager responsibilities. My brother was a lazy bastard."

She wiggled out of Trevor's embrace and stood up. She suddenly felt restless, drained.

"De Luca and his inner circle ate dinner at our bistro every Saturday, and the boss was thrilled to find me working there. He wanted me to marry his son Frank and unite our families, but I was playing it coy." She let out a breath, and began to pace the carpet. "After Joey confessed that he'd been skimming the drug profits, I urged him to leave town, but it was too late. De Luca came for dinner. His son was there too. I was sitting with Frank, laughing, flirting, when De Luca called Joey out and told him he knew what he was up to."

Trevor walked over and grasped her waist to still her nervous pacing.

"Isabel—"

"And then he shot Joey in the head." She shrugged his hands off her and took several backward steps. "He killed my brother and I just sat there and did absolutely nothing to stop it."

"Isabel." He moved closer.

She took another step back. "My dad hates me because I didn't try to stop De Luca or use my resources to save Joey."

"Wait—your dad knew you were FBI?"

"He found out later. The second time I went undercover with the outfit, my supervisor offered my dad a deal. Early release, time served, if he flipped on De Luca. He turned it down. He could have been *free*, but he chose to stay behind bars to protect the man who'd murdered his son. So I went to see him in prison. I told him I was a Fed and begged him to take the deal. He still refused, and the visit only fueled his hatred—he realized I could have used my authority to save Joey, but I didn't."

Another wave of guilt swelled in her belly, making her nauseous. It didn't matter how many years had passed—the pain was eternally fresh, the wound forever raw. Her older brother was dead because she hadn't wanted to blow her damn *cover*. Her father was rotting away in a prison cell, consumed with hatred for her.

Knowing that Trevor had witnessed that hatred firsthand was mortifying. Infuriating.

"You should have told me you saw my father," she said stiffly. "All this time you've been lecturing me about not hiding anything from you, and yet you were keeping secrets of your own. Is that supposed to inspire me to open up to you?"

"I told you—I needed you to *want* to open up."

"Yeah, well, now that's the last thing I want to do, Trevor! You're always telling me I can trust you, but now I find out you dug around in my background? What else have you been keeping from me?"

"Nothing." His brown eyes burned with frustration. "I saw your father. That's it. And everything you just told me about your grandfather and Joey, that was all new information for me. I didn't know anything beyond the fact that they'd both died."

"You still should have said something," she shot back.

"I'm sorry," he said quietly. "I really am sorry I kept my Sing Sing visit from you. But I'm not sorry you finally opened up to me, Iz."

Before Isabel could respond, a loud knock sounded on the door, officially putting an end to their turbulent exchange.

"Sorry to interrupt"—Noelle's voice, and she didn't sound at all apologetic—"but I need you two out here. There's been a development."

They listened to the tape twice, and each time the final *click* echoed in the air, D's muscles tensed with anticipation. He hadn't appreciated Noelle's sharp command to get his ass back to the suite, but after hearing this recording, he was grudgingly grateful she'd called him in.

"This is going down tonight?" Liam asked.

Noelle shrugged. "That's what it sounds like."

"I don't like this," Trevor said uneasily. "We can't go in blind."

D stood in front of the open sliding door and lit up a cigarette, working over the details in his head.

"Play the recording again, Blondie." He glanced at Isabel, who was sitting on the couch with her computer in her lap.

With a nod, she tapped a few keys, and Meiro's deep voice emerged from the speakers once more.

"Are we all set?" Meiro barked.

"Yes. The package is arriving at midnight." The other voice, with its pronounced French accent, belonged to Claude Roussel, who didn't sound happy. "Your presence would allow for a more smooth exchange, sir."

"I told you, I cannot leave the Palace. I'm hosting a high-rollers tournament tonight and it will be suspicious if I don't attend. You've dealt with Barka on your own before, Claude. It's a simple exchange, nothing to fret about."

"And what do you want me to do with our unexpected surprise?"

"Bring him to the cellar at Serena's. I'll pay him a visit

when my business at the casino concludes." Meiro's voice took on an ironic note. "A year's worth of hunting and our prey ends up being delivered right to our door."

"Such is life," the henchman said drily.

"What of the woman? Any developments?"

"No sign of her. It's rumored they went their separate ways in Munich."

Every head in the room turned in Noelle's direction, just like the other two times the recording had been played.

"Well, tell our people to keep looking. For now, we'll deal with her lover. Also, remind Henri to send his workers away when the cargo is being unloaded. We can't have a repeat incident of last time."

"Yes, sir."

"And keep me apprised of any new developments."

Click.

A crackle of static, then silence.

D took another deep drag of his smoke. Noelle's woman had done some digging and discovered that a man by the name of Henri Chastain worked as the night supervisor down at the docks. Odds were good that Chastain was the same Henri mentioned in the recording. Rumor had it that Chastain was the most accommodating man in the city—all it took was a little bribe and he turned a blind eye to any shady enterprises that went down.

Liam spoke up. "So we're assuming Meiro's delivery is arriving by boat."

Everyone nodded in agreement. They were all present except for Ethan and Juliet, who were keeping an eye on Meiro's mansion and the Crystal Palace, respectively. D was happy about the absence of those particular two—he was tired of hearing them bicker. Ethan needed to get over it already and fuck that woman.

"Do we think Morgan is the package?" Sullivan looked troubled as he ran a hand over the thick blond stubble on his square jaw.

"We have to assume he is," Trevor replied. "We can't afford not to check this out."

Noelle shook her head. "No."

Every pair of eyes landed on her again.

"What the fuck do you mean, *no*?" Trevor demanded. "If Morgan's on that boat—"

"He won't be on it for long," she finished. "He'll be delivered to Serena's cellar, remember?"

Sullivan spoke again. "And who in bloody hell is Serena?"

"That's what we need to find out," Noelle said. She turned to Isabel. "Call Reilly. Tell him to start making inquiries. Paige is looking into it as well."

D's gaze followed the blonde's every movement. She was pacing now, not from nervousness but in that brisk, efficient way she did when she was formulating a plan. He'd spent enough time with her to know how her head worked, and although Trevor and the other men looked pissed that Noelle was calling the shots, D had no doubt that every decision she made would be the right one.

So much trust in one little woman . . .

He ignored the mocking voice in his head. Screw trust. He didn't trust the bitch, not in the slightest. Yes, he was confident she wouldn't betray them, at least not in this, but that didn't mean he was stupid enough to trust her. Especially with his life.

But Morgan's life?

The woman could protest until she was blue in the face, but D knew she wouldn't rest until she found Morgan.

Dead or alive.

"I know that port," Noelle said confidently. "Security is a fucking bitch, and it's damn near impossible to breach the docks unseen. If we try to intercept the package there, we're looking at chaos and casualties. I prefer the quieter approach. Let Henri and Meiro's men throw Jim in the back of a van and cart him off to a secondary location—where we'll be waiting."

Trevor's tone was markedly reluctant. "That does make sense."

"Of course it does. All right, so here's where we're at.

Isabel, I want you to contact Reilly and then head back to the Palace. Valerie's absence will be noted if you're gone for much longer."

"Yes, ma'am." Isabel closed her laptop and stood up.

D noticed that she barely glanced at Trevor as she grabbed her cell phone and disappeared into the bedroom. In the back of his mind, he wondered if there was trouble in paradise, but he didn't spend much time entertaining the thought. He had zero interest in other people's love lives.

"It's too late to call your man Luke in, but how do you feel about using Reilly?" Noelle asked Trevor.

D could see Trevor working over the idea in his head, just as he was. D wasn't sure how much he trusted the Irishman, but there was no denying the man moved like a soldier. Probably wouldn't require much direction if he helped them out tonight.

Trevor must have reached the same conclusion, because he nodded. "I'm fine with it. We could use the manpower."

"Good. You, D, Macgregor, and the kid will be in charge of Serena's cellar, wherever the fuck that is." The blonde glanced at Sullivan. "You and Reilly watch the docks. Once the package is on the move, follow it."

Sullivan shot Trevor a quick look, frowning when their team leader nodded. "Yes, ma'am," the Aussie muttered.

Across the room, Liam checked his watch and cursed. "It's nearly ten. How are we supposed to come up with a workable plan if we don't even know where we're going?"

"Fifteen minutes," Noelle said curtly. "If Paige and Reilly don't have anything solid for us about Serena by then, we focus our attentions on the docks."

She concluded the meeting by turning her back on everyone and marching to the terrace. Her arm brushed D's as she strolled outside, but neither of them reacted to the physical contact. After the rest of the group dispersed, D stepped onto the terrace and shut the door behind him.

"When was the last time you were in Munich?"

Noelle shook her head in aggravation. "Whoever Meiro

was referring to, it's not me. I haven't been to Munich in years. Neither has Jim, as far as I know."

"You're lying."

"For fuck's sake—"

"Not about Munich," he cut in. "About you and Morgan not having any common enemies."

She arched a brow. "Says who?"

He advanced on the woman by the railing. "Do you know who I used to work for before I joined Morgan's crew?"

"What do *you* think?"

"Yeah, I figured." He narrowed his eyes. "But you've kept your mouth shut about it."

"How are you so sure I've kept silent?" she taunted.

"Because if you'd told anyone about me, I'd be dead." He shrugged. "Whatever. I don't care what you know, so long as you understand what my past association symbolizes."

She waited for him to elaborate.

"Connections, baby. I still have a lot of those, and I made good use of them after you showed up at our compound last year when Sinclair went missing."

Noelle's blue eyes revealed nothing. "How much do you know?"

"Enough. Wanna fill in the blanks?"

"Not particularly, no." She plucked the cigarette right out of his hand and wrapped her lips around the filter, taking a deep pull. "Look, my past with Jim has nothing to do with his disappearance or the attack on your compound."

"You'd stake your life on it?"

Before she could respond, the sliding door opened and Isabel appeared.

"Sean wins this round," she announced. "He came up with the information faster than Paige."

"Serena?" D asked.

Isabel nodded. "She's the madam at the Sapphire Room, a gentlemen's lounge here in the city. Meiro owns it."

"Whorehouse," Noelle said with a nod of her own. "I remember the madam there being named Veronica."

"I won't even ask how you know that," Isabel replied. "Anyway, Sean's coming by with more details. I'm heading back to the Palace, unless you need me to stick around?"

"No, maintain your cover. We might need Valerie again before this is all over."

Once Isabel was gone, Noelle smirked at D. "Looks like you get to visit a brothel tonight, stud."

He reclaimed his cigarette from her lethal hand and brought it to his lips. "Jealous?"

She laughed. "We both know I could fuck you better than any whore ever could." Her expression became surprisingly impish. "And I'm disease-free."

Now D was the one laughing. "Even knowing that, I'd still feel a hell of a lot safer with the whore."

The Sapphire Room was the corner house in a row of elegant brownstones on the east end of the city. There were no driveways, but a narrow passageway ran alongside the building, leading to a line of private detached garages behind each house. Trevor was situated in the rear, inside a large tin shed in the corner of the alley. The shed smelled like manure and contained nothing but broken gardening tools, which was probably why it had been left unlocked, with its doors wide open. Trevor had usurped the space and was now standing in the shadows as he covered the house.

Ethan had taken to higher ground—the roof of an apartment building behind the brownstone strip, giving him a bird's-eye view of the Sapphire Room. Trevor would have preferred Luke's sniping abilities, but Ethan was a damn good shot too.

D and Liam were stationed at the front of the house. From the dozens of expensive vehicles parked on the street, many of which contained a bored driver waiting for the owner to reappear, it was evident that this was a high-traffic area. No doubt this nineteenth-century town house received the most visitors.

"Okeydokey, mateys, we've got some movement." Sullivan's voice echoed in Trevor's earpiece. Sullivan was at the docks with Sean Reilly to monitor the arrival of Meiro's delivery, but the Australian hadn't had much to report in the last hour.

"What's doing?" Trevor murmured.

"Cargo vessel just moored at the dock."

He checked his watch. A couple minutes past midnight. The bastards were prompt.

"Are we certain it's the one Meiro's expecting?"

"No doubt. Roussel's here."

"You sure it's him?" D's sharp inquiry hissed over the line.

"Affirmative. I'd recognize that Frenchie anywhere."

Trevor bit back a laugh. "Reilly, you copy?"

"At your service, good sir." If voices could display facial expressions, the Irishman's would be smirking. "I'm seeing me a van. White, unmarked, no windows—Ollie and I call 'em rapist vans."

"Contents of the rapist van?" Trevor prompted.

"No clue. Driver parked at the gate, Chastain came out to unlock it and waved the van through. Van parked, driver got out to light a fag. He's on his fifth. Looks bloody bored. There's a passenger, but he's staying put."

Trevor caught a flash of movement in one of the upstairs windows of the brownstone. A light flicked on, a voluptuous silhouette appearing in the gauzy curtains before moving out of view.

"Sweet mother-of-pearl," Sullivan mumbled.

Trevor's eyes narrowed. "What is it?"

"Women. Six of them, with black hoods over their heads. They're being taken to the truck. Knocking on your front door, Irish."

"Got 'em. Yeah, I count six."

"One more party guest being carried off the boat." Sullivan suddenly cursed. "Male, tall, black sweater and pants, black hood. Hands bound behind his back. Wait. Right leg seems to be broken—the thing is at a scary angle, dragging on the ground. Must hurt like a bitch, but dude's not making a sound."

Shit. That sounded just like Morgan's tough-guy style. He never revealed a sliver of emotion, even if he was in excruciating pain.

"Can't see his face," Sullivan added, "but he's big."

"Morgan-big?" Trevor said sharply, picturing their boss's six-foot-plus frame and bulky physique.

"Affirmative. Could be him."

Reilly spoke up. "Passenger out of the rapist van, walking around to open the back doors. Roussel and one goon are marching the captives to the van. Aussie, get over here. We might need to move fast."

"Be there in a jiffy, Irish." Sarcasm rippled over the radio feed.

"The ladies and gentleman are in the van, driver and passenger returning to their respective seats. Roussel's goon is getting behind the wheel of the town car. Roussel's talking to Chastain."

Trevor listened to the reports rattling in his ear. His muscles tensed when Reilly announced that the van had driven out the gate. The town car with a goon at the wheel and Roussel in the passenger seat followed the van, sticking close.

"Don't lose the van," Trevor ordered in a low voice. "If Morgan's in there . . ."

"I know, I know," Reilly said. "The mighty Jim Morgan must be rescued."

Sullivan came back on. "We're on it, Trev. Solid visual on the rapist van, and it'll stay that way provided Irish doesn't screw up."

The duo went quiet, but Trevor imagined there was some good-natured bantering happening in that taxi; Noelle had somehow procured a taxicab for the men to use, a vehicle that wouldn't look out of place near the docks or traveling through the city streets so late at night, should Roussel make the tail.

As much as Trevor hated admitting it, Noelle's instincts were spot-on. He still had no clue what her role in this was, though. She disappeared for hours at a time, which hinted she was conducting her own surveillance, but the woman had yet to divulge her activities to the rest of the team.

It took twenty minutes before the next report came in. Trevor stood quietly in the shadows, a ski mask covering his face and weapons strapped to his body, his trusty SIG in hand as he watched the back of the Sapphire Room.

The house was surprisingly quiet. The brothels he'd visited in the past under his Julian Martin alias had been noisy, with high-pitched giggles and male laughter and faint sounds of sex wafting from the establishment. But he supposed a brothel in such a high-class city would be high class itself. Aside from the various lights that switched on and off, and the occasional female bodies that appeared in the windows to close the heavy drapes, you'd never know the house was full of prostitutes and men who were paying to fuck them.

"You're gonna have company soon," Sullivan said. "ETA four minutes."

Maintaining his position, Trevor checked in with the others. "D, Boston, you good?"

D and Liam responded in the affirmative.

"Rookie?"

"All good. Say the word and I'll put my rifle to good use."

It wasn't long before Trevor's blood coursed with the two A's—anticipation and adrenaline. At times like this, he missed the army. It had always been a rush, carrying out a hazardous op, knowing every decision he made meant the difference between life and death.

"Incoming," Sullivan reported. "We're falling back."

A moment later, Liam checked in. "Visual on the rapist van. Just turned onto the street."

Trevor took a slow, even breath. The distant sound of an engine echoed in the night.

"Van's pulling into the alley," D said.

A moment later, there was a gleam of headlights as the white van approached the paved strip behind the brownstone row.

"Boston, you're with me," Trevor murmured. "Passenger

and driver. Sully, Reilly, town car. D, party guests. Rookie, stand by."

He received a chorus of "Yes, sirs" in response.

Trevor stayed in the shadows. He was ready to strike, but couldn't make a move until Sullivan and Reilly were in place.

The van's engine rumbled as the driver turned around in the wide alleyway and backed up in front of the first garage in the row. A shiny black town car pulled in seconds later; it drove past the van, executed a turn, and stopped near the van, its front bumper aimed toward the street. Smart. Roussel's man had positioned the car in a way that ensured the fastest possible getaway.

"Good to go," Liam said softly.

"Ditto," D muttered.

"Hold off," Trevor ordered.

They waited. The driver of the van killed the engine. The driver of the town car let the engine idle.

"In position," Sullivan reported.

Trevor raised his weapon. "Go."

They sprang to action, swarming their designated targets like a pack of wolves working in tandem to trap their prey. The ski masks they wore shielded their faces from the cameras affixed over the garage, and Trevor basked in his anonymity as he burst out of the shed and advanced on the driver's side of the van.

He reached it just as the driver opened the door.

"Ne vous déplacez pas," Trevor snapped. *Don't move.*

The man froze as the muzzle of Trevor's SIG jammed into his temple.

Shouts of outrage broke out all around them as Roussel and the others found themselves in similar positions. Sullivan and Reilly had come flying over the tall fence separating the alley from the street and were now yanking Roussel and his man out of the town car. Liam had his weapon trained on the van's passenger, while D had swiftly moved to cover the back doors of the van, which remained closed.

And from above, Ethan watched everything go down, his amused chuckle rippling over the comm.

"Nicely done," the rookie remarked, sounding slightly surprised.

Trevor was surprised himself. Not a single shot had been fired. He and the others had efficiently neutralized their targets before the bastards even knew what was happening.

Over by the town car, Claude Roussel was red-faced and fuming. Although his harsh French curses marred the air, the man didn't make a move against Sullivan, whose assault rifle was trained right between Roussel's eyes.

But while the Frenchman was smart enough not to charge the person holding a gun on him, he still felt the need to demand, "What is this? Who are you and what do you want?"

"Just here to inspect your wares," Trevor said mockingly.

He'd answered in French, but clearly his accent left something to be desired, because Roussel's mouth curled in a sneer.

"Américain!" the Frenchman spat out.

Trevor dismissed Roussel from his mind and glanced at D. "Open it," he said.

With a nod, D yanked on the door handle.

Tormented wails and muffled sobs cut the night air. Trevor couldn't see the back of the van, but he heard D's harsh command for silence. It went unheeded, the female cries getting louder.

"Japanese," D announced.

There was a loud thump, and the van began to rock slightly.

"Jesus Christ!" D snapped. "Motherfucker head-butted me. Morgan, if that's you I swear to God I'm gonna—"

D stopped abruptly, and just like that, Trevor's heart sank to the pit of his stomach.

Shit.

The silence could only mean one thing.

"Get out," Trevor told the van's driver.

The man's lips tightened and his eyes flashed with fury,

but he followed instructions. His boots landed on the pavement with a thud.

Trevor gestured with his gun. "Walk."

As he followed the driver around the van, he continued to cling to hope, but D's imperceptible shake of the head was all the answer he needed.

Swallowing a frustrated groan, Trevor peered into the shadowy space and took a good look at the male hostage Tomas Meiro had been so eager to get his hands on.

Tall and built, just like Morgan, but that was where the similarities ended.

The man in the van had a scarred face, salt-and-pepper hair, black eyes—and he was clearly Japanese.

"Shit," Trevor muttered.

No sooner had the word left his mouth than the garage door behind him came to life with a mechanical whir.

And then all hell broke loose.

Chapter 19

Pain jolted through Trevor's left cheek as the driver's meaty fist connected with it. The hostage had taken advantage of the distraction caused by the opening garage door. So had Roussel, whose hand snapped to the gun on his hip the second Sullivan's head turned.

A gunshot exploded in the night, and then Sullivan went down with a hearty thump.

Down but not out—the Australian was squeezing the trigger even as he fell to the ground, sending a spray of bullets into the center of Claude Roussel's chest before the man could take another shot.

Shrill screams pierced the darkness. The captive females dove out of the van, several of them still wearing the hoods. The ones able to see crawled away from the van, screaming as three armed men burst out of the garage, guns blazing.

Trevor dove for cover, taking the driver with him.

Metallic dings echoed overhead as bullets struck the side of the van. The man who'd clipped Trevor in the face tried to crawl toward the driver's-side door. As something hot whizzed past Trevor's ear, he slammed the butt of his gun into the back of the driver's skull, and the man went limp.

Diving forward, Trevor repositioned himself at the front of the van and returned fire just as one of the men who'd emerged from the garage rounded the vehicle, machine gun in hand.

Before Trevor could shoot, a hole appeared in his enemy's forehead.

The report of a rifle echoed from the rooftops. Once, twice, three times, and then the only men left standing were Trevor and his teammates.

Footsteps sounded from the street in the distance. Car doors slammed, engines roared to life, and tires screeched as the patrons visiting the Sapphire Room escaped like rats abandoning a sinking ship.

Stepping over the unconscious body of the driver, Trevor ran to his fallen comrade's side. "Sully, you good?"

Sullivan was flat on his back, palm slapped against his neck to apply pressure to a wound that was oozing blood. "Peachy," the man replied in a careless tone. "I took it in the vest."

Liam appeared and helped the blond Australian to his feet. "And the blood pouring out of your neck? Did the vest get that too?"

Sullivan moved his hand from his neck and replaced it with the sleeve of his black shirt. "Just a graze, mates." His gray eyes landed on Roussel, whose lifeless body was sprawled next to the town car. "That bloody asshole nearly blew my head off."

The howl of sirens could suddenly be heard.

"Fuck," Trevor muttered. "We've gotta get out of here."

From his position by the garage, D cocked his head in the direction of the whimpering Asian girls lying on the pavement. Miraculously, none of the women had been hit during the gunfight. Same went for the man who wasn't Morgan—he was sprawled at D's feet, mumbling wildly into his gag. In Japanese.

Unfortunately, French and Spanish made up the extent of Trevor's language repertoire. D, however, surprised them all by yanking off the captive's gag and addressing him in perfect Japanese.

The sirens got closer.

"D, we've gotta go," Trevor called urgently. "It's not Morgan. That's all we need to know."

"Go," D called back. "I'll be there in a second."

Trevor touched his earpiece and said, "Hey, our hero, you there?"

Ethan, who'd proven himself as skilled a sniper as Luke, chuckled. "I'm here."

"Fly back to the nest."

"Yes, sir."

Trevor glanced around at the bodies strewn on the ground. The driver of the van wasn't dead, only unconscious; he should have a fun time explaining all this to the law enforcement officers who'd be arriving any second.

Guilt washed over him as his gaze landed on the women who'd been transported here from the docks. They must have traveled a long way, judging by their bedraggled appearances.

Every instinct in Trevor's body screamed to go and untie them, to hold each one in his arms and offer words of comfort, but he and his team couldn't afford to be here when the police showed up. The girls would be well taken care of once that happened, and maybe they could even aid law enforcement in shutting down Meiro's sex trafficking network once and for all.

Beside him, Liam seemed equally reluctant to leave the girls. Trevor could see only the man's blue eyes through the ski mask, but that soft expression said it all.

Trevor clapped a hand on Liam's shoulder. "They're safe now. We, on the other hand, are not."

With a nod, Liam tore his gaze away. "I know. We should get the hell outta here."

Fortunately, D's exchange with the hostage had wrapped up. The injured man was now attempting to stand up, but the task proved difficult thanks to his broken leg, which jutted out at a grotesque angle.

It was a miracle the man was able to move at all. As he fell to the ground, he gazed imploringly at D and a stream of hurried words left his mouth.

Trevor didn't need a translator to know that the man was begging for assistance.

"Let's go," D said curtly. He turned away from the pleading man and strode toward the others.

Five minutes later, Trevor, D, and Sullivan were in the sedan peeling away from the brownstone. In the rearview mirror, Trevor caught a glimpse of red and blue lights, and then half a dozen police cruisers and two ambulances sped into view.

Removing his ski mask, he stepped on the gas and put distance between them and the approaching cavalry. Liam and Reilly had taken the taxi and would find their own way back, as would Ethan.

"So what did the Asian have to say for himself?" Sullivan demanded from the backseat.

Sully's sleeve was still pressed to his neck, and since his shirt was black, Trevor couldn't be sure how much blood the Australian had lost. It was hard to tell with Sullivan—the dude could be out five pints and still be functioning properly.

"His name is Takashi Fujiwara," D answered. "He and his girlfriend used to run one of the Tokyo brothels where Meiro ships his kidnapped tourists. Fujiwara screwed Meiro and Hiroshi Tachikawa, the crime boss who handles the Tokyo side of the operation—Meiro sends Tachikawa the blue-eyed blondes, and Tachikawa ships Japanese girls to Meiro's European brothels."

"So Fujiwara and his girl were stealing from Meiro and Tachikawa?"

D nodded. "They stole a shit ton of dough, and sometimes they would arrange for the private sale of certain girls. They'd tell Tachikawa that the women died of a drug overdose, or a customer's beating, or whatever, but really they were reselling them. Fujiwara and the girlfriend fled Tokyo after they got caught. They've been hiding out for the past year." D paused meaningfully. "One of their hideouts was in Munich."

Trevor got the message. So Noelle had nothing to do with any of this.

Hell, maybe Morgan didn't either.

"What the fuck!" Sullivan burst out, voicing Trevor's thoughts. "We show up tonight looking to save Morgan's ass, and we unintentionally thwart a human trafficking deal? Where the bloody hell is he?"

"Good question," Trevor said grimly.

D sounded just as frustrated. "We know that Meiro hired Eddie Lassiter to assemble a team to hit the compound."

"Do we?" Sullivan countered. "We know Meiro hired Lassiter to do *something*. That's it, mate."

Trevor stopped at a red light and let out a breath. This entire night had been one long roller-coaster ride. From the mind-blowing sex with Isabel, to the emotional confrontation that followed, to this rescue attempt gone awry, to Morgan's continued absence.

They'd put all their eggs in this goddamn Lassiter basket, banking on the fact that Meiro had to be responsible for Morgan's disappearance because he'd dealt with Lassiter, but who the hell knew anymore?

In fact, the only real piece of knowledge Trevor possessed at the moment was that they were right back to where they'd started.

Square fucking one.

It was just after one in the morning. Meiro wasn't up in his penthouse sleeping, but on the security floor watching his casino with the vigilant eye of a guard dog. To his great disappointment, the lovely Valerie had remained in her suite all night. He longed to see her, even if it was a fleeting glimpse on a security camera.

Their evening on the *Splendid Lady* had been a rewarding one. He knew the woman desired him—her fervent response to his kiss proved it. And when she'd pushed him away afterward, his annoyance had been rivaled by genuine pleasure. It had been a long time since he'd had to pursue a woman this diligently. Nowadays, women flocked to him wherever he went. Not only was he a wealthy man, but he was also a handsome one, a guarantee that he would never be lacking for female attention.

Valerie's resistance excited him. Aroused him. He was determined to win over the exquisite redhead, with her fiery nature and sparkling green eyes.

Make no mistake, his sweet Valerie would not be leaving his city without first gracing his bed.

Meiro's phone buzzed in his pocket, interrupting his thoughts. Good. Roussel had finally decided to check in.

But the number on the display did not belong to Claude. It was unfamiliar, raising Meiro's hackles.

"Who is this?" he said in lieu of a greeting.

"This is Serena, Mr. Meiro. I apologize for the late hour, but I'm afraid it can't be helped."

Meiro stalked toward the door. In the hall, he waved at his bodyguards to give him some privacy. They moved to the end of the corridor like obedient dogs.

"What happened?" he demanded. He'd heard the note of weariness in the madam's voice, which told him something had gone wrong tonight. "Where is Claude?"

"I don't know. Dead, I assume."

The woman conveyed no emotion. He hadn't expected her to. The years had hardened Serena Theroux—indifference and detachment were common traits among whores.

As Serena informed him of the ambush that had occurred behind the Sapphire Room, Meiro became incensed. "Who were they?" he snapped. "Were they caught on the security cameras?"

"Yes, but they wore masks. And I didn't linger in hopes of seeing their faces. All the guests made it out before the police arrived, as did I, but most of the girls weren't so lucky. Felipe informs me there were many arrests."

Meiro muttered a furious expletive. "Where are you now?"

"The safe house, with three of the girls."

"Stay there. I'll call you back."

Meiro hung up, but before he could dial another number, the elevator at the end of the hall dinged and the doors opened to reveal his wife.

"Renee!" he said in surprise, swiftly tamping down the irritation he'd experienced at the sight of her.

Renee Meiro, née Beaumont, crossed the long hallway with a masculine stride. She wore a fitted black dress that brought out the severity of her face. Her features were too long, too angular, and her mousy brown hair was pulled into a tight bun, drawing not so welcome attention to her too high forehead.

The woman held no appeal, at least not to her husband, but Meiro still greeted his wife with a polite smile and a kiss to her pockmarked cheek.

"What brings you to the Palace, *mon amour*?"

"You were not answering your phone," she said coolly.

Meiro frowned. "I didn't receive any calls from you tonight."

"You did," she insisted. "I phoned several times."

An edge crept into his voice. "I didn't receive any calls from you, Renee."

She reached into her oversize Chanel bag and fished out her phone. She pressed a few keys and handed it to him.

Sure enough, his wife had dialed his number four times tonight.

The number he no longer used.

"I told you to update your contact list, *mon amour*," he said in annoyance. "I had the number changed last month after I misplaced my phone in Venice, don't you remember?"

It suddenly occurred to him what that meant—he and his wife hadn't spoken in nearly a month. How time flew.

"Right. Right," Renee said with a brisk nod. "That was my error, Tomas. Forgive me."

"Always."

Smiling, he leaned in and kissed her cheek again. This time, they both visibly winced, but pretenses had to be maintained. After all, they had the eyes of two sets of bodyguards on them.

"Now, what brings you here?" he asked for the second time.

"The MONA gala is tomorrow evening. I came to remind you of that."

"At such a late hour?"

Renee's face was devoid of expression. "I was out with a friend. The Palace is on the way home, so I instructed the driver to stop."

Meiro resisted a laugh. His wife's secrecy about her lover was almost comical, especially since he'd already known the truth about the woman before he'd married her. Yet Renee still refused to speak of her sexual preferences.

"And how was your friend?" He couldn't help but ask, his tone slightly mocking.

Her brown eyes narrowed. "My friend is quite well, Tomas. How is *your* new companion?"

He lifted an eyebrow.

"The redheaded Brit you've been spending time with," Renee clarified. She offered a soft chuckle. "You have exquisite taste, Tomas."

"As do you." He grinned, a rare occurrence in his wife's presence.

Renee rolled her eyes before lowering her voice. "Now, I know you're enjoying yourself with her, but tomorrow night I will need my husband by my side. I've assured the museum director that we will both be in attendance."

"And so we will."

"Good. We'll finalize the details in the morning." She held out her hand. "Will my husband escort me out to the car?"

"Of course." He linked his arm through hers and promptly led her to the elevator.

"How goes the hunt?" His wife's pointed inquiry made his shoulders go rigid.

Meiro shot a discreet look at the bodyguards standing behind them, then gave Renee a slight shake of the head. "Still hasn't borne fruit," he muttered.

"Pity." She squeezed his arm in an unexpected gesture of support. "You will have your vengeance soon, *mon chéri*."

Renee's words continued to echo in his head as he watched her car and driver whisk her away.

Vengeance.

Oh, how he longed for that. But Lassiter's fuckup had cost him. It was a setback that gnawed at his insides, infuriated him beyond belief.

Finding Takashi Fujiwara had been a pleasant stroke of good fortune, but now even that had blown up in his face.

Roussel, his best fucking soldier, was most likely dead, and who knew what had befallen Fujiwara? Dead as well? Or was he in police custody along with the Sapphire whores?

Meiro's entire body vibrated with anger. Soon. He'd have his vengeance soon enough.

First things first. He needed to clean up tonight's mess and find the assholes who'd ambushed his goddamn whorehouse.

It was six in the morning and spirits were so low one would think a national icon had just died. Isabel had managed to sneak out of the Palace by joining an early-morning yoga class at the hotel fitness center and then ducking out halfway through the session. Now, she was with the others gathered in Noelle's suite at the White Sands, feeling as discouraged as everyone else.

"So the man Meiro has been hunting this past year is a Japanese brothel owner who robbed him?" Juliet said in disbelief.

"That's what it looks like," Trevor answered.

"But that doesn't mean Meiro's not the one who ordered the attack on our compound," Ethan spoke up.

Decked out in black leather pants and a bloodred tank top, Noelle sauntered to the wet bar. She tossed Ethan a look as she walked past him. "I'm with the kid on this. My gut says Meiro hired Lassiter to assemble that merc team."

After seven years of knowing Noelle, Isabel had the utmost faith in the woman's instincts. "So what now?" she asked. "Should Valerie make another move?"

From the corner of her eye, she saw Trevor's broad shoulders tense. He hadn't said much since she'd arrived at the suite, and she was grateful for that. She was still upset about the conversation they'd had in the bedroom last night. Pissed, even. For a man who demanded nothing but honesty from her, he'd been keeping a huge secret by not telling her he'd gone to see her father in prison. How could he have dug into her past like that? It made her mad just thinking about it—if any other man had done that, she would have ripped into him for overstepping his boundaries.

And yet as angry as she was that he'd kept the visit a secret, it still didn't come close to eclipsing the genuine feelings she had for him. But what did those feelings mean? Did she love him?

The answer continued to elude her. All she knew was that the notion of losing Trevor made her heart feel like someone had sliced it to ribbons with a sharp blade.

Could she do what he'd asked, though? Let him in fully? Trust that he would always be there for her, no matter what?

But how could she trust someone who'd pried into her past without telling her? Someone who was a wreck every time she went undercover?

More questions she didn't have the answers for, but at the moment she couldn't dwell on her personal life. This job had encountered yet another dead end, and her only priority right now was figuring out what had happened to Morgan.

"Yes, we need to dig deeper, find out why Meiro hired Lassiter."

Noelle's response snapped Isabel back to reality.

"Valerie definitely needs to turn up the heat," Noelle added. "Call him in a few hours and tell him you want to see him again, but not in public—he's a married man, after all. Invite yourself to his penthouse and see what you can find there."

Isabel nodded. "And if I don't discover anything we can use?"

"Then we'll employ alternative methods to pry the information out of Meiro." Shrugging, Noelle glanced at D. "I assume you're capable of handling that?"

To Isabel's surprise, Derek "D" Pratt grinned.

And boy, that one little grin transformed his entire face. Made him look sexier, warmer, approachable.

Lord, why didn't he smile more often?

She quickly posed another question to herself—did she *really* want to know what had placed that perpetual scowl on D's face?

Probably not.

"I've picked up a few techniques over the years," D said with a shrug of his own.

"I imagine so," Noelle said drily. "Anyway, I'm tired of this shit. Tomorrow we find out once and for all what Tomas Meiro is up to—"

A knock on the door interrupted her.

Every person in the room stiffened.

"Expecting anyone?" Trevor asked Noelle in a low voice.

The blonde slowly shook her head. In her manicured hand, she held a nine-millimeter equipped with a suppressor. Isabel hadn't even seen Noelle grab the weapon, but the gun must have been hidden behind the liquor bottles on the wet bar.

A beeping noise echoed from the front hallway of the suite. The distinct sound of a keycard being swiped.

As the door opened with a faint creak, every gun in the room whipped up.

The guns didn't stay raised for long, but the tension in the air only spiked when the mystery guest strolled into the suite like he owned the place.

It was Jim Morgan.

Chapter 20

Stunned silence fell over the suite. Everyone gaped at Morgan, who looked as healthy as a horse and completely indifferent to the shocked expressions aimed his way.

He dropped a heavy duffel bag on the carpet and ran a hand through his close-cropped dark hair. His midnight blue eyes, always so intense, swept over the room. His chiseled features hardened at the sight of Noelle, the lines around his mouth becoming more pronounced as he locked gazes with the blonde.

After a beat, he cut off the eye contact and turned to Trevor. "What the fuck happened, Callaghan?"

Trevor didn't answer.

Isabel could feel the anger radiating from his tall frame. She was kind of glad he was standing in front of her, because she was fearful of what she'd see in his eyes. Nope, Trevor was not a happy camper. His body language screamed *pissed off* and Isabel got the feeling she was about to witness something monumental—Trevor Callaghan losing his cool.

Sure enough, the explosion came fast and hard.

"You son of a bitch!"

Trevor lunged at his boss and slammed the other man against the wall. The cheap oil painting hanging there toppled to the floor, only to be kicked away by Trevor, whose rage spiked the temperature in the suite.

"Where the *fuck* have you been?"

With one hand bunching up the collar of Morgan's T-shirt, Trevor drew his arm back and sent his fist flying into the other man's jaw.

The sickening crack made Isabel flinch, but Morgan didn't so much as blink. Nor did he strike back. Blood erupted from the corner of his mouth and trickled down his chin, but those blue eyes stayed locked with Trevor's.

"You done?" Morgan said coolly.

Breathing hard, Trevor released him and stumbled backward. His head turned slightly, offering Isabel a glimpse of the fire burning in his eyes, the sheer frustration and overpowering rage.

"We've been calling you for days," Trevor spat out. "And now you stroll in here like you have no fucking care in the world? Why the *fuck* didn't you call back?"

Morgan used the sleeve of his navy blue button-down to mop up the blood pouring out of his lip.

"My phone's at the bottom of a cliff," the man said tightly. "By the time I made it back to civilization and got my hands on a new one, I figured it would just be easier to do this in person."

" 'This'?" Trevor said warily.

"The briefing." Morgan's gaze strayed to Noelle again before returning to Trevor. "What happened to my compound?"

"What happened in D.C.?" D joined the conversation, moving away from the terrace door and approaching Morgan with predatory strides.

Ethan, Sullivan, and Liam trailed after the tattooed mercenary, each one displaying serious aggression. None of the men were pleased with their boss, that much was obvious.

Isabel didn't blame them. Morgan had been alive and well this entire time, and couldn't be bothered to contact his team?

"Why did you bail on your meeting?" Trevor asked when Morgan didn't respond to D's question.

"Something came up."

Isabel wasn't surprised by the answer—Jim Morgan excelled at *vague*.

"Something came up?" Trevor echoed. "That's it?"

"I had something to take care of. I went dark, lost comm, and made contact the first opportunity I had. End of story."

"Are you fucking kidding me? Lloyd and Hank are *dead*. Holden lost his *wife*. Kane's freaking the fuck out trying to set up a new base and coordinate with Castle, who nearly had his head blown off by the hostage you ordered him to rescue."

Morgan frowned. "The extraction went south?"

"The extraction is the least of our fucking concerns," Trevor snapped. "Someone sent a hit squad to kill every man on the compound and instead of being here with us, you've been off doing who the fuck knows what and can't be bothered to check your fucking messages."

Isabel placed a gentle hand on Trevor's arm, feeling him vibrating with anger. His breathing was ragged again, his whiskey eyes glittering with such resentment she feared he might actually say something he'd regret.

"Trev," she murmured. "It's done. He's back. Let it go."

His shoulders sagged, a slight sign of surrender, but his expression continued to burn as he glowered at his boss.

The tension in the room was so thick you could cut it with a knife. The rest of Morgan's men were clearly with Trevor on this—bitter, pissed, and confused. At the bar, Noelle stood in silence with Juliet by her side.

"I'm sorry I was out of touch," Morgan finally said. Remorse filled his eyes. "Where's Holden?"

"Home. Grieving for his wife," Trevor said coldly.

Morgan's blue eyes moved from one man to the next, settled on Isabel for a second, Juliet for another, and avoided Noelle altogether. Eventually his gaze found its way back to Trevor, who looked considerably calmer.

"Look, we can all agree I'm a bastard," Morgan said gruffly. "I can't talk about where I was or why I was there, not because I'm being a dick but because I'm trying to protect my team."

More blood dripped from the corner of his mouth. He wiped it away and gave Trevor a warning look. "That was a freebie, Callaghan. I let it happen because you needed to do it and I deserved it. But you ever lay a hand on me again, and I'll kick your fucking ass."

Trevor cocked a brow. "Even if you have it coming again?"

"Even then." Morgan glanced at Noelle, a mocking glint lighting his blue eyes. "I'm sure you've had a real fun time ordering my men around, but the party's over, baby. I'm the one calling the shots now."

D wasn't at all surprised when Morgan asked for a private word on the terrace a few hours later.

As the two men stepped outside, Morgan closed the sliding door before heading for the railing. He shoved a Camel in the corner of his mouth and lit up, causing D to raise his brows.

"You're smoking again?"

The sun was shining in the clear blue sky, all signs of yesterday's storm clouds gone. Morgan shoved a pair of Aviators on his nose, took a drag of his cigarette, and shrugged. "I've had a shitty week. The nicotine's kept me sane."

"We've all had a shitty week," D retorted. "So forgive me if I don't feel much sympathy for you."

Morgan's blue eyes narrowed. "You're angry."

"Damn right I am."

The boss rested his forearms on the railing and cocked his head at D. "Huh. So you haven't enjoyed the reunion?"

D tensed.

An ironic smile lifted the corners of Morgan's mouth. "Oh, come on, man. You honestly think I don't know what every soldier on my team is doing?" He offered a knowing glance. "Or *who* they're doing?"

D tried not to show that he'd been caught off guard, but

inside, he was more rattled than he'd ever been. "You know about Noelle," he said evenly.

Morgan dragged a hand over his buzz cut. "Of course I know."

"Yet you haven't said a word until now."

"I didn't see the point. You're a big boy. You can make your own decisions—and your own mistakes. But fuck, man, getting involved with that woman? Big mistake. She's a ruthless bitch who'll turn on you in the blink of an eye."

D had to chuckle. "Yeah, and who made her that way?"

The boss looked taken aback. There was a beat of silence, and then Morgan spoke, his tone sharper than the blade of D's favorite hunting knife.

"She told you?"

"She didn't have to." D smiled, but without an ounce of humor. "You're not the only one who's aware of what everyone else is up to. I still have sources."

Morgan's blue eyes turned to ice. "How much do you know?"

"Enough."

The boss stalked to the table to put out his smoke. "So what now?"

"Now we find out why Tomas Meiro hired a hit squad to attack us."

"That's it? Business as usual?" Morgan sounded skeptical.

"Don't worry, Jim. Everything I know . . . it stays between us." D shrugged. "For now, anyway."

They both turned at the sound of the door sliding open.

"Don't mean to interrupt," Isabel said lightly. "But Meiro just called me back."

They quickly followed her inside. D knew she'd left a message for Meiro after Morgan's arrival, but the casino owner had taken his sweet-ass time calling back.

Granted, the man had a lot on his plate, what with the interception of his whore delivery. He'd also taken a hit with the loss of Roussel, his right-hand man. Dude couldn't be happy about that.

In the living room, Sullivan's big body was sprawled on one of the couches, while Juliet occupied the other. Everyone else was standing, including Noelle, whose expression and body language revealed nothing, but D could sense the waves of hostility rolling off her curvy body.

"Meiro insists he's dying to see Valerie," Isabel said, "but he has other plans tonight. He's taking his wife to a charity gala at the Museum of Natural Artifacts."

Sean Reilly, who'd stuck around since last night's excursion to the Sapphire Room, spoke up in his Irish brogue. "Oh, the annual MONA gala is fancy-pants to the extreme. All the big players in Monaco will be there. European elite galore. Last year the event raised over ten million for the renovation of the Fossils Wing."

"Your knowledge of museum fund-raisers is such a turn-on," Juliet said with a grin.

Reilly's green eyes twinkled. "You know it, luv."

"Anyway—" Isabel picked up the conversation. "Unless we want to wait until tomorrow, our best bet is to make a move at the gala."

"We gonna grab Meiro?" D asked, turning to Morgan.

"Sorry to burst your bubble, but the MONA will be more heavily guarded than the bloody Thirty-eighth Parallel," Reilly announced.

"The Thirty-eighth Parallel?" Juliet said drily.

"Yeah, the border between North and South Kor—"

"I know what it is," she interrupted, rolling her eyes. "But who uses *that* as an analogy?"

"I do," Reilly said smugly. "Anyway, the gala will be crawling with guards. There'll be a lot of bigwigs there, including members of the royal family. You'll never be able to crash that party—and if you somehow manage to get in, there's no way you're getting out alive. The Royal Guard will engage at the first hint of danger."

"Getting to him at the casino will be just as tough," Trevor pointed out. "Security there is equally tight."

"He's attending the gala with his wife," Isabel reminded them. "That means he'll most likely pick her up at the West

Egg mansion so they can arrive at the museum in the same car. They have to keep up appearances, after all."

"Which means he'll have to take her home at the end of the night," Trevor said slowly.

Juliet tossed in her two cents. "I say we grab him then. The security on that property is laughable. I've broken in without a single issue the past two nights."

Morgan narrowed his eyes at the brunette. "My men said they were instructed only to conduct surveillance."

"Well, I'm not one of your men, am I?" Juliet replied in a flippant tone.

Morgan turned to frown at Noelle. "If she'd gotten caught, the entire operation would've been compromised."

Noelle met his gaze head-on. "Juliet doesn't get caught."

"Interpol says otherwise," he said coldly.

"I got my hands on her after Interpol. She's better trained now."

Animosity streaked back and forth between them. D found himself oddly fascinated by it. He'd been in Morgan and Noelle's presence only once—last year, when the blonde showed up at the compound. He hadn't seen them together since, but it was clear that nothing had changed between them. The tension in the air was stifling, the intensity of their gazes and the harshness of their tones unmistakable.

Trevor cleared his throat, putting an end to the brusque exchange. "Regardless of when we go after Meiro, we still need eyes inside the museum tonight. Who knows, maybe he's using the event as a cover. He could be meeting with someone, or making another deal about a new hit squad." He glanced at Isabel. "Is there any way to score an invite for Valerie?"

"Even if there was, I'd advise against it. Meiro will be there with his wife. He won't want to be seen with his potential future mistress. I have a feeling that if Valerie did show up, he'd discreetly ask her to leave."

"I might be able to find a way in," Juliet offered. She chewed on her lip for a moment. "But my only suitable alias is the one I used in Lisbon last year, which is where I ran into Meiro at that party. Is it a good or bad thing if he recognizes me?"

"What's the cover?" Morgan asked briskly.

"Italian heiress." Juliet grinned. "Known adulterer."

"We stay away from single women," Noelle said in a no-nonsense tone. "Tonight Meiro plays the part of a loving husband. We don't want to make waves."

D didn't miss the way Morgan's jaw tensed the moment Noelle spoke. The boss was completely aware of every move the assassin made, even when she stood directly behind him.

"So send one of us in," Sullivan suggested. "A single man poses no threat."

"Neither does a married couple," Trevor spoke up.

Isabel quickly voiced her agreement. "Oh, that's good. Julian and Paloma would be all over such a glamorous event. And making a public appearance will help us keep that cover alive." She turned to their respective bosses. "What do you guys think?"

Morgan took a beat before nodding. "I like it."

"Me too," Noelle said, though she didn't look thrilled to be seconding Morgan.

"All right." Trevor's gaze moved back to Isabel. "Looks like it's you and me, then."

Chapter 21

Four hours later, Isabel stepped out of the enormous bathroom of the extravagant suite looking like a new woman. She wore a jet-black wig and dark green contacts. Gone were the pads and makeup that had rounded out her cheeks; her face was now angular, her complexion bronze to reflect Paloma Dominguez-Martin's Brazilian roots.

Paloma's husband was equally transformed. Hair slicked back with gel, left ear adorned with a diamond stud, and an expensive tux hugging his impressive body.

"Love the earring," Isabel remarked as she approached him on four-inch heels.

Trevor flashed the arrogant grin that was Julian Martin's trademark. "Thank you, baby."

The endearment was also a Julian thing, yet it still sent a tiny thrill through her. She had to admonish herself for reacting to him—she was supposed to be mad at him, damn it.

"By the way, you look good enough to eat," he added.

The gold Versace gown she'd chosen to wear to the gala offered a plunging neckline, and she didn't miss the way Trevor's eyes smoldered as he admired her chest.

Stepping closer, she tilted her head back and met his appreciative gaze with a lick of her lips. "Then eat me, *meu amor*," she drawled in her Paloma accent. Impulsively, she cupped his cock over his pants and gave it a squeeze. "I'm feeling hungry myself."

Desire flared in Trevor's eyes. "Don't start anything you can't finish, Iz."

"Hey, that wasn't Isabel. It was Paloma."

He dipped his head and brought his lips right up to her ear. "Bull. Shit. That was all Isabel."

Then he thrust his growing erection into her palm, a bold challenge that unleashed a flurry of shivers inside her.

She abruptly moved her hand. "We should go."

His answering sigh was laced with weariness. "You always feel the need to hide yourself from me, to hide behind your characters, don't you?"

"And you always feel the need to psychoanalyze me." She scowled at him. "Or to go behind my back and visit my father in prison."

Regret flickered in his eyes. "I'm sorry. I apologized last night, and I'm apologizing again now, but I didn't go to Sing Sing out of pure nosiness. I was *worried* about you, Iz. You know, because you fell off the face of the earth for five months?" He shot her a pointed stare.

She experienced her own twinge of regret. "And I apologized for that too."

"Good. So we've both apologized. Maybe now we can finish the conversation we started last night, about how you're planning on walking away from me when this job is over."

Damn. She should've known he wouldn't let it go.

Trevor noticed her expression and responded with a stern look. "You're not walking away, sweetheart. We're good together, and you know it."

"How am I good for you?" she blurted out. "Damn it, Trev, I'm the last woman you should want to be with. I don't have a normal job. I can't cook. I'm essentially homeless now that I sold my apartment. I'm a loner, so I can't even bring a great group of friends to the table, unless you count female assassins. Half the time I don't remember what I actually look like. I'm—"

"Listing your flaws isn't going to scare me off," he interrupted. "Believe me, I've got a list of my own."

She opened her mouth to protest, but he kept speaking. "We'll talk about the future once this Meiro business is settled. Right now we need to concentrate on the present."

Even though the inevitable was only being postponed, relief still washed over her.

"You're right." She grabbed her gold Chanel clutch from the table next to the couch. "The gala awaits us."

Twenty minutes later, Julian and Paloma Martin strolled through the arched entryway of the MONA to attend the city's most prestigious charity benefit. The museum lobby was spectacular. Vaulted ceilings soared above them, and a gleaming mahogany floor stretched beneath their feet. The corridors to their left were roped off, but the entrance to the Earth Sciences Wing bustled with activity. The gala was being held in the main room of the cavernous gallery, which housed hundreds of mineral specimens, including some of the world's rarest stones.

Getting in had been no great difficulty. Thanks to a few phone calls to some well-connected associates, the Martins' names were added to the guest list. All they'd had to do was present their IDs at the top of the massive limestone steps outside the building, and the armed guards manning the entrance had waved them inside.

Since the event was black tie, guests were dressed to the nines. Isabel had never seen so many sparkling jewels and designer gowns.

"Lots of VIPs here," she murmured as she entered the party on Trevor's arm. "Three o'clock—Princess Stephanie of Monaco."

"And her four bodyguards," Trevor murmured back. "Lots of firepower in this room."

Unfortunately, none of that firepower belonged to the Martins. The metal detectors in the lobby made it impossible to bring a weapon into the building, but Isabel didn't expect to need one for a simple surveillance job.

As they ventured deeper into the room, Trevor kept a possessive hand on the small of her back. All around them, the city's well-dressed elite milled about, chatting, laughing, admiring the pieces in the massive glass cases lining the walls. Waiters maneuvered through the crowd with trays of hors d'oeuvres and champagne.

Trevor grabbed two flutes from a passing waiter and handed one to Isabel.

"Cheers, baby." As they clinked glasses, he lowered his voice. "Meiros are here. Eight o'clock."

She shifted her head to the left. Sure enough, Tomas Meiro and his wife were standing near a display of gold specimens.

Meiro looked dashing as always in a crisp black tux, while his wife wore a high-necked black gown that gave her a washed-out look, her tight bun bringing out the harshness of her long features. The woman was truly unimpressive compared to her husband.

As Isabel looked away from the Meiros, she noticed several females in their midst blatantly ogling Trevor.

"You have a fan club," she said before taking a sip of champagne.

"So do you." His tone was flirtatious, but she caught the displeased glint in his eyes. "Every man in this room is drooling over your luscious tits."

With a sassy smile, she came close to her fake husband's side and stroked his arm. "I only have eyes for you, *meu amor*."

Trevor brushed his lips over her cheek. "Come. Let's see what our potential donation will be paying for."

For the next thirty minutes, they mingled. Isabel oohed and aahed over an enormous jade slab from Austria. Trevor chatted with a group of businessmen from Florence. They listened to the MONA director drone on and on about how certain pieces in the museum were in dire need of restoration—therefore, it was imperative that everyone contribute tonight.

The entire time, Isabel kept a close eye on the Meiros.

Tomas and Renee were doing their fair share of mingling, so it wasn't surprising when the two couples eventually crossed paths.

"Look, *meu amor*, a bauble from my homeland," Isabel said in delight as she and Trevor approached a case containing a rare topaz crystal from Brazil.

Trevor laughed. "Bauble? That crystal weighs more than you, baby. But I confess, it is beautiful."

"More beautiful than me?" she teased.

"Impossible. Your beauty is in a league of its own."

A chuckle sounded from behind them. "Ah, finally an American who's mastered the art of flattery."

Tomas Meiro stepped into view, his dark eyes homing in on Isabel's cleavage before fixing on Trevor. "I'm sorry. I didn't mean to interrupt. There aren't many Americans in attendance tonight—I heard you speaking English and was curious about you."

"It's quite all right," Trevor said with an easygoing smile. "You're obviously fluent in English yourself, but I can't place your accent. French?"

Meiro nodded, then looked at Isabel again. "And your accent is clearly Portuguese."

"You have a good ear." She cast that sensual smile she'd perfected over the years. "I come from Brazil."

"What a coincidence—my wife recently visited Rio," Meiro said, gesturing to the woman at his side.

Renee Meiro hadn't yet spoken a word, but her brown eyes had been examining Isabel since the Meiros had joined them. Isabel was slightly unsettled under the woman's scrutiny. It was too intense, and either she was imagining things or Mrs. Meiro was actually checking her out.

"Rio is a lovely city," Renee said in a thick French accent. Something indecipherable flickered across her face as she eyed Isabel. "The people there are quite . . . intriguing."

Isabel's unease continued to grow. Okay. Both Mr. and Mrs. Meiro were staring at her now, each of their expressions impossible to read.

Shit.

Did Meiro recognize her?

"Where are my manners?" Meiro suddenly said. He extended a hand. "We haven't been properly introduced yet. I'm Tomas Meiro, and this is my wife, Renee."

Trevor shook the other man's hand, familiarity dawning on his face. "Tomas Meiro. Are you the Meiro who owns the Crystal Palace Hotel and Casino?"

"One and the same."

"It's an honor to meet you. My wife and I have been hearing wonderful things about your hotel. We typically stay at the White Sands when we visit the city, but we might have to change that on our next visit."

Despite the shrill ringing of her internal alarms, Isabel continued to play her part. "My husband is now the rude one," she teased. "He has forgotten to return the introduction."

Trevor laughed, seemingly oblivious to Isabel's rising apprehension. "Forgive me. I'm Julian. Julian Martin, and this stunning creature by my side is my wife, Paloma."

Meiro's cordial expression didn't change, but Isabel could have sworn the temperature dropped thirty degrees. Her inner warning system went haywire on her.

"It's a pleasure to meet you, Paloma." Meiro reached for her hand, and as he brought it to his lips, an icy shiver skated up her spine.

He recognized her as Valerie.

That was the only explanation for the intensity of his gaze, for the way his eyes never left her face.

Shit.

After a beat, Meiro released her hand. "And what is it that you do, Mr. Martin?"

"Please, call me Julian. And I guess you can say I'm an entrepreneur." Trevor's eyes twinkled. "I own several businesses, but you won't find me sitting behind a desk. I prefer to let other people take care of the everyday details."

"My husband prefers pleasure to business," Isabel said coyly.

Renee spoke up in a bland tone. "I'm afraid my husband is the opposite. All work and no play, right, Tomas?"

Meiro chuckled. "I will not deny it. Business does indeed come first."

When his gaze drifted back to Isabel, she tried not to gulp. Crap. Those were the same words he'd said to Valerie the day they'd discussed the importance of the bottom line.

He knows.

Now Renee was watching her too. "That's a lovely necklace, Paloma. May I?"

Bewilderment joined her anxiety as Meiro's wife reached forward to lift the chunky gold necklace around Isabel's neck. The chain held a square-cut ruby surrounded by a cluster of gold leaves.

As Renee admired the jewel, her French-manicured fingernails lightly ran over Isabel's bare collarbone. "Wherever did you get it?"

"It was a gift from my late papa. An old family heirloom."

The Meiros were staring again.

Isabel lifted her champagne flute to her lips and took a long sip, hoping she was continuing to give off the carefree vibe Paloma usually radiated. But every muscle in her body was coiled tight, and the alarms kept ringing.

Fortunately, the arrival of the museum director put an end to the odd encounter.

"Mr. Meiro!" the man said in delight. *"Nous n'avons pas eu une chance de parler encore."*

"Jean-Paul!" Meiro greeted the director with a hearty handshake before addressing the Martins. "Please excuse us. We will speak again tonight, I'm sure."

Isabel uttered a silent thank-you as the director whisked the Meiros away. The moment the other couple was out of earshot, she turned to Trevor, offered an overly broad smile, and said, "Something's wrong."

"I know," he replied, proving he was an even better actor than she'd thought. He hadn't given a single indication that he'd sensed anything was amiss.

"I think he recognizes me. Did you notice how he couldn't take his eyes off me? And it wasn't in a leering way. He was *staring* at me."

"I saw." Trevor let out a laugh, as if reacting to a joke she'd told. "The wife, on the other hand? Leering."

"I got that same feeling." Isabel took a sip of champagne. "You think she plays for the other team?"

"No doubt. The woman was looking at your breasts like she couldn't wait to get her hands on them."

"She's not the one I'm worried about. Meiro knows it's me."

"I can't see how. You look like a different woman, sweetheart." Trevor's dark eyes swept over her. "The makeup has completely altered your face—your nose looks longer, your jaw is more square, and your eyes even seem like they're a different shape. Not to mention the skin color, the fuller ass, the way you move. You could walk past any member of the team and they'd be fooled."

"Well, Meiro doesn't look fooled." She tried not to bite her lip in worry. "Shit, and now look at them. What do you think they're talking about?"

Meiro and his wife were no longer with the museum director, but standing across the room in deep discussion. To anyone watching, their body language looked relaxed, but Isabel sensed the tension between them. Meiro's smile was a little too tight, and Renee's eyes went cloudy a couple of times.

"I think we might need to abort," Trevor murmured.

"I agree."

As a waiter walked past them, Isabel handed him her empty glass, waving her hand when he offered her another drink.

"Fuck."

Trevor's barely audible curse raised her hackles. She instantly figured out the cause—Renee Meiro was heading their way. Alone.

Isabel swiftly put on her party face, greeting Renee with a beaming smile. "Hello again," she cooed.

Renee's smile was more tentative. "Mr. Martin, I was hoping to steal your wife away for a moment."

Trevor chuckled. "Oh?"

Meiro's wife continued awkwardly. "The museum has acquired a new piece for the Hall of Gems, one I think Paloma will appreciate."

Isabel feigned confusion. "I thought the other galleries were closed for the evening."

"They are, but my late father was one of this museum's biggest donors. Jean-Paul has agreed to let us have a private viewing of the gallery, if you wish it."

Reluctance seized Isabel's chest. She wanted to say no, but couldn't see a way out of it. If Meiro *wasn't* on to her, she didn't want to anger him by insulting his wife. To make matters worse, Renee had stars in her eyes again, damn near confirming their supposition that Meiro's wife was attracted to Isabel.

"Of course she wishes it," Trevor finally said. His tone rang with delight, but the guarded look in his eyes told Isabel he wasn't pleased about this either.

"Wonderful," Renee said. "Come, then, Paloma."

Isabel forced herself not to look at Trevor as she walked away with Renee. She could feel his frustrated gaze boring a hole between her shoulder blades, but there wasn't a damn thing she could do about it, not unless she wanted to offend Renee Meiro and make Tomas even more suspicious.

No big deal. She would simply admire a few jewels, then excuse herself, find Trevor, and get the hell out of this museum.

"You're going to adore this new acquisition," Renee told her as they stepped into the brightly lit lobby.

Renee linked her arm through Isabel's, her two bodyguards following closely behind. Neither man was tall, but they were incredibly bulky, boasting thick arms, barrel chests, and the noticeable bulge of weaponry beneath their suit jackets.

"Have you ever heard of the Lorena Sapphire?" Renee asked.

Isabel shook her head. "I have not."

Their heels clicked on the glossy floor of the spacious

corridor. The Hall of Gems would be around the corner, if the online map Isabel had studied earlier was correct.

"It's one of the most beautiful sapphires in the world," Renee explained. "More than six hundred carats, the most brilliant blue you will ever see."

The turn was coming up, but Renee didn't slow down. Isabel was acutely aware of the two guards walking behind them, but she couldn't angle herself in a way that would allow her to keep an eye on them. Not without arousing suspicion.

Shit. Nothing about this felt right. She needed to find a way out. Now.

As Renee stalked past their destination, Isabel quickly gestured to their left. "Isn't this the gallery we—"

It was just a pinprick.

A little sting to the side of her neck. A beefy hand clapping on her shoulder.

One of the guards had stabbed her with something.

A jolt of panic shot through her, triggering a rush of adrenaline. Isabel spun around, prepared to shove her elbow into the windpipe of the man who'd grabbed her, but whatever he'd pricked her with was fast-acting. Her vision went blurry so fast she couldn't make sense of it, and when she tried to strike out, her arm felt like a lead pipe she couldn't hold up.

She became aware of Renee's annoyed expression, then a grunt from one of the guards, and suddenly the whole world started to spin.

Don't pass out, don't pass out, don't—

Everything went black.

Chapter 22

Trevor knew something was wrong the moment Tomas Meiro strolled up to him looking like the cat who'd swallowed not one but twenty canaries.

"Tomas," he said warmly. "I see your wife has spirited mine away."

"She has indeed." Meiro's smile got impossibly wider. "In fact, I'm afraid the lovely Paloma won't be rejoining you this evening."

Trevor's back went ramrod straight. "Excuse me?"

"You heard me."

Anger rose inside him, growing stronger when he glimpsed the glimmer of satisfaction in Meiro's eyes.

That son of a bitch had done something to Isabel.

The anger turned to rage. Hot, boiling rage that coiled around his insides like a boa constrictor and had him taking a menacing step toward Meiro.

"Uh-uh," the man warned softly. "You don't want to cause a scene, Mr. Martin."

Trevor clenched his teeth. "Where is my wife?"

"Don't worry. You'll join her soon enough." Meiro smiled at a couple that wandered past, gave a careless little wave, and glanced back at Trevor. "Let's go."

He didn't move an inch. Every muscle, every square inch of skin, burned with fury.

Goddamn it. Why had he let Isabel go off with Meiro's wife? He shouldn't have let her out of his sight, for fuck's sake.

Trevor clenched his jaw. "I'm not going anywhere with you."

"Of course you are. You want to reunite with your beautiful wife, do you not?"

Frustration jammed in his throat, making it hard to breathe. Jesus. He couldn't allow himself to lose his cool right now. Isabel's life was at stake.

Damn it. She'd been right. Meiro must have recognized her as Valerie.

Meiro took a step. "Are you coming, Mr. Martin?"

After a second of indecision, Trevor offered a curt nod.

They left the gallery with Meiro's two bodyguards in tow. The casino owner stopped to chat with several people along the way, behaving as if he had not a care in the world.

Trevor, meanwhile, was consumed with worry. Worry and fear and fury, a volatile cocktail that moved like poison in his blood.

"If you harm so much as a hair on her head," Trevor murmured, "I will rip your throat out."

Meiro chuckled. "So melodramatic, Julian. Please, try and relax."

They stepped outside, pausing at the top of the limestone steps. Meiro nodded at one of his guards. "Bring the car."

The evening breeze was chilly, but not as cold as the ice moving through Trevor's body. If he could have done it without causing a scene—or endangering Isabel further—he would have wrapped his hands around Tomas Meiro's throat and squeezed the life out of the bastard.

As it was, he forced himself to remain calm. To smile politely at the guards manning the museum doors. To casually follow Meiro down the steps to the black limo that appeared at the curb.

Meiro's second bodyguard opened the door for Trevor. "Get in," the beefy man said in a monotone voice.

Although his cheeks hollowed in anger, Trevor did as he was told. He slid into the backseat, breathing in the scent of leather and expensive cologne.

Meiro and his bodyguard followed Trevor into the limo. The second the door slammed shut, Meiro's guard had a .45 Beretta aimed at Trevor's head.

"Empty your pockets," Meiro said pleasantly.

Without a word, Trevor emptied the contents of his pockets. Everything was immediately confiscated, including his cell phone, which Meiro handed to the guard.

Less than a minute later, Trevor's phone was sans SIM card, crushed beneath the bodyguard's shoes, and tossed out the window as the limo drove away.

"Pat him down," Meiro ordered.

Trevor gritted his teeth as the bodyguard searched him for weapons. He had none—trying to sneak a gun into the gala would have been suicide, especially with Princess fucking Stephanie in attendance.

"Give me the watch," the guard said woodenly.

Trevor swallowed his frustration. Shit. With his phone gone, his watch was the only chance for the team to find him. It contained a transmitter, along with an SOS button that would raise an alarm to alert the others. As he loosened the heavy silver band and slid the watch off his wrist, he brushed the side of his thumb over that tiny button.

Ten seconds later, his watch met the same fate as his phone, and the limo continued to speed through the city streets. Destination: unknown. But Trevor knew without a shred of doubt this wasn't going to end well.

For anyone.

Across the street from the museum, D sat in the driver's seat of the rented town car and monitored the front entrance. Although the car's windows were heavily tinted, Ethan remained in the backseat so D would be alone up front, giving the illusion that he was a driver waiting for one of the gala guests.

"We've got movement at the service doors." The report

came from Sullivan, who was watching the rear of the building with Macgregor. "Three bodies coming out—two male, one female."

"Shit," Liam said. "Blondie's down."

D touched his earpiece. "What the fuck do you mean, she's down?"

"We're looking at Blackjack's wife"—Liam used the code name they'd assigned Meiro—"and two guards. One's got a package in his arms. Blondie. Unconscious."

"They're getting into a black Bentley." Sullivan rattled off the license plate number.

A flash of movement caught D's eye. "Blackjack just walked out. Julian's with him."

To anyone else, Callaghan's demeanor might appear relaxed, unruffled, but D had worked with the man long enough to pick up on his signals. And right now Trevor was transmitting some serious turbulence.

"Bentley's knocking on your front door," Sullivan said briskly.

Sure enough, the luxury car emerged from the long driveway at the side of the historic building. The driver stopped to let traffic pass, right-turn signal blinking as the car waited.

"Alpha, you copy?" D asked.

Morgan's gruff voice came on the line. "Copy."

"Rookie and I'll take the Bentley."

A limo pulled up at the curb, and the two men at the museum's entrance descended the steps.

"I've got the limo," Morgan replied.

"Orders?" Sullivan's voice.

"Maintain your position. Boston, replace D."

The break in traffic allowed the Bentley to take its turn, and a moment later, D's foot pressed down on the gas pedal and the town car merged smoothly into traffic. He stayed two cars behind, his gaze glued to the Bentley's bumper.

Ethan leaned forward. "What do you think went down?"

"No fucking idea. Maybe Meiro recognized Blondie?"

"Maybe." A pause. "I don't like this."

"Ditto," D muttered.

He grew to hate the situation even more when his cell phone buzzed. So did Ethan's, and the kid let out an expletive as he investigated the cause of commotion.

"Trev triggered his SOS," Ethan reported.

Up ahead, the Bentley took a left turn.

D followed.

His eyes narrowed as he realized where the car was heading. He quickly switched on his earpiece. "They're taking her to the West Egg mansion."

"Limo seems to be going in that direction too." The boss's chuckle echoed over the feed. "Good thing you boys are already familiar with the place."

"Not as familiar as some people," Ethan said darkly.

Now Morgan released a heavy breath. "Right. Someone get Juliet on the line."

Tomas Meiro proved that he wasn't a liar—Trevor was reunited with Isabel less than thirty minutes after they'd been separated at the MONA gala. Only the reunion was not the one he'd envisioned.

"What did you do to her?" Trevor spun around with murder in his eyes.

Meiro lingered in the doorway of the musty cellar, his dark eyes flicking to Isabel, who lay unconscious on the concrete floor. "Don't worry. The drug will wear off soon."

Trevor shifted his gaze from Meiro to the bodyguards flanking their boss. Nobody had bothered to tie him up, and the only reason he hadn't disarmed the bastards and snapped their necks was because he'd needed them to bring him to Isabel.

But now . . . now there was nothing stopping him from killing the bastards.

Meiro must have read his mind, because the man made a *tsk*ing sound and wagged his finger. "One move and my men will put a bullet in your head. They've been ordered to shoot to kill."

"Just like that? You'll kill me before you get whatever it is you want?"

"But that is *precisely* what I want. You, dead." Meiro waved a hand at the floor. "Her too. Make no mistake, you and your wife will die, Mr. Martin. I'd prefer those deaths be of the slow, agonizing variety, but if you force my hand, I'll shoot you down like a dog."

Trevor eyed the pistol in Meiro's hand. He could disarm the bastard in a heartbeat. Spin around, knock the Beretta out of that first guard's hand, then—

"Go ahead and attack," Meiro said pleasantly. "Just know that in those brief moments it takes for you to come after me, my men will have ample time to shoot your wife. Now, I will return shortly. I'm afraid I need to see to *my* wife."

Trailed by his guards, Meiro stalked out of the room. The heavy wooden door slammed shut and a lock scraped into place, shutting Trevor and Isabel inside.

He was at her side in a heartbeat, pulling her unmoving body into his arms and pushing strands of black hair out of her face. His heart pounded as he ran his hands over her body to check for injuries, but she was unharmed. No bruising, no blood, no sign of foul play—except for the red mark on the side of her neck.

They'd injected her with something. Something strong, judging from her pale face and unresponsive pupils.

He drew Isabel into his lap and slid backward until he was sitting against the cinder-block wall. The air in the cellar was damp, the scent of mold and sour grapes permeating it. The wine racks built into the walls were empty, a sign that the Meiros no longer used this room to store their collection of fine vintages. It was completely barren save for a few broken crates leaning on the wall adjacent to the door.

Trevor threaded his fingers through Isabel's hair, his heart in his throat as he gazed at her closed eyelids. Christ, why had he let her go with Renee? They'd both experienced the same sense of unease. They'd *known* something was up with Meiro. Why the hell hadn't he tried harder to keep her by his side?

Guilt clawed at him, making him want to punch the wall. Or himself. Yeah, he ought to be hitting himself. What kind of man allowed the woman he loved to be drugged and abducted from a goddamn museum gala?

What kind of man isn't home to save his fiancée from being murdered by a goddamn burglar?

A wave of agony crashed over him, but he breathed through it. This was different. Isabel wasn't Gina.

Gina was dead, and he hadn't been able to save her.

Isabel was alive. He could feel her heartbeat vibrating against his chest, hear her soft, even breathing. She was *alive*, and there was no goddamn way he was letting her die.

The woman in his arms stirred and let out a soft moan. "Trev?"

Her eyes were out of focus, her movements unsteady as she tried to sit up.

"Easy," he murmured, holding her tighter. "Don't move too fast. You might feel dizzy."

"Dizzy?" She sounded groggy, and her eyelashes fluttered as she blinked repeatedly. "What happened? Why would I—Renee!" Clarity sharpened her eyes. "One of Renee's guards injected me with something."

"I know." He cupped her cheeks and searched her face. "Are you all right? Do you feel nauseous? Light-headed?"

She slowly shook her head. "I just feel tired."

"Follow my finger. Let me see your pupils."

She humored him, and when he was satisfied that she was okay, Trevor pulled her to her feet and the two of them exchanged a grim look.

"He must have recognized me," Isabel said unhappily.

"I don't know. I think it might be something else."

"Like what?"

"I have no fucking idea, but this is about more than you playing Meiro for a fool. This has to do with *both* of us. You and me, Iz. It seems personal."

She glanced around the room. "I assume we're at the mansion?"

"Yeah. Meiro didn't blindfold me. The limo drove right through the gate and we went in through the front door like I was a welcomed houseguest." Trevor held up both his palms. "And they didn't bother tying us up. He's not planning on letting us go. He said so himself—he brought us here to kill us."

A wrinkle dug into her forehead. "He said that?"

Trevor nodded.

"Why? And does he want *us* dead? As in, the real us?"

"I don't know. He keeps calling me Mr. Martin."

"So it's Julian and Paloma he wants to eliminate. But why?" she asked again.

Neither of them had an answer for that. Nor did they have time to continue the discussion, because the door swung open and Meiro reentered the room.

His dark eyes gleamed in approval when he saw Isabel awake and on her feet. "Good, you've returned to us. I was eager to get started."

One of Meiro's guards entered, with a sturdy wooden chair in his hands. He set it down, walked out, and came back with a second chair.

"Sit," Meiro ordered.

When neither of them moved, the guard cocked his Beretta.

They sat.

Meiro smoothed out the front of his tuxedo jacket, then rubbed his chin in a thoughtful pose. "So. Julian and Paloma. I can't decide if I'm insulted or pleased that you don't recognize me."

Trevor shot Isabel a sidelong look, but her baffled expression matched his own.

"Still confused, are we?" Meiro's dark brown eyes flashed with irritation. "Let me spell it out for you then." He took a step closer. "The two of you took something very important from me."

The accusation just mystified Trevor further. He and

Isabel had gone undercover as Julian and Paloma only once before, and that was over a year ago. They'd infiltrated Luis Blanco's compound and freed a dozen captive girls before Blanco could sell them to the highest bidders.

But Blanco had been killed during the ambush. And thanks to Kane and Abby, Blanco's second-in-command, Devlin, was dead too.

So how the hell was Meiro connected to that mission? Was he one of the bidders who'd gotten away?

Trevor pondered the thought. No, Meiro wouldn't have had the money or the power to procure an invitation to Blanco's sex auction. He'd only appeared on the scene recently, so—

Trevor's breath hitched.

"Ah, perhaps you do know who I am." Meiro met Trevor's gaze. "I'm Lorenzo Blanco, you motherfucker. You and this cunt killed my father."

Chapter 23

Isabel stared at the enraged man standing before them. Lorenzo Blanco? How was that even possible? She remembered hearing that Luis Blanco had a son studying abroad, but Lorenzo hadn't stepped up to run his father's empire after Blanco was killed during the auction raid. Blanco's dossier hadn't contained a single photograph of his son, so for all Isabel knew, this *was* Lorenzo.

But if so, why the hell was he pretending to be a casino owner named Tomas Meiro?

"You *do* remember my father, do you not?" Meiro—Lorenzo?—asked coldly. "And please don't insult my intelligence by claiming otherwise. I would recognize your face anywhere, Mr. Martin. I've watched the security tape hundreds, no, *thousands* of times."

"Security tape?" Trevor echoed.

"My father's cameras captured everything. You and your cunt wife posed as interested buyers. You abused my father's hospitality. You stole his merchandise. And you"—he jabbed a finger at Trevor—"murdered him in cold blood. It's all on tape, every last second of it, motherfucker."

"I see," Trevor said evasively.

He didn't sound surprised, and neither was Isabel. They'd known about the security cameras in Blanco's compound, but it hadn't been an issue. It didn't matter if Julian and

Paloma got caught on tape—because Julian and Paloma didn't exist.

"Do you?" Lorenzo mocked. "Do you *see*?" His breathing grew heavy. "You feel no remorse for what you have done? For the life you took?"

"Your father took lives, too. He sold young girls like they were sex toys." Trevor's tone was pointed. "Did *he* show any remorse?"

"My father was a businessman," Lorenzo snapped. "He ran an empire, and then you two came along and destroyed it. I've yet to figure out what your motive was, but believe me, I intend to. And I intend to punish you fittingly. You *destroyed* my legacy."

Isabel scanned her brain, trying to remember the events that followed Luis Blanco's death. "His rivals came out of the woodwork," she said slowly. "They broke up his holdings."

Lorenzo's eyes flashed. "They stole my empire."

From the corner of her eye, she saw Trevor roll his eyes. "You expect us to believe that your father didn't make arrangements for his only son to be taken care of? How many millions did he stash away for you, Lorenzo?"

"Money means nothing if you don't have power," Lorenzo said bitterly. "The vultures robbed me of that power, but they didn't stop there. They knew I would return one day to reclaim my father's legacy, so they came after me. They tried to eliminate me." Triumph rang in his voice. "But they failed. They failed, and I lived to see another day."

Isabel wrinkled her forehead. "So you changed your name and moved to Lisbon?"

The second the question left her mouth, she realized there was no point in asking it. Lisbon. Damn it, *that's* what had bothered her the night on Meiro's yacht.

Because if the man had truly grown up in Lisbon, then he would have known that the Collectors Wing at Lisbon's most renowned museum had been opened only four years ago. He'd slipped up. Claimed he'd visited the wing as a child—but that was impossible. There had been no Collectors Wing when he was growing up.

Shit, how could she have forgotten that?

"I created a new life for myself," he muttered angrily. "I contacted Michel Beaumont, one of my father's associates, the only one who could be trusted. Beaumont helped me start over."

Lorenzo stepped closer and squatted in front of Isabel. An evil gleam filled his eyes. "I tried to bury the past, but alas, I'm not the kind of man who allows slights against him to go unpunished."

Isabel licked her dry lips and shifted on the chair. It would take no effort at all to go on the attack, kick him square in the face, slice her elbow into his temple, but the presence of those armed guards stopped her from making a move. That, and the quick shake of the head Trevor gave her when he saw her readjust her position.

"I've been searching for you and your husband for a very long time," Lorenzo said in a soft voice. "But you went underground like a pair of fucking rats." His eyes gleamed again, satisfied. "But four months ago, you finally surfaced. Or rather, *he* did."

Lorenzo jerked his head in Trevor's direction, but continued speaking before Isabel could make sense of his last remark. "I'm going to enjoy watching you die. I'm going to enjoy it very, very much. Originally I did not want to risk being connected to your deaths, but—"

"But Lassiter fucked everything up for you?" Isabel finished politely.

"I shouldn't have trusted that incompetent fool to get the job done." He looked at Trevor, shrugging. "But I confess, I'm happy to see you survived the attack on your company's training facility, Mr. Martin."

Isabel hid her confusion. Trevor's company? Did Lorenzo not realize he'd sent a hit squad to raid a mercenary compound?

"Because now I have the pleasure of your wife's company as well," Lorenzo went on. "Killing you separately would have achieved the same end result, but this will be more entertaining. I'm going to enjoy hearing you beg me to spare your wife's life." He glanced at Isabel. "And you, your husband's."

Smirking, Lorenzo approached Isabel's chair. "In fact, why don't I give your husband a little taste of what's to come?"

In the blink of an eye, he pulled his arm back and unleashed a blow that connected with her face and knocked her right out of the chair.

As stars danced in front of her eyes and pain throbbed in her cheek, Isabel glimpsed a blur of movement in her peripheral vision. An angry shout echoed, followed by a loud thud and a cry of outrage.

She blinked, her vision clearing in time to see Trevor being restrained by one of the bodyguards. The other guard, a stoic-faced giant with Slavic features, grabbed Isabel before she could make a move.

He jammed the barrel of his gun against her temple and said, "Boss?"

Lorenzo staggered to his feet, holding his sleeve to his nose. "Tie them to the chairs." His hand moved to reveal the blood dripping from his nostrils.

A sideways glance showed the slight smirk on Trevor's face, and Isabel stifled a sigh, wishing he hadn't gone after Lorenzo like that. The man was already pissed off. No need to rile him up even further.

Their captor loomed over them once more, his mouth twisted in anger. "Enjoy the time you have left together. Soon the games will start and while I expect to enjoy every fucking second of your suffering, I can assure you, Mr. and Mrs. Martin, that the two of you will find no enjoyment in what I have planned for you."

"You really have no respect for other people's property, huh?"

D shifted his head at the sound of Ethan's half-sarcastic, half-amused remark, which had been directed at Juliet. The team had just set up across the street from the Meiro mansion, in a gorgeous Tudor-style home that had been sitting empty for the past two weeks and would remain empty for two more while the owners vacationed on the French Riviera.

D was positioned near the large bay window, wearing all black and armed to the teeth, just like everyone else in the room, including Juliet, who answered Ethan with a shrug.

"Hey, if you're stupid enough to rely on SSI for your home security needs, then you deserve what you get."

"SSI?" Ethan echoed.

"Secure Systems Incorporated." She offered a dry smile. "Never trust an alarm company that uses the word *secure* in its name. SSI is every burglar's dream—the easiest system on the planet to circumvent."

From his perch on the other side of the window, Morgan narrowed his eyes at the brunette. "What about the Meiro house? What system can we expect to find there?"

"The Meiros are old school." As she talked, she unsheathed the knife at her hip and absently ran her fingers over the seven-inch blade.

"They've got the good old electric eye. Photoelectric sensors," she clarified when Morgan raised his eyebrows in question. "Transmitter, receiver. Light is transmitted to the receiver, and if the beam is interrupted, even for a nanosecond, the receiver sounds the alarm. You can usually find them in front of doors, windows, long corridors. Smart folks disguise the units as power outlets, but most people are dumb-asses and leave them in plain sight."

"The Meiros?" Morgan asked.

"Smart," she conceded. "But dumb in their choice of lighting components. Instead of UV or infrared, their system uses laser light, which is easier to spot."

"How do we disarm it?" D inquired in a brisk tone.

Juliet grinned. "Already done."

Next to her, Ethan frowned. "How did you manage that?"

"It's all very convoluted and probably way over your heads," she said, waving a dismissive hand. "Let's just say my methods involve dummy components, piggybacking the central station, Paige's technological wizardry, and good old-fashioned deception."

Morgan looked uncharacteristically amused. "Meaning?"

"I've fooled the system into thinking it's working properly, when in fact it is not." She shrugged, still stroking the smooth edge of her blade. "The motion sensors on the exterior need to be manually disarmed, though. I'll go in first and take care of them. Unless you want me to talk your men through it?"

Your men. D didn't miss the distinction—now that Morgan was back in the picture, Noelle had been conspicuously absent. Probably brooding in a corner somewhere.

D got a real kick out of that particular mental image. He imagined the woman was spitting nails that her command had been stolen from her by a man she despised.

"You can handle it," Morgan told Juliet. "Just don't screw it up."

She rolled her eyes. "Yes, sir."

"So how the fuck do we get them out of there?" Liam asked from across the room.

"Shouldn't be too hard," D rasped. "We're looking at four guards. That's nothing."

"Only four?" Juliet looked surprised. "They must know that Isabel and Callaghan are here with a team. Why wouldn't Meiro take stronger measures to protect himself?"

"Maybe he doesn't know who they really are," Morgan said slowly.

She frowned. "If he recognized her as Valerie, then he must know she's an operative. He just wouldn't know who she's working for."

"Maybe he didn't recognize her as Valerie."

"So, what, he was after Paloma and Julian Martin?" Juliet sounded bewildered.

"Possibly." The boss shrugged. "Whatever his motive, the lack of guards works in our favor. Our only obstacle is the motion sensors—once Juliet disarms them, we'll be inside that mansion before they even see us coming."

* * *

Lorenzo strode into the grand kitchen and marched to the sink. He ran a dish towel under the tap and brought it to his swollen nose, the fury inside him rising once more. That motherfucker had the *nerve* to lay a hand on him?

Julian Martin would pay dearly for that.

And the woman . . . so cool and collected, even with the threat of death looming over her. For some reason, he found that infuriating. It was an insult even, as if she truly didn't appreciate the trauma he was capable of inflicting on her.

He let out a ragged breath. Her punishment . . . oh, her punishment would be much, much worse than her husband's.

By the time he was through with her, she'd be begging him to kill her.

"Tomas! What happened?"

Renee's concerned exclamation sounded from the doorway, and then his wife hurried toward him. She was still clad in the dress she'd worn to the gala, even though he'd ordered her to change for the airport.

He frowned. "You're not ready yet. I told you I want you out of this house."

"I don't want to go. These are the people who murdered your father, Tomas. I want to be here to support you."

He knew she called him Tomas only out of habit, and only because they'd agreed never to use his real name, even in private, but it still raised his hackles. He was Lorenzo Blanco. Lorenzo *Blanco*, once heir to the biggest arms empire in South America.

And now look at him—Tomas Meiro. A fucking casino owner. Married to a woman who ate pussy, living in *her* father's house and running *her* father's businesses.

He should be carrying on *his* father's legacy. Not Michel fucking Beaumont's.

"I don't need your support," he said through gritted teeth. "You will leave this house tonight."

"As you wish."

She averted her gaze, but not before he saw the look of displeasure on her face.

Lorenzo took a calming breath and gathered the shattered pieces of his composure. Whatever bitterness he harbored against Renee's father, he couldn't hold it against Renee. The woman had done nothing but offer him support, and he'd come to appreciate her counsel over the course of their marriage. There might not be any love between them, but there had always been friendship and mutual respect.

"You must go." He softened his tone. "I don't want you anywhere near these people, Renee. The revenge I have in mind . . . it will be dished out slowly. Very, very slowly. I can't have you tainted by any of this. Do you understand?"

After a long beat, she capitulated. "I understand."

"Good." Lorenzo leaned in and brushed his lips over hers in a brief kiss that surprised them both. "Trust me, *ma chérie*. You don't want to be around for what happens next."

"So it's been about us the entire time," Isabel said wryly. "Julian and frickin' Paloma."

She didn't bother putting up the pretense any longer. Gone was Paloma's accent, gone were Paloma's speech mannerisms. If the cellar was wired for sound, which she doubted, then Lorenzo would quickly find out that she and Trevor had lied about their identities. Who knew, though? That might work to their advantage. Maybe he'd be inclined to keep them alive longer, for the sake of answers, at least.

Beside her, Trevor released a rueful sigh. "And thanks to me, we're tied to chairs and about to be tortured by Lorenzo Blanco."

Though she couldn't move her arms, legs, or torso, she could still twist her head to look over at him. "What are you talking about? It's not your fault."

"Lorenzo said he tracked me down four months ago. *Me*. I used Julian's ID in Argentina, remember? That's what raised a flag. He's been searching for us since Blanco's death, which means he probably paid off every passport officer at every airport to alert him when Julian or Paloma resurfaced."

"And then what? You unknowingly led his men back to your compound?"

"I must've. I can't imagine how else he could've found it. The place was buried under piles of paperwork and the address is hard to find."

Her brows knit together in a frown. "What did Lorenzo mean when he said your 'company's training facility'? Where did he think he was sending that hit team?"

"I own a lot of different businesses under Julian's name. One of them happens to be a private combat school that prepares military recruits for basic training and teaches civilians combat skills. I've got two locations—one in Sarasota, one in Mexico."

"Wait. This company actually exists?"

Trevor shook his head. "On paper, but I'm thinking Lassiter fucked up and assumed the compound was the Mexican location for Julian's bogus combat school. I can't think of any other reason why Lorenzo hasn't questioned what Julian was doing on a compound with a bunch of highly trained mercs."

Isabel ran her tongue over her bottom lip, which was dry and beginning to crack. The air in the cellar was too damn arid, yet at the same time, moist. And the odor of rotting grapes was beginning to give her a headache.

"It was always about us." As she voiced the thought again, pain circled her heart. "Beth, Lloyd, Hank ... they died because of us."

God, more deaths on her conscience. More deaths to atone for.

"Don't," Trevor said firmly. "Don't blame yourself. This is all on me."

"No, it isn't. I refuse to let you carry the burden alone." Her staunch declaration hung in the room. "If you're at fault, then so am I. There. I shoulder half the blame."

He let out a heavy breath. "You are damn impossible at times—you know that? I just *had* to fall in love with the most stubborn woman on the planet. Fine, it's *neither* of our faults then. Does that sound—why are you looking at me like that?"

Isabel's heart was pounding. "You're . . . in love with me?"

His whiskey eyes flooded with emotion. "Duh."

"Duh?" She gawked at him, torn between laughing and bursting into tears. "That's seriously all you have to say?"

"This can't come as much of a surprise, Iz. I think I've been in love with you for a long time. I just hadn't admitted it to myself until now."

Isabel bit her lip. Wow. He loved her. She still couldn't wrap her head around it. Trevor Callaghan loved her. *Her.*

"Oh," she said.

"Oh? That's all *you* have to say?"

Her pulse kicked up another notch. "I . . . I'm still absorbing it. I guess I—" She halted as a muffled thump echoed right above them.

"What was that?" she demanded.

Before he could answer, they heard the unmistakable sound of a gunshot.

Trevor's voice contained a chord of satisfaction. "*That* is the cavalry coming to our rescue."

Chapter 24

There was a chill in the air as D and Morgan approached the patio doors. The others were covering the front of the house and the street; with only four guards to contend with, a two-man show was more than enough. Make that three guards, D amended. Meiro's wife had been escorted by a lone bodyguard when she'd left the mansion twenty minutes ago.

As promised, Juliet had made quick work of the motion sensors, and no alarms had been raised as the men crept through the shadows of the manicured backyard.

When they reached their destination, Morgan hung back, gun in hand, eyes gleaming with intensity.

D crouched in front of the door, unclipped his pick kit from his belt and tackled the lock. As he inserted a tension wrench into the keyhole, he said a silent prayer that Juliet's "trickery" had indeed taken care of the security cameras. He was acutely aware of the two cameras mounted on either side of the stone patio. Pointing right at them. It wasn't losing his anonymity that he worried about, but the element of surprise.

One of the pins in the lock clicked into place. He shifted the hook pick, applied more pressure with the flat wrench, and thirty seconds later, the dead bolt clicked open.

Palming his H&K pistol, D pushed on the door handle

and slowly opened the door. A glance at his feet confirmed what Juliet had warned them about. Lasers. Four of them spanning the doorway, a crisscross of beams that went up to his waist.

No way to step over them, but D knew he could clear the top beam if he backed up and jumped over it at a run. He didn't want to risk making noise, though. They had no idea where Meiro or his guards were. Fortunately, there was nobody in the kitchen.

He glanced at Morgan, who was also examining the laser field.

D clicked his earpiece. "You sure about the lasers?" His voice was almost inaudible.

A snicker sounded in his ear. "You scared, D? Who would've thought." Juliet chuckled. "The alarm won't go off, boys. Trust me."

He suppressed his irritation and looked at Morgan again. The boss gestured to the red beams as if to say, *you first*.

Fuck. Fine.

D took a deep breath, uttered another silent prayer, and walked right through the beams.

Nothing happened.

Blessed silence prevailed.

Morgan stepped in after him and closed the door. The two men crossed the dark kitchen, communicating with hand signals as they moved deeper into the house. Shadows and silence greeted them at every corner.

Morgan signaled to the light spilling out from the front parlor, indicating that he would take the upstairs.

D nodded and gestured that he would investigate the main floor.

They went their separate ways, moving silently through the mansion. The rooms were furnished with expensive pieces and tasteful works of art, but the house lacked any personal touches. Apparently Michel Beaumont hadn't spent much time here—the man had preferred the casino penthouse, just like his son-in-law. Renee Meiro didn't seem to be around too often either; according to her credit card statements, the woman was traveling most of the time.

D's instincts hummed as he neared the entryway to a corridor bathed in light. He flattened himself against the cream-colored wall, his weapon pressed to his thigh.

He waited. Listened. Became aware of the sound of soft breathing.

Someone was in that hallway.

Morgan was still upstairs, but the continued silence told D that the boss hadn't encountered any problems.

He edged along the wall, inhaled a breath, risked a glance around the corner.

One guard. Short, stocky, curly black hair. Cradling an AK to his chest.

The rifle gave D pause. Trevor had reported that Meiro's bodyguards usually carried pistols. The switch to assault weapons meant Meiro *really* didn't want his prisoners to get away. And chances were, said prisoners were being held beyond the door being protected by the curly-haired goon.

Well. He couldn't keep Callaghan and Blondie waiting.

Keeping a steady grip on his H&K, D sprang into action. He experienced a surge of adrenaline as he burst into the corridor and took the rifle-wielding guard by complete surprise.

Pop.

The suppressor on his gun ensured that the bullet entering the guard's forehead did so with the softest of hisses.

D caught the guard's lifeless body before it toppled to the floor. He was just patting himself on the back for one of his most soundless kills when the gunshots rang out.

Isabel had never felt more powerless than she did now, tied to a chair while chaos reigned above her. She had no idea what was going on up there, but judging by the rhythmic *rat-tat-tat* that was making the ceiling vibrate, she assumed Morgan and the others had launched a full-blown assault on the mansion.

She tugged on her bindings, but the thin cables Lorenzo's men had used to secure her wrists behind her back were too damn tight. As she struggled against them, the cables dug into her flesh and made her wince.

"We have to get out of here," she said in frustration. "That door could burst open any second, and if those aren't our people up there . . ."

No sooner had the words left her mouth than a round of gunfire boomed beyond the door. Isabel's pulse sped up as the doorknob exploded in a spray of wood splinters. The metal knob snapped off and bounced on the concrete floor, and then the door was kicked open and a familiar face greeted them.

"You okay?" D's coal black eyes revealed no emotion as he stalked toward them with purposeful strides.

Trevor rolled his eyes. "We're great. Can't you tell?"

D swiftly sliced their bindings with the sharpest hunting knife Isabel had ever seen. As the blood rushed back to her hands and ankles, pins and needles pricked her flesh. She rubbed her numb wrists and stumbled to her feet. When she heard another muted gunshot, she glanced at D in alarm.

"What's going on up there?"

He shrugged. "Morgan's in the middle of a Wild West shoot-out with Meiro."

"Blanco," Trevor muttered.

"Huh?"

"Long story. I'll tell you all about it later."

"Deal. Let's go," D ordered.

The three of them hurried out of the cellar. Isabel was grateful that D took the lead, because she had no idea where they were going. They raced down a narrow hallway boasting exposed ductwork and the scent of mildew, then reached a set of wooden steps that D climbed two at a time. He'd tossed Trevor a nine-millimeter handgun, but nothing for Isabel, who felt naked and vulnerable without a weapon. She stuck close to Trevor as they emerged onto the main floor.

The house was quiet. No gunshots. No voices.

D signaled for them to stop. He crept toward the end of the hall. Ducked out, then gestured for them to follow.

The corridor they entered was bathed in shadows, but there was a light at the end of it, along with something shiny and silver flashing on the floor ten feet away. No, not silver. Glass. And several bullet holes were visible in the wall above the shattered glass.

Those shards would make their escape difficult. D's boots and Trevor's leather wingtips hadn't made a sound against the parquet, but they didn't stand a chance of staying quiet once they reached those sharp pieces littering the floor.

D must have concurred, because a resigned expression settled on his face. He made a few hand motions to Trevor, who nodded briskly. Isabel knew both men had been U.S. Army at one point—Trevor had served in the Special Forces, D was Delta. She suspected they could carry on entire conversations and formulate complex strategies without ever uttering a single word.

Trevor touched her arm and signaled for her to stay close. He held up three fingers, then pointed to the end of the corridor.

Drawing a steadying breath, she nodded.

Her muscles coiled tight as she waited for Trevor's count.

He held up one finger. Two.

Three.

D took off first, his boots crunching on the broken glass as he charged forward. Isabel kept her head down and ran. The hallway spilled into a large parlor lit by a crystal chandelier that rocked wildly as if an errant bullet had sent it swinging.

Gunfire erupted the second they entered the spacious entrance. A bullet whizzed over Isabel's head. A sharp glance to the left and she saw Morgan duck out of a corridor she assumed led to the back of the house.

"Go," Trevor shouted, practically shoving her toward the front door.

Isabel was two steps from the massive double doors when she was yanked backward.

Lorenzo had popped out of the shadowy living room behind them and was trying to pull her toward him, but although the dress she'd worn to the gala looked damn good, it was the flimsiest garment ever made. The strap in Lorenzo's grip snapped apart, forcing him to make a mad grab for her hair.

For her *wig*, which was ripped off her head, allowing her to dive out of his grasp. She landed on the floor with a thump just as horrified recognition and sheer outrage dawned on Lorenzo's face.

He stared at the wig in his hand, then at Isabel, and she knew exactly what he was seeing—her Valerie red hair slicked back and held in place with bobby pins. Her bangs had sprung free from the pins and now fell across her forehead.

"You fucking *bitch*!" Lorenzo's livid cry bounced off the parlor walls.

She caught a fleeting blur of movement, saw the muzzle of his gun dip down and train on her. Adrenaline sizzled in her blood, but she knew she couldn't roll out of the line of fire fast enough.

Her heart stopped as she prepared herself for the impact, as she watched Lorenzo's fingers curl over the trigger.

But the pain didn't come.

A gunshot blasted and her field of vision turned black. For a second she thought she'd fainted, but then she realized she was looking at the back of Trevor's tuxedo jacket.

"No!" she screamed.

He'd thrown himself in front of Lorenzo's bullet.

Jesus Christ.

Trevor had taken the bullet meant for her.

Isabel watched in horror as his broad body jerked, as he stumbled from the force of impact. She dove forward just in time to catch him, while her pulse shrieked in her head like a banshee and her hands trembled violently.

Five feet away, D lunged at Lorenzo, whose pistol clattered out of his hand. As the two men crashed to the floor locked in battle, Isabel fought back a wave of panic and struggled under the weight of Trevor's torso. Her arms were wrapped around him from behind, and a glance at his abdomen triggered a new surge of terror.

Blood poured out of the bullet hole in his gut, soaking his white dress shirt, pooling on the hardwood floor. No vest. He hadn't been wearing a goddamn vest because of the gala, and now . . . now he was going to fucking bleed to death in front of her.

Isabel's breathing went shallow as she slid her hands down his chest and brought them to the wound. She clasped her fingers together, applied pressure, tried not to weep.

Trevor's eyelids fluttered, opened, but his eyes were out of focus. "Wasn't . . . gonna . . . let you die," he mumbled.

Her heart was beating so fast it was a wonder it didn't burst right out of her chest. Trevor's face was so pale. *Too* pale.

She pressed her hands to his belly and her cheek against his temple. "Don't talk," she told him. "Save your strength, Trev."

There was another crash, then a grunt as D managed to grab the gun Lorenzo had dropped. Isabel jumped when a flash of black whizzed in the corner of her eye, but it was just Morgan, limping up to her and Trevor.

Morgan took one look at Trevor's face and clicked on his earpiece. "Rookie, bring the car right to the front door. Make sure Sully's with you. We need to get Trev to a hospital. Pronto."

The mercenary peeled off his black shirt, crumpled it up, and dropped to his knees in front of Isabel and Trevor. "Move your hands," he ordered.

Isabel barely heard the sharp command. She felt like she was in a daze. Trevor was so cold. And the blood. It was oozing out of his stomach like oil from a leaking car.

"Isabel."

She balked when she felt Morgan forcibly push her hands off Trevor. "No! He's bleeding out!"

"I know," Morgan said grimly.

He jammed his balled-up shirt against the wound, eliciting a low groan of pain from Trevor's lips.

Tears blurred Isabel's vision. Oh God. He couldn't die. He *couldn't.*

Ten feet away, the muzzle of D's gun was trained on Lorenzo's head. The big mercenary cocked the weapon ominously, but Lorenzo was too busy glaring daggers at Isabel to pay attention to the gun at his temple.

"You little bitch," he hissed. "Did you enjoy yourself?"

She felt utterly numb as she looked into Lorenzo's furious dark eyes. Then her gaze dropped to the man in her arms, the man whose skin was now a sickly shade of gray.

"Did you enjoy playing me for a fool, *Valerie*?" Now he was downright smirking, his attention focused on Trevor. "I hope that son of a bitch dies. I hope he dies in your fucking arms, you cunt. I hope—"

The gunshot reverberated in the parlor.

Shock filled Lorenzo's face, only for a nanosecond, and then he was gone. Limp body crumpling to the floor, a bullet in his left temple.

Isabel was stunned as Lorenzo's body hit the hardwood with a loud thump. He landed with his head turned in her direction, offering a clear view of his eyes. They were wide open. Lifeless. A frozen mask of surprise and accusation.

Isabel stared into that vacant gaze for several seconds, then turned to look at D with shocked eyes.

The black-eyed mercenary showed no remorse. "I was getting bored of listening to him talk."

Isabel had no idea what to say, and no time to process what had just happened. Dead, alive, she didn't care about Lorenzo Blanco. Not when Trevor was dying in her arms.

A car engine rumbled outside, and suddenly Morgan was reaching for Trevor.

"No," she growled. "I won't leave him."

Ignoring her, Morgan heaved Trevor over one broad shoulder and carried him to the door.

Isabel raced after them, her legs so wobbly she was surprised she could make them work. But she refused to leave Trevor's side. He was dying.

He was *dying*, and it was all her fault.

He'd taken that bullet to protect *her*.

Oh God. She was going to lose him. Just like she'd lost everyone else she'd ever cared about.

"Isabel, you have to let go," Morgan snapped.

They were on the circular driveway now. The rear door of the sedan had flown open and the men were attempting to move Trevor into the backseat.

She wanted to tell them to hurry up, until she realized that the reason they couldn't get him in the car was because she was clutching Trevor's arm like a life preserver.

"Let go," Sullivan said gently.

Swallowing, she unclenched her fingers from Trevor's sleeve. "I won't leave him," she said in a quavering voice.

You were planning to.

She ignored the accusatory voice and slid into the backseat, where Sullivan hovered over Trevor. Somehow the car started moving, but she couldn't for the life of her pay attention to who was driving or where they were going. Her only focus, her only concern, was Trevor.

"He needs blood," Sullivan said briskly. "How far is the hospital?"

"Ten minutes," Morgan barked from the front seat.

"He might not have ten minutes."

Sullivan's response was spoken so softly Isabel knew he hadn't intended for anyone to hear it. But she'd heard. God, she'd heard every word.

Her heart throbbed with agony as she looked at Trevor's ashen face. His head was cradled in her lap, his hair damp, his forehead clammy and icy cold beneath her lips when she bent down to kiss it.

She looked up and glared at Sullivan. "Give him blood, then. Kane performed a blood transfusion on D in the fucking chopper back in Mexico. You can do it too."

Sullivan's features creased with regret. "We don't have the right supplies."

The Australian continued to apply pressure on Trevor's abdomen, but the look on his face wasn't encouraging.

Trevor's shirt was no longer white. It was crimson, and his skin was so gray Isabel's throat closed up to the point that no air could get in. She drew in a weak breath, then bent over and brought her lips close to Trevor's ear.

"Don't you dare die on me," she whispered fiercely. "Do you hear me, Callaghan? You are not allowed to die on me."

His eyelids twitched, and then those whiskey brown eyes were peering up at her. Glazed, slightly blank, but God, the mere sight of them sent relief shuddering through her.

When he spoke, it was in a hoarse croak. "Don't . . . leave."

She held him tighter. "I'm not going anywhere. I promise."

"No . . . you . . . you'll use it as an excuse." Each word seemed to take a toll on him. "You'll say it's your fault . . . me getting shot. Won't let you."

Her eyes burned from the tears. "No excuses," she choked out. "You're . . . you're the only man, the only *person*, who's ever really, truly seen me. I'll never leave you, Trev."

The corners of his mouth lifted slightly, like he was trying to smile. "Love you."

She swallowed the lump obstructing her throat and whispered in his ear again. "I love you, too."

She knew the other men could hear every word being spoken in the backseat, but she didn't care. She didn't care about being vulnerable, or revealing the emotions she normally kept locked up. She didn't care about anything or anyone but Trevor.

"Again."

His wheezy command made her smile through her tears.

"I love you, too," she repeated.

He gave the slightest of nods, and then he passed out.

Chapter 25

Trevor woke up to find Isabel curled up on the chair next to his bed. Her cheek was resting on her palm, and her hair fell into her face, shielding her eyes from his view.

Groaning, he tried to sit up, but the streak of pain in his lower gut had him sagging back down.

The groan succeeded in waking up Isabel, who was on her feet and at his side in a heartbeat. "You're awake," she blurted out. "Oh, thank God. I'll get the nurse!"

It took all his energy to grab her hand. "Wait." His voice was so hoarse he felt like he'd smoked ten packs of cigarettes. "Don't go."

Her eyes softened. Blue. They were blue again. The familiar color caused a wave of peace to wash over him.

"Trev. I need to get the nurse," she insisted.

"Not yet. Tell me what happened."

"You got shot," she said darkly.

"Yeah, I gathered that." Another groan slid out. "Blanco?"

"Dead. Just like his father."

Her matter-of-fact response brought a pang of satisfaction. He couldn't remember what had gone down after that bullet connected with his flesh, but he did recall the bloodlust in Lorenzo's eyes right before he'd pulled the trigger. The man had wanted to see Isabel dead. He'd *craved* it.

But Trevor had stopped him. He'd saved Isabel. He'd saved her, the way he hadn't been able to save Gina.

"The Meiro mansion is crawling with cops," she added. "But nobody's come knocking on our door. Morgan and Sullivan are out in the waiting room, but everyone else is back at the White Sands. Noelle's ready to bolt. She called a while ago and said she doesn't want to spend one more second with Morgan or his men."

He smiled faintly. "Should I feel insulted?"

"Nah. Trust me, you don't want to spend time with her either. She's mean."

That garnered a laugh, but unfortunately, laughter and a bullet to the gut didn't mesh well. As his stomach clenched with pain, Trevor breathed through his nose and tried to ward off his rising nausea.

"I need to get the nurse," Isabel said firmly.

He tightened his grip on her hand. "Wait." His tone was equally firm. "First I need you to tell me that I didn't imagine it."

"Imagine what?"

"You telling me you loved me. Telling me you'd never walk away from me again." He met her eyes. "Did I imagine it?"

She went quiet for a moment and then a small smile lifted her lips.

"No, you didn't."

Warmth suffused his heart. "So if I let go of your hand, you're just going to leave the room to find the nurse, right? You'll find a nurse and come back, right?"

"I'll come back."

"Promise?"

Still smiling, she lowered her head and brushed her lips over his. "I promise."

Chapter 26

"Where will we live?"

Isabel snuggled close to Trevor, being careful not to jostle him. They were lying together in his hospital bed, despite the surgeon's orders for him to get some sleep. But, of course, the stubborn man refused to heed the doctor's command.

"Wherever we want," Trevor said in response to her question.

"What will we do?"

He planted a kiss atop her head. "Keep working. Be together. Love each other. Get married."

"That's quite a list." She hesitated. "Is that what you want, to get married?"

"Yes. Do you?"

"Yes. But only if you rock the proposal. No hot sauce spaghetti, thank you very much."

He laughed, his arm tightening around her. "I'll order takeout, I promise." Now he was the one hesitating. "Do you want kids?"

Isabel thought about it for a moment. "Yes. I want kids."

"Good. Me too."

A little laugh slipped out. "Is it weird that we're matter-of-factly going over these details? Like this is nothing more than a business arrangement?"

Trevor grabbed her hand and brought it underneath the thin blanket covering their lower bodies. "Trust me, there's nothing businesslike about it. This is *all* pleasure, sweetheart."

Heat rippled through her when she felt his heavy erection. His hospital johnny meant there was no barrier between her hand and that impressive cock, but Isabel found the strength to slide her hand out from under the blanket.

"You're recovering from surgery," she said sternly. "Sexual shenanigans are forbidden."

"Says who? Hasn't anyone ever told you that sex is the best medicine?"

She propped up on one elbow and kissed his cheek. "You're two hours out of surgery, Trev. You're not getting any action for at least twenty-four more."

"You're a sadist." He shot her a crooked grin. "But I still love you."

She still wasn't used to hearing those three words come out of his mouth. And every time he said them, a part of her wanted to ask, why? Why did he love her? Why didn't he care about all the baggage she brought to the table?

But she was making an effort to push those old insecurities aside. She'd meant every word she'd said in the back of that car—she wasn't leaving him. Nope, not going anywhere.

Her worst fear had been realized when Trevor almost bled to death in her arms. She had a man who loved her. A strong, kind, incredible man who *loved* her, and she was going to be a coward about it? She was going to push that amazing man away because she was scared of getting hurt again?

Well, losing Trevor tonight would have hurt. It would have hurt more than anything.

Not having Trevor in her life, she'd discovered, was the most terrifying thing of all. And it was well within her power to avoid that scary fate—all she had to do was open her heart.

"Just so you know, I'm gonna try hard to stop being such an overprotective ass," Trevor said, interrupting her thoughts.

She arched one eyebrow. "Really? Because it was beginning to seem like Caveman Trevor was here to stay."

"Oh, he'll definitely be making an appearance or two." The humor in his eyes died. "This whole time . . . I've been freaking out, scared I was going to lose you. I hated knowing you were putting yourself in danger and that if something happened to you, I might not be able to save you. Same way I couldn't save Gina."

"Trev . . ."

"No, let me finish." Shame filled his expression. "It was borderline disrespectful on my part, Iz. You don't need me to save you, and you certainly don't need me breathing down your neck during a job. You can protect yourself."

She couldn't help but laugh. "You do realize I would've been shot if you hadn't jumped in front of Lorenzo's gun, right?"

"I know, and it would've killed me to see you lying in this bed instead of me, but I need to accept that your job can be just as dangerous as mine. And as I recall, you took a bullet for me in Bogotá, so if anything, I was simply repaying the favor."

The sincerity ringing in his voice made her chest tighten with emotion.

"So, yeah," he finished awkwardly, "I promise not to be such a controlling ass all the time."

"Well, I promise not to be such a coward."

"You could never be a coward. You're the strongest woman I've ever met, sweetheart."

"And what am I?" came a sardonic voice. "Chopped liver?"

Their gazes moved to the doorway, where Noelle had appeared like an apparition. In her black leather pants, off-the-shoulder sweater, and knee-high boots, she marched into the room like she owned it. Isabel didn't bother asking how Noelle had managed to get into the ICU when it was reserved only for family members.

"You? You're the scariest woman I've ever met," Trevor said drily. "How's that?"

Noelle smirked. "It's perfect."

With a laugh, Isabel sat up. "You taking off now?" she asked her boss.

"Shortly. I came to remind Callaghan of the little deal we made back at the ranch."

Isabel's shoulders tensed, and she noticed Trevor's jaw doing the same. No mistaking what Noelle meant. She was cashing in on the carte blanche favor she'd weaseled out of Trevor.

With wary brown eyes, Trevor slid to a sitting position. He winced as he got settled, a sight that infuriated Isabel. Damn Noelle for coming here and interrupting his recovery.

"So what do you want?" he asked darkly.

Noelle sauntered over to the foot of the bed and tapped her bloodred fingernails on the railing there. "I haven't decided yet, but I'm sure something suitable will pop up in the future."

Isabel saw Trevor's eyes cloud over when the blonde did not elaborate.

"By the way," Noelle went on, "I can't say I approve of this blessed union, but clearly Isabel has made her choice and that choice is you, Callaghan. So I can either kill you, in which case I'd be losing one of my best operatives because Isabel would definitely quit—"

Isabel snorted. Quit? She'd claw Noelle's black heart out if the woman went after Trevor.

"—or I can suck it up and let this happen," Noelle concluded.

"How considerate of you," Trevor said sarcastically.

"I thought so." She smirked. "Isabel's one of my mine—you understand what that means, right?"

He rolled his eyes. "It means if I hurt her, you know a hundred ways to kill a man, seven of which involve the testicles."

Noelle was practically beaming. "He's learning." The blonde glanced at Isabel. "Oh, and feel free to take the Vermont chalet. You've always liked it. Callaghan grew up in the mountains, so he'll like it too. And that way I'll know where to find him."

With that, Noelle turned on her heel and strolled out of the room.

"That woman fucking scares me," Trevor remarked.

"Me too."

"What did she mean, take the Vermont chalet?"

Isabel shook the cobwebs of disbelief from her head. "I think she just gave us her house in Vermont."

"Are you serious?"

"Maybe. I don't know. That's sure as hell what it sounded like, though."

She cuddled closer to him, resting her head on his shoulder as he stroked her hair. A comfortable silence settled between them, and it was several minutes before Trevor spoke again.

"I love you, Isabel," he said thickly.

Her heart skipped a beat. "I love you too."

"With that said . . . I don't ever want to live in a house that belongs to Noelle."

"I don't know, Trev, it's a really nice house . . ."

"Yeah, full of booby traps and cameras and little robots that pop out of the closets at night and murder you in your sleep."

She burst out laughing. "Good point. So I guess that brings us back to the question that started this discussion . . . where will we live?"

"Wherever we want."

"And what will we do again?" she teased.

His gorgeous eyes twinkled. "Keep working. Be together. Get married."

She frowned at him. "You forgot the loving-each-other part."

Trevor's lips were warm as he brushed them over hers in a sweet kiss. "Trust me, sweetheart, I didn't forget."

"How cute. Could it be? Does the heartless killer actually have"—Jim Morgan offered a mock gasp as Noelle stepped out of Trevor's room— "a *heart*?"

Setting her jaw, Noelle brushed past him and continued along the fluorescent-lit corridor. She couldn't wait to get out of here. Hospitals were too damn bright. Always left her feeling far too exposed.

Jim fell into step with her. "You're really not going to explain that grand gesture you just made to the happy couple?"

"I don't have to explain myself to you," she answered coolly. "And by the way, eavesdropping is punishable by death in some countries."

She felt those blue eyes piercing her. Probing.

Gritting her teeth, she jammed the elevator button and waited. Ignored the man at her side.

"I got your message," he said gruffly.

She stiffened.

"Wasn't that a blast from the past." He lowered his voice. "I didn't think you remembered that number."

Slowly, Noelle met his eyes. "Like I could ever forget."

Neither of them spoke. Neither of them moved.

The elevator doors dinged open, breaking the spell.

Noelle strode into the car. She expected Jim to walk away and head back to Callaghan's room, but he marched right into the elevator with her.

The doors closed.

"So listen . . ." He shifted awkwardly.

Noelle masked her surprise. It was incredibly rare to see Jim let down his guard this way.

"Thanks for stepping up when I was out of touch. For letting my crew use your safe house. I owe you one."

"You certainly do."

He chuckled. "When can I expect you to collect?"

"Whenever I damn well please." She paused. Curiosity got the best of her. "Where were you, Jim?"

"The Himalayas."

She frowned. "Why?"

"Why do you think, Noelle?"

It took her a moment to make sense of those pointed words. When understanding dawned, her hands trembled with rage. "You're still looking for her."

"I never fucking stopped."

Bitterness whipped through her body like loose cables being flung around by the wind. She stared into his familiar blue eyes, saw the anger in them, the shared resentment, the spark of triumph.

"I hate you," she whispered.

"Right back atcha, baby."

Their eyes locked.

Noelle almost went for the knife in her boot.

The elevator had nearly reached the lobby.

"Except," Jim continued with the smug cock of his head, "you don't hate me at all, do you, baby? That's just what you like to tell yourself."

Her nostrils flared. "I—"

The doors opened with a chime.

Jim Morgan stalked out of the elevator and walked away.

Epilogue

One month later

"Why did we stop?" Renee Beaumont fought a spark of irritation as she glared at the bodyguard seated across from her in the limo.

Looking confused, Marcel reached for the gun holstered to his hip. "I don't know. I'll go talk to the driver."

As the burly man got out of the limo, Renee glanced out the tinted window, frowning when she realized they were nowhere near the private airport where the Beaumont jet awaited her arrival. Rather, they were on a deserted stretch of road with no structures or humans in sight.

She ignored a jolt of fear and reached for her purse, but when she slid her hand inside it in search of her derringer, she discovered the little gun was gone.

Her pulse sped up, her heart beating even faster when Marcel didn't return. Something was wrong.

Had the people who'd killed Lorenzo tracked her down?

No. No, that wasn't possible. They had no reason to come after her. She was nothing more than the widow of a man who'd been gunned down during a bungled robbery. That was the official story—after she'd generously paid off the police captain, of course.

The partition between Renee and the driver suddenly began to lower, bringing a rush of relief.

"It's about time," she grumbled. "Can you please explain why you decided to stop in the middle of—"

The question died on her lips when she found herself staring at an unfamiliar woman with blond hair, blue eyes, and a gun.

"Who are you?" Renee burst out. "Where's Marcel? Where is my driver?"

The woman carelessly waved the gun and spoke in flawless French. "They're around."

Anger spiraled through her and seized her insides. "Who are you?" she repeated. "How dare you hold that weapon on me?"

The woman just chuckled.

"I don't know what you want, you stupid bitch, but I'm calling the police," Renee snapped.

As she made a grab for her purse, the blonde laughed with unrestrained delight.

"If your derringer isn't in there, do you really think your phone will be?"

Renee experienced another flicker of trepidation. "Who are you?" she asked for the third time.

"I'm Isabel's boss."

She blinked in confusion. "Who is Isabel?"

Displeasure flashed in those blue eyes.

Deadly eyes.

"Oh, right," the woman said coolly. "You probably know her as Paloma. Paloma Martin."

There was a beat of silence, and then Renee's arm shot out toward the door handle.

The door was locked.

She jammed her finger on the UNLOCK button, but nothing happened.

She was trapped.

The blonde laughed again. "So you *do* know who I'm referring to. I thought you would, seeing as you funded your husband's search for Paloma. And Julian, of course. Lorenzo wanted *both* his father's killers dead, didn't he, Renee?"

She didn't bother feigning ignorance. "And rightfully so," she replied in a frigid voice. "My husband lost not only his father but his empire, thanks to them."

"Ah, the empire. I figured you'd bring that up. It's why you married him, after all." The blonde slanted her head. "But you had your own empire—what did you need Blanco for? He was ruined, in hiding. Seems like you'd have been better off spending your daddy's money and staying away from vermin like Blanco."

"Money," Renee spat out. "That's all it was. Just money."

"But you wanted the power, huh?" Those blue eyes sparkled. "I totally get that, hon. Power is a very useful asset."

"I was deprived of it my entire life," Renee muttered. "My father was perfectly content with letting me work behind the scenes, but when it came to taking the helm? Oh no, he needed to find a prospective suitor for me. A *man* to run the business."

She had no idea why she was telling the woman all of this—the woman who was pointing a *gun* at her—but the details kept spilling out. Her bitterness thickened the air in the limo, threatening to choke her.

"When I met Lorenzo, I knew he was the right man to elevate me to where I wanted to be. My father had someone else in mind, but I convinced him Lorenzo was the better choice."

"And you convinced Lorenzo to regain his rightful place at the top of his father's empire."

Renee smirked. "Of course. When Lorenzo came to my father for help, he was content to live life as Tomas Meiro, to hide away and let the vultures pick at his former empire. But I showed him the error of his ways, of course."

"Of course." The lethal stranger looked oddly pleased, as if she approved of Renee's course of action.

For some inexplicable reason, Renee felt a spark of satisfaction. Nobody else had even suspected she was the one pulling her husband's strings. Nobody thought her capable of it. But this woman . . . this stranger . . . she recognized Renee as a force to be reckoned with.

The moment of kinship, however, faded fast when the woman cocked her weapon, an ominous click that echoed in the limo. "And were you the one who convinced Lorenzo to hunt down his father's killers?"

"No, that was one of his conditions." Renee's lips tightened. "He refused to reveal himself to his enemies and reclaim his empire until the Martins were taken care of. So I did everything I could to help him find them. The sooner they were taken care of, the sooner my husband and I could be what we were meant to be."

"And what's that?" the woman mocked.

"The most powerful couple in the world."

There was a soft chuckle. "Lofty ambitions. I approve." A sigh now. "Unfortunately, no matter how much I respect your aspiration to rule the world, I can't overlook the disheartening fact that you tried to kill one of my girls."

The fear returned, constricting her throat.

"With that said"—the woman tossed her golden hair over her shoulder and adjusted her grip on the silenced weapon—"do you have any last words?"

Renee's cheeks hollowed in anger. "Fuck you."

"I figured it'd be something along those lines. Anyway . . . nighty-night, Renee. I'm sure we'll meet in hell one day."

And then the blonde pulled the trigger.

Keep reading for a sneak peek at the next heart-pounding novel in Elle Kennedy's Killer Instincts series,

MIDNIGHT PURSUITS

Available soon from Signet Eclipse

Nothing beat a cup of steaming-hot coffee in the dead of winter, at least in Ethan Hayes's humble opinion. As he stepped onto the enormous cedar deck of the chalet-style house, Ethan was unbelievably grateful for the heat of the ceramic mug seeping into his cold fingers. February in Vermont meant biting-cold temperatures, buckets of snow, and frigid wind, but he wasn't complaining about his surroundings. The isolated house and surrounding area were so idyllic, he'd be a total moron to find fault in it.

He approached the wooden railing and gazed at the snow-capped peaks of the mountains in the distance. White mist shrouded the jagged tips, giving off a ghostly vibe, and dozens of feet below the deck, a sheet of pure white snow covered the hills and valleys that made up the landscape. Tall pines jutted proudly from the land, branches swaying in the early-morning breeze.

A postcard. That's what it looked like, and Ethan found it hard to believe that a woman as cold and deadly as Noelle had ever lived in such a beautiful slice of heaven. Then again, she'd given the house to Trevor Callaghan and Isabel Roma without batting an eye, so clearly the blond assassin hadn't been too attached to the place. He just hoped she didn't spring a surprise visit on him while he was here—

Noelle made him damn nervous, and he had no desire to spend any quality time with the woman.

He'd just taken a sip of coffee when his cell phone rang. He wasn't surprised to find Trevor's number flashing on the screen—he'd been expecting the call ever since Trevor and Isabel had rushed out the door in a mad race to make their private charter.

"I already arranged for a new one," Ethan said in lieu of greeting.

An amused male chuckle sounded in his ear. "What are you, a mind reader?"

"Nope, I just know how attached women are to their phones."

Trevor laughed again. "Yeah, Isabel's incredibly annoyed she left it behind. She didn't realize until we got here that it wasn't in her bag."

"You guys are at the airport?"

"About to board the plane. She wanted to drive back and get the phone, but I managed to talk her out of it. She claims she needs it in case of an emergency—aka any minor crisis that requires us to abandon our honeymoon so she can offer her assistance to some poor soul."

Now Ethan laughed. He'd liked Isabel Roma from the moment he'd met her nearly two years ago, and her endless compassion was one of his favorite things about her. It was refreshing when you spent most of your time with hardened mercenaries. But the downside to all that compassion was that Isabel would drop everything to help out a friend, even cut her honeymoon short if she had to.

"Don't worry," he assured his teammate. "Her phone is safe and sound, and I already called the provider to have a replacement ready when you two land in Maui. Tell her to text me the new number, and I'll forward her entire contact list to the new phone."

"Thanks, rookie. You're a lifesaver." There was a snort. "Remember, don't throw any wild parties while we're gone. I'm kind of in love with the house, and I don't want you trashing it."

"Damn, but I was planning a kegger."

"Funny."

"Make a stupid remark and get a stupid answer." Ethan grinned to himself. "Trust me, I'm looking forward to the solitude. Sometimes it's nice to be away from the others."

"Enjoy it while it lasts. I hear Sully and Liam are moving to the compound this week." Trevor suddenly sounded distracted. "Shit, gotta go, rookie. The pilot's waving us over."

"Cool. Say hi to Isabel and have fun in Hawaii."

"Will do."

Ethan disconnected the call and tucked his phone into the back pocket of his cargo pants. He took another long swig of coffee, returning his attention to the picturesque mountain scene before him. The chalet was located in the middle of nowhere, directly on the top of a rocky hill surrounded by dense trees and a creek that hadn't frozen over despite the below-zero temperature.

As he stood there on the massive deck, he couldn't help but feel like the last man on Earth. It was so damn quiet here, a huge change from the noisy jungle he'd been living in for the past ten months. The mercenary team he worked for had previously been based in Mexico, but after the team's compound had been attacked by a private hit squad last year, Jim Morgan had relocated his men to a sprawling estate in Costa Rica, where the air was forever humid and the wildlife couldn't seem to shut up. Thanks to the jungle that bordered one side of the new compound, Ethan spent his days listening to birds squawking and monkeys screeching and his nights listening to the constant drone of insects. Needless to say, the silence was blessedly welcome.

He was actually looking forward to these next two weeks. He couldn't remember the last time he'd been truly alone. For the past three years, he'd lived with his fellow mercenaries, which meant someone was always underfoot—D in the shooting range, Kane and Abby hanging out in the game room, Morgan brooding on the terrace. No matter where he went, he was bound to run into someone.

Normally he didn't mind the company—he welcomed it,

in fact—but every now and then, it was nice to have some quiet time to collect his thoughts. He was off-rotation for a few more weeks, thanks to the mandatory vacation time Morgan regularly inflicted on members of the team, which gave him the perfect opportunity to . . . to what?

He faltered for a moment, his hand freezing before he could raise his mug to his lips. What exactly was he hoping to accomplish during this time off? He didn't quite have an answer for that, but what he did know was that he'd been feeling out of sorts these past few months. Restless, edgy . . . unfulfilled.

But why? What reason did he have to feel unfulfilled? He worked for Jim Morgan, a deadly supersoldier and one of the most honorable men Ethan had ever met. He had friends he'd lay down his life for, a shit ton of money in the bank, a roof over his head, and food on the table. No serious girlfriend, sure, but he'd been casually seeing someone in Costa Rica, a cute tour guide who worked at one of the many resorts dotting the coast. But it wasn't serious, and he wasn't sure he wanted to keep that going anymore.

He wasn't sure what he wanted, period.

A wife?

A house of his own?

A family?

One day, of course, but hell, he was only twenty-five. He had plenty of time to do the whole home-and-hearth thing.

So then why couldn't he stop feeling like there was something missing in his life?

Philosophical this morning, aren't we?

Sighing, he moved away from the railing and strode into the house through the glass doors that spilled into the living room. Isabel had given him a quick tour before she and Trevor had sped off in Trevor's Range Rover, but Ethan doubted he'd spend much time anywhere but this room.

With its high ceilings, wood-paneled walls and big leather couches, the living room was the very definition of cozy. He was looking forward to lazing around in here, maybe grabbing a few books from the tall oak shelves lining the walls and spending the next couple of weeks doing nothing but reading, eating, and sleeping. And maybe hot-tubbing, he had to amend—considering this place offered a rooftop eight-person hot tub, he'd be a fool *not* to make good use of it.

He'd just plopped down on the couch and set his mug on the rustic pine coffee table when an unfamiliar ringtone broke the silence.

Shit. Isabel's phone. He'd forgotten to ask Trevor for the password so he could forward Isabel's calls to Trevor's cell in the meantime. He'd have to ask her for it after the couple landed.

He leaned forward and swiped the phone off the table to check the caller ID, intending to let the call go to voice mail, but he reconsidered when he glimpsed the name on the screen.

Juliet Mason.

Almost immediately, his body reacted, groin stirring and stiffening.

Well, this was a first. He couldn't remember ever getting hard from the sight of a woman's *name*.

But he knew it was less about those eleven little letters and more about the images her name triggered. The long, dark hair and chocolate brown eyes, the tall, willowy body and high, perky breasts. Sassy little smile. Great ass. Endless legs.

What man in his right mind *didn't* get hard at the thought of such a gorgeous woman?

At the same time, his reaction annoyed the shit out of him. Same way Juliet had annoyed him when they'd crossed paths last year. As hot as she was, the woman had rubbed him the wrong way, driving him crazy with her sarcastic barbs and her relentless teasing about his age.

He shifted awkwardly on the couch and willed away his erection, still debating whether to take the call. Isabel's phone didn't require a password to answer, so in the end, he pressed the *talk* button before he could second-guess himself.

"Isabel's phone," he said in greeting.

There was a beat.

Then another one. And another.

But the shallow breaths tickling his eardrum told him she was still on the line.

"Juliet? It's Ethan," he said gruffly. "Ethan Hayes . . . We met last year. I work for Jim Morgan."

Silence.

He suppressed a sigh. "I know you're there. I can hear you breathing."

"I . . . need Isabel."

The moment she spoke, his guard shot up a good thirty feet. Weak. Her voice sounded weak and shaky, not the confident, throaty tone of the woman he'd worked with after his team's compound had been targeted.

"Isabel and Trevor are on their way to Hawaii." His wariness escalated, rivaled only by the concern tugging at his gut. "They won't land for several more hours, but I can tell her to call you when she picks up her new phone. She left this one behind."

"No . . . time . . . Need her now . . . Can't reach Noelle . . . Need help."

Every muscle in his body went tighter than a drum. "What's going on?" he demanded. "Are you hurt?"

"Big . . . fucking . . . mess . . ." To his surprise, a wobbly sob echoed over the line. "He's dead. . . ."

Ethan's back went ramrod straight. "Who's dead?"

Another pause. "Nobody . . . Never mind. . . . Please, get Iz. Tell her to come."

"Come where?" When she didn't respond, a tremor of concern rippled through him. "Juliet," he said sternly, "tell me where you are."

"Belarus. Grenadier Hotel in Minsk . . . room . . . room two-six-four . . . no, two-four . . ." Her voice grew strained. "Two-four-six. Med kit . . . Tell her to bring a med kit. Antibiotics and . . . um . . ."

If he hadn't known any better, he would have suspected she was high as a kite on something, but Juliet hadn't struck him as a user. Besides, the pain in her voice was unmistakable. She was wounded. Fuck, she was wounded and alone on a whole other continent.

"Stay where you are," he finally ordered. "Someone will be there soon."

No response. And no more breathing sounds.

As the phone beeped in his ear, he realized Juliet had hung up.

Shit.

Shooting to his feet, Ethan raked a hand through his hair and quickly went over his options.

Option one: Stay put and pass Juliet's message along to Trevor and Isabel when they checked in hours from now.

But that would mean ruining the couple's honeymoon, because Isabel would hop right back on the plane to help her injured colleague. And who knew what kind of shape Juliet would be in by the time Isabel got there? Not only would Juliet have to wait for Isabel to land in Hawaii, but also for the twelve or so hours it would take Isabel to get to Europe.

His second option was to contact Noelle, but clearly Juliet had already tried that and hadn't been able to reach her boss.

Option three: Get someone else to answer the SOS. He'd call up a few contacts, arrange for a trusted medical professional to tend to Juliet, and while the doc took care of her, one of Ethan's teammates would make his way to the wounded operative. Abby might be able to . . . No, Abby and Kane were heading up an extraction in Bolivia, he remembered.

D was off-rotation, though. Maybe . . . No, there was no point in involving the surly mercenary, especially when Ethan could easily do the job himself.

You don't even know the woman.

No, he didn't know her. In fact, he wasn't sure he even liked her, which was damn ironic, seeing as he was about to come to her rescue.

"For Isabel's sake," he muttered to himself.

Right, he would do this for Isabel. And for Trevor. The couple had gone through so much to be together. They'd earned this quality time, and he'd be damned if he interrupted their newlywed bliss.

With a heavy breath, he glanced around the cozy living room, his gaze resting on the gorgeous stone fireplace he'd yet to make use of.

So much for his quiet mini-vacation.

Looked like he was going to Belarus. In the dead of winter.

Jeez.

It didn't sound at all appealing, but what other choice did he have? Juliet had stepped up and helped the team when they'd needed her last year.

The least he could do was repay the favor.